PARKS PAT MYSTERIES 10-12

PARKS PAT MYSTERIES 10-12

P.D. WORKMAN

PD WORKMAN

ISBN: 9781774689189 (KDP Paperback)
ISBN: 9781774689202 (Lulu Paperback)
ISBN: 9781774689196 (Digital)

ALSO BY P.D. WORKMAN

FIND MORE BOOKS AT PDWORKMAN.COM

MYSTERY/SUSPENSE:

Parks Pat Mysteries
Police Procedural Set in Canada
Out with the Sunset
Long Climb to the Top
Dark Water Under the Bridge
Immersed in the View
Skimming Over the Lake
Hazard of the Hills
Knows the Hills
Spanning the Creek
Sanctuary in the Stream
Echoes of the Engine
Bench with a View
Beneath the Icy Depths
Grounded in the Wind
Reservoir of Secrets
Peril in the Blooms

Kenzie Kirsch Medical Thrillers
Unlawful Harvest
Doctored Death
Dosed to Death
Gentle Angel
Rushin' Death

Posed for Death

Death of a Corpse

Endowed with Death

Shattered to Death

Captured in Death

Currying Death

Healed to Death

Death's Charm

Bleeding Hearts Valley Thrillers
An Abrupt Departure

High-Tech Crime Solvers Series
Virtually Harmless

Cowritten with D. D. VanDyke
California Corwin P. I. Mystery Series
The Girl in the Morgue

Stand Alone Suspense Novels
Looking Over Your Shoulder

Lion Within

Pursued by the Past

In the Tick of Time

Loose the Dogs

AND MORE AT PDWORKMAN.COM

STYLE NOTE

Since my largest readership is in the USA, I have chosen to use US spellings throughout this series. That includes the Americanization of centre to center, even where it is an actual place name, just for consistency's sake. I apologize to my Canadian readers for this.

I have chosen, however, to use Canadian grammar, particularly for Canadian voices. If you see what you think is a grammar error, it may just be Canadian, eh?

CONTENT

Contains discussion of Canadian Residential Schools and other other institutional abuses of children. There are no graphic depictions of violence against children or others, but some readers may be sensitive to these topics.

ECHOES OF THE ENGINE

To those who want to be seen.

CHAPTER ONE

*I*t was a gorgeous day, clear, sitting at ten degrees above zero, so Margie and her daughter Christina only needed light jackets, particularly when running to keep up with Stella, who was greatly enjoying her first visit to Pearce Estate Park. The leaves of the poplar trees were a brilliant yellow, carpeting the grass and the pathways, crisp and crunchy under their feet. Margie loved the fall and, so far, the season had been mild. Calgary autumns could be beautiful and breathtaking or turn snowy and deadly. They were impossible to predict.

The slightly vinegary smell of the poplars mixed with the smoke of portable BBQs set up in the picnic areas. Everyone and his dog were out to enjoy the beautiful day.

"You're so crazy," Margie told Stella as the dog dashed ahead, pulling on the leash to smell another tree, as enthusiastic as if it had been the first she had seen in months rather than the two hundredth today.

Christina laughed and jogged to keep up with them, her long black hair flowing loose behind her. "She's so happy to be here."

They stopped and waited while Stella smelled the scent post and then dashed on to the next one. Bikes whizzed by them on the pathway, the cyclists serious, heads down and eyes straight ahead, focused on their workouts. Margie watched a family with two young children at the edge of the Bow River, pointing and throwing rocks. Their words were too distant to make out.

The ground started to shake beneath their feet. Stella stopped what she was doing and looked around, her tail tucked, worried about the new development.

"It's okay," Margie told her. "It's just a train."

"It's close," Christina observed, looking around.

"It is. It's going to cross the river up there." Margie pointed to the railway bridge stretching over the Bow River. She bent down to scratch anxious Stella's ears. "There's no need to worry, girl. It's perfectly safe."

The rumbling grew louder, and they heard the train whistle. It was a familiar sound. The rumbling transformed into the rhythmic clack of the wheels as they moved over the ties. Then, the train came into view on the bridge. Red engines at the front and varicolored boxcars stretched out in a long line.

The horn sounded again, longer and more insistent this time. Margie watched it, unconcerned. She knew the train was required to blow its horn at every crossing. The crossing at Pearce Estate Park was safe, a below-grade pedestrian crossing that dipped under the train bridge so there was no chance of an unexpected encounter between train and pedestrian. A person could stand right under the tracks as the train rumbled overhead. Though it probably wasn't a good idea with the bicycle traffic going through there. The cyclists didn't always slow down even though they could not see around the curve or down into the dip under the tracks.

Something was wrong. The wheels started to screech, dragging over the track as the brakes were applied. The train had too much weight and inertia to stop quickly. It might take a couple of kilometers to come to a complete stop if it were going fast enough.

Christina looked over her shoulder at Margie. "Why is it stopping?"

"I don't know."

"Is there a switch? Is it changing directions?"

"No. There's no switch here. I don't know why it would be stopping."

They walked closer, watching anxiously. Other park enthusiasts were stopping to look at the train as well. Clearly, Margie and Christina were not the only ones who thought it odd. It wasn't normal for the train to stop there. Margie held Stella's leash tightly as they walked up to the point where they could see the below-grade crossing. The wheels were still screeching as the train slowed and eventually ground to a halt. Then, it was suddenly too quiet. Margie gazed up at the still train, waiting. A train had two options. Forward or backward. There was no reason to stop unless it was loading or unloading and it wasn't doing that in the middle of the park.

Margie looked up the embankment to her left. There was a worn path leading up to the tracks. Not a paved pathway, but a "goat trail" people had used to climb up to look at the tracks in the past.

"Here," she held the leash out to Christina. "You stay here."

Christina frowned, shaking her head and not taking the end of the leash. "Why? What are you doing?"

"I'm just going to go up and make sure everything is okay. But I don't want Stella up there. Please take her."

Christina took the loop of the leash reluctantly. "Mom, you should just stay down here. You're not supposed to go up there."

"I know. I won't be long."

Margie climbed up the slope, ignoring the glares of the other walkers looking on. The train was too quiet. It did not start moving again, but sat on the tracks like a cooling teakettle, creaking and ticking its complaints.

Even before Margie climbed up to the level of the train, she spotted a homeless encampment in the trees to her left: a small tent, a tarp, and a bike with a trailer. Someone who had been on the skids for a while, used to fending for himself.

Margie ignored the various Warning and No Trespassing signs posted beside the tracks and continued to press forward until she could see the dark shape that was partially on and partially off the tracks. She didn't get too close, conscious of the need to preserve the scene.

While her first action should have been to check for signs of life, such an act seemed totally unnecessary under the circumstances.

CHAPTER TWO

Margie stood there for a moment before acting. She wasn't frozen, exactly. She knew what to do next; it just seemed ridiculous, like she was in the middle of a play or a scenario described in a textbook. She should not have been there. This should not be happening during her relaxing walk in Pearce Estate Park.

Eventually, she dialed 9-1-1. When she reached the emergency dispatcher, she identified herself as a homicide officer and did her best to describe the situation and location. In a dispassionate voice, the dispatcher ran through her script, not commenting on how unusual it was for Margie to be the one to call it in.

"A unit has been dispatched," she advised Margie. "Please stay where you are and don't touch anything. Stay well back from the train."

"Yes, I am."

"Do you want me to stay on the line with you?"

"No, I'll be fine," Margie assured her. "I'll wait for them to arrive. Can you transfer me over to the homicide unit?"

"One moment, please."

In a few seconds, there was a click and the sound of a ringing line. Margie waited for it to be picked up.

"Homicide unit, Detective Cruz."

"Cruz, it's Patenaude."

There was a pause while Cruz probably looked at his phone screen again. "Were you transferred by the emergency operator?"

"Yes. There's been an incident in Pearce Estate Park. I called it in, but I thought I would get a jump on the process before the patrol gets here to take a look and agree that it is a homicide case. Are you free? And can you call the medical examiner's office?"

"Murder?"

"Accident, I think. But we'll need everyone in on it to do their part."

"Sure. Fill me in."

Margie gave him a few sparse details, then hung up so he could do his part. She wasn't sure whether to stay at the scene or go back down the goat path to fill Christina in on what was happening. She didn't want to leave her teenage daughter down there wondering what was happening, but also needed to keep her eyes on the scene until someone else was there to help.

She tapped on Christina's name on her phone screen. Christina answered almost immediately.

"Mom? What's going on? People are kind of starting to freak out. I said everyone is just supposed to stay down here, but no one wants to listen to a kid."

"Tell them that the police are on their way and they will be in trouble if they come up here."

"The police are on their way," Christina repeated, warning those with her. "Why? What happened? Did it... break down? Was it sabotaged or something?"

"No. It stopped because it hit something. Just keep everyone there if you can. I'll explain later."

"The train hit something," Christina again announced to her audience. "The police will take care of it."

Margie could hear people complaining, demanding to know why it was a police matter. Getting restless.

"I'm sorry, Christina. I have to babysit the scene, or I would come down and help you. The police shouldn't be too long."

But of course, they couldn't get there instantly. Margie didn't have her radio, so she couldn't hear whether they had scrambled more than one unit. Whether it was a car patrolling nearby or a couple of bike cops from downtown. It was fifteen minutes before a uniformed constable climbed the goat path and joined Margie.

"You're a detective?" he asked as he approached her, black mask in place, eyes moving around restlessly to take in the scene, head on a swivel.

"Detective Margie Patenaude," she introduced herself. "Detective Pat, if you like."

"Constable Morris." His eyes went to her face as he considered her, perhaps noting the facial features she had inherited from her Cree ancestors. "Parks Pat?"

Margie rolled her eyes. "Yes, Parks Pat," she confirmed with a wry smile. "And here I am again… in another park."

"Maybe you should stop hanging around parks," he suggested seriously.

Margie chuckled. "I don't think that would actually stop homicides from occurring in the parks."

He looked as if he might doubt this, but didn't say so aloud. "So… what have we got here?"

Margie made a motion toward the figure on the ground. "It looks as though… pedestrian met train. I don't know anything more than that yet."

"Did you see it happen?"

"No. It heard the train whistle, just the usual crossing signal, and then several more warning whistles. Then it hit the brakes."

"Did you hear the impact?"

"No. The train itself is too noisy. I didn't hear any scream, or impact, or anything like that. When the train stopped, I came up to investigate. I just… had a feeling."

At that point, a man came walking down the tracks. Tall, slim, with a rough-hewn hatchet face. Wearing the train company's logo on his sleeve.

"What's going on here?" he demanded. "You can't be here," he told Margie. He didn't tell the uniformed constable the same. Apparently, he recognized his jurisdiction did not extend that far.

"Calgary Homicide," Margie introduced herself. "Can you tell me what happened?"

"You're a homicide cop? How did you get here so fast?"

"I was in the park. Came up to check things out when I saw the train stop."

The train employee looked around and grimaced, seeing the dark form caught under the train. But he didn't duck into the bushes to lose his lunch. He looked experienced and stood with that particularly tall and stiff stance that suggested he had served in the armed forces, where he might have seen his share of bloody deaths.

"This is a mess," he said grimly.

"I know," Margie agreed. "Are you... the train engineer?"

"No, he's still up there. Supposed to stay put. We can't leave the engine unattended; he will need to be ready to move the train when... when it can be moved. I'm CP Rail security."

Margie wondered whether it was usual for every train to have a security officer aboard or whether they had just lucked out in this case. She knew little about how trains or the railway police operated.

"You'll need to stay well away from the train until the forensic guys have had a look," she told him.

"I need to be a part of this investigation."

"And you will be. But I'm not messing around with the evidence, either. I'm waiting for the science guys to do their thing so I don't contaminate anything."

He grunted and scowled.

"Can you watch the scene for a moment?" Margie asked Morris. "I just need to talk to my daughter."

He nodded his agreement. "Sure." He stood with his feet apart in a wide base, his thumbs in his belt, looking solid and immovable. Margie was satisfied that he could handle anything that came up while she went back to talk to Christina.

She descended the goat path to the paved pathway, where Christina and a large number of bystanders were now waiting, watching, and speculating. A murmur went up with Margie's arrival. Constable Morris's unit was pulled over on the pathway, blocking most of it, lights still flashing, but there was a sliver of pathway to allow pedestrians and cyclists to get by it. Another cop stood at the bottom of the path to prevent anyone from going up. Morris's partner. He frowned at Margie as she descended.

"Where did you come from?"

"I called it in." Margie felt awkward, with no badge or identification to show him. She wanted to do something with her hands. "Detective

Patenaude, Homicide. But I was here with my daughter and want to make sure that she is okay."

He studied her briefly, then nodded and let her pass without another word. Margie slipped past him and gave Christina a hug, quick and tight, assessing her.

"Are you okay?"

"I'm fine, Mom. It isn't like I saw anything."

"No. But it can still affect you. Your adrenaline is pumping. You know something happened."

"Yeah. So what was it? What's going on?" Christina looked around at the other people waiting for her, who were also eager to find out the details. They were nodding and murmuring their questions and encouragement.

Margie pressed her lips together. She couldn't speak for the department. She knew she needed to be careful what she said. She couldn't give anything away, yet she couldn't pretend nothing was happening.

"Well, there isn't much I can say yet. We need to conduct our investigation before I can say anything that might make it to the media. There has been an unfortunate accident. Until we know more, that's all I can say."

"The train hit someone?" Christina asked baldly.

"Well… that *may* be. But we won't know for sure what happened for some time yet."

Christina rolled her eyes. She knew how cops talked. It didn't take much to figure out that was exactly what had happened. Still, the police couldn't say anything until they had informed the next of kin and had word from the Office of the Chief Medical Examiner and the crime scene investigators who would be there shortly to gather evidence. With the involvement of the train, Margie supposed there would also be some kind of accident reconstruction team. The public would need assurances that it wouldn't happen again. Margie wasn't sure what the railway company would do to show that they had increased security and made it seem safer.

"I can't believe that happened," Christina said. "And when we were right here! It's crazy."

"I know. This wasn't what I had planned for the day. I wasn't expecting to have to deal with an incident at the park. I was just supposed to be walking Stella and getting some fresh air."

Margie scratched Stella's ears. Stella wagged her tail hard, delighted with the attention. Margie was sure she was bored standing around.

"Why don't you take her further down the pathway for a walk? Take your time, then maybe when you get back here, I'll be able to tell you something… like how long I'll be stuck here."

"I'll just wait here." Christina looked down at Stella and reconsidered. Stella was a sweetheart, but she could be a real stinker when she got bored. "Oh, all right. But I might have to stop in Inglewood and buy pizza."

That sounded like a good idea. Margie reached for her wallet. "I'll give you some cash—"

"I don't want cash. Just e-transfer me."

Margie shook her head. "All right. Maybe get me a couple of slices, too. I don't know how long it will be before I can think about going home. I might need something to hold me over if I end up being here all day."

"All day?" Christina repeated in dismay.

"I'm sure I won't be here *all* day," Margie assured her, though she wasn't at all sure of that. "I'll update you when I know something. Just keep yourself and this furry beast occupied for a while."

Christina nodded her agreement. "Send me thirty," she advised. Margie didn't argue.

CHAPTER THREE

*C*hristina walked on with Stella. A few of the bystanders tried to get more information from Margie. She kept repeating that she couldn't tell them anything yet, but they weren't in a receptive mood and grumbled about it. Margie left Constable Miller's partner to deal with them and returned to the accident scene.

Detective Cruz wasn't far behind her. A big Filipino cop, a father with several small children, he was one of Margie's favorites on the homicide team. It seemed like nothing fazed him. He was always calm and stayed on an even keel, even in the face of the most aggravating cases.

"Detective Pat," he greeted. "Haven't we talked before about the fact that you don't need to provide your own bodies? We have plenty to do without you seeking out new cases on your own." Even though he wore a black mask, she could see the twinkle in his eye as he teased her.

"Yeah, it wasn't something I planned on. I did have other things to do today."

"Then you shouldn't be chasing after trains. Why don't you show me what you've got?"

"We don't want to get too close until the ME and crime techs have looked things over and gathered any trace evidence. But we can get enough for a glimpse."

She escorted him over to the tracks, staying well back to avoid fouling the scene any more than it already was. The railway security officer was inspecting the wheels of the train as if they might have been damaged in the accident or the sudden stop. Margie grabbed him firmly by the sleeve and pulled him back.

"Look, Mister...?"

"Williams."

"Mr. Williams. You can't wander around here. There will be a number of experts who will be inspecting the scene, and they need to be able to photograph it as is, gather trace evidence, any biological materials... You could be damaging evidence by walking around here. Why don't you go stand with Constable Miller for now?"

"This is my train. I need to check it out. I am responsible for its safety and security."

"There's nothing you can do right now except to wait. It isn't going anywhere."

Williams looked at the train and shook his head in irritation. "Stupid people! There are all kinds of warning signs. There's a safe crossing. What makes people think it's a good idea to come up here and stand on the tracks?"

"We don't know yet what happened."

"Well, look at him!" He flung a hand in the direction of the mess that had once been a living, breathing man. "What do you *think* happened?"

"I don't know yet," Margie told him calmly. "We will find out in time. One step at a time."

Of course, her opinion wasn't any different from his. The few features that were recognizable—a thick, stained overcoat, broad back, and bald pate, suggested that the homeless person who had called this encampment home had, for one reason or another, been standing or lying on the train tracks with the train approaching. Whether they would be able to figure out *why* he had done so was something she could not predict. There was a lot of work to do, but the first steps would not be hers. Her only job right now was to keep control of the scene and not let anyone like Williams contaminate it.

"Go stand over there," she ordered him firmly.

Williams looked at her for a moment, trying to decide whether to object further, and then he finally obeyed, walking over to where

Constable Morris stood guard. Morris nodded to Margie, indicating, she hoped, that he would keep Williams in line.

"Not pretty," Cruz observed unnecessarily, looking at the biological matter that had been spread by the impact with the train.

Margie nodded her agreement. "How long before the OCME and the crime scene techs will be here?"

"Sounded like they would be coming right over. I don't think they are too busy today."

"Did you bring some tape with you?"

"Of course." Cruz produced a thick roll of yellow caution tape from under his jacket. They started to string a wide perimeter, eyes sharp for all of the evidence that would need to be collected or examined. Margie hoped the train had not dragged evidence for a kilometer or two down the line. It could take a very long time to process the scene.

"So what did you see and hear?" Cruz asked as they worked to loop the tape around various trees to enclose an area that encompassed the biological matter they could see, the homeless man's camp, and the top portion of the goat trail leading up to the scene, though it had probably already been trampled too many times to retrieve any useful footprints or other evidence.

"Not much. Just saw and heard the train coming over the bridge. Everything seemed perfectly normal. It whistled for the crossing. But then it started to sound its horn more than normal and hit the brakes. I didn't see or hear anything of the victim until after it had stopped and I came up here. So what happened up here... I'm afraid I can't say."

Cruz looked around at the trees and the railway track. "And no traffic cams around here."

"No. I don't think we're going to have any video or eyewitnesses. Just whatever the forensic guys can tell us."

"Well, it seems pretty clear. He was camped here," Cruz nodded toward the remains. "And for one reason or another, whether he was drunk or hallucinating or upset about something, he walked out onto the tracks as the train was approaching. He didn't move out of the way in time; the train engineer couldn't stop, and..." He shrugged.

Margie shook her head, feeling a pang of sadness at the unnecessary loss of life. If the man had just stayed away from the railway, everything would have been fine. Just like every other day when the train traveled through the park without incident.

They could hear voices approaching. Margie looked toward the goat path to see who was there, hoping it wasn't bystanders who had managed to get by Morris's partner.

She recognized Dr. Galt, a white-haired death investigator with a small white beard currently covered by a medical mask, walking up with a couple of fresh-faced crime techs who looked like children playing dress-up, not nearly old enough to have degrees in science and forensics.

Dr. Galt stopped at Constable Morris's side to check in with him. Morris took down his information, though he seemed embarrassed to do so.

"It's not like I'm *not* going to let the medical examiner's office on the scene."

"It's protocol," Galt insisted. "Always follow protocol. When the detective in charge of the case looks at the logs and sees everybody logged in and out properly, he will be happy. Not so much if it is a mess and you haven't even logged in OCME."

Morris sighed and nodded, making sure to get all of their names down.

MARGIE HAD BEEN LOST in the case and wasn't sure how much time had passed when her cell phone vibrated. She pulled it out and looked at it, even though she didn't like to be interrupted at a homicide scene. Sometimes, the reach of technology was just too far. It would be a lot easier to concentrate without the constant ringing or vibrating of her phone and the various staticky radios that kept cutting in.

She saw Christina's name on the screen and swiped it.

"Christina, hi! What time is it?" She looked down at her screen and shook her head. "Oh, I didn't realize how much time had passed. You and Stella must be bored silly."

"We've kind of run out of things to do. Do you think I could catch the bus around here somewhere and get home? It isn't far, just across the bridge. I must be able to catch the Max Purple on ninth somewhere."

"Uh… let me see if I can do something first. I'll call you back in just a minute."

Christina grumbled and hung up.

It wasn't that Christina wasn't capable of taking the bus on her own or with her dog, assuming they would allow a dog on the bus. Margie wasn't sure what the transit's policy was on dogs not certified as service animals. It wasn't even that far to walk. Christina could be home in less than an hour on foot. But she'd already been walking around for a couple of hours. She was undoubtedly tired as well as bored and Margie didn't want her getting blisters. Stella, too, was probably getting footsore. She wasn't the young pup she once was.

"Is there anyone who could drive my daughter home?" she asked the group of law enforcement officers, a lot of whom were just standing around chatting now. "It's just up Blackfoot to Southview…"

"I could do that," offered Morris, who had been relieved of his duties controlling the scene and should be heading back on to patrol. "Where is she? I didn't know you had a daughter."

"I'm not sure if she came back here or is still in Inglewood. She was going to get some pizza. Let me just call her back and find out."

Margie thought Christina would be delighted to have someone drive her home, but she whined when Margie told her that Constable Morris would pick her up.

"Mo-om! I'm not a little kid. I don't need someone to drive me home. I'm perfectly capable of getting there myself."

"I know you are, Christina. Of course you are. But you've been on your feet for hours already. I just thought it would be nice for you to have a ride."

"I don't need a babysitter!"

"He's not going to stay with you. He's just dropping you off."

Christina made a noise of disgust. "I don't need to be driven."

"You would rather walk and take the bus? Do you know if they'll take Stella? Or will you have to wait for the right driver who will agree to let her on?"

"Uh… some of the buses will let her on."

"All of them? Or will you have to take your chances?"

"Take my chances, I guess," Christina admitted.

"So you might be standing around for another hour waiting for a bus to take you home. Or Constable Morris could drive you."

"Okay, fine. Whatever. I'll let him drive me."

"Good. Where should he pick you up?"

"I'm just outside the pizza place."

"Which one? Inglewood Pizza?"

"Is there another one?"

Margie grinned to herself. Of course there were plenty of pizza places in Inglewood, but Christina was true to her upbringing. It could only be Inglewood Pizza.

"He'll pick you up there in five minutes."

Christina agreed and hung up. Margie reported the details to Constable Morris. Her cheeks warmed slightly at the thought that he might have heard some of Christina's complaints, and she tried to smooth it over.

"She's very independent. It isn't that she has a problem with you or anyone else, just that she likes to get around on her own, to be independent."

"Well… that's good if she's old enough," Morris said doubtfully.

Margie's cheeks burned hotter at the suggestion that she might be too permissive about what she allowed her daughter to do.

"She's sixteen," she said quickly. "She's old enough to take the bus by herself during the day."

"Oh," Morris nodded quickly. "You, uh… don't look old enough to have a daughter that age."

Margie touched her black hair, smoothing the bun she had coiled her hair into when she had realized that it was going to be a workday for her with the discovery of the human remains on the railway track. She knew that her jet-black hair and smooth skin did not give away her age, but she also wasn't as old as most parents of sixteen-year-olds.

"I had Christina when I was pretty young," she told Morris.

"Ah," he nodded. "Well, either way… I would be happy to take her home for you. It will only take a few minutes and then I'll get back on my patrol."

Margie watched Morris walk away, his own cheeks flushed pink. She knew that her blush would not show up with her brown skin. Morris's flush made him look young, barely older than a teenager. He was probably what? Twenty-two? Not that much older than Christina.

Maybe Christina would change her mind about her mother treating her like a little kid by sending Constable Morris to take her home.

CHAPTER FOUR

*M*argie walked up the length of the train. At first, she had thought that the front of the train would be just a few cars ahead of where she was. But it had continued to travel long after the initial impact. It was quite a hike to get to the front of it.

The engineer was still in the engine but, when he saw her approach, he climbed down to talk to her. He was a tall, thin man, and was very pale. He wore a uniform, but he didn't quite match the picture Margie had in her head of a train engineer. She pictured someone dirty from shoveling coal in a steam engine. But of course, the CPR train did not operate on steam, like the train Margie had ridden on at Heritage Park as a child. And even if it had, she didn't think that the train engineer was the one who shoveled the coal.

"Hi, Detective Patenaude," she introduced herself.

"I'm… Clarence Newmeyer."

"Are you okay? You're looking a little…" Margie didn't want to say he was green, but he certainly didn't look good.

"I've never had anything like this happen before," Newmeyer said. "It's a horrible situation. There are warning signs. There is a below-grade crossing. How could something like this happen?"

"I don't know. Can you tell me what you saw?"

"The company is telling me that I need to talk to a lawyer before I talk to you."

"Well… you can certainly do that if you want to. I won't try to dissuade you."

He shook his head. "I just want to get it off of my chest. I didn't do anything wrong. I followed all of the appropriate protocols. If someone thinks this happened because I was careless or did something wrong…"

"No, I don't think you did. It isn't like you can steer the thing."

He nodded at that. "I can slow or accelerate. I can sound the whistle. There isn't really anything else to do. I do my best to keep it running on schedule. Call security if I see anything suspicious, anyone hanging around the train or getting on or off who shouldn't be. It isn't like driving a car or flying an airplane."

"If you could tell me what you saw…?"

He considered for a moment and then nodded. Maybe if he got it off his chest, he would be able to sleep tonight. She could only imagine the nightmares that he would have after what he had experienced.

"I crossed the bridge over the Bow. I sounded the horn for the Pearce Estate crossing, even though there is a below-grade pedestrian crossing. There could still be deer on the rails. People trespassing on the tracks. It happens. Teenagers, usually."

Margie nodded, saying nothing. It was best if he got his whole story out without her saying anything. They could explore any details afterwards.

"I saw something dark on the rails. Thought it might be a dog. I blasted the horn a few extra times, expecting it to move. It didn't. I couldn't tell for sure what it was, but I hit the emergency brake before impact." He swallowed. "I just couldn't stop in time."

Margie nodded. "You did the best you could."

"It wasn't a dog," Newmeyer said, looking sick.

"No, I'm afraid not. A homeless man."

"What was he doing on the tracks? There are warning signs. It's a train track. Everyone knows better than to lie down on a train track."

Unless it was someone who was hoping to be hit. Or maybe the man had been drunk or stoned. Or had passed out for another reason. Diabetic, maybe. High or low blood sugar could both cause problems.

"We're going to figure out what happened," she assured him. "But you can't be held responsible for a man laying down on the tracks."

CHAPTER FIVE

Margie had just sat down with her morning coffee when the desk phone rang. She looked at it, not really ready to deal with any inquiries yet.

OCME.

The Office of the Chief Medical Examiner. Margie picked up the receiver. "Patenaude."

"Ah, my dear Detective Pat," Galt greeted. "How are you this fine morning?"

"Well, I would be better if I hadn't spent my day off dealing with the newly deceased." She wondered whether he had been up all night processing the remains. At least she had been able to go home to relax and sleep.

"Then maybe you should stop finding bodies yourself," Galt told her with good humor. "Leave it to others. Maybe… stay home on your days off."

"Yeah, I might have to."

"I have some preliminary information for you."

"Homeless guy was hit by a train?" Margie suggested dryly.

"In fact, no."

"What?"

"You are wrong in more than one respect."

"He wasn't killed by the train?"

"Let's start with your choice of pronoun. *He* was, in fact, not a he."

"He was transgender?" Margie asked. She supposed she should not be surprised. It was becoming a more common occurrence. Or being more openly transgender was, at least.

"No. She was not transgender. She was simply a woman."

Margie frowned, recalling what she had been able to recognize of the victim.

"But… the victim was bald."

"Yes. She was."

"Oh." Margie thought about that. "Well, I guess there is nothing to stop a woman from shaving her head. Or was she a chemo patient? Or maybe she lost her hair due to some other disease?"

"It was shaved."

"Okay, then. But she wasn't transgender?"

She wasn't sure what reason a woman would have to shave herself bald other than to appear to be male, but she could be entirely wrong on that note.

"Her clothing was, in fact, feminine."

"All I saw was the overcoat. That didn't look feminine."

"True," Galt admitted. "But that was just the overcoat, which is pretty much unisex. Her other clothing was feminine."

"Was there any identification? Do we know who we are dealing with yet?"

"We do not yet have an identification. And we do not yet have an autopsy and cause of death. It took a significant amount of time to collect as much of the remains as possible."

They had still been working on it when Margie had eventually left the site as the sky was growing dark. The railway was not happy about their traffic being held up, but there wasn't anything the police or OCME could do to hurry the evidence collection. They weren't the ones who had hit the man. Or rather, the woman.

"So, will you be able to do that today?"

"Which?" Dr. Galt asked. "Identify the body or do the autopsy?"

"Well, either. But I meant the autopsy, so that we have as much information as possible to identify the victim."

"We will do our best. At the moment, I can offer you only a general description. Woman in her late fifties, tall, heavy build, bald, blue eyes."

"Can you tell me what her hair color was before she cut it?"

"Somewhere in a dark blond to light brown range. Maybe blond as a child, darkening as an adult."

"So it would be listed as blond on her driver's license."

"Possibly."

"I'll see if we have any missing persons that match."

After finishing her conversation with Dr. Galt, Margie hung up and turned to Detective Kaitlyn Jones, whose desk was nearby and who had just sat down with her coffee. She was slightly overweight, with a round face and blond curls that were always escaping her bun and bobby pins. She and Margie had become good friends in the time since Margie had joined the department.

"We need to go through the missing persons reports again," Margie advised.

"You think we missed something? Or that it might have been called in since then? I thought they were going to flag it so that we would be told if a matching profile came up."

"We have to start over again."

"Completely? Why?"

"Because we were looking for men who were reported missing, and the victim was a woman."

Jones stared at her in shock. She shook her head. "That body must have been pretty messed up if you couldn't even tell whether it was a man or a woman."

"It was. You don't even want to know." It had been a nightmare for Dr. Galt and the death investigators to figure out how to get the remains out of the wheels of the train as efficiently and with as little damage as possible. A nightmare that Margie was pretty sure would haunt her dreams in the future. It was one of those things she had never expected to see in her career as a law enforcement officer.

It wasn't all bar fights, domestic disputes, and shootings. There were some things she would never be able to forget.

"Ugh. Gruesome," Jones observed. "I'm glad it wasn't my scene."

"Yes, you are. And if you have any sense, you will not look through the pictures on the file. Focus on the general description, and we'll see if we can find a match. Late fifties, big woman, bald or blond. Maybe homeless."

"If she's homeless, there won't be a missing person report."

"Maybe not. It's still possible that someone noticed she isn't following her normal routine, starts to wonder if something happened to her. Or there may be a much older missing person report from when she first hit the street."

"That could be tricky."

Margie nodded. She jotted a few things down on sticky notes on her desk. "I'll need to go down there again, talk to some of the other homeless in the area, see if they can tell me more about her. Name, if she has family close by, that kind of thing. They should know something about her."

"There are some churches in the area. I don't know which of them open their doors to the needy or have outreach programs. They may be helpful."

Margie jotted it down. "Local businesses might know her. Either because she buys from them or because they didn't want her hanging around their places of business."

"You've got your work cut out for you."

Margie looked at her sideways. "Did I hear you offer to help?"

Jones laughed. "Of course I did, Detective Pat."

CHAPTER SIX

*T*here was a lot of footwork to be done if Margie were going to identify the woman who had been killed by the train. And she wanted to get it done as quickly as possible. Word would leak out as to what had happened, and there was always the possibility that family members would hear about it before being contacted by the police. That was not ideal. It was best if they heard from the police first. And best for the police investigating the death if they got the family's first reaction to the news rather than having their opinions shaped by others before talking to the detectives.

Margie figured that in the early morning, the people most likely to know the victim would be either in the coffee shops or other places serving breakfast along Ninth Avenue or in the park. Not that it was *that* early. Margie was already on her second cup of coffee herself. Christina's school day had started and most office workers were already beavering away at their work.

But there were plenty of people still around the coffee shops. Some of them were inside, lined up at the counters or busily working their phones or laptops at the small bistro tables, but many were outside, hands wrapped about their warm cups, visiting. It was a warm morning for the end of October, already five degrees above zero, but it was still chilly to stand outside for any length of time. But the homeless didn't have any choice. They couldn't stay inside for long, even as legitimate customers.

Margie scanned their faces. It stood to reason that a woman in her fifties would be best known by other women in their fifties. Some faces were covered by masks. Of those she could see, it was difficult to tell how old people were. Many were prematurely aged by hard living. Lots of time in the sun and wind, smoking, drinking, and using drugs. None of those things was conducive to keeping a young complexion.

A woman with a red toque scowled at Margie, meeting her eyes and demanding, "Who are you? And what are you doing here?"

"I'm looking for… I'm looking for help on identifying a woman who was hurt."

Some of them looked at Margie curiously, but most turned away and continued their conversations with each other, unconcerned. Did they already know who she was talking about? Maybe word had spread through the community quickly, even though OCME hadn't been able to make an identification yet.

"Trying to identify who?" the woman asked.

"There was a woman near here yesterday. Over in the park," Margie gestured in the direction of Pearce Estate Park. "I don't have a very good description yet. But it was a woman in her fifties, tall, broad-shouldered. Her head was shaved."

The woman shook her head, staring at Margie. "Her head was shaved?"

"Yes. She looked bald, but it was shaved. But I don't know whether she usually wore a hat or a scarf or wig that covered it…"

Why would a woman shave her head just to wear a wig? Margie had not seen a wig or a hat anywhere at the accident scene. But that didn't mean that there hadn't been one. One might have been thrown into the brush or be wedged in the train somewhere. While the investigators had gathered all the evidence they could, that was no guarantee they hadn't missed something.

"I don't know any bald woman." The woman with the red toque shook her head and looked around at the others gathered there to visit, holding their coffee cups close to their bodies, cold, limbs pulled inward to keep them warmer.

There were headshakes all around.

"Sorry, honey," a man with a dark complexion and prominent lines around his mouth told Margie. He took a sip of his coffee. Teeth yellow, a couple of gaps between them. His fingernails were thick and long, a deep yellow orange. A long-time smoker. "Maybe she was new around here. But I can't think of anyone who matches that description."

"Someone who camped in the park? There was a bike with a trailer and a small tent near the train bridge."

"A woman over there? You should talk to Lewis."

Margie nodded eagerly. "Lewis? Does he normally set up camp in that direction?"

The man with the long nails nodded. "Yeah, he's usually somewhere over there. Don't know if he will be today. There were a lot of cops around there yesterday."

"Yes," Margie agreed ruefully.

He studied her. "Is this something to do with the train accident? No one is saying very much about what happened. Or..." he cleared his throat, "people are saying plenty, but none of it seems very reliable. Just speculation."

"We can't release anything yet."

"So someone was hit?" he guessed. "You're trying to figure out who so that you can contact their family?"

Margie shrugged. She didn't need to confirm or deny it. They would all assume that was the case. They'd seen it enough times before. Margie hoped they could identify the woman quickly, before word spread to the family.

"Lewis is your best bet. But it might take a while to find him. He moves around."

"Do you think he will be over here for breakfast?" Margie flicked her fingers to indicate the avenue. "Getting a hot coffee to warm himself up?"

"No, Lewis keeps to himself. He might stop in for supplies now and then, but he doesn't come around here. Get coffee grounds at the grocery store and make his own."

"Out there in the park?"

"There are ways," the man said with a chuckle. "Not everybody has a kitchen, honey."

It wasn't like Margie hadn't ever had camp coffee. Of course there were ways for Lewis to make his coffee in the bush. A small fire or camp stove, compact and easy to pack into his gear. A folding pot or tin can or cup. It wasn't rocket science.

But she wasn't looking forward to searching the park for the man. It would be easier if she could find him outside one of the coffee shops along Ninth Avenue.

"Thanks, I appreciate the information. You've been very helpful."

He nodded and sipped his coffee. "A bald woman. That's very unusual. You would think that I would have heard about that," he mused.

"There is no bald woman," the lady with the red toque insisted. "I don't know what you're talking about. We would all know if a bald woman was hanging around here."

"Well..." Margie thought about the overcoat. "Maybe she was masquerading as a man. Was there... a man matching that description in the area?"

"Bald? There are bald men."

"A big man. Bald. Blue eyes. No beard or whiskers." Since men living on the street tended to have at least a few days' beard growth, that might stand out to them.

They exchanged looks, but no one offered anything—no bald woman masquerading as a man that they could think of. Margie would have thought that she would stand out.

"The Drop-In Center is just down there," a tiny, wizened woman offered, pointing toward downtown. "You could check with them, see if it is someone who has used their service."

"It isn't far," one of the others agreed.

"I will," Margie agreed. "That's a good idea."

But she was pretty sure that the woman camping near the railway tracks would not be using the Drop-in Center. Not until it got quite a bit colder.

"You can ask around," the man with the fingernails encouraged, "but I think if a bald woman was hanging out in this part of town or the park, we would know about it."

Margie agreed. She expressed her thanks and walked down to the next knot of people down the sidewalk, outside the next eatery.

While some people were helpful and some were not, the answers Margie got were similar to the first group. No bald-headed woman. No bald, clean-shaven man. No one could think of anyone who matched the description. There were a few churches or outreach programs to check with, but Margie wasn't sure any of them would be any help. If the people on the street didn't know the victim, chances were pretty slim that she was known by the programmers at the various agencies. But Margie noted the names of the churches and programs anyway, not eliminating any of the leads she had been given.

Then she was back at the park. While the weather was still lovely, just like the day before, Margie did not enjoy her walk in the park as much as she had with Christina and Stella. The Sunday crowds were gone, and it was populated with only a few pedestrians and cyclists. Everyone back to work again.

CHAPTER SEVEN

*M*argie walked briskly to the train bridge, but kept her eyes open for any sign of Lewis and his camp as she walked. She wasn't expecting it to be obvious, but hoped to see it through the trees. But she had no such luck. It seemed that Lewis's camp was well-hidden. She reached the goat trail and climbed it once more.

No sign of the police presence. All of the yellow tape had been cleared away. Any evidence that they had found had been removed. There was no sign of the police investigation or the remains that had been spread over the area. The crime scene techs had done a very good job collecting all the human biological material.

There was no tent or bike with a trailer. No sign that anyone else had been there. The people Margie had talked to had said that Lewis camped somewhere close by. Maybe not right there, especially after the police had been there all day, but somewhere nearby.

Margie returned to the paved pathway and continued walking toward downtown, watching for any sign of Lewis's camp. It wasn't long before she reached the end of the path, which then adjoined another pathway through the residential area. Not somewhere Lewis would have wanted to camp. Not in someone's yard.

Margie returned the way she had come, walking past numerous people walking their dogs, cyclists, and a few parents with children. There was a large structure that hadn't been there when she was a kid, coming there with her cousins over summer visits to Calgary. It looked like an old ruin but, of course, it wasn't; it was new. A place that could be a castle in a kid's imagination, where families could sit on a bench and shelter from the wind to have a picnic. A couple of people were training dogs, having them jump up on the benches or other formations and walk along them for treats.

Margie stood at the edge of the "castle," peering down at the water where the dangerous, man-killing weir had once been. Replaced with the newly engineered Harvie Passage, it was now safe to boat or raft down the rapids. She could remember watching pelicans from that location. She'd never seen them anywhere else. Did they still come there, even with everything having changed so much?

Margie continued down the pathway. She had apparently missed a fork and kept walking along the river when she should have turned. It seemed like she had been walking for too long, but she wasn't sure until she reached the section of the path that ran under Blackfoot Trail. Another thing that had just been added in the last few years, allowing cyclists to continue to travel beside the river all the way to the bird sanctuary or to turn and ride parallel to Blackfoot on the new bus bridge over the very busy Deerfoot Trail, without ever having to cross traffic. She could have walked all the way home from there.

But of course, that would be silly, since her car was still in the parking lot, and she had more work to do at the office. She stopped and looked for the pathway that would take her back to the parking lot.

"You look lost."

Margie startled. She had thought that she was alone. She hadn't seen the man standing in the shadow of the underpass, smoking a cigarette, watching her.

"Oh. You scared me."

"Sorry, ma'am."

Margie looked him over. Another rough-looking individual. Homeless or just someone who worked hard and hadn't had a chance to clean up yet?

She was pretty sure he was homeless, but it was hard to see details in the shadows.

She blew out her breath. "No, it's okay, I just didn't see you there."

"You need a hand?"

"No… I just need to find my way back to my car…"

He chuckled. "Sounds like a 'yes,' not a 'no.' Where did you leave your car?"

"In the parking lot."

"Which parking lot?"

"Pearce Estate Park. The main part, not by the Fish Hatchery."

He nodded solemnly. "Do you want me to show you the way?"

Margie hesitated. She didn't fear the man, but was still nervous about getting help from a strange man with no one there to back her up. She wished she'd at least had Stella.

"I'm harmless," the man said in amusement.

Margie forced a smile. "I'm sure you are," she laughed. "I'm just overly cautious."

"There are people around. I'm not going to do anything to you out in public. It's back this way, which is busier, more people. More witnesses." He motioned the direction Margie had come from.

Margie was embarrassed by her own reluctance to walk with him. She was a cop. She was trained in self-defense. She was not armed but, chances were, he wasn't either. The homeless in Calgary didn't generally carry. A knife, maybe, for self-protection, but it was rare for them to have firearms.

The man moved out of the shadows of the underpass. Margie gave him another quick assessment. He was both younger and cleaner than she had thought at first. She felt slightly less threatened. He wasn't a teenager, but maybe a few years younger than she was. He didn't have any bruises or other indications that he'd been in a fight or any trouble lately. Not that bruises would have indicated he was guilty of anything.

He walked toward her, and Margie stepped backward to let him pass by her with enough space between them to feel comfortable. He kept walking, then glanced back at her.

"This way. I'll show you."

Margie followed, allowing a little more space to build between them.

"I don't think I've seen you here before," the man commented.

Did he know all of the regulars? Everyone who came through the park? It didn't seem likely. But he was right that she didn't get there very often. Her walk there with Christina and Stella on Sunday had been her first trip to Pearce Estate in years.

"I used to come here years ago," she told him. "But I just recently moved to Calgary... well, a little over a year ago. But COVID, you know. I didn't get out much."

"No wonder you got lost. It's changed a lot since then."

"Well... to be fair... I'm also really good at getting lost." Margie laughed. It was an embarrassment to her. Someone with her heritage should be able to find her way around by the stars or have an inbuilt sense of true north. But both direction and distance seemed to be problematic. She could even get lost following her GPS. That took some talent.

The man laughed. Margie took a deep breath and let it out again, feeling more relaxed. There were more people around them, and she didn't think that the young man was going to do anything to hurt her. "What's your name?"

"What's yours?" he countered.

"I'm Margie." She didn't put out her hand to shake. A large number of people didn't like to shake hands since the advent of COVID protocols. She also didn't introduce herself as a homicide investigator. She was sure she could find her way back to her car on her own, but there was no reason to scare him and lose her guide.

He nodded. "Lewis."

"Oh!" Margie was taken aback. The very person she had been looking for. She was momentarily at a loss for words, unsure whether to say anything now. She stood still, trying to decide how to introduce herself or what she was doing there.

He raised his brows. "Not the usual reaction. You have a cousin Lewis who is an ax murderer?"

"No, uh... I heard your name mentioned earlier today. I was kind of..." She wasn't sure she wanted to say she was looking for him. That might spook him. People didn't like it when people were looking for them or following them. And the homeless were that much more likely to be upset by it.

"You heard my name mentioned?" He frowned. "You heard it mentioned where?" He looked up and down the pathway as if the answer might be there.

"I, uh... well, it might not have even been about you, but I was looking for someone named Lewis who sometimes… has a camp out this way. Or…" she motioned, "toward the train bridge."

"Yeah?" His dark eyes bored into her. He was no longer the causal, friendly stranger that he had been. And Margie couldn't blame him for that. She would not have been pleased to hear someone else was looking for her camp either. "Why would you be looking for me?"

"I'm not actually looking for you. Not primarily, I mean. I'm trying to get a line on the woman who was up there yesterday. Where the train is."

"What woman?"

"There was a woman up there," Margie said slowly, feeling her way through it. "When the train came through."

CHAPTER EIGHT

a woman? Up there when someone was hit by the train?" Lewis asked.

Margie nodded.

Lewis frowned, thinking about it. "Why would a woman be there? Everything is set up so that people walk under the crossing. You can't get onto the tracks unless you really want to."

"I guess she was camped out there," Margie suggested.

"*She* was camped there? No. She wasn't."

"I saw her tent and bike."

He shook his head. "Not hers."

"Really? How do you know that? Unless you were there…?"

"Yeah, I was there," he said in irritation. "That was *my* camp."

"Oh… oh, I didn't realize. I thought… well, when she was first hit, I thought a homeless man had been killed. That whoever's camp it was…" She shrugged. "That you had walked onto the tracks for some reason."

He just stared at her.

"And then this morning, I talked to the medical examiner's office, and they informed me that she was a woman, not a man. So I'm trying to find her identity, asking around, and someone said to ask you, that you hung out in that area and might know her."

"What woman?" Lewis asked, brow furrowed. "It was someone I know?"

"I don't know. You're my best lead right now. She was a large woman. Tall and quite broad shoulders. And she was bald. Her head was shaved."

"A big, bald woman?" Lewis asked. "You're saying that a big, bald woman was killed up there by my camp, and you think it is someone I know."

"Yes. That's the idea."

He shook his head. "I don't know any bald women."

"Are you sure? I wonder if maybe she wore a hat or a wig normally, but it was lost when she was hit... Sometimes, in motor vehicle accidents, people are hit right out of their shoes."

"How big are you talking?"

"Uh... it was pretty hard to tell yesterday when the remains were... being recovered. The shoulders..." Margie tried to estimate, holding her hands out, envisioning the body, and then holding them up for Lewis so he could try to envision a woman with shoulders that width.

He shook his head slowly. "No. I don't think so. No one pops into mind. Most of the women I know out here are quite slim. A couple of fatter older ladies. But they are not tall. Or bald."

"She was probably in her fifties. Older than you, but not... that old."

"Plenty of old women on the street. But big women like that... no."

Margie nodded. "Okay. I don't know what she would have been doing up there. Unless maybe she wanted to see you." She looked at Lewis. "You moved your stuff? Camped somewhere else last night because of the train accident and all of the cops?"

He raised his brows. "The cops stole all of my stuff. You think they would let me walk back up there and get it? After they all left, I went to see if there was still a guard there or if I could get my things, but it was all gone. They figured they could just help themselves, I guess."

"No, we thought it was you who had been killed..." Margie spoke without thinking. "The crime tech guys would have taken it all as evidence. They wouldn't have left it there."

"You thought I was killed. *You?*"

"Well... it seemed like the logical conclusion. Someone was hit by a train there, and there was a camp. We just assumed that whoever was camped there was the one who had been hit. I'm sorry. I can find out what happened to the things they took from the scene and see what I can recover for you."

"You're a cop?" He looked her over thoughtfully. "I don't know any Native cops."

Margie nodded. "There are not a lot of us around. I'm from Manitoba. I'm the only Indigenous woman in my department. I don't know how many there are in the entire Calgary Police Service. Probably only one or two others, if that."

He nodded slowly. "So you're... in what department? You patrol parks? I always wondered if those park cops are *real* cops."

"They are," Margie said. "They work for the province or the city rather than Calgary Police Services, but they are still peace officers. Carry a gun, make arrests, investigate complaints, that kind of thing."

"Where's your gun?"

"I'm not carrying one. I didn't anticipate needing one for a walk in the park or talking to people along Ninth Avenue."

"Would you really talk to them about getting my stuff back? I didn't think there was any way I would ever see any of it again."

"Yes, of course," Margie assured him. "I'm sure once they have had a chance to review it and confirmed that it didn't have anything to do with the accident or the accident victim, they will be happy to return it to the rightful owner."

"I didn't have anything to do with that woman. Whoever she was. I just slept there."

"I'll pass that along. I'm sorry that happened... you can't have had a very comfortable night."

"No," he agreed. "It's getting cold at night. Not even having a blanket or a sleeping bag..."

"Did you go to the Drop-in Center or a shelter? I understand that a few of the churches in the area might be open at night."

"No. I don't go to those places if I can help it. If it's thirty below... Last night, mostly, I just walked to keep warm. Sat on a bench if I got too tired." He stretched and rubbed his neck and shoulders. "Not the most restful night I ever had."

Margie looked for something she could offer him. Some way to make it up to him. But she couldn't think of anything other than retrieving his gear for him.

"Is there… a way I can reach you if I can get your stuff back? A phone number or a friend I can call?"

"If you get it… just put it back where it was. I'll check."

"Just leave it there?"

He nodded. "Just leave it. I'll be back."

CHAPTER NINE

G ot a briefing," Jones informed Margie as she returned to her desk in the bullpen.

Margie stopped in her tracks and looked at Jones. "Really? I just got back."

"I didn't think you were going to get back in time. Yeah, they've made some progress. Want to bring everybody up to speed."

"Who's made progress?"

"OCME. And I got a possible hit on a missing person. We'll put our heads together and see if we can verify it."

"You got a hit? Why didn't you call me?"

"Things have been too crazy. We need a briefing to get everyone up to speed."

"Okay. Give me a minute to get myself together and I'll be in there."

Margie walked back to her desk, unlocked her drawer, put her handbag in, and then relocked it. She wanted to take a minute to see what had arrived in email while she had been gone and to jot down a few notes before she started to forget anything she had learned in her canvass of the neighborhood and the park. But she could see that everyone was already heading toward the briefing room. The notes she had jotted down during her interviews would have to do for the moment.

"Briefing, Patenaude," MacDonald snapped as he moved from the break room toward the briefing room with a fresh cup of coffee.

"Yes sir, on my way."

Margie stood so he would see she was doing as she was asked and not lingering at her desk. She unlocked her screen and clicked the mouse several times to get a quick view of her inbox. She only had time to skim over senders and subject lines when someone else called out that they were ready to begin. She jogged from her desk to the briefing room to enter immediately behind MacDonald. He turned and looked at her, then nodded.

As usual, briefings were "stand-up" meetings. No one took the chairs circling the boardroom table, but stood behind them, waiting for MacDonald to begin. Thinking on their feet. Staying alert. No way to nod off.

"Things are moving on the train accident," he announced. "We are getting feedback from several different directions, so let's take a few minutes to get everyone working from the same copy."

There were nods around the table.

"Patenaude, anything from your end? You've been canvassing the neighborhood."

"Uh, no, not much. There seems to be a consensus that the victim was not part of the homeless population in the area. No one could identify her. I was given the name of the fellow whose tent and campsite were next to the accident scene. We had thought it was the victim's, but it was not." Nods around the table. "And he'd like his house back," Margie added.

Muffled laughter. MacDonald looked at Patenaude.

"Are you being smart?"

Margie shook her head. "No. I talked to him briefly. He has nowhere to sleep. All of his possessions were taken by the crime techs. He spent all night walking to stay warm."

The snickers were stifled, everyone immediately serious.

MacDonald frowned. "Call FCSU and see what you can get back. Anything that isn't obviously connected with the accident, let's get it released. If they are not the victim's possessions and were just articles found nearby that have nothing to do with the accident, we have no reason to hold them."

Margie nodded. "Good. I will."

"Anything else?"

"No, sir. I understand there has been some progress from OCME and maybe a missing person report?"

He moved on, displaying the medical examiner's initial findings on the big LCD screen.

"Victim was basically mincemeat. Dr. Galt refers to massive trauma. Everyone here has seen at least one picture of the state of the body when the train stopped. The good doctor refers to multiple blunt force trauma as well as nearly being transected by the wheels. He has done a preliminary tox screen, with no alcohol or popular street drugs present. More in-depth tox screens and blood and tissue tests were forwarded to FCSU. You know those will take a while to get back."

"No drugs or alcohol?" Cruz repeated in disbelief.

"Not on the rapid screen field tests, no. They'll follow up with gas chromatograph testing, but it looks like the victim was clean."

"Then why the hell was he—or she—on the train tracks?"

"We don't know yet. We don't know the victim's medical history, mental state, any of that. Diabetes, epilepsy, narcolepsy...? They will continue to do what tests they can on the tissue that they have. But as far as figuring out the number of blows or which direction he—she—was lying when the train struck, it is out of the question. The body hit various parts of the train and various moving parts came in contact with the body when it hit the ground."

It was probably a good thing that it wasn't a lunch meeting. Several faces around the table were looking a little green. Margie flipped absently through the pages of her notepad, her mind not registering the words on the paper.

"And the missing person report?" she prodded.

"Detective Jones," MacDonald directed, nodding at her.

"Thank you, sir. So, there were no matches late last night or early this morning when we ran the initial searches. We didn't miss anything despite not having the correct gender. But late this morning, a missing person report was filed for Sarah Thompson, age fifty-six, a large, rather eccentric woman who failed to return home last night or to answer her phone today."

"She did have a home," Margie observed, relieved she had not just been totally inept in her canvass of the homeless population in Inglewood and the park.

"She did have a home," Jones confirmed. "She was a resident of Ramsay." She paused. "For those of you who do not know, Ramsay is a neighborhood that abuts Inglewood. The average residential listings are currently $1.6 million."

Margie coughed to cover a gasp. She had been canvassing the homeless community for a woman who owned a house in the range of a million and a half dollars. No wonder none of them had recognized her from her description.

"Okay, then," she said in a strangled voice. "And what do we know about Sarah Thompson?"

"She matches the physical description down to the shaved head. As I said, she was widely known as an eccentric. That was one of her eccentricities."

"Was another standing on train tracks?" Gagnon muttered.

He was favored with glares from MacDonald and Jones, and ducked his head, looking away again.

"We don't talk about victims that way," MacDonald said. "They are people who deserve our respect. Carry on, Detective Jones."

"Thompson was a well-respected artist. She received multiple awards. Was frequently shown in galleries both in Calgary and in other cities and countries. Her style was…" Jones's eyes dropped to her cheat sheet. "Postmodern symbology."

Everyone was silent.

"What does that look like?" Siever asked when no one else admitted to not having a clue what it meant.

"Umm… so she used a lot of bright colors, flat, with a… postmodern influence, and her works used a lot of symbolism to express her views on society."

Bright and flat and symbolic. Margie could understand that much, at least.

"Did she spend a lot of time at Pearce Estate Park?" Sergeant MacDonald asked. "She lived in the area. She was killed there. Did she wander around the park taking pictures, using a sketchpad, getting inspired in other ways?"

"The woman who reported her missing, her executive assistant, didn't suggest that she might have been at the park or have run into problems at the park. It sounded more like she was reclusive and should have been at home in her studio. We haven't started conducting interviews with her family and friends. Hopefully, one of them can tell us why she was in the park or what she might have been doing there."

"Any other areas we need to follow up on?"

"I don't think so," Jones shook her head and looked at Margie.

"No, the next thing is to talk to the next of kin. Do the death notification. Confirm her routines, if she normally walked in Pearce Estate Park or had reason to be there. Do we know next of kin? What was in the missing person report?"

"There are some distant relations. The person to be notified is this executive assistant."

"Okay. I'll go out to make the notification. Do you want to come with me?"

Detective Jones nodded and smoothed down a few locks of blond hair that were curling up. "Yes. I'll get the information together and we can go over this afternoon. She said she would stay at the house in case Thompson came back."

Margie imagined the executive assistant sitting alone in the big, quiet house, waiting for her boss's footsteps or a key turning in the door.

CHAPTER TEN

Some of the houses they passed in Ramsay were spectacular. Others looked like regular bungalows built fifty or more years before. Margie guessed they were fixed up inside and were at the lower end of the market. The houses that balanced out the five-million-dollar homes to bring the average down to one and a half million.

"Unbelievable," Jones said as she looked out the window at some of the fancier houses. "Can you imagine living in something like that?"

Margie shook her head in response. "You've seen my house."

"And you haven't even seen my apartment. It's pretty basic, and I still have to budget to afford it."

"I'll bet most of these owners don't even have kids," Margie said, looking at them. "Just one or two residents, in all of that glory."

"Sitting at opposite ends of the dinner table," Jones laughed. "Using a butler to pass the salt and pepper from one end to the other."

Margie smiled. "Maybe so."

The house they pulled up to was one of the more splendid houses. Not something that had been standing there fifty years earlier, Margie decided. The owners had knocked down the previous house on the property. Or maybe two houses spread across two lots, and in their place had built up a mansion full of glittering windows. It probably cost a fortune to heat in the winter with all those windows. And to keep it cool in the summer.

But if the owner was an artist, she probably needed a lot of natural light, at least in her workroom.

They got out of the car and approached the house. They didn't need to ring the doorbell, because the door was immediately opened as they started to walk up the front sidewalk.

The woman who opened the door reminded Margie of a greyhound. Skinny, with a pointed nose, looking as though she might dash off at any moment. She waited for them, practically quivering with impatience.

"I'm Violet," she told them breathlessly. "Violet Brody. I'm the one who called it in." She wrung her hands. "Oh, I'm so worried. Nothing like this has ever happened before. Sarah likes to keep to a regular routine. She is very particular about doing everything the right way, the same way every time. She has a very strict schedule and doesn't like deviating from it. So I knew something was wrong when she didn't come home last night. But I thought maybe she had met someone, maybe stayed out for drinks. People can... have fun, can't they? She might have run into an old friend or made a new one." She paused to take a gulp of air. "It could happen."

"It's okay," Margie said soothingly, touching the woman's shoulder to try to calm her. "Why don't we go inside and sit down."

"I can't imagine what's happened to her. This just isn't like Sarah. She's always very predictable. When she didn't answer her phone, I thought maybe she was sick. That she got in late this morning and was still in bed, sick, or maybe sleeping off a hangover. I didn't know what to think, since none of that made sense. But she was human, wasn't she? People can do unexpected things."

Violet led them into a spacious great room. There was a conversation area with a fireplace, a dining room table, a kitchen counter and appliances, everything sleek, modern lines. No clutter. It looked like a showroom rather than somewhere someone actually lived. But Sarah probably had servants that kept it clean without her lifting a finger.

"Does Ms. Thompson drink?" she asked Violet. "Has anything like this happened before?"

"No, nothing like this. I've never known her to take a drop of alcohol or anything like recreational drugs. She believed in keeping her body pure and healthy. She wouldn't contaminate it with anything non-organic, let alone anything intoxicating. But I thought... I didn't know what else to think. I thought that maybe, this one time, she had indulged. People do. Even those who have strong beliefs are sometimes tempted. Slip up."

"Yes. That does happen," Margie agreed.

They already knew that Sarah hadn't had any alcohol or recreational drugs in her system. But the fact that her assistant had suspected it worried Margie. It was something that had to be followed up on.

"Let's sit down."

Most of the chairs in the conversation area looked very uncomfortable, but Margie managed to pick out a seat on the couch that wasn't bad. There was no back support, but she leaned forward with her elbows on her knees and was fine. She readjusted her mask.

"Was there anything about Sarah's behavior lately that made you think she was upset about something? That she might be tempted to drink or take something... to settle her down? Had she been behaving strangely?"

"Well, she was... no, I don't think so. I can't think of anything that had changed or was new. She was just... just *Sarah*. She could be erratic."

"I thought you said that she was predictable? That she liked to follow the same routines all the time," Jones pointed out.

"She did. She always wanted everything *just so*, but her moods were... she was a moody person. She could jump from one thought to another very abruptly and was very hard to follow sometimes. She would be talking about one thing and then would suddenly switch topics and be angry about something completely unrelated. I think... she liked routine because her brain was so... variable. It was her way of trying to keep everything on an even keel."

"Was there anything in particular that she had been upset about lately?" Margie asked.

"I don't know. She was working on a new series of paintings, but I didn't know what they were about."

"What they were about?"

Violet nodded. She paced, unable to settle herself down in one place.

"She painted *about* things. Symbols. Social issues that she felt were important. Things that she wanted her viewers to think about. They weren't just pretty pictures. They were intended to... make people think about the way they saw the world."

"Oh," Margie and Jones nodded. "I see," Margie said. "And she had started a new series of paintings to educate her audience about something, but you didn't know what."

Violet agreed. She wrung her hands some more. "I can't think what could have happened to her. She should be back here. I don't see what this has to do with her paintings or anything else. Something must have happened to her. I've been calling the hospitals, but you know, they really won't tell you anything. I always thought that was what you were supposed to do when someone was missing. Start calling the hospitals. But they just keep citing confidentiality and saying they can't talk to me about anyone who has been admitted. So, does that mean that she is in their system or not? They won't even tell me."

"Could you sit down, Miss Brody?" Margie motioned to one of the uncomfortable-looking chairs. "We need you to sit down and listen for a minute."

CHAPTER ELEVEN

*V*iolet looked at her, frozen. Maybe anticipating the reason for the request.

"What is it? What has happened?"

"Could we sit and talk?"

Violet wrung her hands again and finally alighted on a chair, looking like a bird that would take flight at the least movement from them.

"I'm afraid that something *has* happened," Margie told her gently. "I'm afraid that there was an accident yesterday, and Ms. Thompson was killed."

Violet gasped and swore and covered her mouth. She sputtered, looking for the right words. She sprang to her feet again, far from collapsing like Margie had thought that she would. She held her head between her hands, holding everything in, keeping it from exploding.

"No, this can't be true," she protested. "Oh, no. Oh, no. You don't know how awful this is. Oh, no."

"Are you sure you don't need to sit down?" Jones suggested.

Violet was back to pacing again, frenetic. Unable to keep all of the shock and horror inside. She had to work it out physically somehow.

"No, no. Where is she? What happened? Are you sure it is even her?"

"We're pretty sure. We will need to get some DNA samples to match, if we can. To be one hundred percent sure. But Ms. Thompson was… quite unique in her appearance."

"It could be someone else. Maybe someone was pretending to be her. It could, couldn't it? If you don't have proof, you don't know for sure."

"You know that she didn't come home last night," Jones pointed out gently. "That you can't reach her today. That none of that is in keeping with her normal personality and practices. You already knew something had happened to her before you called us."

Violet wailed, holding her head. "I knew it had to be something awful. She would have been here, unless something horribly tragic had happened to her. She would always be here. Even on a night when she had a showing that went late, she was always here by ten. Like clockwork."

"She needed that routine."

"Yes." Violet sniffled and swiped at her nose. She hadn't started crying and didn't have a tissue in her hand. Margie glanced around the room for a box of tissues. She hadn't thought to bring anything in with her. Usually, she kept a purse pack of Kleenex tissues for just such an occasion. But she had assumed that there would be a box handy in a big house like this.

"What happened to her?" Violet asked with another sniffle.

"There was an accident in the park."

Violet shook her head. "What park?"

Margie had wondered whether Sarah walked there often. Whether that was part of her routine. She might go there to exercise, sketch, or get inspiration, to clear her head before or after a big project. She might consider it "her" park. Maybe she had seen the homeless encampment and had confronted Lewis, wanting to keep her park clean and pristine. Pure, like her body.

"Pearce Estate Park," Jones advised. "Did she go there often?"

"Pearce Estate Park? Over by the river? No, she didn't really like it over there. Said that it was too… urban. Too many people, too many bums. Her words, not mine. Full of sniveling little kids, bums, and cyclists who wouldn't watch where they were going."

"So she had been there," Margie observed. "But she didn't enjoy spending time there."

"She liked wilderness areas. When she needed to get back to nature, she would go on a retreat. Sometimes, between art projects, as a sort of palate cleanser. Get back to nature. Clear her head. She would go to these places that were really wild. Where there weren't a lot of computers or tourists."

"I get the feeling she didn't really like people," Margie suggested, giving Violet a little smile in the hopes of taking the edge off the question.

"Well, no. She would be the first one to tell you that, so I can't very well tell you otherwise. If I did, someone would just tell you the truth anyway. I think she liked people better than she pretended to. She could be... tender at times. She often inquired after my parents, and it wasn't just the sort of casual friendly inquiry that you are supposed to say 'fine' to and go on with the conversation. She really wanted to know. She had a lot of expectations of the people she worked with, a lot of high expectations. But if something happened... if you were sick, or had a sick kid or parent, or a death in the family, she expected you to take the time off. There was no question about it. She treated people... the way she would want to be treated, I think."

"Tough but fair?" Jones suggested.

"Yeah. She had high expectations of herself, too. It wasn't just like everyone around her was there to serve her. She wanted... for people to have expectations of her, too. To hold her to a high standard. She demanded that we always tell her exactly what we thought, whether it was about one of her paintings or something else."

"And she tried to keep her body pure, and to educate people through her art," Margie said, starting to build a picture of this woman in her mind. Tough. Hard to please. But tough on herself, too. Expecting herself to attain or surpass the standards she set for others around her.

"Yes. She was always trying to improve herself."

"Any idea why she would have been in the park?" Jones asked. "Anything you can think of that might have led her there?"

"I can't think... unless it was something about her new project. Sometimes, she had to do research at a particular location. Or to meet someone. She was very hands-on. She expected all of her work to be... authentic. Even if it was symbolic."

"I wonder if we could see some of her work," Margie suggested. "Maybe we can understand it better."

"Yes, of course," Violet agreed. "Yes, come with me and I'll take you to her studio."

Margie and Jones rose to their feet.

CHAPTER TWELVE

*J*ones and Margie followed Violet out of the great room and up the stairs to the next level. Almost the entire second floor was one open room, with windows lining each wall so that the room was awash with light even in the afternoon light of the fall. There were a few easels with current work on them. Paintings that would never be completed now. Maybe Thompson's most priceless works.

There were several clusters of gallery walls that looked like the dissected pieces of a labyrinthine maze, different sections jutting away from each other at right angles, forming intersections and corners. A painting or two was displayed on each piece of wall.

"Start over here," Violet instructed, walking over to one of the displays.

Margie and Jones studied the paintings. As Jones had explained in the briefing, they were brightly colored, flat images. Not cartoonish, exactly, but without the shading and detail Margie would have expected from a great artist. Pictures that would have worked well in a literary magazine or on the cover of the latest women's fiction offerings.

On the display walls were a number of paintings with subjects such as a tree stump, smokestacks, and dead or injured animals. Margie shifted uncomfortably. They were disturbing. Especially the ones with animals in them. Despite her upbringing in a hunting and fishing society, Margie had a very tender heart where animals were concerned. Stella was a member of her family, not a lower creature. Christina had been experimenting with vegetarianism, and Margie had not pushed too hard back against it, other than telling Christina that she needed to make sure she got all of the iron and other minerals her body needed. Margie would probably never go vegetarian herself, but she didn't mind eating mostly vegetarian meals with Christina. It was ridiculous for the two of them to make two separate meals.

"It's about... industrialization?" Jones suggested. "About the negative effects of industrialization."

Violet nodded her agreement. "Of course. It's not exactly subtle. She wanted people to understand what it was about, how she felt about the subject."

They looked at that set of paintings for a few minutes, and then Violet pointed to another collection. They all walked over to the little cluster of brightly colored paintings.

Most of them featured houses with dark windows. Some were big and empty. Others were small and in poor repair. Margie stared at them, picking out some of the other symbols in the pictures. There were a few that showed forged iron chains, thick and chunky. Others showed outstretched hands, either grasping or cupped, begging to be filled. Margie looked at Jones, who gave her a look that said, "This one is yours."

Margie grimaced, trying to decide what to say about it. "My first guess would be that this one is about... the housing market... homelessness... lack of affordable housing...?"

Violet nodded. "Not bad, detective." She seemed far more comfortable touring them around the showroom than she had answering questions downstairs. Margie assumed it was something she had done many times before. She knew what she was doing here, on solid ground.

"But..." Margie looked around and made a small movement to indicate their surroundings. "Making a statement about the disparity between the rich and the poor and the affordability of housing for the working poor while living in a house like this...?"

Violet nodded. "She was aware of the hypocrisy. She knew her own failings, but that didn't stop her 'talking' about it in her art. Of course, when she created this series, it was before she lived here. She was in a much more modest house at that time, before she really hit it big. She went through her own struggles to reach this level of success. And she knew that... other people could not afford houses like this. That just blocks away... they are sleeping on sidewalks and in doorways."

"Or in the park," Margie suggested.

"Yes, I suppose they probably are, though I haven't been there myself to see them."

Jones gazed at the paintings. "It is a very engaging style. You want to look at it for a long time. To work out the symbolism of each individual piece as well as the overall effect."

"Yes," Violet agreed.

"How long have you been working for Ms. Thompson?"

"Oh, that's a good question... maybe... eight years. Since the divorce."

"The divorce?" Margie asked sharply. Spouses and ex-spouses were always at the top of the list of homicide suspects. "I didn't know she had been married."

"You won't find much out about it in mainstream media," Violet admitted. "She worked hard with public relations companies to neutralize any articles that mentioned Jonathan. To make sure that he didn't show up in anyone casually searching for information on Sarah."

"How do you do that?" Jones asked. "I thought that you couldn't delete anything from the internet."

"There are ways to get articles deleted, especially for someone wealthy and powerful. But even then, there are still records in archive systems. The Wayback Machine and things like that. If you know what you're looking for. But mostly, the idea is to create so much other content that anything you don't want to be revealed is pushed to the fifth or sixth page of results. No one looks past the first page or two. The top three hits comprise sixty percent of the traffic. No one looks that far into their search results, so it is effectively erased from the internet's memory."

"And she didn't want people to know she had been married?" Margie asked.

"She had a lot of choice things to say about marriage and society's expectations of women," Violet said with a shrug. "She didn't want to be seen in those traditional roles of wife or divorcee. She wanted to be seen as a strong, independent person, not burdened with all of those expectations. She didn't want to conform to gender roles."

"Is that the reason for shaving her head?" Jones suggested.

"I suppose…" Violet thought about it. "I always thought of that as 'Sarah just being Sarah,' but I guess it is all tied up into that same package. She wasn't one to do anything just because of society's expectations."

Jones nodded. "Tell us about her ex. Jonathan."

"He was a mistake. A youthful indiscretion, except that they'd gotten married. Sarah said many times that she wished that the two of them had just had a torrid affair, gotten it out of their systems, and gone their separate directions. But she had gone down the path dictated by our society and regretted it almost immediately. They were married for… twenty years? Twenty-five?"

"Wow. That long. And she regretted it the whole time?"

"To hear her tell it, yes. I don't know whether it was the truth or just bitter feelings in the end. It was messy. She said that Jonathan was just a leech, wanted all of her fame and fortune for himself."

"So instead of letting him ride the coattails of her success, she erased him," Margie said, feeling for her notepad. She needed to get a few details down on paper before she forgot anything.

Violet nodded, looking down. "There were a lot of bitter feelings, I know. But… that was Sarah. She didn't really care if people hated her. She thought we should be able to decide who we like or don't like for ourselves and not have to pretend to like and get along with everyone. That it's better to be honest about our feelings than to hide them."

Margie had seen what brutal honesty could do to a marriage. She hadn't experienced it personally, but they'd had a case not so long ago, and she could attest to how unrestrained expressions of honest feelings could tear apart a previously good relationship.

"How can we reach Jonathan?"

"I have his number on my computer. I can get it for you."

"Good." Margie nodded. "And who else should we know about who had bad feelings toward Sarah?"

"Well… I can try to get a list together."

"How many are there?"

"I don't know… a few."

A few people or a few dozen?

"I'd appreciate whatever information you could give us."

"Has she received any threats?" Jones inquired.

"Some. Not a lot."

Since most people didn't get threats, any number was significant.

"Did you keep a file? Report any of them to the police?"

"No. She said just to delete them or throw them in the trash. There would always be people who resorted to threats of violence, but she wasn't concerned anyone would actually follow through. Mostly, they were anonymous or obviously fake names."

Jones and Margie looked at each other.

Was it possible that Sarah's accident could be something other than an accident? They had been approaching it from the angle of someone who had just happened to be on the tracks when the train had come along. Maybe she hadn't been drunk or high, but maybe confused for another reason. A reaction to a medication. A psychotic break. Possibly suicidal. But was it possible that someone had intentionally killed her?

MacDonald would not like it. From the beginning, no one had seen it as anything other than a tragic accident.

"Is there anyone other than her ex-husband that we should be talking to? That had significant resentments? Do you know who was named in her will?"

Violet walked over to the next collection of paintings, frowning and staring at them like she'd never seen them before.

"I thought you said… it was an accident," Violet said. "What do you mean?"

"It was, as far as we can tell. But we need to be sure. For the sake of a thorough investigation. We need to eliminate all other possibilities."

"What kind of accident was it? I thought… maybe she tripped and fell. Or was she hit by one of those insane bikers? Or those electric scooters. Everything now has to have electricity. Power. No one can just walk anymore. Those things zip all over the place and are bound to kill someone sooner or later. Sarah hated them."

"No." Margie licked her lips and tried to think of the gentlest way to put it. There was no point in trying to keep it from Violet. It would be one of the first things that hit the news. Local celebrity killed by train. It wouldn't be possible to avoid it. "I'm afraid… it was not a scooter or a bike. Or a fall. It was a train."

"A train?" Violet repeated. "The train doesn't come this far. Only the buses go through Inglewood."

"Not the c-train," Jones clarified. "The regular train. The railway bridge that comes across the Bow in Pearce Estate Park…"

"That train? But how? It goes over the bridge. The pathway goes underneath the tracks."

"She circumvented the safety features. Climbed the hill up to the tracks."

Violet stood there with her mouth open. Everyone was quiet for a while. Margie thought that Violet needed some time and space to work through all of this. It wouldn't be easy to find that the person she had worked with for eight years had been killed in such a freakish, violent accident.

If it was an accident.

CHAPTER THIRTEEN

*M*argie went over to one of the easels with work in progress. "So, is this one of the new series you mentioned?"

Violet walked over slowly, feet dragging as if they suddenly weighed twenty pounds each. She looked at the painting for a few minutes, as if seeing it for the first time. Margie waited, looking at the bright colors.

The cheerful tones were at odds with the subject matter. It was a portrait of an unhappy-looking male artist with slashes across it as if it had been cut with a razor blade. The slashes appeared realistic from a distance but, upon closer inspection, they were clearly brushstrokes.

"Yes," Violet agreed. "This is the new series that she was working on."

"What was it about?"

She shook her head slowly. "Sarah didn't tell me exactly what it was about. She never shared her inspirations or plans before she started a new project. She would dig in, do her research, make mock-ups and plans, and then she would paint, paint, paint, and no one was allowed to see them until she was done."

"But you could, since you were here with her."

"Well, yes, I would see what she was working on. But I didn't hang around while she was painting. I would let her work on them by herself. Keep interruptions to a minimum. I *never* commented on the paintings, never asked her about them. It was important to stay out of the way and not interrupt the process. Be invisible."

Margie nodded slowly. "Do you know who this is in the picture?"

"No. It might not be anyone. It might just be out of her imagination. She didn't usually do portraits of living people. She certainly never had anyone sit for her. She might have taken pictures of someone but, if she had," Violet looked around, "she would have it posted somewhere nearby to refer to."

"Are there others in the series?"

Violet pointed to another easel. Margie looked at the painting sitting on it. Cheerfully painted crayons, pens, and paintbrushes, all broken. Margie stood looking at it for a minute. A third easel held a canvas with only the beginnings of shapes sketched onto it. Trees in the background. Something else in the foreground that looked like pop cans and bottles.

"So... broken art tools and a slashed painting. Someone who is... destroying art?"

"I guess so. I hadn't talked to her about it. So I don't know what the inspiration was or where she was going to go with it. I wish I could tell you more, but... she didn't like to share those things before she had a final product. She didn't share ideas, only the final product. Anyone who wanted to see the inner workings..." Violet shook her head. "No one was allowed into that world."

Except for Violet herself, of course. It seemed like she kept forgetting to put herself in the equation. So the police wouldn't include her in the suspect list? Except that there was no suspect list. There was no murder case—just a woman who had died in a tragic accident.

A woman who was notorious, received plenty of threats, spoke out against social issues even though she was part of the group she was attacking, had secrets, and had an ex-husband. And the price of all of her work was about to skyrocket.

"Did Ms. Thompson have a will?"

"I guess so. I'll have to check through the files. She was very careful about documentation and filing, so I'm sure if she had a current one, it will be in the file system."

"Okay. We'll want a copy of that and the ex-husband's phone number. The names of anyone you can remember who threatened her life." Margie looked at Jones. "Am I missing anything?"

"DNA sample. Day planner, if she kept one. We should probably look at her office, if she had one here. Any medications she was on."

Margie nodded. "Yeah. All of that. Could we get her toothbrush and hairbrush?"

Violet nodded her agreement. "Yes, I can get those for you. But I don't understand why you need them to make a positive ID. There are plenty of pictures of Sarah around. You can compare them."

Margie shook her head. "Unfortunately, no. And you don't want to know the details, so you should just leave it there. We will need DNA for comparison."

Violet stood staring at her for a minute, then finally gave a single nod. "Yes. Fine. You can come upstairs to her office, her bedroom, bathroom, and look at whatever you want to. Take whatever you need."

Margie wasn't going to turn down a blanket permission. So much nicer than having to get a warrant to go through Sarah's office and personal living space. "Thank you. That's very helpful. If you want to look for that will and see if she kept any copies of any of the threats, that will be helpful and save us some time."

CHAPTER FOURTEEN

*M*argie uploaded the last of her notes into the shared workspace for the Thompson investigation, and looked through the various other bits of evidence that the lab had already processed. There wasn't a lot to go on yet. Some litter had been collected along with the biological matter at the accident scene, but nothing that seemed to be connected with the accident itself. Nothing that obviously belonged to Sarah Thompson. No indication that anyone else had been in the area around the time that she was killed.

Other than Lewis, the homeless man, and Margie was pretty sure that he had absolutely nothing to do with Sarah's death. There wouldn't have been any reason for him to attack her. Sarah apparently did not want to hang around anywhere there were "bums," so it was doubtful that she would have climbed that hill up to where the train was and then stayed there knowing that Lewis was around or could be back at any minute. She fought for the cause of the homeless but didn't want to be around them. Not an uncommon sentiment.

Margie called the Forensic Crime Scenes Unit to talk to them about Lewis's possessions. She didn't want him to be awake all night again, trying to keep warm and safe. He needed his gear back.

"The contents of the tent and shopping cart that were collected at the

Thompson accident scene, have those all been inventoried?" she asked FCSU Investigator Dunn.

"On a preliminary basis. We haven't had a chance to go through and do any testing yet. No idea what is or isn't relevant right now."

"As it turns out, they are not the possessions of the victim. So if there isn't anything to indicate a connection with the victim or the accident, then they should be released."

"We were told that they *did* belong to the victim."

"That was when we thought that the victim was a homeless male. It seemed to make sense. But as it turns out, the victim was a rather wealthy woman who just happened to choose that place to die. She didn't live there. None of that belonged to her."

"You know who they do belong to?"

"A man named Lewis Riley."

"You got his contact information?"

"No, but I know where to take the stuff for him."

"Hmm." Dunn didn't sound too happy about the situation. "I'm all for giving the guy back his junk if it isn't related to the case. No point in us storing it here. But we like to have the owner sign a claim slip. Giving it to one of the detectives without any receipt to say that he's got it…"

"I'll sign your claim slip."

"That's really not procedure, detective."

"I know that. But we need to be reasonable about this. He can't get down there to pick it all up. I mean, he could, but he'd have to walk, and we're the ones who took it away from him in the first place. We shouldn't be putting him out to return it. And I'd have to find him, bring him in, and take him back today, because he needs somewhere to sleep tonight. It's much more reasonable for me to just take it to him."

"I suppose. If you're going to sign all of the papers. It's not policy, so you'll take all the heat if he complains or sues us."

"He's not going to do that."

"You hope not."

"I talked to the guy today. He's very reasonable. He just wants his stuff back. If he gets it back with minimal fuss, he'll be a happy camper."

"Ha." Dunn gave an unenthusiastic laugh at her unintentional pun. "Like I say, if you're willing to take all the heat, I'm fine with that. I'll say you bullied me."

Margie laughed. "Fine, you do that. I'll back you up."

"I'll see you soon, then."

Margie looked at the time on the phone and started to pack her things to leave. She would need to drive to FCSU, pick everything up, take it to Lewis's campsite, and then drive home to spend the evening with Christina, assuming she didn't have too much work to do.

"Heading home?" Cruz asked, walking by Margie's desk with a fresh cup of coffee from the breakroom. He should be going home to his wife and kiddos pretty soon, too.

"Not quite yet. I have to run over to FCSU and then the park. Hopefully, everything will be ready to pick up, and I won't have to wait."

"Good luck with that," he said cheerfully.

"Thanks," Margie laughed.

❧

THERE WAS a lot of work to sort everything out. Margie hadn't even thought about the shopping cart and how she would get it to the park. Her first thought was just to leave it behind, because the rest of the gear would fit into her little car easily. But then how was she going to carry it across the park and up the embankment to where Lewis would be expecting to find it? It was way too heavy and awkward to transport everything without the cart.

Dunn assisted in folding down the seats and emptying the trunk, which proved to be the most suitable place for the cart. He then secured the cart and trunk lid, ensuring that Margie could drive somewhat safely.

"Just go slow," he advised, "and don't go over any bumps."

Luckily, it was only a short drive to the park. Unloading everything at the park was a little easier. She carefully packed all of Lewis's possessions into the cart and little trailer, hitched the trailer to the cart, and then started to pull the whole contraption down the paved pathway to the train bridge.

She probably should not have been surprised at the glares and slurs she heard from the various park patrons she encountered when walking through the park pulling the cart despite her clean and neat appearance. No one looked past the cart. She was pulling a cart full of junk through the park and, therefore, she was a homeless person. And not just a homeless person, but a dirty Indian. Someone who was obviously just a drunk —lazy and unable to hold down a job. Her face was flaming hot. She didn't waste her time stopping to educate people. Those who reacted that way were not about to be convinced by logical arguments or evidence. They believed what they believed.

She reached the train bridge and looked up the embankment. She would probably need to take the trailer and the cart up separately. And she probably needed to unload the cart at least halfway to get it up there. It would take at least three trips, and she hoped she wouldn't end up stuck or tipping over the cart.

She unhitched the trailer and took it up the slope first, which was pretty easy. She went back down and looked at the cart.

"Give you a hand, detective?" said a voice in her ear.

Margie turned and saw Lewis standing there, smiling at her.

"Oh! I'm glad you're here. Yeah, with two of us, we can probably get it up there without unpacking everything first."

He nodded. "Much easier with two people," he agreed. He started up the embankment, grabbing the front of the cart. Margie stepped forward to grab the cart handle and push it forward. Lewis kept it from getting mired in the soft earth or stuck against any roots, and Margie kept the forward momentum. It only took a few minutes, and they had it back up under the trees where it had been before.

CHAPTER FIFTEEN

*T*hank you, Detective Pat."

Margie looked at Lewis curiously. She didn't remember introducing herself to Lewis as Detective Pat. Of course, he could have just shortened Patenaude to Pat on his own. It was a common solution for people who had problems remembering or pronouncing her last name. That was, of course, why she used Detective Pat in the first place.

But had she even introduced herself to him as Detective Patenaude? She couldn't remember telling him her name.

"You're welcome," she said with a smile. "I didn't want you to have another uncomfortable night. At least now you have time to set up before dark and to have a safe place to sleep."

"Yes. It would be nice to get *under cover* before the temperature drops too much."

Margie stared at him. Was her mind just jumping to unwarranted conclusions? Or was he trying to tell her something? She glanced around. There wasn't anyone else within earshot. They had effectively escaped the other park patrons who might have eavesdropped on them if they were still down on the paved pathway.

"Under cover?" she repeated.

Lewis chuckled. "It's not the most glamorous assignment I've ever had."

"*You're* a cop?"

He nodded. He didn't pull out a badge to prove it, but he was suddenly standing up straight, his whole demeanor changed. No longer the Lewis she had met earlier. She didn't need proof that he was who he said he was.

"After all this work, I went to get your equipment back to you," she griped to Lewis. "I just had to sign my life away to get this stuff all back. Drove here with the shopping cart sticking out of my trunk. Everyone I saw along the way, pulling the stupid cart behind me giving me the stink eye and thinking I was some shiftless, drunken Indian. Why didn't you tell me this morning you were a cop?"

He shrugged. "I needed to check you out first. Make sure you were okay. Get permission to talk to you." He looked at the cart full of his camping gear. "And I'm sorry people treated you that way." He shook his head grimly. "It really is eye-opening to see how the homeless are treated."

"I had an idea... but I had no idea."

He laughed again and nodded. "It is shocking," he said soberly. "But I have to admit, this is as good a cover as I've ever had. Nobody looks at me twice. Nobody looks at me *once*, I'm invisible."

"So what are you doing here? What are you investigating? Am I allowed to ask that?"

"You can ask, but I can't give you much of an answer. Street crimes. Drugs, mainly. But whatever else I happen to witness or overhear. Like I say, people don't even see me. They don't worry that I might be listening to their conversations. I am just a nobody."

"I'm sorry you're experiencing that," Margie said, sympathizing with his observation about the mistreatment of the indigent and homeless. "Even if it benefits your investigation."

He nodded his agreement. "It's just one of those things that I need to develop a thick skin about. I can't be worried about what people think of me or how they treat the homeless. Just be glad that I am so invisible and do the job that I've been sent here to do."

Margie nodded. She looked up at the train tracks, frowning and trying to formulate her questions. Initially, of course, she had thought that the person who had been killed by the train had been a homeless man. But that had changed when they had identified Thompson from the missing person report filed by Violet. Now, that opened up new questions. As did the fact that Lewis was an undercover cop.

"And thank you for treating me like a person when you saw me this morning," Lewis said. "I know I startled you and your instincts warned you that I might be dangerous. But you were kind and followed through on getting my equipment back for me. Not many people would have gone to such lengths."

It would have been modest of Margie to demur and say that she was sure that anyone would have done the same and that it had not been a big deal. But she knew that it wasn't true. Even most of the detectives in Homicide, who were good, moral, kindhearted people, would not have gone the extra mile to make sure that Lewis got back his camping gear so that he would have a place to sleep that night. They would brush it off and say he could go to the Drop-in Center, another shelter, or one of the churches that kept its doors open at night. Or he could wait another day or go to an outreach program that would provide him with a couple of blankets until he managed to beg, borrow, or steal what he needed to replenish his stores.

Margie shrugged uncomfortably and did her best to take the compliment gracefully. "Thank you. So… I have a question."

Lewis stared up at the sky, not looking at Margie. "What was she doing up here?"

Margie nodded. "Yes. Exactly."

"I'm afraid that I'm responsible for that." He cleared his throat and shook his head. "I don't understand why she was here that day in particular, or how she ended up in the path of the train. But she must have been here looking for me."

"So the two of you *did* know each other."

Maybe she had been in contact with Lewis on a previous project. The one on homelessness and poverty, for example.

"We were in art school together." Lewis saw the surprise in Margie's eyes. "Yeah. Believe it or not, I was once a promising young artist. On my way to becoming one of Calgary's elite creative minds, to quote the Calgary Herald Entertainment section."

Margie tried not to look too surprised at that. What had happened to change the course of Lewis's life from art to law enforcement?

"You have questions, I'm sure," Lewis acknowledged. "That's not the usual path into the police force."

"Well, no. Not exactly. What was it that changed your mind?"

He was still staring at the sky instead of looking at Margie. Deception? Or did he not want to look Margie in the eye because he felt vulnerable and exposed?

"A lot of things happened. The art scene is… quite a bit more cutthroat than you would imagine. It isn't all free-love hippie stuff. If you want to get into galleries and magazines, to have your work shown across the US and Canada, it is a lot of work, and the competition is fierce. Only a few—like Sarah Thompson—survive it."

"And the rest go into law enforcement?"

He laughed. "Well, it wasn't exactly a straight path. But after several forks in the road, that was where I ended up."

"And do you wish that you had stayed in art? Pursued those opportunities with more vigor?"

"Hell, no. I'd rather be shot than eviscerated."

Margie laughed, startled at the vehemence of his quick reply. "Okay, then. No. But you stayed in touch with Sarah Thompson?"

"No. I left the art scene and didn't see her again for years. In person, that is. I had seen her in the news, maybe even attended one of her shows in downtown Calgary, but I hadn't seen her face-to-face in many years. And then one day… she saw me here."

He spread his hands to indicate their surroundings.

"Right here?" Margie asked, back to the question of what Thompson had been doing off-trail and so close to the train tracks.

"No, not right here. In the park. I think she followed me from the streets in Inglewood after spotting me at random. An artist—she was good at recognizing people, even if I had changed a lot since we had seen each other last. She approached me. We talked a little."

"You didn't tell her you were undercover?"

"No. I probably could have, but she didn't need to know that."

"So what happened?"

"Sarah was pretty upset that I was homeless. She knew how things had gone in art school and after that when we had been trying to make a name for ourselves. That things had not worked out and I had eventually given up and gone another direction, while she had stayed in the business and been able to establish herself."

"She felt guilty about it?"

"No. She was angry. At the way that artists treated each other. We all have similar goals and should be lifting each other up instead of competing. There is an audience for all of us. Patrons don't just choose one artist to follow in exclusion of all others."

"And when her accident happened… you think she was up here looking for you?"

"I had told her that she could find me here. I didn't think she would take me up on it, but it was a nice idea, the thought of someone from back in the heydays coming up here to talk art. Maybe do a few sketches. And then I heard the train stop and saw all the police activity. Couldn't get up here without breaking my cover, so I stayed out of the way. But I was afraid from the start that it was Sarah." Lewis shook his head. "I can't figure it out. I don't know why she would be near the tracks. Unless she was… drunk or drugged or having a psychotic break. I still can't fathom what happened."

"The preliminary tox screens say that she wasn't drunk or drugged. Did she have a history of mental illness? Seizures? We'll be getting medical records now that she's been identified, but if you are aware of anything…?"

Lewis ran his fingers through his hair, making it stand up in messy waves. "Like many creative types, she struggled with her demons. I know she suffered from depression, but I don't know any diagnosed mental illness. Whether she was bipolar or schizophrenic or anything. We weren't that close. Not something that you ask someone you are only casually acquainted with."

"Well… we'll keep investigating. It might be something as simple as that. Coming up here to talk to you and then experiencing some… episode while she was waiting for you. It's not your fault."

He pressed his lips together and met her eyes for the first time. "I appreciate that. But… if not for me inviting her here, it wouldn't have happened. If she killed herself—"

"It could have happened somewhere else. She could have wandered out into traffic. Into the river. Jumped out a window or off a balcony. Have you seen her home?"

"No, never seen it. I gather it was quite something, but she never invited me over." He gave a wry smile. So even Sarah had exhibited signs of some of society's anti-poverty sentiments. She had not thought it appropriate to invite a homeless man into her house, even though they had known each other for a long time.

"Yes. It's pretty amazing. Very large, lots of windows. Nice and bright for an artist. But it could be dangerous if she is someone who experiences... breaks with reality."

"But that isn't what happened. What happened was that she came up here to see me and, after waiting for me... was hit by a train. Did she want to tell me something? To say goodbye? Ask for help?"

Margie held Lewis's gaze. "I'm going to find out what happened. But it wasn't your fault. You would have done anything you could to keep her safe. You would never have done anything that you thought would put her life in danger."

"No. I would never have done that."

CHAPTER SIXTEEN

$\mathcal{M}$argie was climbing into her car when her phone started vibrating. She readjusted to pull it out of her pocket. Christina.

"Hi, sweetie. I'm just getting into the car. I'll be home in a few minutes."

"Okay, good." There was something wrong in Christina's tone of voice. Margie tried to analyze it.

"Is there something the matter? You sound funny."

"I'll see you when you get here. If you're on your way, that's easier."

She hadn't said that nothing was wrong. Margie wanted to demand to know what was going on. But as Christina had said, it would be easier face to face, when they could see each other's body language. So she would just have to wait ten minutes.

"Umm, okay. I'm just at Pearce Estate, so I won't be long. See you in a few minutes."

"See you," Christina agreed, and hung up.

Margie's stomach was a knotted mess all the way home. She had a horrible sinking feeling that something was very wrong. Christina hadn't wanted to tell her what it was over the phone, but she needed her mother home right away. That sounded serious. Not just a homework problem.

Not just asking if she could go out tonight, even though it was a school night and she knew the answer would be no.

Had Christina failed a test? Been expelled? Found out she was pregnant?

So many things could go wrong in a teenager's life. Margie wasn't late getting home, but she still felt guilty. Had she not been spending enough time with Christina? Not maintaining their relationship, so that Christina had felt like she needed to go elsewhere for attention and approval?

But Christina did want to talk to her, so that was a good sign. She wasn't just shutting Margie out. She hadn't run away.

It didn't seem like it had been that long since Margie was a teen. She remembered how she had wanted to run. How she just wanted to get out of her life and be somewhere else. She remembered feeling disconnected from her family, as if adults couldn't understand teenage problems or what she had been through. If Christina was reaching out, calling Margie, wanting to have a heart-to-heart tonight, then she wasn't at that point yet. Whatever might have happened, it was still salvageable.

Finally, the light changed to green and she could turn off of Seventeenth Avenue to Twenty-Sixth Street and then, with a couple more turns, she was home.

Christina was not standing at the door waiting for her.

Margie locked the car and dashed up to the door. When she opened it, Stella immediately started barking and ran over to see who it was. She nuzzled Margie's hand to encourage scratches and rubbed against her legs so vigorously she nearly knocked Margie down. Margie laughed and petted and scratched her to get her to settle down. Then, when she was finally calm, she turned to Christina, standing by waiting, her arms folded and a serious expression on her face.

"Okay," Margie said. "Lay it on me. What's up?"

"It's Moushoom."

Margie blinked. She held her hand over her rapidly beating heart. "What? What about Moushoom?" Her brain immediately went into catastrophizing mode, thinking of the worst things that might have happened. Topping the list, of course, was that her grandfather had died.

"I took Stella for a walk, and we stopped by to see him. But the home wouldn't let me in. They said that they couldn't tell me anything because I was not next of kin and wasn't authorized for them to give me information. So I don't know *what's* wrong. But they wouldn't let me in."

That did not put any of Margie's fears to rest. She nodded quickly and pulled out her phone. Her fingers were numb as she tried to navigate to her contacts list and find the nursing home's phone number. She kept getting the wrong buttons and having to correct her mistakes. Eventually, it was ringing through. The receptionist answered.

"This is Margie Patenaude," Margie told her in a crisp, clear voice. "I'm calling to find out what's happening with my Moushoom. Mr. Patenaude. My daughter stopped by to see him today and wasn't allowed in."

"Oh, yes. One moment, Ms. Patenaude. I will put you through to the director."

Margie had to wait while they tracked her down. Her stomach continued to do backflips as she worried about what was going on that the director needed to inform her of. Why couldn't the receptionist tell her? Was it that bad?

Christina was still standing there with her arms folded, waiting. Margie realized that Christina wouldn't be able to be a part of the conversation, and Margie would have to repeat whatever information she got back to her. She hit the speaker button and held the phone between them so that Christina could hear for herself and participate in the conversation. Christina moved closer, nodding her thanks, but still looking very serious.

"Ms. Patenaude," a nasal voice was broadcast over the speaker. Margie remembered the older woman with skirt suits and chiseled, masculine features. "I'm sorry. Thank you for holding."

"Can you tell me what's wrong? Why can't I see Moushoom?"

"I'm sorry to have to tell you this, but your grandfather is quite ill. He has pneumonia."

"Pneumonia? He was fine when we saw him two days ago."

"It came on quite suddenly."

"Is it COVID?" Margie demanded. "Delta variant? He had his first shot already. He was vaccinated."

"We have had several residents come down with COVID in the last week," the director told her. "We haven't yet put a general quarantine in place, so families can still visit their relatives who are not sick, but I think within the next week or so, we're going to see all of the nursing homes put on restrictions and no one will be able to get in."

"Does Moushoom have COVID?"

"His test isn't back yet. But I suspect so. We are monitoring him carefully. He's on oxygen. He is still waking up and responding to questions. If he gets worse, we will have him transported to the hospital. But the hospitals are overflowing; they have no rooms and very few emergency beds, so we'd rather keep him here where we know we can take good care of him and he won't be exposed to any other viruses. Of course, if you prefer that he be sent to the hospital for treatment, we will do whatever you wish."

"Okay." Margie took a deep breath. She swallowed hard, trying to keep the hot lump in her throat from bringing tears to her eyes. She looked at Christina. "I think we should probably leave him there, in his own room with the nurses that he knows. In the hospital, he would just be in a hallway, and who knows how much attention he would get. What do you think?"

Christina raised her brows, apparently surprised that her opinion was being sought. She considered Margie's question carefully, then nodded.

"Yeah. I think that's the best right now, too," she agreed.

"Okay. We'll leave him with you right now," Margie relayed to the woman. "And trust that you will know the right time for him to be sent to the hospital if he needs more care than you can provide. Please do everything you can for him. Don't just let him go because he's old."

"I understand, Ms. Patenaude. We will provide all life-saving measures we are able."

"Can we come see him?" Margie asked, though she knew very well that the answer would be no. He would be quarantined. And as the director said, the whole facility might soon be quarantined. But she wanted to make sure that Christina understood that it wasn't just because she was a minor.

"I'm sorry," the director said. "He cannot have any visitors right now. We are limiting contact as much as possible, with only one worker per shift providing care, unless he ends up needing something more extensive. The fewer people in contact with him, the less chance it will spread through the facility or that another virus will be carried in to him while he is in a weakened state. No one will be able to see him until he has all clear tests. And you will need to provide us with clear tests and proofs of vaccination before you can see him then."

"Okay. Thank you for taking such good care of him. Will you tell him we love him and would be there if we could?"

"I will have his worker pass a message on to him for you. Is there anything else we can do for you?"

"I would like Christina Patenaude's name to be added to the list of those authorized to get updates on his condition and care."

"Isn't Christina a minor?" the director asked in a disapproving tone.

"Christina is old enough to get updates on how he is doing."

"Well… okay. I will put her name on the computer. She is welcome to call in and get an update anytime."

Christina looked at Margie, her eyes swimming with tears, but a smile of appreciation.

"Thank you," Margie told the director, and she ended the call.

"Mom… thank you," Christina said, a couple of tears dripping down her cheeks.

Margie wiped them away with her thumb. "Do you have the number on your phone? Make sure you put it on. If you want to call during school because you're worried about him, do it. You heard her. You can call any time."

Christina sniffled. "Yeah. Give me the number."

Margie read it to her, and Christina tapped the number into her phone. Margie gave her a quick, tight hug. "Thank you for going to visit him. He loves seeing you and Stella, and I'm happy you go whenever you feel like it. There's no reason that you shouldn't be able to see how he's doing and, if you're worried about what they say and want to talk to me about it, you call me. We'll figure it out together."

"I didn't think you'd ask me about what to do."

"You know him as well as anyone. You've seen what kind of care they have at the nursing home. You see all of the COVID updates on the news. You're as qualified as anyone to give your opinion."

"Maarsi." Christina offered the hug this time, giving Margie a long squeeze. Then she pulled back. "We should make something for supper."

"Yes, we should," Margie agreed.

CHAPTER SEVENTEEN

argie felt like they were late getting to talk to Jonathan, Sarah Thompson's ex-husband. They should have spoken to him the day that she was killed. But they didn't know who she was until the second day and only learned about Jonathan's existence later. So she had to console herself that they had tracked him down and arranged an interview with him as quickly as they could.

When she had spoken to him on the phone, Margie hadn't told him anything other than that she was a detective and wanted to talk to him about his ex-wife. He could make of that whatever he liked. She would see, when she spoke to him face-to-face, whether he already knew that she was dead.

He arranged to meet them at his home, which, though not far from his ex-wife's mansion, was very modest. Modest was what people said when they meant that it was small and old. According to the internet research Margie had done, he was an artist too, but not an artist like Sarah. He hadn't gained any recognition. As far as she could see, he hadn't done any gallery showings. He hadn't been "discovered."

He supported himself with a low-level job at a warehouse company. They had so many made-up titles that Margie didn't know whether he was a stock boy or forklift operator. It sounded like he was in management but, from what they could find of his financial records, he certainly was not. In the retail world, a "manager" was often nothing more than a sales-clerk with a few months' experience, and the same appeared to be true in the warehousing industry.

He made enough to afford the house that he lived in and little more. Maybe he had a housemate or two and could also afford to heat it, pay for internet, and drive a car. But he must have been choked when he saw what his ex-wife was making as an artist and he hadn't been granted any spousal support. As far as Margie was concerned, Sarah should have been paying for some of his expenses. She could afford it and he had suffered a lot of losses in the divorce, which did not appear to be his fault.

Jonathan's eyes were big when he answered the door. He tried to act nonchalant about a couple of police detectives coming over to visit him, but he didn't quite pull it off. It was clear that he was anxious and that talking to cops did not fall into his usual experience. He didn't wear a mask, but they did, and Margie knew some people found them menacing.

"Uh, come on in," he invited Margie and Cruz, kicking a few pairs of shoes from behind the door so that he could open it wider for them. The house was small. The blinds and curtains over the living room window made it dark. Margie could smell the previous night's dinner, or maybe breakfast, but she didn't think people should fry onions first thing in the morning. Jonathan had not thought to tidy up the living room when Margie had made arrangements to come and see him. So he had to make room for them now, picking up books, discarded clothes, remote controls, dirty dishes, and flyers turning yellow with age.

"Have a seat," Jonathan muttered. "Let me just get rid of this stuff."

He was back in a minute, having dumped everything in a pile some-where in the kitchen. Margie didn't know whether they had ended up on the counter, kitchen table, or floor.

Jonathan sat in his easy chair. At first, he tilted it back as if he were going to watch TV, then apparently decided that was not appropriate and returned it to its upright position.

"So... exactly what is this about?" Jonathan asked. "Some kind of tax thing?"

"What makes you think that?" Margie asked neutrally.

"Well... she's making a lot of money. Maybe she isn't paying all of her taxes. I don't know."

"It isn't about taxes."

"Okay." He shrugged. "What is it about, then?"

"When was the last time you talked to Ms. Thompson?"

"I don't really know. We weren't in regular contact."

"A week, month, year?" Margie prodded.

"I guess… probably like a month."

"And what would you have been in contact with her about?"

"Just… catching up. I don't know."

"You were still friends? It was amicable?"

"Amicable?" Repeating Margie's words meant that he was stalling, trying to think his way out of the situation. Trying to sort out the best answer and anticipate her responses. "Well, I guess amicable isn't the word I would use. But I still saw her around town sometimes. We're both in the art world. There was a school reunion… maybe that was where I talked to her last." He left the statement hanging for a minute, then nodded. "Yeah, I think that was it."

"A school reunion? High school?"

"No, art school. Seeing where everyone is now, what they're all working on, whether people ended up in art or in something else."

"Ah." Margie wondered whether Lewis had gone to that reunion. He hadn't mentioned it. Maybe Sarah had told him about it and tried to get him to go. Maybe she hadn't. "Who else saw you there?"

Jonathan's eyes widened at the implication that he needed to provide an alibi. He rubbed the bridge of his nose, thinking.

"Uh… Daniel Reynolds. Sarah. Me. A couple of our teachers were there. Other students… I don't know everyone's names. We didn't work on a lot of group projects. You really just knew whoever you hung out with. Isaac Smith. A woman, what was her name… Jenna. Can't remember her last name. The alumni people will be able to find it for you. And they must have phone numbers for people. Email addresses, locations."

Margie wrote down each of the names. "How many of you were still in art-related fields?"

"Sarah was the most successful, obviously. Daniel Reynolds, he's quite well-known. You might have heard of him?" Jonathan left his question hanging.

"No," Margie shook her head. "Is he any good?"

"He's great. Better than Sarah, but not as popular as she is. There's a joke in the art world that anything popular can't be very good. It's sort of… stuck up, I guess. A way to make those of us who are not as popular feel good about ourselves."

Margie nodded. She had heard things like that before, and she wasn't even in the art world. She never could understand the more high-brow art, or art that was supposed to be very symbolic or to shock. Sarah's work, though symbolic was, at least, recognizable enough to puzzle out the meanings if you saw enough of the pieces in the series and thought about it long enough.

"What do you know about the latest project Sarah was working on?"

"Nothing. I don't know if she told anyone else at the reunion, but she didn't tell me. She was like that. She didn't want to give too much away until it was completely finished and ready for viewing. She didn't need any outside input. She knew what she wanted and how she wanted it to look when she was done, and she went ahead and did it. She didn't have an advisory committee, a mentor, or talk to any of her friends—or exes—about it."

CHAPTER EIGHTEEN

*M*argie gave Cruz a nod, letting him move forward with his part in the discussion. He leaned forward.

"Mr. Thompson. I'm sorry to have to tell you this, but Sarah Thompson passed away recently. We are looking into her death."

"Looking into it? Does that mean it was..." He cleared his throat. They waited for him to finish his sentence. "Murder?" Jonathan finally asked.

"It initially looked like an accident," Cruz told him. "But we need to investigate all eventualities. Is there anyone that you are aware of who had a grudge against Ms. Thompson?"

Jonathan's mouth opened and closed a few times.

"Well, other than me, you mean? I guess so. Sarah never minced words. If she had a problem with someone or with their opinion, she would tell them. Some people find that refreshing. Others find it offensive."

Depending solely on whether her opinion of them was complimentary or critical, Margie assumed.

"Do you know if she had trouble with anyone in particular?"

"No. If you want to know that, I would ask that assistant of hers. Violet. She knows everything. She would be able to tell you if anyone was bothering Sarah."

"She said there had been threats, but she hadn't kept track of any of them."

Jonathan shrugged. He spread his hands apart. "I don't know any more than that. I'd heard rumors that she'd gotten threats. But Sarah wasn't the type to be cowed by someone writing poison pen letters, hiding behind anonymity. She would have been pretty disparaging about that."

"She thought that if you had something to say, you should say it face-to-face and not mince words," Margie suggested.

"Yes, exactly. But she wasn't a mean person. There were plenty of times when she just kept her mouth shut and didn't say anything. She wasn't one to run down other artists' work; I'll say that for her. I never heard her say a derogatory word about someone else's work. And believe me, we had plenty of opportunities in school to critique each other's work. Sarah was always very professional about it. Others in the class… never did get the hang of critiquing without it sounding like a personal attack."

After Lewis's comments about how cutthroat the industry could be, Margie could understand what he was talking about. She pondered the new series of paintings Sarah had been working on. A slashed canvas of an unhappy artist. Broken art implements. Could the series have been about someone destroying an artist with unfair criticism or personal attacks?

"Do you know of anyone who had criticized Sarah that way?"

"Recently?" Jonathan considered for a moment, then shook his head. "No. But there's always criticism in the art world. The more you're in the spotlight, the more people will be jealous and make personal attacks. Hold you up as the worst representative in your genre."

"And with the internet, it is easier than ever to get the word out," Cruz said, "and still hide behind anonymity."

Jonathan looked in his direction and didn't agree or disagree. Margie thought she detected a red flush around his throat. Maybe he'd been more involved in attacks against his ex-wife than he wanted them to know about.

"Where were you Sunday afternoon?" she asked Jonathan.

"Sunday?" Jonathan stalled, repeating the question and scratching the back of his head as if it were a difficult question to answer. "Gee… I don't know. I lose track of what day it is…"

"You work. Was it a workday?"

"No. I never work on a Sunday."

"So you weren't working. What did you do on the weekend?"

He swallowed, still considering the question. "Is that when she died? Is that why you're asking? You think that I was involved somehow in this accident, and you want to see if I have an alibi?"

"We are investigating your ex-wife's death. We would like to know where you were when she died," Cruz said in his tough-cop voice.

Margie kept her face expressionless, but she was inwardly amused. Cruz put on a good tough-guy act, but she knew he was a family man, compassionate, even-tempered, and abhorred violence.

That didn't mean he couldn't handle himself if a situation required it. He was just as good with a gun or methods of subduing a violent offender as anyone else in the department. But it wasn't like on TV. No one was going to take Jonathan into a room lit by a single bulb and beat him until he confessed.

"I was... at an art show. Downtown. One of the guys in our class. Isaac. Isaac Smith. You can look it up. The gallery will tell you he had a show."

"Will the gallery be able to confirm that you were there?" Margie asked.

"Well... not the gallery. I didn't introduce myself to the owners."

"But Isaac can confirm it."

"I don't know. I said 'hi' to him, but he was busy with a lot of other people—potential buyers or patrons. So, I wasn't his focus. I waited a while for the others to show up, but no one else did. I had a few drinks, some crackers and, eventually, went home. I had work of my own to do. I still paint, but I can't do it when I'm at work, obviously, so I have to fit it in evenings and weekends."

"What others?" Cruz asked.

"What?"

"You said you were waiting for the others, but they didn't come."

"Oh. Some of the others from the art class. We had talked about going together. Or meeting up there, rather. But I waited around for them, and they didn't show. I thought that we would all talk to Isaac at the same time, congratulate him, tell him what a good job he did. You know, give him a boost. But the others didn't show up, so I just... I just left without really spending any time talking to him. I didn't want to interrupt his conversations with people who might actually buy his art. Because I wasn't going to be buying any of it."

"Who else from your class was supposed to be there?"

"Sarah, of course, but I never thought she would show up. Especially not when I was planning to be there. She didn't exactly want to hang out with me. Uh. Jenna what's-her-name. Daniel Reynolds."

"Sounds like you guys were the core group from your class."

"Well, the classes weren't huge. You got to know the people that you did projects with. Yeah, I guess we were kind of 'the gang.' We did stuff with others. Invited them along. But it was usually me and Sarah, Daniel, and a couple of other people that I've kind of lost touch with."

"So they could tell us that you were all supposed to meet up at the gallery... but not that you were there, since they didn't show up."

Daniel's mouth twisted into a scowl. "I can't help if they didn't show up. They were *supposed* to."

"Sarah was supposed to be there?"

"Like I said, she was supposed to be, but I wasn't surprised that she wasn't. She had better things to do than to hang out with losers like us."

"Did she give you any explanation? Call you and let you know that she was going to be somewhere else?"

"Not me. Maybe she contacted one of the others. She wouldn't have called me."

Instead of being at the art show, Sarah had been in the park, looking for Lewis. Ending up on the tracks as the train came across the bridge too fast to stop in time. Had someone set her up? Jonathan could have intended for the opening to be his alibi, shown up there, made an appearance, and then gone to the park to meet Sarah. He could have taken one of the motorized scooters that were rented out downtown and made it to the park very quickly.

"Do you have phone numbers for Isaac and the other art students who were supposed to be there?"

Jonathan shook his head, but when he opened his mouth to say that he didn't have the information or they could find it themselves, he changed his mind. "Yeah... if you give me a few minutes, I can find something for you. Some of them I might only have email addresses for, not a phone number."

"Whatever you have would be good."

CHAPTER NINETEEN

$\mathcal{M}$argie had a number of notes that needed to be transcribed from her notepad and expounded on in her reports saved to the workspace on the server for Sarah Thompson's file. She frowned as she worked through them, trying to make all the necessary connections.

"You ready to close on the Thompson death?" MacDonald questioned, standing in front of Margie's desk with a fresh cup of coffee. She was used to being called into his office if he had any questions about a case. Hovering over her was not his usual practice.

"Uh... well, things aren't quite as straightforward as they looked initially."

Margie had to look way up at her sergeant. He ran a hand over his close-cropped gray hair.

"A woman lying on the tracks was run over by a train. How is that anything other than an accident? Or suicide? You should be able to clear it pretty quickly. We're getting calls from reporters and people in the art world. She was quite the big name, as it turns out."

"Well, we are pursuing it. Interviewing acquaintances, getting the details nailed down. I'm sure the people asking for information and updates wouldn't want us just to ignore any red flags and sweep it under the rug."

"Of course not," MacDonald agreed with a scowl. "What makes you think that it was anything other than an accident?"

"It could still be... but some things concern me. She was getting threats. She was a local celebrity in the art world, and I guess there was a lot of competition. A lot of people who probably would have liked her out of the way. And there is a bitter ex-husband living in a hovel, while she lives in a huge mansion. She didn't change her will after getting divorced."

MacDonald opened his mouth to counter this point, but Margie raised her hand. "I know that the divorce means that the provisions she made for the ex in her will are revoked, but that doesn't mean the ex knows that. He may think that he's now due a pretty good nest egg."

"Okay," MacDonald nodded at this. "Fair enough. Most people don't know enough about Alberta estate law to know how that works."

"The ex does not have a good alibi. But we also don't know who has been making threats—whether it was him or someone else, or several other people. Like you say, she's quite well-known in the art world, and I'm sure that has caused some jealousies."

"Are you trying to track those down?"

Margie looked at her screen. "It's on my list. The personal assistant should be able to help with that, but she says that Thompson always just told her to delete or garbage any threats, so we only have her memory to work from, or if they were received in email and are still in the trash folder."

"Is there any indication that it was homicide rather than an accident? Other than the fact that people had made threats and there is a lot of money to be divvied between people now."

"The question of what she was doing on the tracks in the first place. The train engineer puts her lying down on the tracks, not standing on them. ME says that there was no alcohol or drugs in her system. Her medical records say that she didn't have epilepsy or diabetes or something that would conceivably make her fall or lay down on the tracks."

"But she did battle depression."

"Right. So, it's possible that she was suicidal. But she didn't go out there to commit suicide."

MacDonald shifted his stance and took a drink from his mug.

"And just how do you know that?"

"The homeless guy whose gear was at the scene. They were old friends. Went to art school together. Then the homeless guy—who is actually an undercover, by the way—ran into her one day, so she knew where he camped out. She went out there to talk to him, not to commit suicide."

"You can't know her purpose for going there."

"No. But why would she go to her friend's campsite, his 'home' to commit suicide? She went there because she wanted to talk to him about something. And then… something happened. I'm not sure what that was. But something made her change from visiting an old friend to lying on the tracks."

"The homeless guy is undercover?"

Margie nodded. "He didn't break cover to tell anyone. But when I went back there with his gear, we talked. He doesn't know why she went to see him."

"But he didn't see what happened?"

"No."

"And he didn't see anything at the scene to make him think that it was murder or suicide."

"No. He wasn't there until it was all cleaned up."

"Okay…" MacDonald stared off into space for a few seconds. "Continue with your investigation. Keep me informed. In ninety percent of these cases… it's the spouse or the ex."

"I know. I'm looking at him."

MacDonald nodded and headed back toward his office.

Jones looked over at Margie from her desk. "These background searches are interesting."

Margie blinked and looked over at her. "What? Which one? Sarah's ex?"

"His is pretty innocuous. He's not very well-known. No one is showing his stuff. He just dabbles. Posts in some art discussion groups. And works in a warehouse. But one of the other ones that you had on the list… Daniel Reynolds, he's a different story."

"What did you find on him?"

"He has criminal charges for art theft and fraud, for starters. When I look for deeper background, it's interesting…"

Margie stood up and walked over to Jones's desk to look over her shoulder. "What's interesting?"

89

"Well, he's got lots of good press. Like Jonathan said, he's well-known, though not as much as Sarah. He doesn't have a distinctive style, but is known for being able to pull off a lot of different looks. I guess that wins and loses him points. Anyway, a good amount of positive press. But when you start looking for stuff that has been buried, you start to get a different picture."

"Like Sarah burying her divorce?"

Jones nodded.

Margie leaned in to read the small print on the screen. They were not major news sources. A few posts buried here and there in social media. A small website that specialized in exposing art forgery. Little snippets of conversation that had taken place over the years and been buried by Daniel's more successful projects.

"Maybe it isn't the same Daniel Reynolds," she said. "There might be a few of them around."

Jones clicked on one of the articles and, when it expanded across the screen, Margie could see it was the same face, albeit somewhat younger. She skimmed through the information on the screen. "He was accused of copying or stealing other people's work while he was at school?"

Jones nodded. "Exactly. He pleaded ignorance to the school administrators. He said that he was just copying other people's work to learn, which is a long tradition of artists. And that he hadn't intended to pass off anyone else's work as his own. He just wanted to see how it was judged if both his work and someone else's were submitted at the same time. Something about exposing biases."

"So it was all a mistake. They just misunderstood his intentions. He wasn't trying to pass off anyone else's work as his own."

"That's right," Jones agreed with a grin.

"Interesting. Is there anything about whose work he was 'borrowing' or learning from?"

"Not really. I got the impression that they didn't want to bring anyone else's names into it in case they got tarred with the same brush as Reynolds. Anyway, it sounds like he has some wealthy relatives, and things were smoothed over, and even though he lost his scholarship and was cited with 'code of conduct' demerits, he was allowed to stay in school and finish his degree."

"And then went on to become a successful, well-known artist. Left all of that nasty business behind."

"I guess no one held it against him. He was just young and foolish and learned the error of his ways."

"I'll bet."

Margie looked at Jones's search page when she clicked back to it, and made a couple of notes. "Can you save those to the workspace?"

"Sure, of course."

"I'm going to do a little bit more digging…"

Margie returned to her seat and thought about what searches might get her to the next step. Looking at her list of names, she decided to pair them together in a few searches. The media outlet that had published the story that she and Jones had looked at together had refrained from listing anyone else's name in the article, but other sites might not have been so careful. A combined search might tell her if any other art school students had been targets of Reynolds's fraudulent activities.

She started plugging in "Daniel Reynolds and Sarah Thompson," "Daniel Reynolds and Isaac Smith," and so on through the various names on her list.

No hits on any of them. Either Reynolds had been stealing from other artists further afield, or everyone had agreed to leave the other names out of the story.

Remembering that Lewis had said that he and Sarah went to school together, Margie keyed in "Daniel Reynolds and Lewis Riley."

There were a few hits. A couple of them just seemed to be articles where the two of them were mentioned as participants in a show or recipients of scholarships. Margie saw pictures of the two of them across the top row with others from their program.

Margie clicked on a Calgary Herald article praising Lewis's work, saying he was on his way to becoming one of Calgary's elite creative minds. Margie smiled, remembering Lewis quoting that line proudly. But then something had happened. The cutthroat business had been too much for him, and he had diverted to a career in law enforcement instead.

The same article was not nearly as complimentary toward Daniel Reynolds, saying he was derivative, uninspired, and lacking natural talent.

Looking for anything else related to the article, Margie found a social media thread with commentary on the article. Most of the posts were by Reynolds himself, decrying the article and the biases of the reporter. He not only pumped up his own work, giving quotes from various other sources who thought he was the best thing since sliced bread, but also denigrated Lewis's work. He did more than critique it professionally, as Jonathan said they were encouraged to do. Instead, Reynolds went way overboard, cutting down Lewis's work, him as a person, his ancestry, and anyone who might dare to have an opinion that conflicted with his.

Far from being an up-and-comer or having any creative talent, Lewis Riley is stuck in the last century, as was the author of the article. Lewis's work, produced after many long hours of blood, sweat, and tears, looks like something a five-year-old could have drawn with a box of crayons. The reporter is clearly enamored with his long and respected heritage in one of Calgary's "royal" families. The Rileys may have been artists in days of yore, but what have they done lately? Lewis's insipid works with little form or substance, will not cut it. Lewis should get out of the program while he can still save face.

Margie winced and shook her head. "Look at this," she told Jones. "Now, if Lewis Riley had killed Daniel Reynolds, I might understand it…"

Detective Jones hung over Margie's shoulder this time, slowly shaking her head. "Ouch! I'm surprised they let him post something like that and didn't delete it."

"Some groups or boards don't have very much moderation. People can pretty much post whatever they want."

"If I was Reynolds, I would probably have deleted this post later. I certainly wouldn't leave it like that."

"He may have completely forgotten about it. Especially if it had the hoped-for effect of getting Lewis out of the class and into another career."

"Did it?"

"Yeah, he's the undercover. He went into law enforcement, and he told me that he left the art world for this very reason," Margie flicked a finger at the monitor. "Because it is too cutthroat."

"I always thought that art was all… creative touchy-feely. I didn't think it was competitive like this."

"It probably depends on whether you are trying to get ahead or just make nice pictures. If they are fighting over a few sweet gigs and are afraid that someone else is getting ahead…"

But she had to admit that it was over-the-top and shocking. She would not have expected such venom between two young artists.

"The question is, then, if there is any connection between this nastiness and Thompson's death. I can't see a straight line between them."

"No," Margie agreed, studying the words on her screen. "Not yet."

CHAPTER TWENTY

$\mathcal{M}$argie and Christina were working together to get dinner on the table, Margie chopping vegetables with her head in the clouds, working through the puzzling case.

"Mom?"

"Hmm?" Margie looked at Christina, aware she had missed some part of the earlier conversation. "I'm sorry, I was thinking about something else. What was that?"

"That cop that drove me back here on Sunday. What was his name?"

"Oh…" Margie thought back, trying to remember back that far. What had been the name of the young constable? "I think Morris? I remember associating it with that old detective series. I think it was Constable Morris."

"How would I get ahold of him if I wanted to thank him for dropping me off?"

"I don't think you need to do that. He was happy to be able to get away from the scene, I think. And it doesn't hurt to be escorting such a lovely young lady."

Christina rolled her eyes. "Still, he was very nice. I think I should thank him for helping me out. You always say to be polite, and I was kind of cranky that day, after having to wait around and then having to be driven by someone I didn't know, like a little kid."

Margie turned her head to look at her daughter, a smile spreading across her face.

"I thought you already had a boyfriend."

"Mo-om! Tracy isn't my boyfriend. He's just… a friend."

"Who is a boy."

"Yeah, well, you told me I should never judge someone by their gender. I should see what kind of a person they really are inside. What does it matter if he is a boy?"

Margie had been concerned with how close the two friends were, and the level of physical intimacy between them when Margie was not around to supervise. On the one hand, she was happy to hear that Christina and Tracy were "just friends," but, on the other hand, Christina could be lying about that. There was no way to know unless she actually saw something between them, and they had been careful not to let her catch them so far.

And regardless of whether she and Tracy were involved, Christina was now showing interest in someone else. A man who was not the same age as she was, but several years older. The fact that he was a cop did not make Margie feel better. She knew plenty of cops who were reckless and willing to break the rules. A lot of adrenaline junkies who loved to take risks and feel that rush. The risk of breaking the law and getting caught was a thrill.

"I'll see if I can find his number," Margie told Christina, though she had no intention whatsoever of doing so.

Margie dumped the vegetables into the hot pan, where they sizzled and released their enticing aromas.

"I could just call the main police number," Christina pointed out.

Checkmate. Christina wasn't fooled. Now that Margie had given up Morris's name, there was nothing she could do to stop Christina from making such a call.

"How is your homework coming along?" Margie asked, trying to distract her from the conversation about Morris.

Christina grimaced. "It's just fine," she said. "I'll get it done."

"I know. You've been doing pretty well in all of your classes." She was grateful to Tracy for the help he gave Christina with her homework. Her marks had gone up since getting to know him. "And how about the Indigenous Fair?"

Christina chewed on her thumbnail. "What if Moushoom doesn't get better in time to take part? I really wanted him to help out. To do some of the jigging and chanting... storytelling, talking about his residential school days, stuff like that."

"We have to be more concerned about his health than whether he can do the fair or not."

"I know," Christina agreed quickly. "I wouldn't want him to try to do it when he's sick. That's why I asked if you thought he would be well in time. I just... I want him to get better. And I want him to be able to go to the fair. But if he can't help, that's okay. I have some other dancers. I really want people to get to know him, though. He's so cool."

"I'm sure everyone would love to meet him." Margie sighed. "Right now, I'm just hoping they don't shut the schools down again. They keep saying that they won't, but there are so many kids and teachers going down with COVID that I don't see how they can keep ignoring it."

"They're not ignoring it. We still have to wear masks and not sit too close together."

"But as soon as you're out of school, you take your masks off anyway."

Christina smirked and shrugged. "And if they shut down the schools, do you think we are going to stop seeing each other?"

"We're lucky not to have had quarantines enforced by the military like they did in some other countries."

"I know. But maybe if they'd done it that way, we wouldn't have Delta now." Christina shrugged. "People are so tired of restrictions. They just don't want to do it anymore. Nobody wants to keep masking and social distancing."

"Yeah. I know. I see it every day."

"Moushoom sent his love," Christina said suddenly, her tone brightening. "I forgot I didn't tell you yet!"

"You talked to him?"

"No, but the nurse gave him our message and he sent one back. He said that he loves both of us, and we're supposed to 'be true to ourselves.'" She smiled, eyes sparkling. "That sounds like him, doesn't it?"

It would figure that Moushoom would be more concerned about giving his granddaughters advice about how to live their lives than he would be about his own health and what his chances of survival were as an old man with pneumonia and COVID.

"So what does that mean?" Margie asked, curious what Christina would come up with. "What does it mean to you?"

"Just… I don't know. Make the family proud. Be strong and make the right choices; don't let other people talk you into making bad ones."

Margie nodded. That was a good answer. "People can really do each other a lot of harm with their words," she observed, thinking about Reynolds and the damage he had done to Lewis's art career. And about the other people involved in the case and the choices they had made. Sarah, advocating for the poor while she lived in a mansion and her ex-husband lived paycheck to paycheck in a dump. Acting as if she cared about what had happened to Lewis, but what had she done to help him? Had she intended to do something concrete to give an old friend a hand up? Or was that just talk? Why had she gone to visit him the day she died?

CHAPTER TWENTY-ONE

*D*aniel Reynolds looked like he did in the news articles and internet searches they had done. A little older, maybe, but he wasn't a fifty-year-old trying to appear in the media as if he were twenty or thirty years younger. His face was narrower and more wrinkled, and his short sideburns a little grayer. But still easily recognizable from his PR materials.

"I'm not sure exactly what I'm doing here," Reynolds said as he was led to an interview room and sat at the table. He looked around the bare room, eyes eventually returning to Margie. "From what I can understand, you are looking into the death of Sarah Thompson. That's great, but... I thought it was an accident, and I don't know what insight you think I might have into it. Sarah and I met for cocktails occasionally, of course. Ran into each other at some of the same boring fundraisers, but we weren't close."

"Were you close with anyone in your old art class?" Margie asked, ignoring his pompous manner.

"Close...? No, not really. I do run into some of them from time to time, but we haven't stayed close friends. There were a lot of... a lot of different personalities. Artistic temperaments. They lead to some clashes. I'm sure you know what I mean. Creative types can sometimes act like toddlers."

Margie chuckled at the image of the artists she had met on the case, envisioning them as toddlers, perhaps bopping each other over the head with big foam bats.

It was better than envisioning Reynolds or one of the others hitting Sarah over the head with a blunt object and leaving her on the tracks unconscious.

"So, you saw Thompson sometimes. Who else?"

He shook his head. "I really don't know. I guess her ex, Jonathan. Sometimes Jenna or one of the others. Isaac just had a showing, but I wasn't able to get to it. Last-minute emergencies, you know. Smoothing out issues with my own shows and public relations."

"You didn't make it to Isaac Smith's show? I thought that you and some of the others had planned to be there together as a show of support."

"I was supposed to be there but, at the last minute, I couldn't make it."

"But you have someone who can testify as to where you were? You were working with someone else on an upcoming show."

"Well," his brows drew down and he shifted slightly. His chair wobbled a little and he moved again in irritation. "I didn't say that I was with someone else. There was a lot to be done and, as an artist in today's world, you really need to be your own manager, ready to step up and take control when things go off the rails."

He licked dry lips and looked concerned. "Off the rails—I mean—when things don't go the way you had planned."

He clearly didn't want her to think he was making light of what had happened to Sarah. An allusion to railway tracks might not be appropriate.

"So you don't have someone who can verify where you were at the time you had been expected at Isaac's show?" Margie deliberately did not refer to the time of Sarah's death.

"Uh... I was at home. There was a lot to do. I couldn't really go out. But I didn't have anyone else... I don't have an administrative assistant like Violet."

"Oh, you know Violet?"

"Sure, sure. She'd been with Sarah for eight years. Violet was the best option if you wanted to get in touch with Sarah. She ran a tight ship."

"We noticed that you've had a number of calls with her when we pulled phone logs."

He looked left and right. "Calls with Sarah? No…"

"Calls with Violet."

"Well, sure. Like I said, she ran things. She was the person to talk to."

"And she was the only person with access to Sarah's work in progress. So that you could keep track of what she was working on."

"Sarah never shared her work before it was complete. She was very adamant about that."

"So I understand. So the only way to know what she was working on was through her employee."

"I never talked to Violet."

"I thought you just said that you talked to her when you wanted to get in touch with Sarah. She ran Sarah's schedule."

"Um, yeah. That's what I mean. Just to talk to Sarah or meet with her. I never have asked Violet anything about Sarah's work in progress."

"Is that what Violet will tell us?"

Of course, Violet had already said that she never told anyone about what Sarah was working on. But when people said things like that, they just meant that they limited the number of people they told about it. What were the odds that Violet had actually been able to keep her mouth shut about Sarah's latest project? And what were the chances that the calls between Reynolds and Violet were just to set up meetings with Sarah?

Margie figured Violet would be singing a different tune when she was brought in to have a serious chat in the CPS Homicide offices about her involvement with Reynolds. It was something that made most people pretty anxious. They tended to want to unburden themselves and straighten out any misunderstandings.

Reynolds cleared his throat and licked his lips again.

"Can I get you a glass of water?" Margie offered.

He said no, but right after that, he nodded his head. Margie went to the breakroom to fetch a glass of water for him, then returned. She sat down at the table.

"So no one can vouch for where you were or what you were doing when your friends were expecting you at the show."

"They really aren't my friends."

"No. I gathered that. It didn't seem like any of you liked each other very much. I'm surprised you still planned to do things together, like supporting Isaac at his show."

"Well… it's the nice thing to do. Being a supportive friend."

"Probably not your idea. I understand. What did you think of Isaac's work?"

"Well, considering his training and how long he has been trying to break out… I expected more from him. It was all very basic. Not really any more… elevated than it was when we were in school. And that was a long time. I guess his persistence paid off, because I don't think it was his talent."

"Did you tell him your opinion?"

Reynolds hesitated. "He didn't ask me my opinion. I try to be honest when people ask me."

"So no one asks you anymore."

He pressed his lips together. "So it would seem."

"What did Sarah think of your honesty?"

"Sarah demanded honesty," Reynolds said, perking up at the mention of her name. "If you didn't like a piece or a series, she wanted to hear it in plain language. No waffling around or trying to be nice."

"So the two of you got along well."

"Her work was better than Isaac's. I can't say I understand what all of the fuss was about. I don't think it was brilliant or inspired. But she would tell me that wasn't what she was going for."

"What did she think of the way that you critiqued other artists' work?"

Reynolds took another drink. "Like I said, she prized honesty."

"She told you that you should be brutally honest about *other* artists' work?"

"No, not exactly."

"What did she think about how you ripped into Lewis Riley back in the day?"

Reynolds shook his head. "I don't remember the name. Sorry."

"One of the men you went to art school with. He is now homeless, living in Inglewood or Pearce Estate Park. Sarah had run into him and recognized him. She must have told you about it."

"No. Why would she tell me about it?"

"Because she blamed you for destroying his artistic career, maybe resulting in his homelessness. You took his future away. I would be very surprised if she had said *nothing* to you about it."

Reynolds shrugged and didn't protest, but his meaning was obvious. He still was not admitting that he had talked to Sarah about it.

"If that's all you have, Detective, I have other work to do."

"And then you talked to Violet. And she told you about the new series Sarah was working on. A man whose life and art you had destroyed and who lived in the park, picking bottles."

"I had no idea of any of that."

"I don't believe that."

"Well…" He shook his head. "I can't help what you believe. If you don't know the truth when you hear it…"

"It's amazing the technology we have at our disposal these days, isn't it?" Margie asked, unlocking her screen and looking down at her phone.

Reynolds looked at her. "What do you mean?"

"I mean, you can call each other, text messages back and forth, even pictures or videos."

He gulped and said nothing.

"And at the park, they used to have a lot more issues with security, but that has been reduced since they put up cameras in the parking lot. They're everywhere now; you don't even see them. But if you are on your way to confront or possibly kill someone, you really should keep your eyes open."

He turned a pasty gray. He held the cup to his mouth but couldn't seem to drink.

"I don't understand," he finally croaked.

"You don't have an alibi, but we actually do know where you were before Sarah's accident."

Margie turned her phone around to let him look at it. A nicely framed picture of him walking through the parking lot at Pearce Estate Park.

CHAPTER TWENTY-TWO

*R*eynolds stared at the picture on Margie's phone. Sweat broke out on his temples, though his face remained smooth and impassive.

"I don't know where or when that was taken," he said, with only a slight quaver in his voice.

"Of course you do," Margie told him, in a calm, reassuring voice. "You realized that Sarah's new series of paintings was about *you*. That it would reveal what you had done to Lewis and others. That people would find out about you stealing and copying other artists' work. You spent all of this time building up your reputation and fighting for recognition, and she was threatening to take it all away from you."

"She was such a hypocrite!" Reynolds exploded. "She acted like she was so much better than anyone else, that she was educating the public about social issues that we all needed to be aware of and work to abolish. It's easy to see what's wrong when you look at what everyone else is doing. Yes, we have poverty and addiction and mental illness and all of those other things that she was so intent on 'exposing.' But what can I do about that? As an individual, what can I really do?"

Margie nodded encouragingly.

"She advocated for programs for the homeless and supporting people at poverty wages. All while she lived in that monstrosity. She decides she's going to ruin me because of something that happened years ago to Lewis? Someone she hadn't even bothered to keep track of? What right does she have to be judge and jury and destroy my life?"

"You just wanted to talk to her," Margie suggested.

"I didn't go there to hurt anyone," he insisted. "I wanted her to see what she was doing, to be reasonable. What good would it do to ruin me? How would that help Lewis? If she wanted to help him, why didn't she give him money? Or a job? Why didn't she invite him to stay in that mansion of hers? She lived alone. Violet didn't live in. Sarah broke up with Jonathan and kicked him out. She was all by herself in that huge mansion that could have housed thirty immigrant families. If she felt bad about Lewis, then why didn't she do something about it?"

"No one could change what had happened in the past," Margie agreed, careful to keep passive voice. Not what Reynolds had done to Lewis but what had happened to Lewis. No accusation, no hint of responsibility.

"No," Reynolds agreed. "That's exactly right. Ruining me wouldn't change Lewis's situation. What would it achieve? She would be able to stop anyone from getting their feelings hurt in the future? She would change the face of the art community? Her paintings were not going to change anything."

"Except for you. You were afraid that people would identify who it was that she was painting about, and that they would turn on you."

"What does it matter what I did back in school? When we were all still starting out? This isn't something that I did last week. I was a stupid kid, I'll admit that. I didn't know how to handle myself. But it isn't all on me." He looked affronted, as if Margie had accused him unjustly. "People have to make their own choices in life and to live with them. Lewis didn't have to leave art. He didn't have to make whatever other choices he made to end up on the street. He could have done what the rest of us did, working at it and struggling and finding a way to pull ourselves up and get what we wanted. It's not my fault that he made the choices he did."

"Actually," Margie said, "Lewis isn't really homeless. He's an undercover cop. He decided to go into law enforcement. He's only living on the streets temporarily as part of his cover."

Reynolds's mouth dropped open. He looked at Margie in horror. At first, she didn't understand why he felt so strongly about it. But she followed the logical progression. He had killed Sarah because she was painting a series that exposed his past and his unethical or illegal practices. Sarah had chosen to paint the series because she had seen Lewis living on the street and in the park and sought some kind of justice for what had been done to him back in art school. But Lewis wasn't a broken man living on the streets because Reynolds had destroyed all of his dreams. It was just an act. Reynolds had done what he had for no reason at all.

"Tell me about how the conversation with Sarah went," Margie prompted him.

It was a difficult barrier for him to cross. He had as much as admitted that he had been there. That he had hurt Lewis in the past. That he was angry with Sarah for trying to ruin him for no good reason. But if he were to recount the conversation with Sarah Thompson, he would have to admit what he had done to her.

Was there a way out of it? Could he just keep denying it? His best bet was to just tell Margie what had happened. She would see that he had been justified in what he had done. He would be able to shed his burden and they would find a way to move on. Someone would understand and he wouldn't have to keep hiding, worried that every call was going to be someone who had figured out his secret.

He had held on to a lot of secrets in the past. Maybe that was the way to connect with him.

"What happened in school happened a long time ago," Margie said.

He nodded eagerly. "Yes. It was a lifetime ago. I was a different person then. Do I regret that Lewis took my words so personally and decided not to pursue a career in art?" He considered his own question seriously. "I guess that on one hand I regret it. I would never want to harm anyone. But on the other hand, I didn't say anything that wasn't true. And he could have chosen to just work harder. To listen to someone else's opinion instead of mine. They were writing nice things about him in the paper. Why not focus on that instead of on a few throw-away comments that I made?"

"I don't know if that's what made him leave art," Margie said generously. "Who knows. He may just have decided that it wasn't for him. It's not an easy scene to break into, is it?"

"No. It's not. And not everybody is cut out for it. He probably decided that he needed a regular paycheck. Living as a creative is extremely difficult, and I went through a lot of lean years before I managed to break through the barriers."

"You struggled with other areas too. He might have been more talented than you, who is to say? But you had to pay your dues too. You had to deal with not having your own particular style, but borrowing from others instead. You had to figure out how to make that work. There were a lot of detractors. A lot of people who wanted to keep you down. Laws and rules of ethics that were murky and contradictory."

Reynolds nodded. "Why is it okay to copy the old masters, but not anyone more current? Why is copying a valid learning method, but only to a certain degree? When is following someone else's style valid and encouraged and when does it cross the line into copying or derivative works or art plagiarism? There is no clear line."

"It wasn't like you were trying to do anything unethical. You were only trying to build up your catalog, to be noticed. To find a way to make a living."

"It seems like it is so easy for some people," Reynolds complained. "They just walk right into it and everyone welcomes them with open arms, like Sarah. And someone like me, who has just as much talent as she does, is kept down. I have to keep struggling against these arbitrary rules about what is creative and what is copying."

"It must have been very frustrating. You just wanted to explain that to Sarah."

"Yes. I wanted to tell her that I was just doing what I had to do to succeed. And that what had happened to Lewis all those years ago... it wasn't my fault. She needed to just back off and leave me alone."

His words at the end were stronger, angrier. He was working himself back up into a self-justified, righteous anger. Margie could use that.

"So you knew she was going to be at the park. Maybe Violet told you. And you went there to discuss it with her. Away from offices where others might overhear you and misinterpret what was being said. Away from all of the pressures and distractions, people wanting to be involved in what was none of their business."

"I'm not a big nature buff," Reynolds confessed. "I like landscapes, but I'm not someone who needs to walk outside in the dust and the smog to regenerate. But I thought that if I could see her there, I could explain it all. I could convince her that what she was doing was pointless and would just hurt more people."

Margie nodded.

Reynolds looked like he was expecting her to guess the rest of the story for him, but Margie just sat there, waiting. He had started his tale. If she didn't say anything, he would need to fill the silence. He'd gone too far to just stop and not explain himself now.

"I followed her to that place, the campsite beside the railway tracks. She said that I needed to grow up and stand on my own two feet."

He shook his head, the movements tight and angry. "Stand on my own two feet! Grow up! I am just as much an adult as she is. Was. She said if I was a man, I'd be able to take my own medicine. Actions have consequences." He growled, a wordless, feral sound. "Well, her actions had consequences too. She couldn't just paint whatever she felt like when it affects someone else. Isn't that what all of those civil rights people are always saying? Your right to swing your fist ends where my nose begins? You can't harm other people. That's going too far. And here she was, ready to destroy me completely. She didn't have the right!"

"You felt like it was a personal attack."

"It was!" Reynolds agreed, his voice going up. "That's exactly what it was. A personal attack. I had the right to defend myself."

"And how did you do that?"

"I told her that I wasn't going to let her finish the paintings. She mouthed off about how I couldn't stop her, blah blah blah. She told me to go away or she would call the cops. Did she think that they would come? That she could tell me I was trespassing when she didn't own the property? You can't make someone else leave a public place just because you feel like it. She didn't own it."

Margie nodded and waited for him to go on.

"She tried to push me away, back toward the pathway. Told me to leave her alone, that I couldn't stop her from expressing herself, from 'educating' everyone as to what kind of a person I really was. She said I had no talent," his tone was outraged, "and that everything I had ever created was a copy of someone else's work. And that's not true!"

He nursed his anger for a short time, breathing heavily. "I shoved her back. She laid hands on me, I had the right to defend myself. She fell over backwards. Fat old broad had had zero athletic abilities. Just keeled over when I barely even touched her." He apparently decided that "shoved" was too aggressive a word. "And... she hit her head."

"And...?" Margie prompted, when he didn't continue. Reynolds surely had a cell phone to call for help. He could run back to the pathway where there were other people, get someone to help him with first aid. The usual reaction to someone falling down and hitting her head was not to drag her to the railway track and leave her there.

Reynolds shook his head. "She didn't move. She didn't get up. I checked, but I didn't think she had a pulse or was breathing. There was nothing I could do then. It was just an accident. And I didn't really push her, I just, you know..." Reynolds demonstrated a small, gentle movement in the air, "It wasn't my fault."

"Where did she fall? What did she hit her head on?"

"I don't know. A rock, I guess. I didn't know what to do. I just... got out of there."

"Was she on the railway tracks when you left?"

He swallowed. "I guess she was."

"So if she wasn't dead from the fall, you intended to kill her with the train?"

"No, that wasn't the way it was... I just... there wasn't anything I could do, so I got out of there."

"I see." Margie stood up. "Well, you're under arrest, Mr. Reynolds. If you'll please stand. We'll get you booked."

CHAPTER TWENTY-THREE

*M*argie's phone had rung several times while she had been interviewing Reynolds and getting him taken care of. Now that Reynolds was out of the way, Margie had to focus on typing her reports and ensuring that his recorded interview confession was properly linked in the workspace. Once that was done, she supposed MacDonald would want to have a small press conference or, at least, issue a press release and call one of the papers to let them know that Sarah Thompson's killer had been arrested. It would make a big splash, considering that up until today, the media had been told that it appeared to be a tragic accident and nothing else. Margie wasn't sure what time she would be able to go home.

But she knew that at least one of her missed calls had been from Christina, so as soon as she sat down at her desk, she looked at the display on her phone and saw that Christina had called not just once, but several times.

Her stomach clenched. She always tried to get back to Christina as quickly as possible, but sometimes she couldn't leave what she was doing. Was there a problem at school? Or worse, with Moushoom? Margie had thought it was a good idea for Christina to be able to talk to the nursing home about Moushoom's condition whenever she wanted to, but what if he had taken a downturn and Christina had no one to talk to about it?

Margie immediately tapped Christina's name on her call log.

"Christina?" she spoke as soon as the call connected. "I'm sorry I couldn't answer right away. Is everything okay?"

"Oh, Mom." Christina's voice sounded a little wobbly. Margie held her breath; the phone clenched in her hand so tightly it would take a crowbar to pry it out. "I called to see how Moushoom was doing."

Margie's worst fear. He had gotten worse. Had they taken him to the hospital? Had they made the wrong choice and waited too long, and now it was too late for the hospital to do anything? She thought of the pictures she had seen of gurneys lining the halls of the hospital.

"What did they say?" she asked, trying to keep her voice steady.

"They took him off of oxygen."

Margie gulped. Did Christina mean they had removed all support and were just going to let him go? She had told them to do everything possible for him.

"They what?"

"He's doing better. He's getting enough oxygen without the machine. They said that his pneumonia is clearing up. They might put him back on oxygen at night; they're going to watch his numbers and see how he does."

Margie let out a sob of relief. "Oh, that's really good news, sweetie. Thank you for letting me know. They think he's on the mend, then."

"Yeah. They got his COVID test back, and they said it was negative. It was bacterial, and the antibiotic is clearing it up."

Margie had been worrying about long COVID and the possibility of permanent lung and heart damage. Now she could let that worry go too.

"Wonderful. Oh, I'm so glad to hear that. Did you tell them to say we love him and miss him?"

"Yes. He might be able to have visitors in a day or two, as long as the facility doesn't go on lockdown."

It would be good to see him again. She looked forward to telling him all about the case that had begun with their walk in Pearce Estate Park.

She was sure he would find it interesting.

PEARCE ESTATE PARK

Pearce Estate Park is a 21-hectare natural haven nestled in a curve of the Bow River in southeast Calgary, seamlessly blending urban convenience with serene wildlife and plant life. The park features reconstructed wetlands, ponds, and streams that support a diverse range of plant species such as willows, Water Birch, and cattails.

Nature enthusiasts can enjoy birdwatching with species like White-breasted Nuthatches and Northern Flickers making frequent appearances. Families will appreciate the playgrounds and open spaces perfect for picnics or leisurely strolls along well-maintained pathways. Additionally, the adjacent Bow Habitat Station offers an immersive experience into aquatic ecosystems through its Sam Livingston Fish Hatchery Visitor Centre.

The author has spent many hours in Pearce Estate Park, beginning with when she and her husband were dating and gathered with other young adults for a fire and songs accompanied by guitar. She also went on numerous nature walks there with her son and frequently watched a medieval re-enactment group sword fighting.

BENCH WITH A VIEW

To those laboring against all odds to save souls.

CHAPTER ONE

*M*argie really didn't like early morning calls.

The sunrise was so late in the autumn and winter that she really couldn't expect the sun to have risen before she got to every homicide site. But she never could understand people getting up so early to run or walk their dogs, coming across fresh bodies when it was still too early for Margie to drag herself out of bed.

She had been doing better about getting out to run before work herself but, sometimes, she just kept snoozing her alarms until it was too late to get out. She had stumbled across a body herself on one of her early-morning runs, so who was she to criticize anyone else for doing the same thing?

Margie sat up and grabbed her phone from the nightstand. She used her thumb to answer the call and held it to her ear.

"Patenaude."

"I'm looking for Parks Pat," the dispatcher told her cheerfully.

"This is Detective Pat," she acknowledged, trying not to groan. "Does that mean you've got a body in a park?"

"Carburn Park this morning. DB on a park bench."

Margie envisioned a homeless person sleeping on a bench and dying from hypothermia overnight. It had been a mild fall so far, but Calgary weather was not kind to those who preferred to sleep rough.

She covered a yawn before speaking again. "Where is Carburn Park?"

"Not far from you, actually. But it's one of those little gems that is kind of tucked away, and you don't know about it unless it's in your neighborhood or someone tells you about it."

"Okay." Margie cleared her throat. She picked up the water bottle from the nightstand and had a drink. She was not an early-morning person. "I will punch it into my GPS and get there as soon as I can. Tell them I'm on my way."

"Will do, detective."

"Has OCME been called?"

"Yes. They will be behind you. I'm not sure how long you'll have to wait. Take coffee."

"Okay. Thanks."

Margie didn't need to terminate the call; the dispatcher had already hung up. Margie rubbed her eyes. She knew better than to lie back down or even just sit on the edge of the bed waiting until she was fully awake. It was a sure way to fall back asleep.

She went to the bathroom to splash water on her face and quickly do her hair, coiling her long braid on top of her head. She didn't start the coffee machine in the kitchen. It might wake up Christina. Instead, she would stop by Tim's and get a box of coffee for herself and the other professionals already on the scene. She had learned that the Take 12 worked better than taking a tray of filled cups, when she could only carry a few at a time.

"Mom?"

Margie stopped in Christina's bedroom doorway as she left the bathroom.

"Go back to sleep, honey. It's not time yet."

"You got a call?"

"Yeah."

"I'll call you when I get up."

"That would be great. Let me know how you are doing."

Christina murmured a reply and fell back asleep. They had agreed that Margie would not wake her up before leaving when she was called out, but often Christina woke up anyway when she heard Margie getting ready. Christina would get the details when she was up and getting ready for school or riding the bus.

Stella, though, was a different story. However excited the dog was when Margie got home from work or took her for a walk in the morning, she did not stir if Margie got up before seven—a dog after Margie's own heart.

CHAPTER TWO

*W*ith her Take 12 in the footwell of the passenger seat, Margie set up Carburn Park on her GPS and headed out. The electronic voice directed her south on Deerfoot Trail, which was busier than Margie would have expected so early in the morning. But at least she didn't have to contend with rush hour traffic. The drivers of the cars out on the road were happy to let her zoom over the Calf Robe Bridge and down to Glenmore, even without flashing lights.

She didn't need emergency lights or siren to get to a homicide scene. What difference would it make if she arrived five minutes later without a siren? The victim was already dead. The Office of the Chief Medical Examiner death scene investigator would be behind her somewhere, and the other crime scene investigators wouldn't have much reason to be there before it was light and they could see what they were doing properly. It wasn't like a kidnapping or hostage situation where seconds counted. The victim would still be dead when she arrived.

What had looked like a fairly simple route to the park turned out to be a lot of twists and turns, and then, finally, Margie reached the park entrance.

It was right in the middle of a residential area. Probably a lot of walkers liked to take their turn around the park every day or two. Lots of witnesses who could help narrow down the time of death. Though there had probably been only a few walkers out that late or early.

Margie drove in slowly and parked her car with a cluster of other vehicles. A young constable with a traffic wand indicated the direction she should go. "Around the pond here, ma'am. Clockwise is shorter. Just keep hugging the pond on your right. Can't miss it."

Margie could see large lights being set up partway around the pond. She would have to be blind to miss them. "Thank you," she told him and offered the Tim's box. He took a cup and she filled it.

"Thank you!" he said, pulling down his mask to drink and giving her an appreciative grin.

Margie switched the box of coffee from one side to the other as she walked around the pond. It wasn't that heavy, but it got heavier the farther she walked.

As she approached, she studied the scene, brightly lit in the middle of the dark park. It was a strange sight, like a play or tableau with spotlights on it. She had imagined an old man in voluminous coats lying on the park bench, having passed away in his sleep. Not too much to investigate. Just a natural death. Sad, but something that inevitably happened at least once a year in Calgary, usually in the depths of winter when it was 35 or 40 below. Some homeless person sitting in a bus shelter to avoid the wind and snow.

Instead, the victim appeared to be sitting up. As if he were just looking out onto the pond and had fallen asleep, never to wake up again.

As Margie got closer and again switched the Tim's Take 12 from one hand to the other, she realized the victim was a woman rather than a man.

It didn't take long to reach the bench. At her approach, the other law enforcement officers looked up and fell silent. Margie stopped a short distance away to put on protective gear. She wasn't as sure now that it was just someone who had died of hypothermia or passed away in her sleep.

"Here, someone better take this," Margie offered, showing the Tim's coffee. A couple of officers hurried to take it from her and set it on a table with folding legs that had been set up away from the scene. Margie saw a garbage bag that already contained a few discarded coffee cups.

Free of her offering, Margie approached the bench to have a look at the victim.

It looked at first glance as though the woman were merely sleeping on the bench. Her face was at rest, her eyes closed. Her body was leaning slightly to the side but not falling over. As if she might jerk awake at any moment. The bright white lights were not flattering, but she did not have the gray pallor of many of the victims Margie saw. Her skin was a rich golden brown and had not yet taken on the chalkiness Margie expected. She was probably around Margie's age, in her thirties, and was not a homeless person. Her hair and skin were well-cared-for and her overcoat was pristine and good quality. Margie couldn't see the brand and didn't know enough about fashion to immediately identify it, but guessed it was LL Bean or a pricier brand.

"Well, this is not at all what I was expecting," she told the others.

"What were you expecting?" one of the patrol cops asked, taking a sip of the fresh Tim's coffee.

"The dispatcher said a body on a park bench, and I just figured... an old homeless man."

"That'll teach you not to jump to conclusions."

"Do we have a name yet? Does anyone know how long she's been here?"

"No identification yet. But we haven't touched anything other than to make sure that she was dead. Waiting on you and the ME's office."

Margie was not going to go poking through the woman's pockets either. She would wait until the death investigator had a chance to examine the body in situ and to check her pockets and handbag.

"Does she have a purse?" Margie asked, looking around.

Everyone looked at the woman, under the bench, and scanned the nearby ground.

"Nothing immediately obvious. We'll need to check the bushes and water when it's light out."

"Yeah." Margie took another step back and carefully looked around. There was no sign of the woman's personal possessions. "Is she wearing any jewelry? Watch?"

"You think it was a mugging? Doesn't look like any mugging I've ever seen," disagreed a cop with a short, grizzled beard that showed around his mask.

"No, I'm not making any assumptions. I'm in the information-gathering phase."

Margie stretched medical gloves over her warm gloves and gently pushed back the sleeves and collar of the coat to expose the victim's wrists and throat.

She was wearing a pretty but practical wristwatch. It was not a big name, nothing Margie recognized, and probably the jewels inset in the bezel were nothing more than zircons. No wedding ring on her finger. No necklace.

"No gloves," the younger cop noted.

Margie nodded. "It might be unseasonably warm, but I still wouldn't walk to this side of the pond without gloves, much less sit down to watch the ducks or wait for someone to meet me with bare hands."

She had made sure she had her gloves on before she stepped out of her car and picked up the Tim's box. Had the woman walked over and sat down without gloves? If so, why? Had it been a rush trip and she'd forgotten? Had she dropped them? Had someone taken them? With a jacket like that, she had to have gloves. Probably leather. Real leather, not the synthetic stuff.

Margie made a mental note of the missing purse and gloves. She didn't want to take off her own gloves to write in her notebook yet; it seemed like it took forever for her fingers to warm up again once they'd gotten good and cold. Policing in the cold weather was not at the top of her list of favorite things to do—especially middle-of-the-night or early-morning callouts.

CHAPTER THREE

*D*o we have any witnesses? Anyone who can tell us how long she's been here?"

"Not yet. Found by early morning walkers. But I don't know how many people walked by here before someone realized she wasn't just resting her eyes. The woman over there is the one who called in." The cop nodded to an older woman standing a short distance away, outside the area that had been cordoned off with yellow tape. She looked cold, but was waiting to see if she needed to answer any other questions.

Although Margie figured there was little she actually needed from the woman, and she'd probably already told the cops who were first to the scene everything she knew, it was best to talk to her anyway. Show her that her opinion was valued and that they were listening to her.

She approached the woman. "Hi. Detective Patenaude. I'm sorry to keep you waiting here. I'm sure you want to get home and get warmed up. How are you doing? Can I grab you a coffee?"

"Oh, no, I'm fine," the older woman said with a gentle smile. "I just wanted to make sure that you had all of the information you need before I go anywhere. I want to be a good citizen."

"I certainly appreciate you calling it in and waiting around to help us out. Why don't we start with you just telling me your story, start to finish, and I'll ask you some questions afterwards."

"Okay. My name is Betty. Betty Mitchell. I walk here most mornings. Got to keep myself in shape, and you don't do that by just sitting around all day. I spend an hour walking every morning, and it does wonders for my health. And helps to keep off those pesky pounds."

"Which is a big health benefit by itself," Margie agreed with a nod. "Funny how the pounds start to pile on any time you let down your guard."

Betty nodded. "Oh, just you wait until menopause." She rolled her eyes. "That's when the battle really begins!"

"Oh, don't tell me that. But I said I wouldn't interrupt. You got here like usual this morning."

"I have a headlamp," Betty tapped the headband light that she had turned off now that they were under the bright police lights. "So it doesn't matter what time of the year it is, I can get out and exercise even if the sun doesn't rise until eight-thirty."

"Good plan."

"I generally go at the same time every day and, when you do that, you get to know the regulars. Even if you don't talk or walk together, you smile and nod and say good morning. You get to know the people and the dogs, since there are always a couple of dogs here."

Margie could see a few lone figures still taking their regular walks, not stopping to gawk at the police, but keeping an eye on what was happening. There were a few walkers with dogs.

"When I walked past the bench the first time, I was a little surprised to see that young woman here. She isn't a regular. And when it is dark, people don't usually sit down to enjoy the pond. They keep moving, unless they have to stop to tie a shoe or something. And with the mornings being so *brisk*, no one stops for long. If you keep moving, you stay warm. She's not dressed to sit down for very long. She would get cold." Betty pressed her lips together and shook her head. "It just didn't seem right. When I made a second circuit of the pond, she was still in exactly the same position, like she'd fallen asleep there and hadn't stirred. It didn't feel right. I was worried about... well, that she could be drunk or maybe diabetic."

"What time do you think you got to the park in the first place?"

"Five-thirty, maybe. Around then. I shook her, tried to get her attention, you know, and she didn't move, and she was stiff..."

"And you knew that she wasn't just having a nap."

"I feel terrible that I did not realize something was wrong the first time and just left her there."

"You couldn't have known. She does not look like most of the bodies that I deal with. I would not say that she has been dead for very long, and her dark complexion keeps her from looking gray."

"You're..." Betty looked at Margie, hesitating as she searched for the appropriate term. The politically correct terminology changed over the years and those who were older and didn't keep track often used words that had fallen out of favor. "You are First Nations yourself, aren't you?"

Margie nodded. "I am," she agreed. "Métis." Even with her mask on, her heritage was obvious. She looked toward the woman sitting on the bench, waiting for someone who would never come. While it was impossible to be absolutely certain, the woman's dark skin, black hair, and high cheekbones made her look Indigenous as well. She had more delicate features than Margie, and might have some Asian influences. She was not from just a white European heritage; that much was certain. "And she looks like she is."

Margie saw a white van approaching from the parking lot down the paved pathway toward them, moving very slowly—the Office of the Chief Medical Examiner.

"That will be our death investigator. So you don't remember seeing the deceased here before?"

"No. I think I would have remembered. She is very attractive. Those of us who are usually walking around the pond in the morning... well, you've just rolled out of bed. Maybe combed your hair before putting on a toque. No makeup. No... fashionable clothes. Just some sweats and walking shoes, maybe a warm shell to keep off the wind as it gets colder."

The deceased woman did look out of place, when Margie thought about it like that. She certainly had not just rolled out of bed and thrown on her comfy workout clothes to go for a walk. Lipstick, maybe some eye shadow, smooth and neat black hair. That pretty overcoat. Margie looked at her feet. No sneakers. Blunt-toed flats, so she hadn't come from a cocktail party. No impossible-to-walk-in spiked heels. But not what one would wear to exercise or walk the dog. Maybe shoes for the office or a casual dinner out with friends.

There was something that seemed familiar about her, but the more

Margie concentrated on it, the more ethereal it became, slipping away to hide in the back of her mind. If she ignored it, she was more likely to have a flash of insight later.

"Did you see anyone else that you didn't recognize? Today or sometime in the last few days?"

"No, I don't think so. Not that I remember."

"And did you see anyone else close to this bench? Stopping to look at her, shake her by the arm, roll their eyes at you over someone falling asleep in the park at this time of day?"

"No, everyone was just doing their own thing like usual. Independent of each other, but used to being here around other people. It's safer with more people here." She bit her lip, worrying it. "At least, I always thought it was safe. There's never been any trouble here before."

CHAPTER FOUR

*T*he white van with OCME emblazoned on the side of it pulled up to the edge of the yellow-taped perimeter. Margie put her hand on Betty's arm. "Did you give the constable your contact information?"

"Yes, I gave him everything."

"You can get on with your day, then. I have everything I need for now and, if I have any follow-up questions, I will give you a call."

"Okay, thank you. Good luck… I hope you find out what happened." She cast a glance toward the deceased woman, still looking as if she were just at rest. "Maybe it was natural causes. She just had a seizure or an aneurysm or something. She looks so peaceful. I hope she was just sitting here looking at the pond and then… she was gone."

Margie's heart gave a little squeeze. "I hope so too."

But the missing purse gave her pause. Maybe there was a good explanation. Maybe the woman had everything she needed for a short walk and meditation by the pond in her pockets. The keys to her house nearby. Her phone and wallet.

Maybe it was just something simple and unexpected. Something quick. So that the victim hadn't even known that anything was happening, and then she was just gone.

Margie walked over to the white van as the occupants stepped out. She saw that the death investigator was Dr. Kahn.

"Hello, doctor. You got here pretty quickly. You must not have had anything else to see tonight."

His eyes crinkled in a smile. "No, and I would have been up in another hour anyway, so I even had a good night's sleep. Had to roll this one out of bed," he tilted his head toward the technician who had come with him. "I suspect he was up late partying."

"I was not," the tall young man objected, his voice slightly muffled by his mask. "I was just… working on the computer late."

"Working?" Dr. Kahn challenged.

"Well… I did have a campaign I needed to finish."

"Are you running for mayor or gaming?" Margie asked, laughing.

"I *might* have been gaming."

They all laughed. "Oh, the foibles of youth," Dr. Kahn proclaimed. "One day, you'll discover that sleep is more important to your health and success than all the games or movies, no matter how much you enjoy them."

The doctor's slender assistant shrugged. "I know. But sometimes it… pulls me in."

"Well, let's have a look at our newest case and see what we've got."

Dr. Kahn looked at Margie and raised a brow questioningly, but she didn't fill him in on any details. She wanted to hear what he had to say about the woman and what had happened to her. Without any preconceptions or biases.

The two of them got out soft-sided equipment bags and, after suiting up appropriately, walked over to the victim on the bench.

"A lovely young woman," Dr. Kahn observed, dictating through his lapel mike to the recorder in his pocket. "Thirties, slender build, average height, Indigenous or mixed race. No sign of violence on the face or outer clothing."

His assistant took a large camera from his equipment bag and started snapping pictures, moving around to capture all angles.

Dr. Kahn touched the woman's wrist briefly. "No pulse. Rigor is setting in. Dead for a few hours." He looked at the other man. "Do you need to take any more of her clothing and position before I touch anything?"

"You're good to go, doctor."

Dr. Kahn unbuttoned the woman's overcoat slowly and deliberately, then opened it up.

"Do you think it was natural causes?" Margie couldn't help asking. "An aneurysm or something like that? There is no sign of an external injury."

"Much too early to tell," Kahn told her. "We're just getting started. No blood is apparent from this position. That doesn't preclude me finding any as I examine her. Sometimes cause of death is not immediately obvious."

"No, of course," Margie agreed.

She was glad that it didn't appear to be a violent death, though. Maybe this would be an easy case to close.

Dr. Kahn shone a flashlight on the victim's face, moving it back and forth slowly and looking at it from different angles.

"There may be some residue on the face. Let's get some swabs around her mouth and nose."

They worked together carefully, the technician anticipating Dr. Kahn's needs and supplying him with additional swabs and collection vials.

"Clothing appears to be disturbed," Kahn observed. He turned to the law enforcement officers looking on. "Did anyone touch her? Open the coat to search for identification? Check her neck for a pulse?"

They all looked at each other. Margie shook her head. "Certainly not while I've been here. I touched her sleeves and lapels to check for jewelry. I wore gloves. No one unbuttoned the coat."

Kahn moved back while the technician took more pictures, noting that the woman's clothes under her coat had been pulled around. Margie swallowed as she looked on, wondering whether that was an indication of sexual assault. But she waited for the doctor to do a further examination and give them additional information. After the additional pictures had been taken, Dr. Kahn and the technician carefully removed the overcoat. Then Margie could see what Kahn had been talking about. One of the woman's sleeves was pushed up. Maybe it had just happened when she had put on her coat and not bothered to fix. Sometimes, when Margie pulled on her coat, her sleeves would ride up if she weren't holding on to them. The woman might have been distracted or in a hurry. It might have been as easy as that.

"Injection mark," Dr. Kahn observed, exposing the inner arm at the elbow joint.

"Is she an IV drug user?" Margie questioned in surprise. The woman certainly didn't look like an addict. Not that one could always tell. If the woman were a covert drug user, then she would probably have chosen a less conspicuous place to inject. Between the toes, maybe.

"No, I wouldn't say so," Kahn said. He examined the injection site. "No sign that she has injected any other time recently. No scarring, no tracks."

"She doesn't look like a drug user," Kahn's assistant offered.

"Never make an assumption. Just because she doesn't have open sores or meth mouth, that doesn't mean she's not an addict or occasional drug user."

The younger man nodded seriously. Kahn examined the woman's other arm and all visible skin. "Nothing else stands out on examination in situ. We'll see what we can find on the table in autopsy. Do some tox screens, look for any other signs of IV drug use, any signs of assault or recent activity."

"Does she have a wallet?" Margie asked. "Phone, keys?"

Kahn felt each of the woman's pockets and shook his head. "No, nothing. Probably in her purse." he glanced around. "Wherever that is."

"So someone took her purse after she died."

"Could have been opportunistic. Someone saw the woman asleep or dead, the purse on the bench next to her, and decided to snatch it to see if there was anything valuable in it."

Margie nodded. She looked at the LEOs who were there to preserve the scene. "Chances are, they grabbed anything valuable and tossed the rest. Check nearby garbage cans as well as behind bushes or anything between here and the parking lot." She looked at the pond. "I don't imagine we'll be able to dredge the pond for it but, when the sun comes up, if everybody could take a quick look to see if it is near the shore."

They nodded, but no one moved to do anything just yet. An evidence-collection team would come once it was light.

Margie's phone rang. She pulled it out of her pocket and looked at it. She hadn't realized so much time had passed.

"Hi, honey. *Boon matayn.*"

"Hey." Christina yawned loudly. "How's your morning going?"

"Well, it could be worse. It's not thirty below."

"That's good. Where are you?"

"Carburn Park."

"Where's that one?"

"Not far, actually. It's in the southeast, in a neighborhood called Riverbend."

"Any water?"

"A pond, at least. And the river is close by. I can't see it from here. But then, I can't see anything much. It's still dark."

"Yeah. So you're okay?"

"I haven't even been thinking about it."

Christina knew about Margie's irrational fear of water. But Margie was getting used to most of the Calgary parks either being beside the river or having a water feature. She ran around the Valleyview Park pond several times a week and was able to do it without any fear of falling in or anything bad happening to her.

"Good," Christina pronounced. She yawned again. "I'm getting ready for school. Took Stella out, so she's fine, but you might want to stop and see her before you go downtown, if it's on the way."

"Sure, I should be able to do that. How are the arrangements for the Indigenous Fair coming along?"

"I can't believe we're so close now. I keep expecting everything to fall apart. That they'll just cancel it, or all of the performers will come down with COVID or something. Or they'll close the schools again."

"I don't think they're going to close the schools. I think they decided it didn't really help that much the last time, and it put a lot of kids in jeopardy."

"Put them in jeopardy?" Christina repeated skeptically. "How did it put them in jeopardy?"

"Because kids who live in violent homes or with pedophiles were trapped twenty-four hours a day with their abusers, who were at home because they were furloughed or working from home or lost their jobs. There was a huge increase in domestic violence and child trafficking during the lockdown." Margie swallowed. "For some kids, school is their only safe place."

"Oh." Christina's voice was quiet. "I didn't know that."

"Really, only law enforcement was aware of it. And maybe some of the school administrators. It didn't make big news."

"It should have."

"Yes. I think it's important for the public and those making decisions for society to know things like that."

"So you don't think the schools will shut down again because of that."

"Probably not. It would also be a problem if they close the schools without imposing another general lockdown, because if people are still working, they need childcare. And for many people, their only childcare is the school system. What are they supposed to do if the schools close and they still have to work? Leave kids at home alone?"

"Yeah. I guess I can probably stop worrying that they're going to shut down and we won't be able to do the Indigenous Fair." Christina gave a low chuckle. "I can worry about the other disasters instead. People getting the date wrong. Fire or flood. You know, more realistic things."

"It will turn out okay. Even if it isn't everything you want it to be, it will still be more than what would have been done if you hadn't planned anything."

"Doing something is better than doing nothing."

"Always."

"Okay." Christina sighed. "Getting my coffee and then I'm out of here. Have fun with your body."

CHAPTER FIVE

*T*he forensic techs should be arriving any time," she told the small group of LEOs who remained at the scene. "Let's take a quick look around before they come to see if we can find the purse or any other evidence. Then we'll be able to point out any other areas they need to process."

Now that it was light out, everyone seemed agreeable to walking the area outside of the yellow tape, looking for additional evidence rather than just standing in one place. They had run out of coffee and people were restless.

When the crime scene techs got there half an hour later, they'd had no luck in finding the purse or any other evidence that seemed to relate to the dead woman.

Margie briefed the techs and told them about the missing purse. They talked to Dr. Kahn about the victim, and the techs went to work documenting and seeing what else they could find.

Once the techs had done an initial review, Kahn and his assistant returned to the van to get out body bags and a gurney. They went to work moving the stiff body into the inner and outer body bags to contain any fluids. There was no blood on the bench. Nothing that Margie could see on the back of the coat. She still didn't know what had happened to the woman, but she hadn't been stabbed or shot. Dr. Kahn would have to complete the autopsy and tell them what he found. But it did appear that drugs had been involved somehow, which dashed Margie's hopes that it would be a natural death. Bizarre, but explainable.

Margie looked at the victim one more time before Dr. Kahn and his assistant finished wrapping her up in the body bags and transporting her back to OCME.

There was something so familiar about her. Margie motioned for them to stop before they zipped up the bags, staring at the woman's face and trying to figure out why it seemed so familiar. She motioned to the other LEOs.

"Do any of you recognize her? She seems very familiar to me, and I'm wondering if she is a public figure or something like that. Do you know her face from anywhere?"

Everyone came over and took a long look at the woman's face before shaking their heads and walking away.

"She looks kind of like you," one of the constables offered.

Margie thanked him, but shook her head in irritation. It was a well-known phenomenon that people had trouble recognizing faces across racial barriers. Also known as "all you people look the same" syndrome. The young man saw two Indigenous faces and saw only their similar skin color and black hair, not the finer features that would indicate a familial relationship.

"Sorry," she told Dr. Kahn. "It was worth a try. I'm sure I've seen her somewhere, but I have no idea where. Hopefully, it will come to me."

"I will let you know if we are able to identify her through fingerprints or a missing person report. As soon as we have an identification, I'll get back to you with the name."

"I appreciate that. Thanks."

She watched them finish bundling her up and load the body into the van.

It would be easier to spot any evidence now that it was light. Still, there was also an increasing number of people walking around the park, and Margie was concerned that their scene wasn't sufficiently protected by the yellow tape. They had the primary area quarantined, but they didn't yet know where the purse had been dumped, or if there were any evidence showing how the victim had arrived or whether anyone else had been with her.

CHAPTER SIX

*E*ven though Margie had been called out in the early morning hours, she did not get into the office until late morning. She had missed the usual morning briefing, but gave the bullpen a quick rundown on the scene she had been at that morning.

"Maybe she was killed by beavers," Cruz suggested, deadpan.

Margie's face heated as the rest of the homicide team laughed. She tried to keep her expression blank.

"Well, I did see a lot of beaver trees and a small dam there," she told him. "I'll talk to MacDonald about having you follow up on that line of investigation. Get you some hip-waders, and you can go right down into the water to talk to them and see if they can lead you to the missing purse."

She liked the mental image of the Filipino detective struggling through the mud and bullrushes in hip waders, playing Dr. Dolittle with the beavers. From the chuckles around the room, others appreciated it as well.

Cruz shook his head. "Oh, Detective Pat," he said, sadly, shaking his head.

"So, no identity on the deceased yet?" Siever asked, trying to get them back on track. He liked things to be done in an orderly way and, like all of the detectives, he was disturbed when they could not identify the victim. He could be very tenacious in chasing down missing information. He had a knack for seeing patterns and identifying missing pieces.

"No, not yet. OCME will be checking for any matching missing person reports, but it wouldn't hurt to have a second set of eyes going over them in case there is a piece of information that doesn't quite seem to fit."

"I can do that. Have you entered her vitals in the workspace?"

"Not yet, I just got in. If you're lucky, Dr. Kahn might have gotten to it already. Otherwise, you'll have to wait just a few minutes for me to catch up and get my notes transferred to the computer."

He nodded. "Fair enough."

Margie turned to Detective Katelyn Jones, her best friend in the unit, who sat at the desk next to hers. Jones pushed a lock of blond hair that had escaped her bobby pins back behind her ear. She opened her mouth to ask a question, then her eyes slid to the side, looking past Margie at someone else.

Margie turned to see who had entered the bullpen. He removed a black mask and smiled at her.

"Oh! Lewis!" It had taken Margie an instant to recognize him. The last time she had seen Lewis, he had been undercover as a homeless man; unshaven, in dirty, worn clothing. It had been a difficult case for him and she hadn't seen him in a few weeks. It was odd to see him in a white shirt now, clean-shaven, smelling like laundry soap and aftershave.

"Wow!" She motioned for him to come into the bullpen and indicated him to the rest of the team. "Guys, this is Lewis Riley. The undercover officer I met on the Sarah Thompson case."

"Oh, the woman who met the train," Cruz said. "And you knew her personally, didn't you? I'm sorry, that must have been a real heartbreak."

"It was," Lewis agreed with a nod. "But… I'm doing my best to move on and to fill my free time with all of the things that I have always planned to do someday. Seize the day and all that. No more putting things off until I have time or am retired."

Cruz nodded. "You're a pretty young fella. I wouldn't recommend waiting for retirement!"

"But you do, you know? You say that someday you'll get around to it. When I'm grown up, I'm going to… When I'm retired and have all the time in the world, I'll take up this hobby or travel to that place. You know how it is. So I'm not doing that anymore."

Margie nodded. "Good for you. But what are you doing here?"

Lewis laughed.

"I didn't mean 'what are you doing here?' I meant… it's nice to see you—what are you doing here?"

"That's okay. I heard about your new homicide this morning, the woman discovered in the park. I wanted to follow up and get some more details about it. And I thought… I wanted to see you again, so I would just come over here instead of calling or emailing."

Margie noticed that he had buried the comment that he wanted to see her again in that statement and her face got warm again, but not in embarrassment this time. She smiled and tried to stay focused on what he had said.

"What do you want to know about it? And what does it have to do with your cases? I have to say, by the way, that you clean up pretty good."

"You like this better than Eau de Garbage?" Lewis teased, motioning to himself.

"Well, just a little, yeah."

"You know that I was stationed in Pearce Estate Park. There has been a faction using parks for meetings or dead drops, so I was keeping an eye on things at Pearce Estate, thinking that it was a pretty good bet based on its proximity to downtown. Others have been watching Prince's Island and other downtown parks. But now I'm wondering if… they managed to misdirect us, or we made some false assumptions. Carburn Park was on the list of parks to check out, but it was further down the list."

Margie's stomach knotted. From the beginning, she had worried that there was more to the woman's death than just an accident or natural causes. It had just not felt right.

"What kind of a 'faction' are we talking about?" she demanded. "And who is 'us'? What department are you working for?"

"Shall we sit…?" Lewis motioned to a spare chair that floated around the bullpen.

Margie sat at her desk and motioned in front of it for him to wheel the chair over.

Seeing that they were sitting down to have a private discussion, the other detectives returned to their own work. Margie would, of course, keep them updated on the case through the shared workspace, morning briefings, and whatever other methods were necessary to keep everyone on the same page.

Lewis sat down and he put an expanding folder he had been carrying under his arm on her desk with a thunk. Documents that might relate to her case? If so, it had just taken a huge leap forward.

"What do you know?" Margie asked. "Please tell me that the woman who died was not a cop. I thought she was familiar, and if she was another undercover cop…"

He looked startled by this question. "Uh, no, not as far as I know. I don't know every undercover cop in the city, but if this was related to our case, I should know all of the UCs, and I'm sure I would have heard if one of them had not reported in."

But they both knew that someone could be killed and her body discovered before anyone knew that she was gone. She could have been on her way home to bed, but was killed before she was missed.

They both pretended this was not the case and the woman could not have been a cop.

"Good," Margie pronounced. "You scared me for a minute there. So tell me what you're investigating."

He glanced around the room to ensure no one was listening. Why would he be concerned about someone listening in from the homicide division? Maybe it was just a reflex—something all undercovers did. Margie had not done any significant undercover work herself. Nothing where she had been in position for days or weeks. A few times when they had needed an Indigenous face to blend in, but only for a few hours.

"I'm from ALERT," he explained. "We are investigating new activity by the Alberta Warriors."

ALERT, the Alberta Law Enforcement Response Teams, was an integrated law enforcement agency that focused on organized crime and included the Special Enforcement Unit that focused on gang-related crime.

Margie's throat tightened. She grabbed the water bottle beside her monitor and took a couple of swallows of the stale, lukewarm water.

She cleared her throat and looked at Lewis with wide eyes. "The Alberta Warriors?"

CHAPTER SEVEN

*Y*ou've heard of them?" Lewis asked, taking in her reaction. "Most Alberta law enforcement agencies won't even call the gangs by name. They won't do anything that might 'legitimize' them."

"You think pretending they don't exist makes anything better?" Margie demanded. "You don't *invoke* them by calling them by name."

"That's just the viewpoint here. Don't legitimize them, and you limit their scope. Keep people from giving them any respect or regard."

"Well, I came here from Winnipeg. And trust me, I know all about the Manitoba Warriors." She clenched her jaw.

Lewis nodded slowly. "Yeah. The Alberta Warriors are an offshoot of the Manitoba Warriors. And unfortunately, no less violent."

Margie felt sick. She shook her head. "I thought when I left the Peg I was leaving all that behind."

"You can't escape it. You could go to Yellowknife and still have to deal with organized crime."

Margie shook her head. She wanted to say, "At least they wouldn't be Indigenous gangs," but she was sure they were. Other countries ran their cocaine through the territories, and she was sure that Indigenous criminals facilitated it. As much as she would like to suggest that her people were only victims of crime in Canada, particularly at the hands of organized crime, she knew that the statistics didn't bear her out. Most violent crime against Indigenous people was perpetrated by other Indigenous.

She rubbed her forehead, feeling the fatigue from getting up too early that morning starting to weigh on her.

"So you think that the Alberta Warriors are using Calgary parks as hubs for their business and that the woman killed in Carburn Park might have been the victim of that activity?"

"I can't tell you anything. Since all that I know right now is that there was a death in the park, and that it wasn't a homeless person or someone known to the police in the area. I need you to tell me the details."

Closing her eyes, Margie recounted the basics of the case as succinctly as she could. When she opened her eyes, she saw that Lewis had taken out his notepad and was scribbling down notes about what she had related.

"There wasn't any obvious sign of gang activity," Margie said. "We can go back and look for it, but... I didn't see any gang tags or anything else. We walked the area pretty carefully looking for the victim's purse. I thought it would be in a bush or garbage can nearby. Or thrown in the water. But we didn't turn it up."

"And you don't yet have an identity on the victim."

"No."

"But she did have an injection mark," Lewis mused. "An injection suggests drug and possibly gang involvement."

"She looked as clean-cut as anyone I've ever seen," Margie protested. "She was not an addict or a drug runner. She was not a gang member."

"They can clean up pretty good. They don't all look like the Manitoba Warriors you ran into in Winnipeg."

"No. I'd swear it. She was not involved in a gang."

"But she *was* out of place."

Margie thought about it. "Yeah. Yeah, right from the start, I didn't feel like she belonged there. She wasn't a walker. Most of the people through there... they're walking their dogs, getting some exercise themselves, whatever. But she looked like... an office worker, I guess. White collar. Just home from work. Flat, sensible shoes. Nice looking, but not spikes. Something she could work in. Nice clothes, she could certainly live in the area. Be a neighbor of the park... but I still would have expected her to put on sweats or something comfy before going for a walk in the park."

"She was sitting on the bench. Why? Watching the sunset? Birding?"

"Waiting for someone," Margie guessed.

"What makes you think that?"

"Just because she looked out of place, I guess. Like someone told her, you go here and you wait at such-and-such a time, and so she did and, while she was waiting…" Margie trailed off. "I don't know. It looked like she fell asleep and never woke up. But I know that's not what happened. Someone came along and… gave her an injection and took her purse? It really doesn't make much sense yet."

"No. If she wasn't a drug user, then most likely, someone else injected her. But why? People don't generally go around injecting each other with drugs to kill them."

Margie heard what he had been too polite to say.

"Unless they are in a gang."

Because gang violence didn't make any sense. It was just violence. Violence for the sake of violence. Violence to intimidate. To bully their way to the top. To get what they wanted. It didn't have to be measured or logical. They just did whatever it took to get their way. And an organization like the Manitoba Warriors…

Margie shook her head. She should have known that working in homicide, she would never be completely free of the gangs. She would know about it whenever they were involved in a murder. And there would be gang murders. As long as there were Warriors, there would be murders.

"I'm sorry to have to tell you all of this," Lewis said apologetically. "I wish I could just tell you it had nothing to do with the Warriors. That it was just a random act of violence. That you could walk any park in this city just as safe as could be."

Margie laughed bleakly. "I guess I had kind of thought that I was leaving it all behind. The city streets and parks were perfectly safe. Any homicides that I would be investigating would just be domestic or random. I knew there would be organized crime. I knew there were gangs everywhere. Indigenous gangs included. But I had my own little fantasy where I never had to deal with any of them."

"You're sure that the woman was Indigenous."

"Pretty sure, yeah. Looked like it. I could always be wrong. Maybe she was Asian or some mix that just happened to look Indigenous, but I don't think so."

"And you thought you might know her?"

"Well, I feel like I've seen her somewhere before. Like I've seen her on TV or something. Sometime in the past... I don't know. I can't be much help identifying her."

"Do you get together with groups for... *tribal* stuff?" Lewis turned a little bit pink as he fumbled for the right words. "Like community dinners or dances, stuff for school kids to meet each other..."

"Normally, yes, but we got here during lockdown. Large gatherings have not been permitted. We keep saying that we're going to go to the Native Friendship Center, that we're going to get together with cousins that we haven't seen since we got here, all that kind of thing. But we haven't been able to. My daughter Christina, she's organized an Indigenous Fair at her school, and they're getting a bunch of people to talk about their cultures, perform, make crafts and food..."

"What a great idea. It's important to get to know each other's cultures. And even your own sometimes, if you weren't raised doing cultural things or exposed to your language. A lot of Indigenous kids I meet were never a part of a traditional family, haven't been to a reservation, seen a dance, gone on a hunt..."

Margie nodded. "Some of them have really been deprived of their culture," she agreed. But they were getting off-track. Lewis wasn't interested in the plight of the Indigenous in Canada. He was concerned with stopping an Indigenous gang, breaking up their drug networks, the sex and gun trafficking that went with it hand-in-hand. He wasn't fishing for an invitation to a high school awareness day.

"So, did you meet any of the people that your daughter has been making contact with for this Indigenous Fair?"

"Oh... well, yes, I have. She doesn't drive—or, she can, but she only has her learner's right now, and roads like Seventeenth Avenue and Deerfoot make her nervous. So if she has to go anywhere to meet with anyone, then I drive her."

She thought of Christina sitting on a park bench waiting to meet with someone, while Margie sat in the car waiting for her to have her meeting and come back—thought of her falling asleep on that bench and never waking up.

She shook her head to rid herself of this vision. "So, yes, I've met some of the people she has been talking to about the Indigenous Fair."

"Any chance that the victim was someone your daughter had met with? Or the sister or friend of someone she had met with? Even just someone in the background?"

"Well, I can't say no. Of course it is possible." Margie closed her eyes and tried to picture the victim's face and where she might have seen her. She just kept seeing children or youth groups. Had she been an activity coordinator? A public relations person? Where had Margie seen her?

"I'll have to keep thinking about it. I don't know where I saw her. If I saw her. Maybe she just looks similar to someone that I know. That does happen. Two people who look alike but have no connection."

"Of course. Well, if you identify her, please let me know. And if you find anything in Carburn Park that might relate somehow to the Alberta Warriors or a rival gang. I'll leave this with you." He indicated the expanding folder full of paper. "Don't say we didn't share with you in the spirit of openness and cooperation. ALERT can't function without sharing resources. And we aren't going to solve this murder—if it was murder—without sharing information. You know who to call. My contact information is in there. Or you can call ALERT and ask for me by name. If you want to confirm that I am actually who I say I am."

Margie couldn't imagine anyone who wasn't working for the agency would just walk into the homicide unit and sit down with her for a conversation. The Alberta Warriors didn't plant him there. That kind of thing happened on TV thrillers, not in real life.

CHAPTER EIGHT

When Lewis left, it was time for lunch and, even though Margie felt like she had just barely arrived, she had to get something to eat. She'd only had coffee for breakfast and hadn't stopped to eat when she had gone home to walk Stella. She should have, but she had wanted to get into the office as quickly as she could to get a good start on her paperwork.

The paperwork was not done, but she was famished.

"I'm going for Subway," she announced to Detective Jones. "You want anything?"

"Meatball sandwich?" Jones returned with a smile. "That would really be awesome. I don't want to stop what I'm working on, but if you're going out anyway…"

"Yeah, sure. Meatball sandwich." She already knew Jones's favorite toppings.

"Great. I'll e-transfer you."

"Anyone else?" Margie raised her voice so that the others could hear. "Subway run."

Cruz and Siever both placed their orders as well, and then Margie was on her way to pick everything up.

AFTER EATING and furiously typing all of the information she could to the shared workspace before she opened Lewis's folder and immersed herself in the information about the Alberta Warriors, Margie made one call to OCME to see if Kahn had been able to come up with anything that hadn't been posted yet. She knew it was a long shot and he would probably be irritated with her for calling before he had anything. But there was always a chance he had something already.

"Office of the Chief Medical Examiner, Dr. Kahn speaking," Kahn's soft, pleasant voice answered.

"Oh, hi, Doctor. This is Detective Patenaude. I know it is too early to know anything, but I wondered if…"

"If I knew anything?"

"Yes," Margie laughed at herself. "Exactly."

"Well, I have not yet had a chance to do much. I can confirm that there were not any apparent injuries. I did full body X-rays as well as gross examination, and we are not looking at blunt force trauma, stabbing, or shooting. There are no external signs of strangulation, though I may look a little further for that if circumstances dictate. However, I do have initial testing on the swabs and blood toxicity, and I would suggest that your girl died of a massive fentanyl overdose."

"Fentanyl."

"A synthetic opioid," Dr. Kahn provided.

"I know what it is. How could I be in law enforcement and not know? I think even elementary school kids know what fentanyl is. But she didn't look like a drug user."

"No. I agree. There are no signs on her body that she is a regular fentanyl user. There are no other injection sites, just the one."

"So… someone else injected her. We're looking at a homicide."

"I think we are looking at a homicide rather than an accident. But my examination and report are not anywhere near complete. I cannot rely on field tests for my final report. Samples have been sent to FCSU to test the blood and hair strand levels and give us a nice report with all the bells and whistles. But the field test strips reacted very quickly and definitively. I would guess that the concentrations are high."

"Which is another reason to suspect that she was given the injection rather than taking it herself."

"Yes. If you decided to experiment with IV fentanyl use, I would expect you to start with a very low dose. Its potency is well known. You know the risk of overdose. So unless you were actually trying to kill yourself..."

Margie thought about the woman's body sitting on the bench, looking out into the water. A peaceful, pleasant scene. Was it possible that something had happened in the woman's life and she *had* decided to commit suicide there? Away from her home so that she wouldn't be discovered by her family. In a familiar, pleasant setting where her last sights and thoughts could be about the beautiful yellow and orange leaves rather than whatever had driven her to the act?

"Do you think it was suicide?"

"I haven't made a finding yet, so I can't tell you my final determination. But... I suspect it was not suicide. I told you that the swabs were also positive. The swabs of her face," he reminded her. "I had thought there was something on her face around her mouth and nose. And the swabs of the skin were positive for fentanyl."

"How would she get fentanyl around her mouth and nose?"

"Because someone forced fentanyl powder into her mouth. She inhaled and ingested it."

"And *then* she was injected?"

"Yes," Kahn's voice was grave, and Margie could imagine his sage nod as he confirmed her understanding. "I would suggest she was accosted, forced to ingest fentanyl and, once she was overcome by the effects, was given another dose by intravenous administration, which resulted in cardiac arrest."

Margie could picture it in her mind—the violence of it. Someone coming up behind the woman as she was sitting on the bench, putting an arm across her neck and a hand full of fentanyl powder over her mouth, holding her until the fentanyl did its job and incapacitated her. Then, the attacker would only have had to open her coat and pull one arm out of the sleeve in order to inject her.

Then, whoever it was had taken the time to put her arm back through the sleeve, button up her coat, and leave her in a position where she looked like she had just been peacefully staring into the water. With the massive dose of fentanyl, she had probably been dead by the time he had finished adjusting the body.

Why? To make it look like she had died of natural causes? Did he think that they would miss the injection mark and not do an autopsy, but just write it off as a natural death? Was it to prevent people from discovering the death immediately, giving her killer time to stroll around the pond at a leisurely pace without being identified as a threat or suspicious person?

Or was it a warning? If Carburn Park or Calgary parks in general were known as the new stomping grounds for the Alberta Warriors, maybe she was a sign, a warning to others not to cross the gang.

If that were the case, then what had the victim done? How had she crossed the Warriors?

"That's about all I can tell you at the moment, Detective," Kahn advised.

"That's a lot more than I expected. We can start putting together a profile of what happened there and investigate it right away instead of waiting for weeks to get the tox reports back from FCSU and realizing that we should have talked to more people, pulled surveillance video, and all that. This will help to guide the investigation. It obviously was not just a natural death."

"That is correct," he agreed.

"This would have been... quite a violent attack. If other people were nearby, they must have seen what happened, wouldn't you think?"

"I would expect so. Fentanyl overdose is quick but not instantaneous. There would have been a struggle. It would have been difficult to disguise it as a friendly tussle or anything other than what it was. But given the state of rigor mortis, I would suggest that she was killed several hours before she was found at five o'clock. I don't imagine there are many people in the park at two o'clock in the morning."

"No." Margie frowned to herself. What had the woman been doing there in the wee hours of the morning? Like Betty, she would probably have needed a headlamp or flashlight to find her way around safely. It would be isolated. Spooky. She hadn't been attacked in the middle of the afternoon, sunning herself on the park bench while she watched the waterfowl.

"We'll have to see what surveillance video we can get from the park or doorbell cams from residences around the park. Maybe we'll be able to identify when she went to the park and who entered around the same time as she did. I can't believe that there were very many people accessing the park at that time of the day."

"Parks are officially closed from eleven until five. I imagine that if residents noticed unusual activity, they might have reported it to the police or 3-1-1."

Margie nodded and made a note. "I'll need to check that," she agreed.

CHAPTER NINE

*M*argie had already gone home and was working on making supper with Christina when the call came in. The caller ID on her phone was Unknown, which she knew could mean that it was someone else in the department. So she tended to answer the phone even when she wasn't sure who was calling.

"Patenaude."

"Detective Patenaude?"

"Yes, how can I help you?"

"Officer of the Day, ma'am. We've just taken a Missing Person that matches the description of your park victim."

Margie looked at the time. Six o'clock. It was, at least, less than twenty-four hours since the discovery of the body. Longer than she had expected, considering the well-cared-for appearance of the woman, but not long enough to be concerning. The victim obviously had people in her life who cared about her and had quickly noticed that she was not where she was supposed to be.

"Great. Can I get the name and the details of the person who filed the report?"

"Missing is Laura Clothier. Husband Alexander filed the report in the last hour." She gave him the phone number and address of the husband.

"Missing Person detective who has been assigned to the case is Amelia Banks. Will you be calling her?"

"Yes, I'll need to coordinate with her. Has she been in contact with the husband already?"

"Just to follow up on the missing person report, let him know she's been assigned."

"Is there a picture of the missing woman?"

"I'll send it to this number?"

"Yes, just text it here. Then I can make sure we're both talking about the same person before we give the husband a heart attack, telling him that his wife is dead."

When she finished the phone call, Margie put her phone down and waited for the picture to be sent.

Something was bothering her.

The name kept echoing in her brain and she was sure she had heard it before. Just like she had been sure she had seen the woman's face before.

She tried to put them together. But her brain just wouldn't cooperate.

Her phone vibrated and the message notification flashed across the screen. Margie tapped the message to bring the picture up.

The picture that Alexander Williams had provided of his wife was much more recognizable than the dead woman's face. It was always more challenging to identify a dead person. The relaxation of the muscles, change in skin tone, and other factors all contributed, Margie knew, to giving anyone who knew the victim a sense of *jamais vu*, the feeling her face was foreign and unfamiliar. Sometimes, loved ones had to rely on birthmarks, tattoos, gaps in the teeth, and other such details to identify a loved one because they seemed so unfamiliar in death. Even a skilled funeral home cosmetologist could not always achieve the level of reality needed for loved ones to recognize the deceased.

But the picture of Laura Clothier in living color was a different story. Her eyes were bright, she had a big smile, and her hair was pulled back in a braid. Margie had not seen her since they were children, but she knew those eyes, that face.

She sat down on one of the kitchen chairs with a thump, misjudging the height of the seat. She stared at the picture of Laura, the name and the face finally connecting.

Laura.

"Mom? Are you okay?"

"I just…" Tears sprang to Margie's eyes and ran down her cheeks. She was too shocked to be able to stop them.

"Mom?" Christina hurried over to her, bent down, put an arm around her shoulder, and looked at the picture on Margie's phone. "What is it? What happened?"

"This is… Laura."

Christina nodded. She rubbed Margie's back in slow circles. "Who is she? A friend of yours?"

Margie swallowed. "A cousin. Yes. We used to get together when I was in Calgary. A long time ago." She wiped at the tears that were tracking down her cheek. "I didn't know her. I didn't recognize her. I thought she looked familiar, but it wasn't until I saw this picture that…"

"You didn't know her where? Did you run into her?"

"She was killed. She was the victim I was called about this morning."

"Oh no!" Christina's voice was sharp with the shock of it. "Oh, no, Mom! I'm so sorry."

Margie grasped her hand. "I know. It's okay. I will be okay. It's not me, it's her husband…"

"She was married?"

"I think she has a child, a little boy. Younger than you." She touched Christina's cheek, trying to dredge up all the details. "Six or seven, I think. Oh, that poor boy."

She tried to stop her eyes from leaking, but the tears continued to come. Christina sat beside her, dragging her chair as close as she could to put her arm around Margie. Worried by all of the sniffling, Stella came over to comfort Margie, putting her head in Margie's lap and licking her hands or face whenever they got close enough to reach.

Margie only allowed herself a few minutes, then cleared her throat and stood up.

"I'll need to go over there to give him the death notification. I won't leave them wondering all night what has happened to her."

"Can't someone else do that?"

"No, I want to do it. He should have a friendly face. Someone who knew her."

"Can I come with you? I don't want you to go by yourself."

"No, you really can't, sweetie. It wouldn't be appropriate for me to bring my daughter."

"But they are family."

"Maybe I could take you back another time, when I am not on duty, and we can talk to them as family. Comfort them. But I need to do this officially first."

Margie was still crying. But it was time to get ahold of herself. She blew her nose and walked around the house a bit, trying to get her emotions back under control. She couldn't cry at a death notification. She had a cold glass of water, which helped. She held the cold glass to her hot forehead and looked at the contents of the fridge. They still needed to eat, but she didn't have the time to make something. She needed to eat quickly and get over to Alexander Clothier's house.

CHAPTER TEN

*M*argie focused on following her GPS instructions back to Riverbend to find the Clothier home. With something to do, it was easier to stay in control. But she still wasn't sure how she would manage when it came to breaking the news to Alexander. Would it be easier for him if the news came from a family member, or would it make it harder? Sometimes, the next of kin felt the need to attack the person who delivered the news. To shout at and abuse her because they didn't want to believe it. Because it was such a terrible injustice.

She had given the Missing Persons detective, Amelia Banks, a bare outline of the circumstances of Laura Clothier's death in the park and the fact that she had known Laura years ago and wanted to be the one to break the news to Alexander. But Banks had still wanted to come along. Even though the missing person file would only be open for no more than a couple of hours, she wanted to do her part.

A car pulled in across the street from the Clothier home, and Margie waited for a moment before getting out to see if it was the Missing Persons detective. The woman who got out of that car and looked around was clearly not a resident, but was there to visit or meet someone. To meet Margie and pay a visit to Alexander.

They met in the street to nod to each other briefly, avoiding shaking hands.

"Are you sure you want to do this?" Banks inquired, giving her an out if she wanted to take it. "You don't have to be the one. I can tell them that we have tentatively identified the victim in the park as his wife and then get confirmation with DNA or dental."

"No. He should know that it is more definitive than that. I know her. I recognize her. I know her face and her name. We'll still do a positive ID based on science, but he should be allowed to put his doubts to rest. Hope is not a solace in this situation."

She thought of the little boy. His life was also about to change forever.

They walked toward the house with its porch light on and living room still brightly lit. The door opened as they walked up to the house. Of course Alexander was watching the door. Waiting for his wife to return home. Unaware of the news he was about to get.

"Mr. Clothier?" Banks inquired, holding out her hand.

"No, no. Clothier is my wife's name. I'm Alexander Williams. She kept her name." His eyes drifted to Margie's face. "She was very proud of her heritage."

Margie nodded. She felt bad that they were wearing masks. She wanted him to see her face. To know how she felt when she told him the news. She didn't want to be a faceless monster.

"Oh, I'm sorry. I'm Detective Amelia Banks. This is Detective Patenaude. We're here to follow up on your missing person report. Can we come in?"

He stepped back, opening the door wider and motioning them in. Relieved, Margie thought. He was relieved that they were there, taking his report seriously. That maybe it meant they would be able to find his wife and bring her home to him.

"Let's sit down," Banks suggested gently. The living room was spotless. Margie wondered whether it always looked that way or whether Alexander had cleaned it while he waited for someone to show up, needing something to do to keep himself busy.

It was a nice little bungalow, a single-family home, probably three or four bedrooms. Just the right size for a family to grow into. But that would never happen for Laura now.

"Did you have questions?" Alexander asked. "I have more pictures. The woman at the police station said that they only needed one, but I have more. It was hard to pick out just one that you would be able to

155

recognize her from. I don't know what else to tell you about where to look... I guess you can call the hospitals. They keep telling me they can't give me any information for privacy reasons. Especially if there is anyone who hasn't been identified. How do they expect to be able to identify anyone if they won't tell you details?" He shook his head.

"No, we don't need any other information, Mr. Williams." Banks looked at Margie, inviting her to give the notification now that they were all sitting down.

Margie nodded and cleared her throat.

"Mr. Williams... I'm sorry to tell you that your wife's body was found in Carburn Park early this morning. She had been attacked. She did not survive the assault."

She waited as Alexander tried to process these unexpected words. It was a shock, though he had surely been wondering what could have happened to her. Why hadn't she come home? Why wouldn't she answer the phone? How could she just disappear and not tell anyone where she had gone? He had surely already decided in his own mind that she had either been killed or kidnapped, because what else would have kept her away from her family?

Even if he had been expecting to hear at some point that she had been injured or killed, that didn't make it easy to hear. It didn't make it any easier to reconcile himself to the truth that he was now alone. No longer coupled. Left to raise their child on his own.

"How can that be?" he asked, bewildered.

"We're still trying to sort it all out," Margie said. "I understand that it's difficult to understand. I am a homicide detective, and I will be working on your wife's case. Doing everything I can to bring the people responsible for this to justice."

"People?"

Margie nodded. "We don't yet know who or why. I hope you'll be patient while we investigate. These things often seem like they are taking an inordinate length of time. Even when you know who the killer is in a case, it can still take years to bring them to justice."

"Years? Do you know who did this? I don't understand. How could she be dead? Attacked in the park? Who would do that?"

"We are looking into it. We already have leads we are following up. This is going to be a very difficult time for you. I want you to know that you can call me anytime." Margie already had out her business card and handed it to him. "And... I'm very sorry, Mr. Williams. I want you to know... I knew your wife a long time ago."

His eyes widened. "You knew Laura?" He sat up straighter, looking down at the card, holding it at arm's length like he was farsighted. "Patenaude." His eyes flicked to her face. "Can you take your mask off? I don't think we need them on here. There's plenty of air circulation."

Margie and Banks took their masks off. Margie saw Banks's face for the first time. Firm lips. Soft eyes. Worry lines on her forehead and around her mouth. She looked older than Margie. Most detectives were older than she was.

Alexander barely gave Banks a glance. He studied Margie's face, cataloging her skin tone and features. Margie swallowed.

"Laura was my cousin," Margie explained. "I used to see her when I came here from Winnipeg over the summer. We played together as little children. Explored the city as teens." She licked her dry lips. "We kind of fell out of touch when I stopped coming to Calgary. I had my daughter and needed to get my life in order. I wish I had gotten back in contact with her when we moved to Calgary, but it was in the middle of the lockdown and I didn't do anything more than let people know that I was moving here."

His expression brightened a little, as if this were familiar. "Yes. Yes, I remember her saying that one of her cousins was moving to Calgary and that maybe when all of this stuff was over..." He made a gesture indicating the mask Margie held in her hand. "When this all settled down, maybe she would be able to get together with her. You."

"I'm sorry that didn't happen. I wish we hadn't put it off."

He nodded slowly. "She would have enjoyed it, I'm sure. She always spoke fondly of her cousins."

Margie nodded. She didn't know what else to say, and just sat there in the growing silence, trying to think of what a person was supposed to talk about when she found out that her estranged cousin had been murdered. All of the things that she usually said to the victim's family seemed to fall short.

"She would be happy you're running the investigation," Alexander suggested.

"I don't know. Would she? Maybe she would rather that it was someone else, outside the family. Someone unbiased, with no emotional involvement."

"No. She'd be glad it was you. She was proud of her cousin, the police detective."

"Really?"

He nodded seriously. He looked around, his hands moving restlessly like he needed to pick things up and tidy his surroundings, to occupy himself with something that was needful. But there was nothing left to tidy. He made an effort to fold his hands quietly in his lap. He took a deep breath and let it out. He didn't cry. That would come later. He was too much in the "disbelief" stage now.

"So, tell me what you know and what you need to know from me," he said practically. If he couldn't clean, maybe he could help with the investigation.

CHAPTER ELEVEN

I can't tell you very much yet," Margie said. "Let's start with a few questions. What was it that Laura did? I thought I remembered from social media that she was a social worker?"

Alexander nodded. "That was her training. What she was doing most recently was supervising at a halfway house. She liked to be home with Quinn when he wasn't at school, so she worked nights at the halfway house, just making sure that everyone was where they were supposed to be and someone was there if there was a problem."

Margie nodded. She was aware of nurses, police officers, and others who preferred to take the night shift so that they were available for their kids during the day. Getting enough sleep was a perpetual problem, but that was probably true of most parents.

"What was her shift? How did your schedule work?"

"She took the morning shift. Three until ten. I work nine to five. So I was here in the morning when Quinn would wake up, and I would get him off to school. Then Laura was available if there were any problems with school and was home when he got off. She slept while he was at school, unless something came up. We would have supper and the evening together. She would be able to put Quinn to bed and watch a movie with me. I would go to bed, and she would have a couple of hours to herself before going to work again."

He shook his head and rubbed the center of his forehead tenderly.

"It's a very strange schedule, I know, but it worked for us. She was able to sleep during the day. One of us was always here for Quinn. If he woke up with the flu, I would call in to the office and let them know I would be late, and she would leave early if there were enough people to cover at the halfway house. The only time we overlapped was a couple of hours in the morning."

"That sounds really creative. Laura was an outside-the-box thinker."

Alexander nodded. "It seemed like it worked so much better for us than both working during the day and having to find after-school care."

"So were you aware of Laura going to Carburn Park between when you went to bed and her going to work? Was that a regular thing?"

"She sometimes went over there… I wouldn't say I liked it. I knew it was closed and she could get in trouble for being there. And it was so isolated. She said that was what she liked about it. She could be there all by herself, like it was her own little sanctuary." He sniffled and wiped his nose. "I said that we had a perfectly good garden and fishpond in the backyard, and she could sit there, and I would be much happier about her safety."

They all chuckled a bit about it, even knowing it had ended tragically. What if Laura had listened to her husband and just sat in the backyard when she wanted some time to think and meditate in nature?

But Margie knew that wouldn't be the same. For Laura, as with Margie, being in nature meant more than sitting in the backyard. Even the parks were a compromise. Finding something in the city that would do. They both remembered what it was really like in the wilds. When Kokum and Moushoom or someone else in the family would gather all of the kids together and take them out onto Crown Land or the reservation. Where things were really wild and untouched. They could learn how to watch and listen for the animals, follow a trail, and learn about the different plants and trees and their medicinal properties.

Margie had lost so much of that knowledge in the years since Christina was born. She was just returning to her roots now, getting Moushoom to teach her some of the things that she should know. And teaching them to Christina, so that she wasn't a complete city girl, but knew a bit about how to live with nature.

And as far as following a trail and learning how to orient herself in the wilderness… Margie had been hopeless at that part. She had absolutely no sense of direction, something that had sent Laura into peals of laughter time after time. Margie getting lost on family outings in Calgary was a regular occurrence. She knew her surroundings a bit better in Winnipeg, but they had never spent much time in the wilderness in Manitoba. In the city, she knew her streets and could find her way home or ask for directions. There were only a few wild places they ever went to, and Margie learned them the best she could and stuck like glue to her mother or one of her aunties if there were any chance of her getting lost out there.

"So as I said, that's where she was when it happened," Margie said apologetically. "In one of her favorite places. Being one with Mother Earth."

"It was just random?" Alexander asked. "She never even ran into anyone out there. It was just… the deer and the night birds, the splash of the beavers in the water. Sometimes, she told me what she saw there but, usually, there wasn't anything exciting to announce. It was just… a good place to get centered before going to work."

"She would want to have that before going to a halfway house. What was it like? What kind of offenders was she dealing with?"

"It was a juvenile halfway house. So she wasn't dealing with hardened adult offenders. Kids who had served their time and needed something to help integrate back into society. She called them her kids. She was really close to them. A lot of young offenders are Indigenous. Forty to fifty percent of them. I guess I don't have to tell you that."

Margie's chest tightened as she nodded. It was one of the reasons that it had been so important to get Christina out of Winnipeg, where violent crime was the highest of anywhere in Canada, with the majority of the victims and the offenders being Indigenous. Calgary was better, but still bad. As much as she wanted Christina to be part of the Indigenous community in Calgary, she was actually happy that she didn't have many Indigenous friends, and those she did have did not seem to be in gangs or any trouble.

But that didn't stop an obviously Indian teen from being picked up just for walking down the street, with charges that started with loitering, increased to resisting arrest when she protested, and escalated to assault if she tried to defend herself. In a few minutes, a dark-skinned, black-haired, obviously Indigenous girl like Christina could go from being a model citizen to a violent offender.

"Had she ever run into any trouble at the halfway house? Threats? Violence from any of the participants?"

"Some of that is bound to go on," Alexander admitted. "I was always worried about it. But Laura said I didn't have anything to worry about. They were good kids; they just needed help getting settled in and integrated back into society."

"What were their stats like? Reintegration and recidivism? Did the kids get out and stay out, or…?"

"You would have to look it up or ask them. I don't actually know. They had successes. But I know that a lot of kids went back into the system, either while they were at the house or shortly after."

Margie and Banks both nodded. The odds were not great that someone who had been incarcerated for a few years, especially at a young age, would stay out of the system for that long. Once the damage was done, it was hard to get them back on a productive path, and to help them to stay there.

"How did…" Alexander started. "I mean… how did it happen? Did they…? I mean… out there in the dark where it was so isolated? I suppose that they were just after one thing."

Margie held up her hand, shaking her head. "No," she assured him. "No sign of sexual assault. It was a very strange case and we are doing our best to unwind it so that we can figure out what prompted the attack, if anything. It was actually a drug overdose." She saw Alexander open his mouth to protest, the anger tightening in his face. "We know she wasn't an addict. We know she wasn't using. It was a forced overdose. And we don't know why."

He sat there just looking at her. Margie tried to read his face. His dark eyes and skin glistened in the lamplight.

"I'll do my best to find out why, as well as who. But sometimes, it is just random violence."

Alexander nodded mutely. Banks made movements like it was time to go, but Margie was not ready.

"What would Laura have had with her?"

"With her?"

"What possessions? I assume she carried a purse, wallet, cell phone…"

"Yes. Of course. Keys. A little breakfast to eat while she was there. She could have eaten breakfast with the residents, but she said that they had so little funding, she didn't want to take food out of the mouths of her kids. Sometimes, she took food *to* them. She'd make a big batch of cinnamon buns or peanut butter cookies and spoil them. She said that someone needed to show them some love."

Margie smiled at her cousin's generosity. She had seen some social workers and group home or halfway house supervisors who were very hard. Bitter and disillusioned. When they found out that the system didn't work the way that it was supposed to and that kids kept getting hurt and offenders kept reoffending, the compassion fizzled out and they built up walls to protect themselves. Laura was the other kind. The kind who just kept doing more and never stopped caring.

"Do you track her phone?"

Alexander blinked at her. "No."

"Do you have friend locations or 'find my phone,' or any of these other apps that would tell you where her phone is now? Or earlier in the day?"

"I don't know." Alexander pulled out his phone and looked at it. "I'm pretty useless at these things."

"Can I see?"

He unlocked it and passed it over to her. Margie wasn't a big techie either. She got Christina to show her how to do things on her phone, or played with the settings until something either started working or broke. But she knew enough to start searching for apps that shared locations and might show the location of Laura's phone. In all likelihood, it was at the bottom of the pond and would never work again. It wouldn't lead them directly to the killer's lair. But sometimes criminals were stupid. Killers were *frequently* stupid. A stolen iPad or phone had led the police to a thief or killer more than once in the past.

CHAPTER TWELVE

Scrolling through screens, Margie managed to find Alexander's *Find My* app, which, if they were lucky, would be set up to find the other devices in the household, including Laura's phone. Since Alexander was not familiar with the app, it was just as likely that she would not be able to find anything with it, that it would think it was alone in the world. But she still held out a little hope. Devices were smarter and smarter and, if she were lucky, the phone would know what other devices were regularly logged in to its home network and would have been granted permission from Laura's phone to track its location in case it was lost or stolen.

She waited while the splash screen appeared and things whirred in the background. A map appeared on the screen, and *Finding your devices* was superimposed over it as a status report. Then, several triangles appeared on the map.

Laura's Phone

Margie tapped on the icon. It wasn't far away, and she was afraid that the last known location would be the home's WIFI network. It wouldn't help her much if the last time Laura's phone had made contact with her cloud account had been when she was at home. She might not have background location tracking turned on.

Margie knew that location tracking could be turned on and off easily enough. Christina had granted Margie location tracking on her phone but, sometimes, when Margie tried to see where Christina was when she was late coming home or just wanted to make sure she had gotten to school safely, her phone was unreachable. She never knew whether it was a network issue or if Christina had intentionally blocked the transmission of her location so that she could sneak off somewhere.

Kids did that. It was completely normal for kids to want their privacy and not be tracked constantly. They needed to explore and test their boundaries in order to grow more independent and self-sufficient.

That didn't mean she had to like it.

Margie zoomed in. The last location of the phone had been that morning just after three o'clock. Which was after the time that Laura would have gone to the park. Her work at the halfway house started at three, so she would have gone to the park an hour or more before that.

And she had not left the park until OCME had transported her body later that morning.

She waited for the background map to resolve. It looked like a residential street between the park and the house. Maybe thrown into a garbage can or some bushes. Margie tapped the triangle to obtain a GPS reading and then dialed Siever's number on her own phone.

"Detective Siever," he answered, sounding vague and far away.

"Patenaude," Margie said briskly. "I need you to look up some map coordinates for me."

"What? Okay." Siever returned to the real world, coming to attention. He was a techie at heart. Anything involving computers or devices was his wheelhouse and would be far more interesting to him than touchy-feely human nature or relationship stuff.

Margie read the coordinates to him. She could hear Siever tapping the numbers into his computer as she read them out.

"Okay," he said, confirming that he'd gotten the location. He read the address it was closest to. "What do you want me to do?"

"That is the last known location of Laura Clothier's phone. We need to get someone over there to look for it. Looks to me like it was probably dumped there. It isn't showing up as inside the house—probably the yard or a garbage can. And you never know when a garbage can is going to be emptied. It will be easier to find it while it is still on the street than in the municipal dump."

"Who is Laura Clothier?"

"Oh—the identity of our Carburn Park victim. Sorry. She was just identified in the last hour."

"Laura Clothier," Siever repeated, trying to embed it in his memory. He agreed. "Sure, I'll call it in. Maybe… I'll head over there and see if I can find anything myself. It's dark, so getting a team out there isn't going to happen until the sun is up tomorrow."

Margie looked at the window, remembering that it was after supper. It was nighttime. She must have reached Siever at home.

"Oh, sheesh. I lost track of the time," she told him apologetically. "I was thinking I was getting you at the office. You don't need to do this tonight. Yes, in the morning, once the sun is out, will have to do. Garbage pickup isn't likely to be before that."

Even though the garbage trucks frequently reached Margie's house before dawn. She pushed that thought aside. She needed to be reasonable. Some things just were not going to happen on her timetable.

"It's okay," Siever said. "I wasn't doing anything that can't be put aside. I'll go over there. I probably won't find anything, but it's worth checking out. If I don't find anything, I'll get a team looking in the morning. If I do, then we can have the tech guys working on it as soon as they open in the morning."

It probably pained him that he couldn't be the one to force the phone to give up its secrets. But the detectives were supposed to leave that for the techies to do in a way that no evidence was destroyed. That involved things like dumping the internal memory of the phone onto a computer and manipulating it there, rather than directly on the phone, so that no data could be accidentally overwritten. Siever could check if there were any messages on the lock screen of the phone, as long as he didn't touch them. And maybe he could discern something from the state of Laura's purse and its contents, if the purse and the phone were still together.

"I really appreciate that," she told Siever sincerely. He was going out of his way to help with the case. While they all worked long hours in the beginning of a case, checking out clues as quickly as possible, he wasn't obligated to drop his evening plans to look for a phone in the dark, when chances were he would find nothing.

"No problem. Where are you?"

"With the family. Just grabbed the location from her husband's phone. Last contact with Laura's phone was at three this morning."

He grunted. "Might still be there. I'll see if I can find anything."

"Thank you."

She disconnected the call. Putting down Alexander's phone, she took a couple of pictures with her own phone to document the information, then handed it back to him.

"Thanks. We'll probably subpoena that information from the cloud service as well, but these things take time, and it is good to act on it as quickly as possible. I appreciate that."

Alexander nodded. His eyes were misty. He was far away, probably thinking about his wife and how his life was going to be totally different from that point in time forward.

"I wonder if I could also take a look around here," Margie said gently. "See if there is anything to indicate trouble in Laura's life. The possibility that she was aware of a crime, or a threat had been made, or anything like that."

Frown lines appeared between Alexander's eyebrows.

"Yes... of course." He shook his head as if trying to clear the mental fog. "Do you mean... that it was targeted? That this wasn't just some random mugging?"

Margie nodded. "Someone forcibly administered a drug overdose," she reminded him. "That isn't a mugging. We think it was related to a gang."

"A gang?" He shook his head. "We don't have gangs around here. In this neighborhood. This is a good neighborhood."

"I'm sure it is. And that there isn't a lot of violence to worry about. But there are gangs in Calgary, and ALERT has been aware of gang activity in some other Calgary parks, so we need to take that into account in our investigation. And since there isn't reason for a gang to target a woman sitting on a park bench randomly, we have to investigate the possible reasons for the attack."

Alexander stared off into space, and Margie thought she had lost him. It wasn't the right time to explain their theories. He couldn't take it in right now.

"You can look around," he said slowly. "Whatever you want, of course. But the house was already searched."

Margie's heart pounded. She looked at Banks, startled and wanting to make sure she had heard correctly. Banks looked just as surprised as Margie felt.

"What do you mean it was already searched?"

"Quinn called me at work when he got home because he couldn't get into the house. I called Laura and couldn't get an answer. I was really worried. But I thought she might still be asleep and just hadn't woken up when he rang the doorbell. Or maybe she had the flu. Quinn has a key, but Laura usually gets up and has the door unlocked for him and he doesn't have to use it. So he called me, crying that she didn't open the door. I got him to let himself in with his key… and she wasn't here. I was home in… fifteen minutes, maybe." He gave her an embarrassed look. "I might have broken a couple of speed limits on the way. When I got home, I looked around and couldn't figure out what Quinn had been looking for." He made a gesture to indicate the house around them. "Drawers were open. Some papers scattered around. It wasn't like on TV when someone's house gets tossed and there are ripped sheets and upholstery slashed and everything overturned. Not like that. But someone had been looking for something…"

"And you thought it was Quinn."

"Yes… but he said he wasn't. He said it must have been Laura. That she had been looking for something, and then she'd had to leave. And she forgot that he was coming home from school." Alexander shrugged and shook his head. "We were both very upset. I was trying to keep him calm and not let him see how concerned I was about her being gone. He felt abandoned because she wasn't there to let him in and take care of him, so he was trying to make up a scenario that explained it."

"And did you think that he was the one who had left everything open? Or that it was Laura?"

"I don't know." Alexander blinked a few times as if trying to remember something that had happened a long time ago. "Nothing made sense to me. So I was just trying to… make everything normal. I closed the drawers while I made Quinn an after-school snack, like Laura would have done. I didn't go through anything or try to figure it out. I was…"

"You were in shock. You were afraid that something terrible had happened. You didn't want it to be true. So you just continued as if it was normal."

"Yes... something like that. I picked up any papers or anything that had been disturbed, and I took the dishes out of the dishwasher and started to think about supper. I called Laura a few times, but couldn't get her. I didn't want Quinn to see how worried I was, so I didn't call her too many times in front of him and I didn't call the police to report her missing until after supper when he was off playing on his computer. I know you're supposed to wait twenty-four hours, but..."

"No, you don't need to wait twenty-four hours. You knew her schedule and that she wasn't where she was supposed to be. That something was wrong or she would have been here for Quinn. You did the right thing."

"Do you think so?" he asked, sounding pitiful.

"I wouldn't have been able to identify her if you hadn't."

He looked surprised. "She's your cousin."

"I know, but I haven't seen her since we were kids, and it's harder when..." she trailed off and shrugged. She didn't want to explain to him how corpses looked different from live people. He didn't need to think about that. "You did the right thing," she repeated. "It would have delayed our investigation if you had waited. Now I have a line on the possible location of her phone and purse. I can take a quick look around here for anything that might give us a clue of if she had been getting threats or hiding something. And I can follow up with the halfway house to see if there is any possibility that this is related to her work."

"I don't see how it could be anything other than... just bad luck."

"Don't worry about that. That part is my job. You have enough to worry about. You let me sort out what happened."

He shrugged and looked away from her. Margie hated to think about the list of jobs that he had to do with his wife dead and a young son to raise on his own. At least it wasn't like it had been a hundred years ago, when a man left to raise children himself would more than likely have to parcel them off to neighbors or relatives. There were lots of single dads. There were ways for him to do it. His son was at school during the day and, if he needed to put in extra hours, maybe he could do so remotely after the boy was asleep.

She rose to her feet. "I'll just look around, if you don't mind. Do you want to walk through and tell me what drawers were open and what things you picked up and put away?"

"I don't know if I can remember everything. It was kind of a mess and I was panicking."

"Just tell me what you can remember. Any little thing might help. If you remember something else in the next few days, you can call me and tell me. There's no pressure for you to remember right now."

He nodded. Banks didn't know what else to do, so she tagged along with them, listening in and looking around. Maybe something would catch her eye and she could contribute to the investigation. Otherwise, her role in the case was over. The missing person had been found. Her case would just funnel into the homicide case.

CHAPTER THIRTEEN

*A*lexander pointed out various drawers that had been pulled out. All of the top drawers in the kitchen, the drawers in a writing desk, and the top drawer in a bureau of the bedroom. Nothing in Quinn's room or the guest room. Alexander couldn't remember for sure what papers had been on the floor, and Margie paged through all of the papers on the counter by the back door, which appeared to be where the family's mail was generally deposited, and the writing desk.

Alexander blinked and looked around, frowning. "Did Laura take her computer to work with her? She must have, but she didn't usually."

"Her laptop is missing?"

"Yes."

"What about yours?"

He considered for a moment. "No. I had mine at work. But also... the tablet. Unless Quinn has it."

"Do you want to see?" she prompted him.

Alexander was reluctant to do so, but eventually nodded. He knocked on Quinn's door and then opened it to peek in.

"Mom?" Margie heard Quinn inquire immediately, his high child's voice piercing. Then he saw that it was only his father. "Oh, Dad. Did Mom answer her phone yet?"

Margie could see him through the door. Older than she had remembered. She had put him at five or six, but a glance showed he was older. Eight or even ten. His mother's high cheekbones. Two slender braids. Dressed in a black band t-shirt and jeans.

"No, sorry, bud," Alexander told him. "They... we'll talk about it later. I was looking for the tablet. Do you have it?"

"No, I'm playing on my computer."

"Have you seen it? Who had it last?"

"I dunno."

Alexander stood there for a moment longer, but Quinn, apparently absorbed in his game, didn't make any suggestions. Alexander withdrew, shutting the door again.

"I don't know what to say to him," he told Margie. "I don't know when to tell him or what to say."

"If you want, I can do it."

Alexander shook his head immediately. "Oh, no. That wouldn't be good at all. Laura would never agree to that. It's my responsibility. It would be terrible coming from a stranger."

"Then... maybe after we're gone, ask him to come have a bowl of ice cream with you when he's done his game. Then... just tell him gently, but clearly. Don't use phrases that could be construed more than one way. Don't say 'she's gone' or 'they found her body.' Say 'she's dead' so that he doesn't wonder what it really means or hope that she'll come back."

Alexander put both hands over his face, covering up a grimace of grief. He stood there for a minute like that, and Margie waited for the tears and sobs, for the breakdown. But he eventually lowered his hands again, face composed.

"Thank you. That helps."

Margie didn't find anything unusual in Laura's writing desk or bedroom. The mail waiting to be dealt with consisted of household bills, subscriptions, and routine stuff everyone had. A notice from the CRA that no one wanted to open.

Alexander couldn't identify anything else that was missing or anything else that had been out of place when he got home. She hoped he would get through the night okay.

"Is there anyone you can call to stay with you? So the house doesn't feel so empty? In case you want to talk about it?"

Alexander shook his head. "I don't have any family here—only

Laura's. And as far as friends, they're all work colleagues. I'm going to have to call them tomorrow and tell them. I'd rather be on my own tonight."

"You have my card. If you need to talk…"

He nodded. "Thanks."

"I'm family. You can call me anytime, even at two in the morning. I take middle-of-the-night calls."

"Okay. I'll have Quinn tonight. He'll probably want to sleep in our bed anyway."

Margie said a reluctant goodbye, and she and Banks walked out together.

❧

SHE WAS in her car when Siever called back.

"I found it," he announced proudly.

"You found the phone? That's fantastic! Good job, Detective."

She wished she could see Siever's face, since he didn't say anything to acknowledge this. She hoped that he didn't think she was being patronizing, because that hadn't been her intention. She was delighted that he had managed to find the evidence..

"Tell me all about it. Was it in a garbage can?"

"Yeah, a bin for collection out on the street, so I assume the truck will be around in the morning. Good thing we acted on your instinct and followed up on it tonight."

"Wow. Good. And was it just the phone, or the purse too?"

"Purse too. I've commandeered the bin and I'm having it picked up. I'd take it in myself, but I've just got a little car."

Margie remembered a recent trip in her car with a shopping cart hanging out of the trunk and understood his problem. They should all drive pick-ups. Little compact cars were great on gas, but not so great for moving larger items.

"The techs should be the ones collecting it anyway. You don't want to obscure any fingerprint evidence. There might be fingerprints on the inside of the handholds."

"I wore gloves. Can't promise I didn't smear anything, but I did my best. I pulled the phone out, but I left everything else in place. Looks like

173

the contents of the purse were dumped, and I didn't want to lose any trace evidence on the little bits."

"Wallet?"

"It's in there."

"So they didn't want the wallet or the phone."

"I didn't open the wallet. Don't know if they took her cash and credit cards. That's all they usually want. Not the wallet itself or any of your reward cards or ID."

"No, you're right. I guess we'll hear tomorrow what all is in there. Anything unusual on the lock screen of the phone?"

"Just dozens of calls and texts from the husband. Appointments that hadn't been cleared. A few other calls, but I don't know what they are. After they are processed, we might have some people to interview."

"Great. I'll check in at her work tomorrow. And someone has been through the house."

"Oh?" Siever sounded surprised or interested, or maybe both.

"The husband had already straightened up, but the top drawers of the kitchen and bureau and the writing desk had been opened. And a laptop and iPad are missing."

"They were looking for electronics," Siever deduced immediately. "Maybe a thumb drive."

"I was thinking that too."

"Hmm. So she was killed because of something she knew? Something she had written down or saved somewhere."

"Certainly looks that way."

"Why did they ditch the phone, then?" Siever mused.

"Whatever they were looking for wasn't on it."

"How did they know?"

He sucked on his teeth. "Must have unlocked it."

"How?"

"Fingerprint or face scan."

Margie grimaced, thinking of the attacker pressing Laura's thumb to the phone screen before or shortly after she died. From what Margie understood from the medical examiner, it was easier to get a fingerprint scan on a conductive screen from a live body than a dead one. She supposed whoever had killed her knew that, too. The fingerprint scan had probably been done after he had incapacitated her, before he killed her with the injection.

This case was going to give her nightmares for sure. She tried not to think about Laura and how close they had once been. How could anyone kill such a bright spirit? Laura was one of those people who was always more concerned about other people than herself, who reached out the first time she thought someone might need a boost, and who never tried to raise herself up over anyone else.

Why did it have to be Laura?

She cleared her throat and tried to speak without giving her emotion away to Siever. Though he was one of those people who didn't always get nuance.

"I need to hang up now to drive. Thanks so much for finding the phone and purse. I hope you don't have to wait too long for the bin to be picked up."

Margie knew she should probably drive the few blocks to meet him and wait with him, but she needed to get back to Christina.

"That's okay. My car is warm and my phone is charged. I can sit here comfortably for a couple of hours."

"I owe you one."

He disconnected without any further comment. Margie nodded to herself. That was just like him. She wiped her eyes, pretending to herself that the burning was just fatigue. It had been a long day that had started very early. Fifteen minutes to drive home, and then she could head to bed if she wanted to. If she thought she would be able to sleep.

But she might just as easily be spending the night in front of the TV, waiting for the fatigue to do its job.

CHAPTER FOURTEEN

*M*argie had consumed a couple of cups of strong coffee before heading to Second Step, the halfway house where Laura had worked. She knew that the coffee did all kinds of bad things to her digestion, but it was her preferred delivery vehicle for caffeine. Wake-up tablets were not nearly as tasty. Hopefully, after putting in a full day's work, her brain and her body would decide that they'd had enough and she could go to sleep.

She certainly wasn't the first homicide detective to pull an all-nighter. Though she wished she had been more productive the previous sleepless night. There hadn't been much to do other than worry about the case and process whatever memories she could of Laura.

None of which was particularly helpful. Whatever they had done together as children when Margie came to Calgary on summer vacations had nothing to do with whoever who had ended Laura's life.

They had not been involved in anything remotely related to gangs, not the Alberta Warriors or any other street gang or an unofficial group of similarly aged children. They hadn't been born into families that were already part of the gangs. They hadn't hung out with gang kids or been recruited by older kids to participate in any activities.

Maybe that was why Laura had ended up where she had, a social worker helping kids leaving juvie to find their place in the community.

She had been able to stay out of the gangs, so she had what it took to help other kids back into a normal life.

She had always had a strong affinity for good and had always been a rule follower. Not someone that Margie's mother had ever worried would lead her astray. Margie's summers in Calgary had influenced her life positively, not negatively. They hadn't kept her from making any wrong choices, but it had helped. Maybe that was why Margie had brought Christina to Calgary.

She rang the doorbell at Second Step, and she and Lewis stood there waiting for someone to answer. It wasn't unexpected that it took a lot of yelling back and forth between residents before someone was eventually harassed into answering the door. In a place like that, it was always someone else's job to answer the door, and everybody was too busy.

The door opened three inches and a slim, Indigenous young man stood on the inside looking out at Margie, ready to shut the door again if it were someone trying to sell a natural gas plan.

"Detectives Patenaude and Riley. Here to see Angie Craig," Margie advised.

The boy looked back over his shoulder. "Missus Craig?"

Margie couldn't make out whether there was an answering shout.

"Somebody here," he shouted. "Couple cops."

If they expected an uproar over the fact that there were cops at the door—displays of fear, panic, or guilt—they were disappointed. No one seemed to care. Eventually, the boy stepped back, pulling the door open the rest of the way.

"I guess you may as well come in," he conceded.

Margie and Lewis entered the house.

It was about what Margie had expected. Carpet worn almost through to the floorboards. The stale smell of cigarette smoke, even though she was sure the house probably had rules about not smoking in the house. Combined with old cooking smells, onions and chili. Lots of people on the move, talking to each other, negotiating with the supervisors, doing chores. Furniture nearly as worn as the carpets.

"Could you get Mrs. Craig or direct us to her office?"

"Uh… yeah, sure. She's just back there," he pointed toward the back right corner of the house.

He drifted away from them.

"Thank you," Margie called after him.

Lewis chuckled. They found their way to the bedroom the boy had pointed to, finding that it had been transformed into several office cubicles, all of them too small for a meeting.

"We're looking for Mrs. Craig?"

A woman with masses of gray hair working at a computer looked at them.

"Oh, are you the detectives? I'm sorry, I didn't know you were here. I hope you haven't been waiting long."

"Is there somewhere we can talk?" Margie suggested.

"Well…" Angie Craig looked around. "Not really anywhere private. Maybe… we should go for a walk."

So, back outside they went. Margie had left her hat and gloves in the car, expecting to be inside the warm house. She burrowed her hands down into her pockets and hoped they would keep up a brisk enough pace to keep warm.

"I was… I was so sorry to hear about Laura," Mrs. Craig said. "I don't know what to think. What a horrible thing to happen. Crazy."

"She was supposed to be here at three?"

"Yes, that's right. When Laura didn't get here, we left a few messages on her phone. Couldn't get through to her. I thought maybe her phone service was out. Probably home with a sick kid and…" Mrs. Craig trailed off. "I couldn't find something to explain it all satisfactorily, I guess, because if she was staying home with Quinn, she would have called one of us, explained what was going on, and ensured we had someone to cover for her. She was always very considerate. She never just… failed to show up. I said it was nothing, but I was worried."

"You didn't feel the need to report her absence?"

"To who?" Mrs. Craig mused. "Her husband?"

"A supervisor. I don't know how things work here. Maybe someone, when they couldn't reach her, might try the police. Ask them to do a welfare check."

Mrs. Craig shook her head. "That all seems a little… intrusive."

"You weren't worried enough to follow up on it?"

"We were floundering to cover for her. Dealing with everything here. It isn't easy to get coverage at three in the morning. She left us in the lurch. I mean, now I know that she didn't, but at the time, how were we to know the difference? We couldn't stop to worry about that. We needed to make sure that everyone was supervised and everyone's needs were met."

Margie nodded. It was a small organization. Just a few supervisors trying to cover all of the shifts. Laura's failure to show up for her shift had been more of an inconvenience than something they needed to deal with. It wasn't unusual for a workplace to be the first to report a missing person to the police. But it usually took a few days. Someone who didn't have a spouse or other family members in the home.

"Can you tell me what Laura did here?"

"The same as any of us do. Keep an eye on things. Make sure that the kids are complying with their release requirements. Report those who aren't. Help them enroll in school, find jobs, find places to live when they are ready to transition out of here. And then... be a sort of a den mother as well. Break up fights. Teach kids how to communicate with each other. Coping skills. Life skills. Get them referrals to doctors, help them keep track of their meds. Be a listening ear."

Laura would have been good at that. Margie had been surprised that she only had one child; Laura was the sort of person she would have expected to have a whole house full of kids. And she had. It just happened to be a halfway house rather than her own.

"How long had Laura worked here?"

"Oh, she's an old hand... Maybe five years? I would have to check her employment records. She wasn't a newbie. A lot of people bounce after a few days or a few weeks. It just isn't what they expected it to be, or they find that they can't handle it for one reason or another. Laura was steady. She was born to this kind of work."

"Had she had any problems lately? Conflicts with any of the kids? Trouble at home? Any... outside threats?"

"Nothing unusual, no."

Margie waited, letting Mrs. Craig think about it. Her answer had been too quick.

"She had been... I don't know if the right word is depressed. She seemed more moody than usual. Not quite as patient as usual. But people do burn out. She'd been here for a long time. She might have felt like it was time to move on to something else."

"Had she talked to you about that?"

"No, no. I just thought she seemed a little stressed. A little... moody."

"Did she talk about something that had happened to worry her? Even if it wasn't related to the kids here. Something that was on her mind. Distracting her."

"She didn't say what it was. But..." Mrs. Craig looked around, as if expecting someone to be listening in on them. "There was Patrick Belcourt. Laura seemed to be talking to him a lot lately. I wondered what was going on with him, but she didn't draw anything to the attention of the staff about him. And Ceci McKay. She said that we needed to keep an eye on Ceci. She didn't say why."

"What are their histories? Patrick and Ceci?"

Mrs. Craig was hesitant to disclose anything. "Well, I suppose you have access to their criminal files..."

Margie nodded. They didn't always have the access they wanted to young offender files, but they could ask for court orders to have them disclosed. If they were pertinent to the case. If they were worried that the youths might be a danger to others. If there was evidence they might have had something to do with Laura's death. It was a stretch. Much easier if Mrs. Craig just filled them in on what she had been told.

"Well... Patrick is Métis and Cec is Blackfoot." She nodded toward Margie as if to emphasize their Indigenous heritage in case they didn't understand. "They both had very rough upbringings. A lot of... I don't want to say neglect, but many of these families don't really know how to parent or how to provide for their children. It is a legacy they have struggled with for generations. We break up families and then expect them to know how to be families." She shrugged. It was not something she had personally done to them, not something she could change. Just one of the facts of life she had to deal with at the halfway house.

"And their charges?"

"Patrick... assault and gross bodily harm. Cec, a number of drug charges. She had a very long history of stuff she had served little or no time for in the past, and then a judge got tired of it. Decided to really hit her and make her realize she couldn't continue to go on that way. So she ended up serving four years."

A long time for a youthful offender.

"Personal drug use, or...?"

"She was dealing. Probably started out with running drugs for a family member as a child. By the time she was old enough to charge, she was well into the business. But a sweet little thing who could charm cops and judges and convince them that she would change her ways if they just gave her one more chance."

She could probably no longer masquerade as a sweet little thing after four years of prison time.

"And Laura was spending a lot of time with these two?"

"Not a lot. But… maybe more than the other kids. She was closer to them."

"Because they were Indigenous?"

"More than half of our kids are. There seemed to be something about these two in particular that had drawn Laura's attention."

None of them said anything for a minute, walking and thinking.

"Gang affiliations?" Lewis asked finally.

Mrs. Craig raised her head to look at him. "Gang affiliations?" she repeated.

"Do you know their gang affiliations?"

Mrs. Craig didn't say anything at first. Maybe she wanted to deny that they had any affiliation or that anyone in the house knew anything about it. Margie was surprised that Lewis had asked the question so directly, but she was quiet, trusting that he knew what he was doing. She didn't want to get in his way.

"Alberta Warriors," Mrs. Craig said finally. "Both of them."

CHAPTER FIFTEEN

*L*ewis took the lead in questioning Patrick. He was a tall, loose-limbed Indigenous youth with an acne-pocked face who looked at them warily and was not inclined to trust them. He did raise his brows, however, at the fact that Margie was also Indigenous.

"I don't know any Indian cops," he said. "I didn't know there were any. Other than the ones on the rez, and they are useless, you know? No one wants to talk to them and they're either acting all high and mighty over everyone or joining you for a drink and pretending that they are just one of the guys and not looking to narc on you or bring you before the council."

"There aren't a lot of us," Margie admitted. "I really wish that there were more. I think that it would be easier to address Indigenous issues if there were more Indigenous cops. But the fact that our own people are not likely to listen to us and just see us as Oreos or traitors... that makes it pretty hard to have the effect we would like to on the community."

"Indians don't belong on the police force."

Margie shrugged. "Maybe not. But I'm not giving up any time soon."

He nodded slowly.

"So... we're here because of Laura Clothier," Lewis inserted, not interested in a philosophical discussion of Indigenous bands self-policing. They had an actual case to investigate. A dead woman. A widowed husband and motherless child. Those things were real and concrete, and were what they needed to focus on.

Patrick looked genuinely saddened at the mention of Laura's name. "I heard about that," he said, shaking his head. "That is bad business." His eyes drooped halfway, hooded, not looking at either of them. "Mrs. Clothier was a good person. She really cared about the kids here."

He looked around for a moment, identifying anyone who might be close enough to overhear the conversation. "Not all the adults here care. Some of them…" He trailed off, thinking about it. "It's complicated." He rubbed the bridge of his nose. "But Mrs. Clothier was solid."

Margie and Lewis nodded. Margie waited to see if he would offer anything else without prompting.

"Did you hear anything about how she died?" she asked eventually.

Patrick cleared his throat. "No."

It was clearly a lie. Margie and Lewis waited for him to consider his answer and confirm or deny it.

"I heard it was, like, a mugging," Patrick said eventually, bouncing his leg nervously. "Like, she was in the park after dark, and she got ambushed, and they took her stuff. I don't know why she was there, and she wouldn't carry around a lot of cash or something late at night in the middle of the park. She's just coming here; she doesn't spend anything when she's here."

"She wasn't mugged," Margie told him. "This wasn't someone who held her up and she fought back or the mugger got too jumpy. This was a targeted attack. A premeditated murder."

"No… that couldn't be." He pressed his lips together, frowning worriedly. "No one would do that to Mrs. Clothier."

"I think she knew something," Lewis said. His voice had an edge to it. A toughness that Patrick would know from prison. "And I think it was to do with the Alberta Warriors."

Patrick swallowed.

"I understand you're with the Alberta Warriors," Lewis said. "So maybe you can tell me what it was about."

Patrick was too late to hide the AW tattoo on the back of one hand and 1-23 on the back of the other. Margie didn't know if he would have hidden them if he could. The ink declared his affiliation to anyone who knew them, and hiding it would have been pointless. He'd chosen to make that affiliation public and couldn't take it back now.

"I don't know of any beef the Warriors have—had—with Mrs. Clothier. Why would they care anything about a halfway house night supervisor? You can't get much *smaller* than that."

"She was killed in AW territory with a fentanyl overdose," Margie said. "Do you really think that could lead us to any other conclusion?"

"Fentanyl?" Patrick swallowed and wiped his mouth with the back of his hand. "Why would they do that?"

"I think they wanted to make it known that she was interfering where she wasn't wanted," Lewis contributed. "Where she had no business being. As a warning to anyone else who tried to get in the middle of gang business."

"What could she get in the way of? What could she know?" Patrick protested.

"Maybe you can tell us," Margie suggested. "You're AW and you were in close contact with her. Maybe you said something to her. Or maybe you had something to do with her murder."

"I never! I wouldn't do anything to hurt her. I told you, she was good to us. She helped to protect us and to help us get on the right track. She didn't want us in gangs. So maybe they didn't like her trying to take kids away from the gang, but she didn't make enough of a difference for them to care. What difference do one or two kids make to the organization?"

"You haven't heard anything through the grapevine? About why she was killed? You never said anything to anyone that might have set off alarm bells?"

"I would *never* do or say anything that would get her hurt," he protested.

"You're loyal to the Warriors, aren't you?" Lewis pressed. "If you had to prove your loyalty to them, you would turn on anyone you had to. And that includes a lowly nighttime supervisor at your halfway house."

"I'm loyal... but I would never let them do anything to hurt her. If I knew... I would have warned her."

"Maybe you didn't know beforehand," Lewis said, "But you know now. Aren't you going to do anything to avenge her murder? Help bring her killer to justice?"

Patrick's face was a mask. It was all hard, unfeeling planes. "I can't do that," he told them. "I can't go against the Warriors."

"That's what I figured," Lewis said. "You say that you liked Mrs. Clothier and that she's good people, but when it comes down to it, you really don't care. Your little gang is more important to you than anything that happened to her. You don't care about the people you took her away from. Her husband. Her little boy. Do you know what it is like to lose your mother when you're just a little boy?"

Patrick cleared his throat. He scratched at a pimple on his cheek. "Yeah, I do."

"But you just don't care. Too bad for him."

"I can't change it. I can't take it back and give her back to him. Doesn't matter how bad I feel about it, she's still going to be dead and he's still not going to have a mom."

"You can stop them from killing someone else. You can let them know that justice has been served."

"I can't do anything about it."

"You could tell us who killed her. Who ordered it. You knew her. You knew who she was in contact with through this house. If you didn't have anything to do with it, then it was likely someone else in the house. So step up. Be a man. Look after your own."

Patrick looked around. "I can't talk. I can't tell you anything. They know who I am. They would know if I talked. You think I want to go out that way too?" He shook his head. "Actually, they wouldn't kill a traitor that way. That was a nice way to go for someone like her. A traitor..." He trailed off and let them think about how the Alberta Warriors would deal with a traitor. Someone they knew had talked. Torture him? Cut out his tongue? A long, painful death. Maybe, in the end, the mercy of a slit throat. Everyone would know that he had betrayed his gang. His family. His community.

How many more people in the house were Alberta Warriors? They hadn't asked Mrs. Craig. She probably would have been able to tell them. Most of them, anyway. There would always be those who didn't talk about their affiliation but remained loyal to a faction behind the scenes.

"Patrick. We can take you in," Margie told him. "You don't need to talk here. We can take you in on some charge and you can tell us in the police station, where no one will overhear you and no word can get back to the gang."

He looked at her for a minute, maybe even considering it, but in the end, he shook his head again. "I can't," he told her, his voice strained.

"She was my cousin," Margie told him. "A sister to me. You killed my sister."

He swallowed hard, his Adam's apple bobbing up and down. "I didn't have anything to do with it. I swear."

"Your family killed her. Your gang killed her. That makes you guilty of it, too."

He shook his head wordlessly, eyes glistening. But he didn't break down and tell them who the responsible party had been.

CHAPTER SIXTEEN

*J*f Lewis thought Ceci would be easier to question because she was a girl…

Margie knew that Ceci would be that much harder. She knew gang girls. And she knew how they used their feminine wiles to make their interrogators think that they were frail or vulnerable. She knew how fake and underhanded they could be, hiding their true natures behind smiles and simpers and begging for help. Then, when they walked away, they would laugh with their girls about how easy men were to manipulate.

So Margie wouldn't let Lewis take the lead in the discussion with Ceci. Ceci who had a long, long list of charges before a judge had finally seen through her act and cracked down on her.

Ceci was not the nice little girl that Mrs. Craig had described, who had been able to charm cops and judges. As Margie had expected, she had changed during her years in prison. Margie could still see the outer shell that had fooled people in the past, but the Ceci she saw now had a hard face, piercing black eyes, and the smooth movements and caution of a feral cat.

She was a product of the prison system. It sounded like she had a family history with the gang as well, or at last with the drug trade, so she had probably been hard before prison.

"Hi, Ceci. Can I call you that? I'm Detective Pat."

Ceci nodded uncaringly. "Call me whatever you like."

"I wanted to talk to you because of what happened to Laura Clothier. She was my family." Margie said it in a hard, flat tone. Staking out her territory. *Alberta Warriors killed my family.* So Ceci would know that she had a real stake in this.

Ceci looked surprised. She played with a stud in her lip.

"I didn't know Mrs. Clothier had family here."

"Did you know she was married? That she had a little boy?"

Ceci looked away. She wrapped a long lock of hair around her finger and let it go again, repeatedly.

"Well, yeah. Everybody has somebody," she said eventually.

"Not everybody has a ten-year-old boy who has to grow up without a mother now."

"I don't even know why you're talking to me. Do you think I had something to do with her getting killed? Look at the check-in sheet; I was here, just like I'm supposed to be, before curfew. We can't sneak out of here to go murder someone." She pulled on the lock of hair. Long and hard so that it made Margie wince. Ceci leaned forward. "And if I wanted to kill her, why would I go to the park? She was coming here."

"I don't think that you killed her directly. But I think your gang did, and that's the same thing."

"I didn't have anything to do with it."

"Tell me who did."

Ceci laughed. "Even if I knew, do you think I could tell you? You think I want to be killed, too?"

"Why target Laura? She was a good person. She was here to help you. She called you all her kids, and I understand she gave you special attention. Why would you just stand by and say nothing while your gang killed her? Why would you let them get away with it?"

"What makes you think it was Alberta Warriors?"

It was Lewis who answered. "I have been undercover at the parks for months. I know which gangs are involved. I know that she was killed by the Alberta Warriors. I'm not sure why—probably over a drug shipment, considering the way she was killed. The question is, what did she know that could get her killed?"

Ceci sat back in her chair, arms folded across her chest. "What do I know? I'm here to rehabilitate, you know. To transition from prison to respectable society. Mrs. Clothier didn't want us associating with anyone from the Warriors."

"And so you didn't?" Lewis questioned, his face twisting into a sneer. "You never talked to anyone from the Warriors? Do you know how ridiculous that sounds?"

She didn't like being mocked and told that she sounded ridiculous. No one, especially a tough gang girl, wanted to look ridiculous in front of others, even if they were strangers.

"I can't help talking to anyone in the gang," she pointed out. "Not when they're in my own house."

Margie and Lewis sat there looking at her. She knew that she had said too much, but it was too late to take it back, and trying would just make her look weak. So instead, she tried to bluff her way through it.

"AW is everywhere you go," she told Lewis. "She knows," Ceci jutted her chin at Margie. "You can't get away from them. They're in every prison, every community, every family. And I'm not going to blab to the police and have them take action against me."

"So you'd rather that Mrs. Clothier's killer just went free."

"I wasn't the one who hurt her. I wouldn't have ever done that." Ceci looked at Margie, and her hard expression melted slightly, her chin quivering just a bit. "She was really your family? Your cousin? You're not just saying that?"

"Yes. My cousin. I lived in Winnipeg, and I used to come to Calgary during the summer, and she and I would spend days together. Exploring the city, having a fun time, going to Cochrane for ice cream with Moushoom. She was so…" Margie struggled to think of the right word. "So nurturing. I don't mean she was like a mother, because she wasn't. But she was just… ready to be my best friend, someone I could always call on. Someone who always buoyed me up."

Ceci nodded. "She was like that."

"Was she to you too? I'm glad. She was a special person, and Alexander told me how much she loved 'her kids' here. You were her family too. She chose to spend the time with you."

"It was her job," Ceci said dismissively.

"It wasn't just her job. She could have done a lot of things. You think that someone like her had nothing else she could do? That was the only thing she could find? She didn't need to be babysitting juvies. She *chose* to be here. But you and the others... you're acting like none of that mattered. I guess she didn't mean anything to any of you. You think what AW did was okay. Maybe you think she deserved it for sticking her nose into someone else's business." Margie leaned forward and slowed down her speech, trying to emphasize each word. "But you know she was trying to help you."

Ceci looked away, blinking. She shook her head. "She got herself into trouble. It was nothing to do with me. I wouldn't have turned her in. I'd never have betrayed her."

"But you'll betray her memory. You'll let her little son spend the rest of his life wondering who killed his mother and why nobody cared enough to stop it or to tell the police what had happened."

"She was in the park," Ceci said.

"Yes."

"She knew it wasn't safe there."

"She was in the park near her house, where she always went to walk or think. Why should that be dangerous for her? She was on her way here. Just stopping to look at the frozen pond for a few minutes. To meditate and get her head on straight so that she would be one hundred percent there for you and the others. Even if you were sleeping, she still wanted to make sure that she had done everything she could to prepare herself. Take that extra few minutes."

Ceci shook her head. "She wasn't sitting on that bench to meditate."

"What, then?"

"She thought she could stop them. She was stupid. One person can't stop the Warriors. She should have stayed out of it."

"What was she doing? How was she trying to stop them?"

"I don't know." She shook her head, looking steadily away from Margie. "She shouldn't have gotten involved in whatever it was."

"It was drugs," Lewis said, looking at Ceci. "I know that much. Was there a big shipment coming in? Is that what she was trying to stop? And what did you get out of it? What did you get for turning her in?" He stared at her steadily. "A couple of hits of fent?"

"I'm no addict. I'm clean." She held out her arms, inviting him to look. They were covered with stick-and-poke tattoos she had undoubtedly gotten while in juvie. But there were no obvious injection marks or tracks.

"Addicts are switching to smoking fentanyl," Lewis said with a shrug.

"Cheaper, easier, less risk. You get a good high without having to risk needle infections. And without any telltale tracks."

"I don't do fent. Or any other drugs," she told him coldly. "You're just making assumptions based on racial profiling."

"Then I must think that Detective Pat is a drug user, too." Lewis turned and looked at Margie pointedly. "Detective Patenaude, are you a fentanyl addict?"

Margie rolled her eyes. He was being annoying and confrontational, which she didn't think was the best way to get to Ceci. But she didn't want to criticize him in front of a witness, either. Showing a rift between them would not be helpful. Other teams might like good cop-bad cop, but Margie found it was better to work together, staying on the same level, treating the suspect with respect and trying to establish a good relationship. Lewis apparently had other ideas.

"Ceci..." Margie said softly, "A little boy will never see his mom again. I'm never going to see my cousin again, never going to get together over tea and talk about the times we had together here as kids. She's gone. Because someone wanted to deal drugs to kids and she got in the way of it. Have I got it right?"

Ceci's gaze was downward. She nodded slightly.

"Who is the dealer? Is it one of the kids here?"

Ceci shook her head.

"Who, then? And how did Laura find out about it? Did someone come to the house at night when she was supervising? I assume you guys are not allowed to have visitors after curfew."

"I don't know what she saw or heard," Ceci told them unconvincingly, staring off into space.

"How many people in the house are Alberta Warriors?"

She shrugged. "Everyone is affiliated with someone," she said. "If not AW, then one of the other gangs. You can't live in this world without protection."

"Who else is AW?"

She lifted her hands, palms up. "I'm not a snitch. I don't talk."

CHAPTER SEVENTEEN

hey talked to one of the other supervisors before they left. Mr. Gaetz was an older man, with a day or two's growth of beard on his chin and little hair on top. He was shorter than Margie, which was relatively short for a man.

"Is there any way we could get a listing of what kids are associated with what gangs?" Margie asked.

"We have to respect our residents' privacy. And the fact that most of them are trying to stay away from the gangs they were *formally* associated with. It's very hard to break with these guys once you have been accepted into an organization. We try to help them make that transition, but I'll be honest: Most of them are not able to."

"And we would like a list of what those associations are."

"I'll talk to the director, but I'm not sure that's something we can give you. It violates all kinds of rights and policies."

"We want to solve Laura's murder. And it has something to do with the Alberta Warriors. So we need to know who in this house she might have had contact with that arranged for her death. Don't you think that overrides any privacy concerns?"

He shook his head slowly. "Sadly, no, I don't think so. You may feel justified in riding roughshod over people's rights. They're just kids, after all, and we're talking about murder. But that's not the way it works around here. The kids come first."

Laura would have been proud of him.

Rather than smiling at the thought, Margie kept a stony expression. "You speak with your director, then. See how far this institution can push it before the Minister of Children's Services decides that you are not living up to the terms of your charter and shuts down the house or replaces you. If, in the view of Calgary Police Services, you are supporting criminal organizations and putting these kids in danger, you will be shut down so fast you won't know what hit you."

Gaetz shook his head, looking grim. "I'm sorry you feel that way."

But he didn't buckle under and give Margie the information she had requested.

MARGIE AND CHRISTINA had both made time to go over and visit Moushoom. The modest house that Margie had purchased when she moved to Calgary had been selected in large part because it was so close to the nursing home where Moushoom lived. It was within easy walking distance, so either of them could see him at any time, and she was right there in case of an emergency. But he could still maintain his independence as much as possible.

They spent the time immediately after getting home from school or work to make some bannock. They had a little bit of it while they were cooking, and took the rest, still warm and in a towel, to Moushoom's room.

As usual, the nursing staff had left him sitting in his chair in front of the TV. He looked at the door when Margie knocked and opened it, and his face creased into a grin. "My daughters," he called, and held out his arms for them. Margie and Christina took off their masks and both gave their grandfather warm hugs and touched their cheeks to his, whispering in his ear how good it was to see him again.

Stella pranced around them and would not settle down until Moushoom had talked to her and given her ear scratches and assurances that she was a good dog. He got her to lie down at his feet.

"Shut this off," Moushoom directed, motioning to the TV. "What drivel. Show me what you brought me!" He sniffed the air. "Bannock!"

"Can't get anything past this old man," Margie said happily. Of course, most of the time if they brought him something, it was bannock. He loved whatever traditional foods Margie and Christina were able to make. It had been a long time since Kokum had taught Margie the traditional recipes she knew, and the results were sometimes not what she would have hoped. But the bannock always turned out.

She brought Moushoom's meal tray over to him and unwrapped the bannock. There were butter and jam in Moushoom's tiny fridge, as a treat of bannock was not uncommon, and they munched on the still-warm bread, enjoying each other's company.

"How are you feeling, Moushoom?" Christina asked. "You are looking better all the time."

"Yes, getting stronger," he agreed. "It will take more than a little virus to bring this old coot to heaven's gate."

"I hope so! I'm glad you're getting better. We were really worried when you were on the machine." Margie looked over at the small tank of oxygen nearby, which Moushoom only needed now and then at night, if the regular testing during the day showed that his oxygen levels had dipped down too much.

Luckily, it had been bacterial pneumonia and not COVID as they had feared. The doctor said that long-term damage was unlikely.

Margie waited until after Moushoom had finished eating his bannock before bringing up Laura. Then, as gently as she could, she introduced the topic.

"Moushoom, do you remember Auntie Gaye's daughter, Laura?"

"Remember her?" He smiled. "You were two peas. Joined at the hip."

Margie nodded. She rubbed her forehead, focusing on keeping her composure. Christina looked at her with wide eyes and squeezed her hand.

"What is it?" Moushoom demanded. "What is wrong with you?"

"Moushoom..." Margie cupped her hands over her eyes for a moment. "Laura is dead. She was killed a couple of days ago. In a park."

His jaw dropped. He shook his head. "How could this happen? Explain to me what happened."

"We are investigating. I can't tell you who or why. I can tell you…

that she was forcibly given a drug called fentanyl. And that stopped her heart. It would have been very fast, I'm told."

"Why would anyone do such a thing?"

"Right now, we think it was because of drugs. She was trying to stop some... some nasty guys."

"Do not treat me like a child," he warned. "I might be old—I *am* old —but I am not feeble. You explain to me."

"I think it was the Alberta Warriors gang. I don't have any proof yet, and this is not for public consumption," Margie warned, giving Christina a stern look, "but that's what our intelligence tells us."

"Alberta Warriors." Moushoom leaned back in his chair. "A bunch of hoodlums. Why would they do that to Laura?"

"I think she knew something about a big shipment and was trying to stop it. She was working with kids in a halfway house, trying to keep them away from drugs, away from all of the gangs. But she was a threat in some way, so they killed her."

"I don't understand why kids join gangs," Christina said. "I don't understand why there even *are* gangs. Why can't people just think for themselves and get along together? Why do we need to have gangs that are causing all of this violence and running drugs and guns? Why do people have to be so dumb?"

"Kids—and older people—join gangs for protection. For family. Because it is the only thing they have ever known. The Alberta Warriors are an offshoot of the Manitoba Warriors." She saw a flicker of recognition in Christina's eyes at this name, making Margie shudder inside. She didn't want her daughter to have any knowledge of or familiarity with that gang.

"Manitoba Warriors started as a prison gang," Moushoom explained. "Most of the gangs in prison follow racial lines, and these were Indians banding together to protect themselves. When there are Italian gangs and Black gangs and sp—Hispanic gangs, then the Indians need to do something to protect themself. They need to band together and be strong and united. So they did. And the Manitoba Warriors were the biggest and strongest of the Indigenous gangs."

"And how did they get here?" Christina asked. "Why didn't they just stay in Manitoba?"

"They were too much of a problem in the prison. There were too many of them. So the prison decided to do something about it. To split them all up and ship them to other prisons. So they were transplanted to different prisons in Alberta."

"And became the Alberta Warriors."

Margie nodded. "Yeah."

"And they're not just in the prisons anymore, because they let them out?"

"Yes. They get released, and they do the same thing, banding together on the outside for safety in numbers. And because it's profitable. They can work together to set up criminal ventures that are much bigger and stronger than anything they could do individually. The combination of community and power is really strong, and that keeps them running."

"But it would be better for the community if we didn't have all of this violence."

Margie nodded her agreement. "I'm all for law and order," she pointed out. "But I can understand the draw of family looking out for each other and providing for each other. When you have grown up in a place with so much need and broken culture and families, it is really important to belong to something and to have the assurance that your needs will always be provided for and someone will always have your back."

"But like..." Margie could see Christina struggling with this. "Isn't that what the band is supposed to do? And Indigenous outreach and cultural programs? And we have all of these social programs that are supposed to provide for any medical needs and community kitchens and all that?"

"Yes. All of those things help, and we're trying to build a community that supports each other and teaches us how to be better families and how to hang on to our youth and still teach them the old ways, even if they don't seem relevant. But it's a lot to ask. And a gang is much more imme-diate and in-your-face. You need something, they'll give it to you. And then you do something for them in return. And they keep you coming back, giving you protection and drugs to feed your addiction, and a substitute family to replace the one that you grew up with—or didn't have when you were growing up."

"In school, the children had to band together," Moushoom contributed. "We had no parents. No adults who cared about us. We had to do what we could for ourselves and each other. It's the same in prison.

The weak die. Only the strong survive. And the only way to stay strong is by working together."

He smacked his hand on the arm of his chair, making Stella jump and look up at him in concern.

"And now… they got my daughter."

Margie put her arm around Moushoom's neck and leaned into him. "I'm so sorry, Moushoom. I wish that I had known she was in trouble. We didn't see each other. She knew I was a cop, but she never called me or came to me for help. I'm sorry."

"You could not know," Moushoom assured her.

He started to rock back and forth, and then picked up a chanting rhythm. Margie didn't know all of the words in the chant, but she followed it the best she could, listening to him tell of Laura's days spent with them as a child. About how he mourned the loss of another precious child from the family. He prayed for God to take her spirit back to her ancestors and to make her strong, and the rest of them strong in her memory.

Margie listened to him, humming along with the chant, holding Moushoom's hand on one side and Christina's on the other.

CHAPTER EIGHTEEN

*T*hey started for home at a brisk walk. While it was still unseasonably warm, the temperature dropped when the sun went down, and it was several degrees colder on the way home than it had been when they had arrived.

"I didn't know whether we should tell him about Laura," Christina said. "But I'm glad you did. I think it was the right thing to do."

"Well, like he says, he is still strong. We worry about him and how long he will be with us, but his mind is still very strong, and we shouldn't try to protect him like a child." They walked for a minute in silence. "Even if you were a child, I would still tell you," Margie said. "I don't think anything is achieved by hiding the truth and trying to protect people from being sad. We need sad times so that we can be happy the rest of the time. And to help to strengthen us and pull us together."

"I don't like being sad."

"No one does."

As they drew close to the house, Stella's demeanor changed suddenly. She pulled ahead on the leash, casting about for a scent and then, when Margie and Christina started to catch up to her, she turned sideways and tried to push them back and herd them in the other direction.

"Stella," Christina objected. "What's the matter? It isn't time to play. We need to go home now. It's time for homework and bed."

Stella bumped against their legs again, growling when Christina tried to push her away.

Margie's chest tightened. She looked around and pushed her hand into her pocket to find the bright flashlight attached to her keychain. Christina was still trying to negotiate with Stella, and Margie nudged her to stop.

"Shh. Let's look around. See if there is something that spooked her. Trust that her senses and instincts are stronger than yours."

Christina was immediately quiet, her muscles stiffening. Margie found the switch on the flashlight and turned it on. She shone it toward the house, panned back and forth across the yard, and then pointed it at the car. They had just walked over to Moushoom's as they usually did, leaving the car at the house.

Margie saw glittery bits of ice on the sidewalk beside the car.

"Stay here," she told Christina, and walked ahead to the car. Stella barked a warning at her. Margie looked around, staying alert, watching for anyone lurking in the shadows.

Every window in the car had been smashed. The windshield was mostly one big sheet of crazed glass. The others had big holes in them. The broken glass lay in little rectangular pieces, reflecting Margie's flashlight beam.

Margie shone the flashlight at the house again, wary. She didn't see any sign that someone had been inside. The door still seemed to be secure. But her cop training told her not to go in without backup. And Christina and Stella didn't count.

She walked back to them, and they stayed huddled close together, heads on a swivel, taking in their surroundings. Margie took one good look around before raising her phone to her ear, and gave it voice commands rather than dropping her eyes to look at the screen.

Within a minute, they could hear the first siren. Margie shivered. It wasn't that cold out. Not cold enough for either of them to be hypothermic after such a short period of time. But the adrenaline was doing things to her. Her senses were all keyed up, alert for the slightest noise or shadow.

Once they had a few cops there for support, Margie went with them up to the house and checked the door. It was still locked and there were no broken windows at the front of the house. Margie inserted her key into the lock and the other cops went ahead of her, turning on the lights and clearing each room.

Once they confirmed it was safe, Margie ushered Stella and Christina back into the house. Stella was anxious, whining and barking and growling if anyone got too close to her people.

"Keep her on the leash," Margie told Christina. "Just until everything is settled down and we are alone again."

Christina sat on the couch and gave Stella ear scratches, trying to calm her down.

"Who would do that?" she demanded. "That's really stupid. Do you think it was just some random thing?"

"Maybe."

But Margie didn't think so. People who committed random acts of vandalism didn't confine it to one car. There would be a series of cars along one block that had all sustained similar damage. But she had looked around at the other vehicles, and none of them appeared to be touched.

Her phone rang, and she looked at the face. A number that she didn't know and hadn't linked to a contact. It was probably Cruz or one of the other homicide cops who had heard about the incident. She swiped the call and answered it.

"Patenaude."

"Detective Patenaude?" a nervous male voice said tentatively.

"Yes. What can I do for you?"

"It's Alexander." A pause. "Alexander Williams."

"Oh, Alexander. I'm sorry, I was distracted. How are you doing?"

"There was... an incident. A rock was thrown through our window."

"Oh, no!" Margie's mind immediately went to her broken car windows. A coincidence? Doubtful. "Are you okay? How is Quinn?"

"We're okay. Just a little bit scared. I think this is related to Laura. There was a note. Saying to mind our own business." He cleared his throat. "I haven't done anything to anyone. Why would they be telling me to stay out of their business?"

"Have you called the police? I'll send someone over to have a look around and to take your statement."

"Yes. They are already here. But I thought that I should tell you, give you a heads-up."

"Thank you for thinking of me. That's very kind of you. We've had...

an incident of our own. Can I call you back after we've had a chance to process it? Are you okay for now?"

"We're okay. No one is going to do anything with all of the police here."

"Okay. I'll call you back in a bit."

When one of the officers who had shown up at Margie's distress call walked into the living room, she already had a pretty good idea of what he was going to say. He produced a brick and a piece of paper.

If you know what's good for you and your family, you'll keep your nose out of anyone else's business. Close the case and go back to your life. Keep investigating, and people you love could die.

CHAPTER NINETEEN

*E*ven though Margie had been warned by Alexander, she was still unprepared for her gut reaction to the note. She couldn't have been prepared for it. Her muscles clenched so tightly that they hurt. She tried to avoid grinding her teeth. Her heart was beating hard and fast and she felt like throwing up.

Christina looked at her, eyes wide. "Mom?"

"It's okay, Christina. It's going to be okay. We've got lots of people here to look after us and make sure that we are safe."

"You don't think we're safe?"

"We're safe, baby. I won't let anything happen to you. These guys are not going to get away with threatening me. They might think they can intimidate me, but they're wrong."

"But you know that they…" Christina swallowed. She scratched Stella's ears and held the dog's face in both hands, avoiding eye contact with Margie. She couldn't finish the sentence, but Margie knew what it was anyway.

You know that they killed Laura.

They weren't just threats. They were not going to stop at a brick through the window and a little vandalism. They weren't just going to make a threat and fade into the background. They were prepared to act.

"Nothing is going to happen to us," she promised Christina. "We'll get through this. Just like we have before."

They had dealt with threats of violence before. With a stalker who they knew had killed and who had easy access to them in the neighborhood. They had gotten through that. They could get through this, too.

Never mind that the Alberta Warriors were an organization, not a lone stalker. They could have men—and women—all over the city, in many different places at once.

Margie had the police force behind her.

She had truth and justice behind her.

"Okay," Christina said, but her voice was not convinced. "We'll get through it."

IT WAS ANOTHER SLEEPLESS NIGHT. Christina went into her room and shut the door after a while, but Margie suspected that she was probably just watching movies on her phone, not actually sleeping. But at least she was trying for a semblance of normality.

Detective Jones came over when she heard about everything and installed herself on Margie's couch. Police patrols were driving by the house regularly. Margie was not normally armed while she was at home, but she did not lock her gun away.

She tried to sleep. Jones took watch in the living room and sent Margie to bed. She did her best to sleep but, whenever she managed to drift off for a few minutes, it was into restless dreams of danger, and she would jump awake, heart pounding, ready to defend herself and her family against an immediate threat.

In the morning, she was up earlier than usual, making coffee and trying to figure out her next steps. How was she going to deal with the threats? How were they going to move the investigation forward?

They would be canvassing neighbors for any doorbell camera footage that might show who it was that had vandalized the car and left her the threatening note, but Margie already knew what the footage would show. A shadowy figure in dark winter clothing that obscured the vandal's build, and a hood, hat, or mask—or all three—to hide any facial features. There would be no way to identify the perpetrator.

She didn't wake Christina. They had a standing deal that Christina could sleep as late as she wanted without being disturbed, as long as she got to school on time. Margie would not harass her about sleeping in until two minutes before the arrival of the bus as long as she got there. And today, Margie didn't think school was on the list of priorities. Christina could sleep for as long as she liked.

But she was just pouring herself and Jones each a cup of coffee when she heard Christina's door open. She expected Christina to stumble to the bathroom, bleary-eyed, and then to return to her bedroom again a minute later with perhaps a grumble of greeting, and return to sleep for a couple more hours. But Christina was dressed for the day, her hair neatly brushed and braided. She used the bathroom and then joined Margie in the kitchen, pouring herself a cup of coffee.

"Morning," she greeted in a soft voice.

"Did you get any sleep?" Margie touched Christina's cheek briefly, looking at the bags under her eyes.

"A couple of hours."

"You can go back to bed for a while. You don't have to be up yet."

"I can't sleep anymore. Besides, the bus will be here soon."

"Under the circumstances..."

Christina raised her brows. "I still have school."

"I think today you might want to stay home. While we get this sorted out." Margie looked out the window. "I don't know if going to school today is the best idea."

"Are you going to work?"

"I don't know... I suppose so. I can work from here for a while, but I think I will need to be there for the morning briefing and to coordinate the investigation. I can do some work remotely from here, but I might also need to do some interviews." Margie tried to sort out in her mind what different directions the investigation would go. She wouldn't be able to do everything herself, but the detectives and other law enforcement officers they had access to would be putting all necessary resources into tracking down who had made the threats and making sure that Margie, her family, and Alexander and Quinn were all protected.

Christina nodded. "I'm not staying here alone."

"I'll make sure that you have protection. One of the other detectives, or someone else. We have the support of ALERT on this case and what-ever other resources we need to draw on."

"I'm safer where there are a lot of people, though, right? Not just sitting here by myself. I mean… obviously they know where we live. I'm not just going to sit here waiting for them to pick their time. I'll go to school, where I'm surrounded by people. They have a resource officer. Teachers. Other students. It would be a lot harder for them to track me and do anything to me in the school."

Margie couldn't fault her logic. "But you're also harder to guard if you're in a big place like that with lots of other people and multiple exits."

Christina shrugged. "You don't need to guard me," she said. "I'm not letting these people scare me. If they were going to do something, they would have done it last night, wouldn't they? Why threaten us and break the windows instead of actually doing something about it? They could just as easily have been lying in wait in the house. They didn't do that."

Margie had to admit that she had been thinking the same thing. The Alberta Warriors had killed Laura. They hadn't wasted their time making threats, at least not as far as Margie knew. They had just approached her in the park and taken care of business. But Margie and Christina and the others were not a direct threat to them like Laura had been. Laura had known specific information. She'd had something to use against them. Information that could disrupt their operation or be used against specific people in the organization.

So far, Margie couldn't point the finger at any one person. She couldn't prove exactly who had killed Laura. She didn't know the informa-tion Laura had known. She was asking questions and knew what she was looking for, but she was not getting anywhere in questioning the halfway house residents. She couldn't use any of the information she knew to justify an arrest.

"We can give it a day or two to see if it blows over and to try to get information on who did this," she told Christina. "You can miss a couple of days of school. Get notes and assignments from your friends and catch up again next week. I would just like to be sure that you're safe."

Christina sipped her coffee. "I'm going to school."

CHAPTER TWENTY

*I*t wouldn't do much good for Margie to lay down the law and tell Christina that no, she wasn't allowed to go to school; she had to stay at home under guard until they had solved the case.

It might take weeks or months to break the case and arrest the people who had been involved in Laura's murder and the threats against Margie and Alexander. She couldn't keep Christina home indefinitely. And Christina was too old for Margie to physically keep her at home. Even if she tried to and left someone there to guard Christina while she went into the office for the morning briefing and to conduct some interviews, she couldn't stop Christina from leaving the house. She wasn't under arrest. She wasn't even grounded. She hadn't done anything wrong.

Margie shook her head. She caught a grin from Jones at Christina's response.

Like mother, like daughter. Margie had been quite defiant during her own teenage years and, while Christina was more stable and had a better relationship with Margie than Margie had with her own mother, she still possessed a strong-willed and independent nature. Regardless of whether it was innate, genetic, or influenced by Margie's upbringing, there was no denying that Christina was her own person. She might listen to Margie's opinion or advice, but she would make her own decision.

Margie took a deep breath and let it out. She took a couple of large gulps of coffee. Too bitter and too hot. It seared all the way down.

"I'll walk with you to the bus stop."

"Seriously?" Christina objected. "I'm not a little kid that you need to walk to the bus!"

"Nobody said you're a little kid. Was Laura a little kid?"

Christina looked at Margie. She opened her mouth to raise another argument, but apparently couldn't come up with a good counter to that.

Laura had been a grown woman. Someone who could take care of herself and who presumably knew that she was in danger. Whatever precautions she had taken had not been enough. Being by herself in the park had not been a good idea.

Christina shook her head. "I don't see what difference it makes."

"Maybe not. But we need to do what we can. I want to have eyes on the neighborhood. I want to make sure that you get on the bus safely and that no one is watching you or following you. It's not a perfect solution, because it won't be hard for them to figure out where you go to school, but at least if they can't follow you directly…"

Christina just drank her coffee. Margie knew that she had all kinds of objections to this approach bubbling up in her brain, but she chose not to express them in the presence of Detective Jones, whom Christina liked and wanted to impress. She would want Katelyn Jones to think she was a smart, independent woman, not a rebellious child.

Christina pulled out her phone and scrolled through her social media or watched videos until Margie was sure that the bus was supposed to be there. She didn't say anything. If Christina missed the bus, she missed the bus. Then she would have to stay home, where they could keep better track of her, or find another way to get to school.

"Okay, I'm heading out," Christina said finally, walking toward the door.

"I'll come along."

Christina didn't object or wait for Margie. She walked at a brisk pace to the bus stop, which was about a block away. Margie looked around her, eyes alert, head on a swivel.

There were the neighbors who had become familiar to her over the last months, out walking dogs and going to work or school. But there were other faces that she didn't know. Indigenous faces, like her own, many of them hidden behind black hygiene masks or bandanas.

Christina didn't appear to notice anything out of the ordinary. She stationed herself by the bus stop sign, looking down the street for the arrival of the bus.

A young man strolled up and stood nearby. Margie moved between him and Christina, giving him the eye. He pretended not to notice.

"Mo-om!" Christina protested in a low voice, expressing her displeasure with this overprotectiveness. Margie stayed where she was.

When the bus pulled up to the stop thirty seconds later, Christina got on board. The man moved to join her, but Margie blocked him. The young man's eyes glittered. "Excuse me."

Margie shook her head. He shifted his feet to get past her, but Margie blocked him more aggressively.

"Are either of you getting on?" the bus driver demanded.

"No," Margie told him firmly.

The bus driver looked uncertain of this. The man eyed Margie. She put her hand on her holster. He took a step back, shrugging. "I'll catch the next one."

The bus pulled out. Margie watched the man rather than watching her daughter's bus heading to the school.

The man smiled.

It was a cool, crisp morning, and he wasn't wearing a jacket. His shirt sleeves were rolled up, showing off his ink.

"Get out of my neighborhood," Margie told him through her teeth. "Unless you want to be arrested."

"For what?"

"Loitering. Harassment. Stalking. Criminal mischief. Whatever I want to arrest you for."

"That's not very neighborly."

"You and the rest of the Alberta Warriors can stay out of my way. I'm not going to put up with your harassment. You stay away from me and my family."

He looked in the direction the bus had gone. "You think I don't know where that bus is going?"

"I'll know if you show up there. Stay away."

He smiled and walked away from her.

Margie watched until he was out of sight and then a while longer. She looked around, noting anyone else who was out of place, and walked back to her house with her hand on her firearm. When she reached the house, Jones was standing on the front step, looking worried.

"What happened?"

She could see the bus stop from where she stood, but obviously could not see any details or hear what they had said.

Margie motioned her back into the house grimly, away from any listening ears.

"Hang on for a second," she told Jones, and called the school and then the police dispatcher to request that a law enforcement officer meet the bus on the other end and make sure nothing happened.

She did not hop into her windowless car and drive to the school to meet Christina on the other end and make sure she got off to her classes safely. Christina would be mortified. And what could Margie do that another law enforcement officer couldn't? It was more productive for her to stay on the case and try to get the culprits at the center of the drug trafficking and murder plot. She wouldn't get anywhere by trying to swat at the flies buzzing around her head.

She dumped her coffee cup and refilled it.

"So what happened?" Jones pressed. "What made you suspicious of that guy?"

Margie shook her head. "Oh, it was pretty subtle."

Jones raised her brows. "Oh?"

"Maybe the fact that he's got AW and 1-23 inked on his shoulders."

"And he wanted you to know it."

"Oh, yeah." It would have been easy enough for him to roll down his sleeves to cover the tats or to wear a jacket. But the whole point of the exercise had been so that Margie would see she was surrounded by them, that they could hang out in her neighborhood and she couldn't do anything about it. So she would see just how close they could get to Christina. Even Christina hadn't understood the danger that she had been in. She had thought that Margie was just confronting a random stranger who happened to want to take the same bus as she did.

Parents could be so embarrassing. Especially parents like Margie, law enforcement officers who thought that they knew everything and that it was their job to patrol the world and enforce everyone's behavior.

"I hope they're taking protecting Alexander and Quinn seriously," Margie said. She took several swallows of her coffee. Quinn wouldn't be going back to school today, would he? He would be staying inside, where they were shielded from whatever Alberta Warriors were hanging out in their neighborhood. And there were probably even more of them there, if Carburn Park was the place they were using as a central meeting hub and exchange site.

"We can call them," Jones suggested.

"Yeah. Yeah, let's do that." Margie pulled her phone back out. It vibrated while in her hand. She looked at the incoming call. Moushoom's care center. Her heart plummeted. First they had tried to harass Christina at the bus stop, and then they were causing problems at the care center too? How had they known about Moushoom? What were they doing over there?

She looked at Jones, panic probably evident in her eyes.

"You take that," Jones instructed. "I'll call to make sure Alexander is being looked after."

Margie nodded her thanks and swiped to answer the call from the care center.

CHAPTER TWENTY-ONE

*M*rs. Patenaude?" the woman from the care center greeted cheerfully. "I'm sorry to bother you during the day."

"No, that's fine," Margie said, taking a deep breath. If the woman's demeanor was any indication, then nothing was wrong. They didn't have some Alberta Warrior over there threatening to shoot the place up. No one had come to take Moushoom away on an imagined outing or take him hostage by force. "What can I do for you?"

"Your grandfather asked me to call you. I tried to explain this to him, but he didn't understand, and he said you would."

"Yes?"

"He got a package in the mail today from one of his other grandchildren. It is a USB drive with some photos or something for him. But of course, he doesn't have a computer, and the TVs in the rooms are not sophisticated enough to have USB ports. I told him that I could put it on my computer to see what it was for him, but we would have to print the pictures out, if it is something else, we would have to find a device that we could use to play it back for him. I thought that you and your daughter might just want to bring a computer with you the next time you visit him…"

It took a while for Margie's brain to catch up with what the woman was saying.

"Wait, let's back up a bit. Who sent this package?"

Margie's mind immediately went to letter bombs, poisons, and other terrible thoughts. But of course, it had already been opened and no one had been hurt. It was just a USB stick with some photos on it.

"I'm not sure who it was from. He has the packaging in his room and the USB doesn't say anything on it. One of his grandchildren, I think. We don't know everyone as well as you; most of them only visit once in a blue moon."

"One of his other grandchildren. But you don't know which one? And you don't know what is on it?"

"I was going to check but, honestly, we aren't supposed to connect any outside devices with our computers in case they could have a virus that could damage our systems. I know it's kind of over-the-top, but..."

"No, that's probably the best. Look... can I come over right now and get it? Would you mind?"

"Well, of course not. That would be perfectly fine. I just assumed that you would be at work."

"I'm working from home right now. But I could come over to pick it up."

"Certainly. Just ask for Mirabelle at the reception desk. I'll bring it to you. Or if you want me to return it to your grandfather, I can leave it in his room, and you can get it from him and explain what it is. I think he understood that it might have pictures on it, but when I said it could be a video or some other document or database, he said that you should be the one to look at it."

Margie's heart was pounding. "Yes, he's absolutely right. If you'll just hang on to it, I'll be right over."

She grabbed her laptop and was looking around for her laptop bag to put it into when someone came in the door. She whirled around, her heart leaping and her hand jumping to her gun before seeing that it was Detective Lewis Riley.

"Oh." She blew out her breath. "You startled me. Man. Okay. My heart is fine now."

"Everything okay?"

She gave him a look. Was everything okay? He had to know that everything was not okay, that with her and her family being threatened at every turn, everything was most definitely not okay.

"Sorry," Lewis held his hands up in surrender. "Bad question on my part. I didn't think. I take it that things have not improved since the report of your car being vandalized last night?"

"Not just vandalized. They included a brick with a note threatening my family. And in case you didn't notice out there," Margie motioned to the door and the street outside, "The neighborhood is crawling with Alberta Warriors, which I cannot do anything about. And one of them tried to get onto the bus with my daughter this morning."

"Oh. Yeah, I can see how that could make you jumpy."

"And I just got a call that someone sent a package to my grandfather, and I have no idea what might be on the USB drive that they delivered to him. I don't know how they would even know where my grandfather is. Unless one of them was following us last night, which I guess is completely within the realm of possibility."

Lewis noted the laptop in her hand and nodded to it as Margie found a soft-sided case and slid it inside. "You're going to find out?"

"Yes. And don't try to talk me out of it or tell me that I shouldn't be putting some unknown device into my computer when I don't know what will happen. I'll keep it offline so it can't infect anything else, but I need to know what's on the USB drive right now. I'm not going to wait for a forensic team."

Lewis nodded. "Fair enough. Do you want some company?"

Margie took a steadying breath. "Sure. Yeah."

"Shall we take my car?"

"It's only a couple of blocks away."

"Oh, that's nice and handy. With the neighborhood crawling with Alberta Warriors, do you really want to walk over there and lead them all directly to him?"

Margie stopped and looked at him. "No."

"Hop in my car. We can zip down Deerfoot, make it look like we're going over to Alexander's house, and then loop back around when we're sure we don't have a tail."

Margie didn't have the time to analyze every aspect of the suggestion, but it sounded like a better idea than just walking into the care center with a half dozen Warriors on her tail.

"Okay. Sounds good."

"I'll stay here until we have a plan," Detective Jones said, lowering her phone from her ear. "Alexander is fine and Quinn is staying home. They're not going anywhere until things settle down."

❧

LEWIS WAS a good driver and an effective agent. By the time they looped around, Margie was certain they didn't have anyone on their tail, so she could rest easy that they were not leading the fox straight into the hen coop. The woman at the desk called Mirabelle, one of the nursing aides, who brought Margie the USB drive quickly, not making them wait an extended length of time while she completed other duties. Margie was grateful not to have to wait.

Margie inserted the drive into her USB port and navigated to it on the file system. She did not have the computer set to autorun anything inserted into the port. When she double-clicked the drive icon, she was prompted for a password.

"Do you know what the password is?" Lewis asked unnecessarily.

Margie thought about it. How many chances would she have to get it right? Unlimited attempts? Three? One?

If it was a USB drive sent to her by the Alberta Warriors via Moushoom to damage her computer or get her information, then she had already bypassed that by not allowing it to autorun.

But what had Mirabelle said? She had said that it had come from another grandchild.

What if it had?

"Let's go see him," Margie said, picking up her laptop and heading toward Moushoom's room.

Lewis followed her immediately. "Yes, ma'am."

Margie knocked on Moushoom's door and poked her head in. "Moushoom?"

He was not in the middle of a bath or a meal, but was parked near the TV as usual. His face crinkled into a big smile.

"My daughter!"

Margie motioned Lewis in behind her. "Detective Riley, this is Moushoom. Moushoom means grandfather."

Lewis nodded his head respectfully. "Lewis, sir."

"Sir," Moushoom chuckled. "You got here fast, daughter. I didn't expect to see you here during the day."

"I was working at home, so I thought I would just come over. Do you have the package this came in?"

He nodded and gestured to the garbage can. "It is over there."

Margie pulled on a pair of gloves before picking it up. It was a media mailer, stiff cardboard that could be picked up at any Staples store in bulk. She turned it over and saw that it was addressed not to her grandfather, but to Margie in care of Moushoom. She blinked at that, frowning to herself. She looked at the corner for the sender's address and saw Laura's name hand-lettered. She remembered Laura's neat printing. It hadn't changed in the years since they were teenagers.

She sat down, her knees suddenly weak.

"What is it?" Moushoom questioned. "Are you okay?"

Margie nodded. She tried to speak calmly and clearly around the lump in her throat. "It's from Laura," she said. "And it's directed to me." She checked the postmark to confirm it was mailed before Laura's death, but the imprint was unreadable. She didn't even know if they were dated anymore. Or just some machine-readable marking that the naked eye could not decode.

"From Laura?" Moushoom's expression softened. "What would she have sent?"

"I guess she knew your address but didn't know mine, so she sent it to you instead."

"She sends Christmas cards," Moushoom explained.

"So she had your address on her Christmas card list." Margie swallowed hard and looked at Lewis.

"You still need the password," he reminded her.

Margie nodded. It had been addressed to her, not to Moushoom. Therefore, the password was something that she would know. She opened her laptop back up and tapped the password in. The contents of the drive were listed on the screen.

Lewis's brows went up. "Well, that was quick."

"We had a secret handshake, too."

He smiled.

Moushoom was leaning forward in his wheelchair, trying to see what Margie was doing.

"Is it pictures? Mirabelle thought that it was probably pictures."

Margie scanned through the short list of files. "There is a video. But I don't think I should play it here."

"A video from Laura? Maybe it's of Quinn."

"No, I don't think so. She sent it to me. We hadn't been in touch much recently, and I think it was probably something that she wanted me to look into as a police detective. Which means that it isn't a video of Quinn. It might be something disturbing. Not something I would play for you."

Moushoom scowled. "I am not a child," he reminded her. "I have probably seen far more disturbing things than you have."

She would have agreed with him if she hadn't been a law enforcement officer in Winnipeg for ten years. She was sure that Moushoom had seen some terrible things in his time, especially in his residential school years, but she wasn't about to show him a video that might include torture or murder.

CHAPTER TWENTY-TWO

*D*espite Moushoom's objections, Margie and Lewis returned to his car before playing the video. Margie held the laptop on her lap and angled it so that they could both see it.

As it turned out, there was no need to see the video. The camera was pointed at a wall in a dark corner. It was the audio that Laura had been capturing—a couple of voices discussing the arrangements for the arrival of a large shipment of drugs.

The first time through, Margie tried to make out each word. Some of the conversation was quite muffled. She could get the overall shape of it, but she wished she could understand more.

The deal was to go down tonight, so they wouldn't have a lot of time to prepare for it, if they wanted to disrupt the Alberta Warriors' pipeline right away. There were enough details there to be able to stop and confiscate the drugs. But Lewis was more concerned with being able to get the person giving the orders.

Margie played the recording again. She listened carefully for every clue she could find about who the people discussing the deal were. Unsurprisingly, she didn't know all the players involved. She had only been dealing with homicide since transferring to Calgary and, while some of those murders had been connected with the Alberta Warriors, they had been lower-level deals, and she didn't know any of the really big players in the organization.

But Lewis had been undercover, trying to get all of the details he could about the Warriors' involvement in drug trafficking in the province for some months, and he would, Margie hoped, have a better idea of who the players were.

The car was cool, but Lewis reached over and turned off the heater. Margie played the recording again and, this time, without the noise of the heater fan, it was a little clearer.

"How did Laura find anything out?" Lewis asked, giving Margie a stern look as if she had been arguing with him about the case. "How would she know anything about the Alberta Warriors and what was coming down the pipeline?"

"Well…" Margie thought about it. "She was working with the kids in the halfway house. A good number of them were Alberta Warriors."

"But they wouldn't have any knowledge of a big shipment like this. They might be aware of what was going on through the juvenile facility, maybe even the halfway house. But in Carburn Park or one of the other parks nearby? How would she hear about that?"

Margie stared at him for a minute, trying to understand what he was encouraging her to see. Then, as she played the audio again, it clicked into place. Her eyes met Lewis's.

§♠

THERE WERE two separate police actions, both timed to go down simultaneously so that one party could not tip off the other. As planned, there was a team in place to stop the deal going down in the park.

And downtown, Margie was with Lewis at the halfway house, where he knocked politely on the door some time after curfew. It was a while before the door was opened. They didn't hear yelling back and forth this time. Everybody was, Margie suspected, in their bedrooms with their lights out, so they weren't allowed to go to the front door to take callers. It was Mrs. Craig herself that opened the door.

She looked in confusion at Margie and Lewis. She shook her head.

"What? I don't understand what you're here for. You must know that it's after curfew. None of the kids can talk to you right now."

"We aren't here to talk to the kids."

"What is it, then? Can't you wait until morning?"

"You were very helpful when we were here before," Lewis said. "What has changed?"

"I don't think this is appropriate. You shouldn't be here after curfew. And I don't think I should let you talk to any more of the kids. They can't help you. They're all just working on their own rehabilitation. If they know anything about what happened to Laura—and I don't think for a minute that any of them have any knowledge about it—then you should come back during the day and make sure that they've had a chance to talk to their court-appointed advocates before you start asking them more questions. I just don't like the way you're taking advantage of these kids."

"Or maybe you're afraid they'll pick up on what's happening in the house or slip up and tell us something we don't already know. Like they did yesterday. No matter how careful they are and how hard they try to obey what they've been told, kids still make mistakes and, once the cracks start to show… people like Laura figure out what's going on."

"I don't know what you're talking about," Mrs. Craig said, shaking her head. "Why don't you come back in the morning with a warrant? I'm not required to let you into the house and I don't think it is a good idea. If you are going to bully and take advantage of these kids, I'll go to the papers. I'll go over your heads and report you."

"You mean one of these?" Lewis held up a piece of paper folded lengthwise. The backer was headed "Warrant."

Mrs. Craig's eyes widened. She hesitated, not sure what to do. Slam the door in their faces and hope they wouldn't break it down? Throw out accusations or try to confuse them? Let them talk to the kids and hope that they didn't really know enough to cause anyone any trouble?

"Mrs. Craig?" Margie held out her hand to shake, and Mrs. Craig mirrored her movement, muscle memory responding before her body could process the competing directions from her brain. Margie took Mrs. Craig's hand. "You're under arrest." She snapped a bracelet over the supervisor's wrist and immediately turned her and reached for the other arm. Mrs. Craig resisted.

"No, what are you doing?"

She was too slow to pull back, and Margie had the other bracelet in place. She held Mrs. Craig still and searched her pockets, waistband, bra, and any other hiding places normally utilized by the criminal element.

There was disruption from within the house, kids shouting back and forth. Margie looked at Lewis, bracing for trouble. She guided Mrs. Craig out of the house into the waiting hands of the other law enforcement officers. The others breached the house, hurrying in the door and spreading throughout the house to check for any other trouble. They hoped that by flooding the house immediately with as many LEOs as possible, they could prevent any further violence and protect those who were not actively involved in the gangs from those who were.

One other supervisor was present that they hadn't met on their first visit to the house. Lewis sat her down in one of the cars lined up in front of the house and called in to the members of his ALERT team who were standing by to find out if she had any criminal record or known association with gangs in Calgary or in the rest of the province or any of the neighboring provinces. It would likely take a few hours to be sure that she was clear, if she was.

All of the youth were removed to the police department until they could be cleared and returned, once there were adults who could properly supervise them once more. They were down at least two supervisors, possibly more.

Lewis was talking with Patrick. Margie took on Ceci, hoping to do the investigation justice. Ceci had been put in an interview room by herself, keeping her isolated so that she didn't have a chance to talk to anyone else in person or on the phone. Her phone had, of course, been confiscated for the investigation. All properly papered.

Ceci looked at Margie as she entered the room, her eyes dark and suspicious. She had not washed her mascara off before going to bed, or else she hadn't gone to bed yet. It was smeared and streaked now.

"Is it true?" she asked immediately. "You arrested Mrs. Craig?"

Margie nodded. "She has been arrested for her involvement in the drug trafficking that Laura was trying to stop, and in Laura's murder."

She observed Ceci for her reaction to this news.

Ceci blew out her breath and her shoulders slumped. "Really? It's over?"

Margie nodded. She sat down across from Ceci. "Why don't you tell me what happened? How did you get involved in this?"

"I wasn't involved," Ceci said immediately. "I was trying to get out of the gang. Mrs. Clothier was helping me. She said she could help me to get out and they wouldn't bother me anymore. But..." She shook her head, blinking and swallowing hard. "We couldn't tell her about Mrs. Craig."

"If you had..." Margie didn't finish.

Maybe Laura wouldn't be dead.

"*I* would be dead," Ceci declared. "If any of us had said anything about her..." She just shook her head, choked up, and wasn't able to say anything further.

"Laura was trying to help you."

"You think I don't know that? She was *real*. She meant it when she said she wanted to help. It wasn't just words. But it was too big for her. I knew she suspected someone else in the house was leaking information, but she figured it was one of the other kids."

"But then she figured out it was Mrs. Craig. And she recorded a conversation between her and one of the bosses late at night."

Ceci scrubbed at her eyes with her fists. "She shouldn't have done that. She should have just stayed out of it."

"She wanted to make things safe for you and the others."

"How did you find out?"

"She sent me a copy of the recording."

"She did?" Ceci shook her head. "I didn't know. She said she would take care of things, but I didn't think she knew."

"You knew she knew about the trafficking through the park."

Ceci looked for a way to deny it, then finally nodded. "Yeah. She had seen things going on in the park near her house. She said she knew they were Warriors. She said that if you wanted to stop it, you had to stand up to them. That if everyone stood up and said they wouldn't put up with the gangs and trafficking in their community, they could drive the gangs out." She pressed her lips together, obviously not in agreement. Look what had happened to Laura.

"'The only thing necessary for the triumph of evil is that good men do nothing,'" Margie quoted.

"She said that," Ceci admitted.

"She believed it. Laura always stood up for what she believed in."

CHAPTER TWENTY-THREE

*I*n Carburn Park once more, Margie watched the small group of mourners grow as they were joined by other members of the community, law enforcement officers who had worked on the case in various capacities, and members of the extended family whom Margie hadn't seen in years. She couldn't identify them all, but she continued to smile at them despite her mask and to give hugs and handshakes despite the risk of infection. At least it was an outside gathering. She didn't think they were breaking any of the gathering restrictions meeting there for the small memorial service.

Christina was in charge of Moushoom's wheelchair and pushed him back and forth between people so he could say hello to all the family members he had been missing. He was clearly one of the social centers of the gathering. At the other nucleus, Alexander and Quinn did not appear to know as many of those who had come to celebrate the life of his wife. But they continued to nod and shake hands anyway, meeting many of them for what would be the first and last time.

Eventually, much later than planned, Margie called for everyone's attention and held the microphone in front of Moushoom's face.

He started with a short introduction, thanking everyone for coming and telling them about Laura and her escapades as a child. He looked at Margie a few times, and she nodded for him to continue. She had to switch the position of the microphone a few times due to sore muscles, but she let him talk for however long he wanted to.

Eventually, he started a smudge, burning herbs on a salver and waving the smoke, offering it at each point of the compass. He chanted in Michif and Cree, flowing from one to the other without any apparent effort. Margie could understand most of the Michif but little of the Cree. More that she needed to learn if she wanted to keep the traditions of her forefathers alive.

He switched to English once more and prayed to the Great Spirit to watch over Laura and guide her to her fathers and her father's fathers. There, she would watch over her husband and son until they could join her someday. He looked at the young people assembled to one side. Not cousins, but residents of the halfway house. He blessed them to be strong like Laura and always stand up for their beliefs. There were tears in the eyes of most of those prison-hardened faces.

Eventually, he was finished. Margie thanked him and invited everyone to stay as long as they wanted to and to enjoy the park Laura had loved and reclaim it from the men who had committed violence there.

She drifted over to Lewis, nodding and not sure what to say to him after the ceremony. She had no idea what he thought of her traditions.

She looked toward the kids from the halfway house. "I'm surprised at how many of them came."

"They really were her kids. They knew she cared about them."

She looked over their faces. "Patrick didn't come. I thought he was one of her special cases. I thought he would."

Lewis's lips tightened.

Margie waited for him to say what he was thinking, but he didn't.

"Do you know why he didn't come?" Margie prompted.

"He's gone."

"Gone where?"

"That remains to be seen."

"You think he's gone to the Alberta Warriors somewhere?"

"I talked to him after Mrs. Craig's arrest. He was in pretty bad shape. Relieved that she was gone, but I think…"

Margie waited.

"*Someone* told them that Laura had recorded their conversation."

"You think that was Patrick?"

He nodded.

Margie sighed. "That poor boy."

"That poor boy?" Lewis repeated. "You feel bad for him?"

"He didn't know how to get out. These kids have been wrapped up in gangs from the time they were young. It was how they grew up. How they survived juvie. How they would survive after they got out. What happened to them is the fault of the adults who used them. The fault of the circumstances they grew up in. They wanted out. They didn't want to be responsible for someone else's death. The death of someone who cared for them. But it was a matter of survival."

Lewis shook his head. "You're more forgiving than I would be."

Margie let out a long breath. "Someday… we'll get rid of these gangs."

LEWIS SHOOK HIS HEAD. "The gangs will always be there."

CARBURN PARK

Carburn Park, located along the Bow River in Calgary, is a sprawling 135-hectare natural oasis that offers a rich blend of constructed and natural environments for outdoor enthusiasts. The park features two man-made ponds, walking trails, and a regional pathway that meanders through diverse habitats, including a riverine deciduous forest, shrublands, and open spaces.

Nature lovers will appreciate the chance to observe various species of fish-eating birds like Belted Kingfishers and Great Blue Herons around the ponds, as well as diving ducks such as Common Goldeneye in the river channel. With its mix of narrow nature trails flanked by lush greenery and fast-flowing river waters, Carburn Park provides a serene escape where visitors can immerse themselves in Calgary's natural beauty

The author recalls BBQ and canoeing at the park with her son's Cub Scout troop, and running to, around, and back from the park while doing half-marathon training.

BENEATH THE ICY DEPTHS

To those fighting to take back the cold, dark nights.

CHAPTER ONE

*M*argie was working at her desk. Snoozing, if she were to be honest with herself. The bullpen was warm and Margie had hit her midafternoon slump, trying to push through some paperwork but making little progress.

The phone ringing jolted her awake. She nearly fell out of her chair. She reached for the receiver, looking at the phone number on the display as she did so. The number was familiar, but she couldn't put a name to it until she picked it up and heard the voice.

"Detective Patenaude," she greeted.

"Detective Parks Pat," Gagnon's French-accented nasal voice drilled into her ear. "They're asking for you at this scene."

She knew that Gagnon had been called out to a newly discovered body an hour or two earlier. She had envied his going out, even though she didn't much feel like standing outside in the cold today. At least it was something to do.

"They're asking for me?" she repeated.

"They need your particular area of expertise."

Margie's area of expertise was nothing more than having been called out to attend a few murder scenes at Calgary parks, which had led to her being dubbed Parks Pat, and now she was the expert on bodies found in parks and wilderness areas.

She also attributed it in part to her Métis heritage. It gave her a bit of mystique, with people thinking that due to her European explorer and Indigenous Cree ancestry, she must have some special connection with nature and have learned tracking and lore at her parents' knees.

She was doing her best to learn more about Mother Earth and her secrets from Moushoom, her grandfather, but Margie had grown up a city girl and was woefully bereft of instinct in the area of tracking or even following a map. It was a standing joke how easily she could get lost, even following GPS directions.

But, despite Margie's lack of skills or specialized knowledge, she was the proclaimed expert on deaths in parks, and they would keep calling her out to the scenes of murders or accidents in Calgary parks for as long as she worked homicide in the city. There was no shaking the name and reputation now.

"We're at Bowness Park," Gagnon told her. "You know it?"

"Sure, I know Bowness Park," Margie agreed, happy she was familiar with this one. She remembered visiting Bowness Park as a child on vacations to Calgary. Most of her trips there had been during the summer, when they had enjoyed picnics and BBQs, riding the zip line, and playing tag on the other playground equipment. The couple of Christmases that she had spent in Calgary, they had gone skating on the lagoon in Bowness. There had been fires and hot chocolate, and it had been a lot of fun. Margie had enjoyed skating and had not been bothered at all by her fear of water. Frozen water held no terrors for her.

Boating during the summer was another story. But skating in the winter was a good memory. She had loved spending that time with her cousins and other members of her extended family.

"So you can get out here?" Gagnon pressed.

"Yeah, you bet. I have my car. It should take me about… half an hour to get down…" Margie hazarded a guess, even though she had no idea how long it would actually take.

"Dress warmly," Gagnon warned.

Margie had her toque, gloves, and other winter gear in the car, so that wouldn't be a problem. The weather had been mild the last few days, but she knew it would be colder in Bowness Park than downtown.

"I'll be there as soon as I can," Margie promised.

As Margie stood up and got ready to go, Detective Katelyn Jones was returning to her desk after getting coffee from the breakroom

"Parks Pat is on call," Margie advised Jones. "Bowness Park."

"Have fun," Jones told her cheerfully. "Don't worry about the rest of us, stuck at our desks flipping through dusty cold cases."

"Well, I guess I've got a cold case of my own," Margie laughed.

CHAPTER TWO

*M*argie worried at first that she had taken a wrong turn, it was taking so long to drive to Bowness Park. She didn't remember it being so far west. She had thought it just the other side of Crowchild Trail, but it was a long way past that. The GPS wasn't objecting that she had missed a turn, so she kept going, following the instructions as they were dictated to her and shown on the screen.

Then she did miss the turn into the park. The entrance was well-hidden. Margie swore when the GPS instructed her to perform a U-turn to get back to the park.

After she got turned around and took another run at it, she found the initial descent into the park familiar even after all the years since she had been there as a child. Margie knew she was in the right place.

She spotted a police car in the main parking lot and an officer stood nearby with a black mask, high-vis traffic vest, and orange baton, chatting with park patrons. It was evident that there wasn't much for him to do there. All of the experts were probably there ahead of Margie.

She drove up slowly, waiting for him to finish talking with an older couple before turning his attention to her.

"Detective Patenaude," Margie announced herself after rolling down the window and letting the brisk air in.

"Ah, Detective. You are this way," he pointed the baton to the roadway she should take. "Just keep following it around. You won't be able to miss all of the other vehicles."

"Thank you."

She rolled the window up again. Gagnon was obviously right about her needing to dress warmly. It was always colder near the water and there was a brisk wind.

She followed the road around and, after a couple of kilometers, found the site of the accident.

She had a lot more winter gear in her trunk than she needed walking only from her house to the car and the car to the office. But she always preached preparedness to Christina. A person couldn't trust that the car would always work and that she wouldn't have a breakdown or get into a motor vehicle accident and end up standing at the side of the road or pushing the car out of an intersection. Margie pulled on ski pants, swapped her shoes for boots, put a puffy vest on under her coat, and bundled up with her warmest gloves, hat, and face covering.

She felt like the Michelin Man as she walked to the line of vehicles and the people gathered there ahead of her. She found Gagnon with a couple of patrolmen with red noses and Tim's coffee cups.

He was a heavy man, made to look even rounder with the bulk of his winter jacket. His face mask was pulled down to drink the coffee, and there was frost in his mustache.

He nodded a greeting to her. "I'm sure everyone knows Parks Pat," he said, without bothering to introduce any of the other law enforcement officers to her. "Found it okay?"

"Yeah, no problem." Or only one, anyway. Margie gazed out at the river. While there was ice and snow at the edges, there was still a wide channel of dark water running down the center. Too early in the season for it to be completely iced over. Even when it was, people would need to be careful and know how thick or thin the ice was. She had seen cars drive on the river when it was fully iced in, but she wouldn't choose to walk on it herself. She would stick to the pond, lagoon, or irrigation ditches. Nothing with fast-moving water. She knew enough about the river to respect it.

There were a number of figures out on the ice dressed in dark coats, too far away for her to make out the insignia. A yellow raft had been inflated but sat unused on the ice. Some men in wet suits stood around talking as if they didn't have a care in the world and were completely unaffected by the cold.

"So, what have we got?" she asked.

"Body discovered in the river," Gagnon pointed to a bright fleck of color at the edge of the ice. "Got caught on a log. They're going to attempt to retrieve the body in a few minutes."

"Did anyone see it happen? Do we know who it is?"

"No. Someone walking over the bridge saw it," Gagnon shifted his pointing finger to the wide bridge past the body caught on the log. "They called it in and, gradually, we got everyone out here to discuss the best way to retrieve it. The ice is thick enough over here," he pointed to the larger group of people, "but not out there," he indicated the men in the wet suits. "They are trained in cold water rescue, so this is their thing. I don't know yet whether they will go out in the boat and approach it from the water or see if they can crawl out on the ice and pull it in that way."

Margie shuddered. "Better them than me. I don't think I'll be volunteering to be part of *that* team."

"Wouldn't get me out there either," Gagnon agreed. "I had a friend drown when I was a teenager. Playing on the ice before it was safe." He shook his head. "Ice opened up right in front of me. Water was as black as pitch. Like a gateway to hell."

Margie shuddered, even though she was warm in her winter clothing, at the thought of seeing something like that happen right before her eyes. Or worse, having it happen to her. She could imagine the ice water closing in around her, chilling her to the bone and pulling her under.

"That's horrible," she told Gagnon.

He made one of those indescribably French grunts of acknowledgment. "Oui."

Margie smiled. "We say *oui* too, but we spell it w-i-i."

He raised his brows inquiringly. "What?"

"In Michif. The Métis language. We say *wii*."

"Ah." He nodded. "It is all a bastardized French, is it not? Pidgin?"

Margie resisted the urge to snap at him. He knew something about Michif at least, and was making an inquiry to understand more. It was good to ask questions, even if she didn't like his approach.

"From my understanding of the definitions, it is a creole, not a pidgin."

"Creole like New Orleans?" He shook his head. "It's not the same."

"A creole is two different languages joining to become a new language. A pidgin is a simplified version of a language. Some say Michif is creole and some say it isn't. But it is a mix of French and Cree and some other influences."

Gagnon nodded. "I see."

The men out on the ice began to move. Margie watched the men in wet suits begin to push the raft. But they didn't push it out into the river as she had expected them to. They pushed it along the ice toward the point where the body was caught on a branch or log. Margie and Gagnon watched, both tense.

As the men in wet suits got closer to the body, Margie heard the ice cracking. She looked down at her feet as if cracks might appear there, but she was standing on the shore and didn't need to worry that the cracks in the ice would extend to her feet. Then she looked at the other law enforcement officers and techs standing halfway out. What if the cracks in the ice extended to them?

But they watched, seeming unconcerned. Maybe someone had measured the thickness of the ice and had already established that it was safe at that point. There were a lot of them standing too close together for Margie's comfort, putting a lot of weight on that one part of the ice. She could just picture the shelf breaking off and floating down the river with them still on it.

There were louder pops and cracks of ice under the raft, sounding like gunshots in the distance. There were shouts from the men in wet suits, and then, all at once, the ice beneath the raft broke, and they all slipped into the raft, as graceful as swans, as if that was what they had planned to do all along. Maybe it was.

They controlled the movement of the raft with paddles and poles and snugged it up against the log so that a couple of them could work on freeing the body while the other held the craft in place. Margie was breathing through her open mouth, panting as hard as if she were the one doing all the physical work.

If they went into the water, they would be fine. They were dressed for it. They had trained for it. But she could barely breathe, waiting for them to fall in. Gagnon too was tense, looking like he would grab her if things did not go well. They made a good pair.

Margie blew out a shaky breath and tried to laugh at herself, but the high giggle that came out of her would not fool anyone.

With a great heave, the rescuers managed to pull the body into the raft. They then pushed it away from the log and continued to travel downstream. A few meters farther down, there was a clean shelf of ice. They got close to it, and then two of them jumped out, grabbed the ropes along the side of the raft, and pulled it up onto the ice.

They pulled the raft to the shore, laughing and shouting as if they were having the time of their lives. Margie supposed they were high on adrenaline after tempting fate in the icy water.

Once the raft was pulled to the shore, everyone moved toward it, picking their way through the brush and rocks to reach it and look inside.

"There's your ice queen," one of the men in a wet suit announced. "None the worse for wear."

"Nicely done," said one of the law enforcement officers who had been watching the operation from the safety of the ice. "What about other forensics? Trace on the log? Any other foreign materials caught in the branches?"

"Nothing obvious. Just her and some twigs. Flotsam."

Margie was close enough to see that the man who approached the body first was a crime scene tech she had run into at other sites. She stayed back and waited for him to take pictures and examine the woman's outer clothing.

The victim had obviously not intended to go for a swim. She wasn't prepared for the possibility like the men in the wet suits. The heavy clothing she wore would have pulled her down immediately, dragging her under the water. The icy water would quickly have incapacitated her and made it impossible for her to get herself back to safety. Margie's throat closed as she thought of being dragged under the surface by the weight of her clothes.

The tech muttered to his companions as they examined the body carefully, documenting everything.

"Was her coat torn before you pulled her off of the branch?"

The foremost man in a wet suit shrugged. "It was after we pulled her off."

The tech shook his head in irritation.

Margie thought that the men had done well, considering the circumstances. No one had been hurt or ended up in the water, and they were able to retrieve the body on the first try and not dump her back in the water. All in all, it was a pretty successful venture and not one that she would have volunteered for.

The tech eventually unbuttoned the heavy winter coat to give them a better look at the body.

It was a woman, as the rescuer had indicated. She had long hair frozen into intertwining sticks in a mass around her head. She had a couple of scrapes and bruises on her pale white face. The body under the coat was not slim. Not all of the bulk was the coat—a lot of it was the woman herself. The rescuers must have both been pretty strong to be able to move a woman of her size, especially a dead weight, clothing soaked in water.

The tech described the woman into a hand-held digital recorder, estimating her height and weight.

"She doesn't look like she's been dead long," Margie said. She had seen bodies bloated up in the water, features unrecognizable. Maybe it took longer when the water was so cold.

"No, don't think so," the tech told her after turning off his recorder. "Last night, probably. And she wasn't completely submerged, snagged on the log like that."

Margie nodded. She didn't take out her notebook to note down this information. She would save as much writing as she could for when she was back in her car with the heater on and the doors shut to keep out the wind. Her gloved fingers tingled from the cold despite the layers of insulation she had bundled herself in.

"Any identification?" Gagnon asked.

The tech patted her coat and shook his head. "Will have to check more carefully at the morgue. No obvious wallet. But most women carry their wallet in a purse, not coat pockets."

"No purse?" Margie asked. "Nothing caught on the log?"

"No. Might want to conduct a search downriver, see if it washed up on shore."

CHAPTER THREE

*T*here wasn't much to be discovered at the scene. The techs scouted both upstream and downstream, hoping to identify the spot where the woman had gone into the water or whether any of her possessions had washed up, but the snow and ice obscured any evidence of the accident scene. There were numerous animal tracks along the way where birds had landed or other animals had walked out to drink from the river. Quite a few human tracks, too. Margie was surprised by the number of people who had walked out onto the ice without any apparent concern for their safety. It was impossible to tell when the victim had crossed the ice or where she had entered the water.

"Accident?" Margie proposed to Gagnon as they stripped off their winter gear at the office. The indoor air seemed almost too warm after her time in the frigid outside weather.

"We'll see what the Office of the Chief Medical Examiner has to say," Gagnon said with a shrug of his bulky shoulders. "OCME gets the final say."

"But that's what it looked like to you?"

"Not a shooting or a stabbing, no apparent injuries other than a smack or two on the head. She could have been drunk or drugged. A lot of people who die of hypothermia are."

Margie hadn't smelled any alcohol, but she wasn't sure that she had been close enough to. "She seemed well put together. Good clothes, manicured nails."

Gagnon nodded. "Doesn't rule out being drunk."

"No, of course not," Margie agreed. Plenty of rich people got drunk occasionally or were closet alcoholics. The same held for drug use. And since the legalization of marijuana, there were a lot more people experimenting or indulging on special occasions. People in all walks of life, some taking it for recreation and some for chronic pain or nausea.

"What was someone like her even doing at the park at night, though?" Gagnon asked.

"We haven't established for sure that it was at night."

"No, but you would think that if she had gone in the water during the day, someone would have noticed and called for help. Or would have told her to stay off of the ice or away from the edge."

"True," Margie conceded. She couldn't see how either scenario worked. She couldn't see a reason for the woman to go to the edge of the ice on the river during the day or the night. Maybe she lived in one of the houses near the park and had sleepwalked into the water. It had been known to happen. The cold water would have woken her up but, once she was in the water, it was too late. Margie just couldn't see any other way it might have happened. Unless... "Suicide?" she suggested. "Maybe it was intentional."

"What a way to go," Gagnon said, shaking his head. His dark eyes were haunted. Remembering the friend he had lost? The ice opening up like the gates of hell in front of him? She wondered how the experience had affected him over the years.

"Not the way I would choose," Margie agreed. "But it would be quick. And no way to change your mind once you were in."

§.

CHRISTINA CALLED to check in with Margie when she got home from school. "We're getting close to the Indigenous Fair," Christina commented before either of them had a chance to talk about how their days had gone. "I can't believe it. When it was rescheduled, I thought we had plenty of time to get everything done, and now... there's no time left!"

"Not much," Margie agreed with a smile. "You'll be glad to have it off your plate when it's done."

"Will I ever. I feel like I haven't done anything else this year, just organizing the darn thing. It was a lot more work than I thought it would be. I pictured… putting a few posters up and people volunteering to do booths or presentations, and that's it. It would all just come together by itself. But it's been such a lot of work."

And soon, she would need to study for her first semester final exams. Margie hoped Christina would use some of the Christmas break to do practice tests and prepare for finals. Everyone was anxious about whether the kids had learned everything they were supposed to during the COVID lockdown and then so many students and teachers being out sick during the Delta wave.

They had been through a lot.

"So, how are you, Mom?" Christina asked, probably having heard Margie's sigh over the phone line.

"Caught a new case today. Bowness Park."

"Parks Pat is at it again," Christina said lightly. "What happened?"

"Drowning. In the river, last night probably."

"Oh, great case for you," Christina sympathized, knowing of Margie's phobia of water.

"Well, luckily, I didn't have to get too close. There was a water rescue team to get her out, so I just stayed on the shore and watched. But it was still… whew… It still affected me."

"Of course," Christina agreed. "That's scary. Do you know who she was? How did she get in the water? Did she fall out of a boat?"

That was one scenario that Margie hadn't considered.

"No, I don't think so. It's not completely iced over—there is a channel down the center where a boat could go—but I don't think many people would do that this time of year; I don't think it would be safe. And a lot of people would notice. We think… well, we're still figuring out what we think, but we think she fell through the ice. It's too thin for people to walk on yet, and maybe she didn't know that."

She could practically hear Christina rolling her eyes. "If there is a channel down the center, you'd be pretty stupid to think it was thick enough to walk on."

"Yes. But we don't know. It could have been night and she couldn't see across. She could have been sleepwalking. It could have been suicide. Or just… I don't know; sometimes people don't think about what they are doing. 'I walked on the ice yesterday and it was fine, so I can walk on it more today…' "

"People are stupid sometimes," Christina admitted with a sigh. "So, does that mean you won't be home for dinner?"

"I think I should still be home for dinner. Let's plan on it, and I'll try to give you a heads-up if things change."

"Yeah." Christina didn't sound like she believed Margie. "Just let me know if you're running late."

"I will."

CHAPTER FOUR

"OCME has posted preliminary results," Gagnon announced from across the bullpen.

Margie frowned as she looked across the room at him. "Really? That's quick."

"I don't think it was that complicated a case. Maybe there were no other autopsies waiting and they were able to jump right into it."

Margie opened the workspace on her computer screen, and the first thing she noticed was the name.

"And she was identified?"

"She must have had ID on her after all."

Gagnon walked over and looked at it with her. He apparently preferred looking over Margie's shoulder at the result.

"Julia Louise Robertson," Margie read, "Do I know that name from somewhere?"

Jones gave a little gasp and turned toward Margie with wide eyes. "Julia Louise Robertson? She's an investigative reporter."

The gears in Margie's brain were turning. How did an investigative journalist end up drowning one night in Bowness Park? Everything suddenly took on a new light. Somebody who was just stupid and happened to be walking on the ice where it was too thin? She recalled the woman's elegant attire and perfectly manicured nails. No. It hadn't just been a casual walk, going out farther onto the ice than was advisable. She was too smart for that. And too wealthy for that neighborhood. She was a celebrated journalist, the kind who had won multiple awards and rubbed elbows with the country's rich and famous. She would not be living in Bowness. Margie had seen a few really nice houses there where people had built mini mansions for themselves, but the ones in the immediate neighborhood to the park were much more modest, and Margie couldn't see someone like Julia Louise Robertson living there.

"Do you think that's why they pushed the autopsy through so quickly?" Jones asked. "They figured out who it was and decided to prioritize it?"

Margie nodded. "It's possible. They probably want to have a preliminary answer before people start calling in demanding answers. This is one where the mayor will be calling, maybe even the prime minister. You don't want to put those guys off too long." She breathed out. "Julia Louise Robertson!"

"You're not going to find anything else out saying her name," Gagnon said irritably. "Click on the preliminary report by the ME."

Margie obeyed. There was no point in swooning over the identity of the victim. Where was that going to get her? She clicked on the report and skimmed it.

"Consistent with drowning. Water in the lungs. Likely incapacitated by the cold when she fell into the water. Scrapes and bruises on her head and face, both antemortem and postmortem."

"Got banged up in the river," Jones contributed.

"Running into a log will do that," Gagnon agreed.

"No defensive marks on hands. No other marks on the body. All consistent with accidental drowning."

"Tox results," Gagnon ordered. "I want to see the tox results."

Margie scrolled down. "Preliminary tox results. Field tests only. Negative for alcohol and the most popular recreational drugs."

"Negative." Gagnon was breathing on Margie's neck. His voice was tight as if he were angry. "I was sure the woman had been drinking. Why else would she end up in the river?"

Margie scratched the back of her neck and put her hand over it to keep Gagnon's breathing from raising goosebumps on her skin.

"So are they finding that it was an accident?" Jones asked. "I don't hear anything that rules out homicide or suicide."

"It wasn't homicide," Gagnon disagreed. "There is nothing to indicate any violence. She was out there by herself."

Jones looked at Margie, brows raised, to see what she thought. Margie shook her head. "I don't know. No preliminary manner of death. Just that the cause was cold water drowning."

"No point in looking for something that's not there," Gagnon said flatly.

"No," Margie agreed. "But this is not the final report. And we haven't completed our investigation."

"What's to investigate?" Gagnon challenged. "I'm ready to close it."

"Well, now that we know who it is, maybe interview her family and friends, see what her state of mind was lately. What she was working on. If anything unusual was going on in her life. If she regularly walked along the river."

Gagnon grunted. "I suppose we're going to have to go through the motions. Since she's someone famous. They'll accuse us of being part of a conspiracy if we don't."

"Yeah," Margie agreed. "Exactly. We don't need that kind of publicity."

Jones chuckled.

Margie clicked through the other files on the workspace—pictures of the autopsy, the clothing, jewelry, and pocket contents. Margie's own notes and Gagnon's were there as well, but she already knew what was in them.

She scrolled through the pocket contents and found that they included a reporter's notebook. Not just a cheap loonie store notebook, but a good quality one that hadn't dissolved when it got wet. The ME had carefully pressed and photographed each page while they dried. Most of it was in the reporter's shorthand. She abbreviated words and used initials to signify the people she was interviewing. She quickly jotted phrases about things that she wanted to be able to remember, but that didn't mean anything to anyone else. Margie scrolled to the end to see what the last thing was that Julia Louise Robertson had written.

CHAPTER FIVE

ENCOUNTER WITH THE ICEBERG

*M*argie stared at the words, trying to decipher their meaning. She was, of course, misreading something. Robertson hadn't been concerned about an iceberg. She wasn't on the Titanic. Maybe it was the title of a piece she was planning to write. Something about a problem that was mainly beneath the surface. Menacing. Margie hoped to uncover its meaning when she reviewed the remaining notes in the reporter's notepad.

"What is it?" Jones asked, unable to see Margie's screen from where she was sitting.

Gagnon leaned closer to the screen to squint at the words as if they were too small and he couldn't make sense of them.

"Encounter with the iceberg," he read to Jones.

"What the heck is that supposed to mean?"

"I don't know," Margie said. "Probably the title of an article she was writing."

"Oh, that would make sense, yeah."

Gagnon withdrew again so his face wasn't right beside Margie's. "Who knows what a reporter is thinking," he said as if reporters were a mysterious species of their own.

"It's just weird," Jones said. "That she would write about an iceberg and then fall through the ice and drown…"

They all considered this.

"Yeah," Margie admitted. "It is weird."

"Do you think it was a premonition? Maybe she'd had a dream about it?"

Margie looked at her. She had never known Jones to be superstitious before.

"I don't know what it's about, but I'm sure it will make sense once we've had a chance to read the rest of her materials. Maybe we can request the files she was working on from the network."

"Good luck with that," Gagnon said. "They'll never give up her files, even with a subpoena. You know how reporters are."

"But if something about it got her killed…"

"There's no indication that this is a homicide, so how are you going to persuade a judge of that? We're lucky to have the notebook that was in her pocket. Maybe there will be something interesting in there. Hopefully, something a little more enlightening than 'beware the iceberg.'"

"It didn't say 'beware the iceberg.' It says, 'encounter with the iceberg.'" Margie corrected, clicking back on the note to ensure she got it right.

"Whatever. If you're going to encounter an iceberg, you'd better beware." Gagnon snorted at his own cleverness.

Margie and Jones shook their heads. Margie looked at the time on her phone. "Well, I'd better be getting out of here. Kiddo is expecting me."

"Have a good night," Jones chirped. "Say 'hi' to Christina for me. I'll see you tomorrow."

Margie nodded. She started to get ready to go, closing the workspace and her other apps, locking her screen, and getting her purse out of the desk drawer. Gagnon was still standing behind her. She looked at him.

"Was there something else?"

"You'll do interviews with me tomorrow?" he asked.

"Yeah. Of course. You can call and set up whatever you can tonight. I'll be here in the morning, and we can go after the stand-up meeting."

He nodded his agreement. "*Oui.* Tomorrow then. *Bon.*"

"*Boon,*" Margie agreed with a smile.

CHAPTER SIX

*M*argie checked the clock on the dashboard as she arrived at the house to ensure she was not too late. She had left the office downtown in good time, but there had been a couple of traffic snarls on the way home, so she ended up being later than she had expected.

The front light was turned on. Margie let herself in. Stella leaped off the bed in Christina's room with a thump, and her paws drummed against the floor as she raced across the house. As soon as she reached the door, she started barking excitedly and jumping around Margie.

"Hi, Stella," Margie stopped to give her pets and scratch her ears. "Who's a good girl? Were you a good girl while I was at work today? Of course you were a good girl. You're always a good girl, aren't you?"

Stella settled down so that she was sitting quietly in front of Margie, her tail beating the floor.

Christina was a bit slower getting to the living room to greet Margie.

"Hey." She looked a little sleepy, and Margie wondered whether she'd been having a nap before Margie had arrived home. "I didn't start on dinner yet because I didn't know what time you were *actually* going to get home. Sometimes when you have a new case..."

"I know. Things can get crazy. But I'm not the lead on this one, and I said I needed to get home. We'll be doing interviews tomorrow. There isn't much I could do tonight anyway."

"Well, good," Christina approved. "Do you want to make something or go out for food?"

They almost always made their own food, and Christina rarely asked to go out for fast food, so it was an unusual question.

"Did you want to go out somewhere?" Margie asked, pausing in unbuttoning her coat.

"Well, we could. If you're too tired to make dinner."

"I could make dinner. But you sound like you wanted to go somewhere."

"I just think it's been a long time since we went for pizza or anything."

"You're right, it has been. Do you want to go out? Get a nice veggie pizza?"

Christina nodded. "Yeah. It would be nice to get something tonight."

"Delivery?" Margie asked.

"No, we should pick something up. So much cheaper."

The family finances were not usually Christina's concern either, though Margie tried to involve her in decision-making. It was just the two of them, and Margie wanted Christina to have some say in how their finances were handled. What things they saved money on and where they splurged. She wanted Christina to understand how finances worked when she moved out on her own.

"Okay," Margie agreed. "We'll go for pizza, then."

She had to wonder if there were something more behind Christina's suggestion to go out for pizza. Like she was going to bring up a topic that she would rather bring up with other people around so that Margie couldn't yell at her.

She remembered using that strategy on her own mother. It had, unfortunately, not worked out as well as she had hoped. She had still been in trouble. She had been embarrassed in front of friends and strangers instead of just in front of her family members at home.

"Everything going okay at school?" she asked tentatively once they were in the car, driving slowly down Seventeenth Avenue to pick out a pizzeria.

"Yeah, just like I said. Trying to get everything to work out for the

Indigenous Fair. I'm afraid people are tired of hearing it now and will just want to drop it. But some of the kids still seem excited about it."

"That's good. Don't worry about the rest. Even if you only educate one person, you never know how far that can spread and how much good it can do."

"Well, I hope I educate more than one person."

"I know."

More silence.

"And you're going to get some studying done over Christmas break?" Margie suggested. "So that you'll be ready for finals?"

"I really don't want to write finals," Christina groaned.

"Nobody does. It's just one of those things we have to put up with."

"I'll study," Christina said tiredly. "Let me get through the Indigenous Fair and Christmas first."

She sounded worn out. Margie resolved to keep a better eye on her mood and whether she was getting enough sleep.

"Don't look at me like that," Christina growled. "There's nothing wrong with me."

"No, I'm just concerned. You'll tell me if you're feeling burned out or depressed, won't you? We can do things to manage it. But I don't want you trying to handle things alone. People who try to manage all of their emotional issues by themselves end up getting in trouble."

"I'm not depressed. I'm just tired."

Margie looked away from the road to study Christina for a long moment at a red light.

"Okay," she agreed. "Just let me know. I'm here any time you need to talk."

CHAPTER SEVEN

*A*s soon as Margie walked in the office door, she was accosted by Detective Gagnon. He wore a scowl, black brows drawn down.

"We have a lot of work to get done today," he told her as if she were late getting in. "Interviews are lined up, and the bigwigs are already manning the phones, asking why it is taking us so long to get traction on the case."

"Robertson was only identified yesterday," Margie pointed out in consternation, "and the ME has only released preliminary findings. Exactly what were we supposed to have done already that we haven't?"

"Press and politicians are not well-known for their logic," Gagnon said sourly. "But they *are* known for being impatient and making a lot of noise. So we need to get to work."

Margie motioned toward the briefing room. "We still need to do morning briefing. We can't exactly get started before that is done."

"I've briefed MacDonald privately. We need to hit the pavement."

"No stand-up meeting?"

"Not for you and me. MacDonald will fill everyone else in; we're to get started."

"Well, okay." Margie had been unbuttoning her coat, but she stopped. If they were going back out again right away, there was no point in taking it off. "Just give me a minute to grab a coffee, and then we can head out."

Gagnon nodded impatiently. But Margie was already dressed and ready to go, and he was not. She was sure it would take her no longer to get her coffee than for him to get his coat and other winter gear on.

He was faster than she expected and was waiting at the door, looking at his watch when she stepped out of the breakroom.

"All right, ready to go?" Margie asked him, as if she had been waiting for him to get ready. Otherwise, he would make more impatient noises at her for having to stop to get coffee. But she needed the boost to get her brain going, especially if they were interviewing right away, without a chance to warm up and bounce ideas off of the other detectives and make sure that they had all of their bases covered.

Gagnon led the way to his car. He looked sourly at Margie's travel mug as she settled it into one of the cup holders. But she hadn't spilled a drop on the pristine surfaces of his car. Which were actually not all that pristine. She hadn't noticed the smell of cigarette smoke clinging to Gagnon before, but either he or someone else smoked in the car, and several cups and food wrappers hadn't been cleared out of the car. So what objection could he have to her drinking coffee in the car?

"Who are we seeing today?" she asked briskly.

"First off is John Calver, ex-husband,"

Exes were always a good bet when looking into an unexpected death. If it turned out that there had been foul play, the spouse or ex-spouse was always the first suspect.

"What do we know about him?"

"They married before she became well-established as an investigative journalist. So he's not... high society. They were fairly young, fresh out of school, idealistic, you know how kids are."

Margie nodded, thinking of her daughter. How long would she stay passionate and idealistic? She was eager to educate others on her Indigenous heritage and culture and that of the other Indigenous nations in the area. How long would it be before she became discouraged by those uninterested in what she had to tell them? Or would she become an advocate for her people long-term, joining up with the Native Friendship Center or one of the other organizations dedicated to education?

She sipped her coffee and focused on the job at hand. John Calver.

"How long were they together?"

"Twenty years or so. Whether they were together that whole time or not, I'm not sure. Looks like it was a somewhat rocky relationship. He did acquire more than one domestic violence charge."

"Oh, did he?"

Gagnon nodded.

"Well, that's interesting. What was the breakup like? Acrimonious?"

He glanced sideways at her. "Acrimonious?"

"Were they on good terms? Or was there a lot of conflict between them? Bitter feelings?"

"I know what acrimony is."

Then why had he challenged her use of the word? Margie gave a slight head shake.

"I wasn't able to find out too much about it yesterday," Gagnon admitted. "We'll have to see what we can find out from talking to him. We can do a courthouse search on the divorce file to see what documents were filed and what allegations were made if we need to. See what feeling we get from this guy."

Margie nodded. "Okay."

At least they weren't going into it blind. They knew that there had been domestic violence.

"You ever married?" Gagnon asked.

"Me? No. You?"

He snorted. "*Non.*"

There seemed to be a lot hidden beneath his answer, but Margie didn't think she had the time or energy to explore it. Gagnon's personal life was his own. She didn't need to know his history. They needed to find out what had happened in Julia's life.

CHAPTER EIGHT

*J*ohn Calver was also a journalist, though from the small, dirty storefront his paper operated out of, it was a rag. He had not achieved anything near the distinction Robertson had. Margie had never heard of the paper, but that didn't mean it lacked readership. She was only aware of the main city papers and news magazines on TV. Alternative press wasn't something she had any experience in.

Calver himself was a pugnacious-looking, olive-skinned man. No longer a young man, he was going gray at his sideburns and had dark rings under his eyes. The normal state of affairs, or had he been up all night thinking about his dead ex-wife?

"Mr. Calver, good to meet you," Margie greeted pleasantly. She didn't offer her hand and, in keeping with the times, neither did he or Gagnon. Calver wasn't wearing a mask, but didn't object to Margie and Gagnon wearing theirs, which suited Margie just fine. That allowed them to see his expressions more clearly, but to better keep their own thoughts more private.

"Our condolences on the passing of your ex-wife," Gagnon offered.

Calver pointed to a flimsy-looking table in the middle of the floor surrounded by mismatched chairs that might have been scrounged from a back alley.

"Things were over with Julia and me a long time ago."

255

Margie wasn't sure it was true. He looked pretty rough for someone who had not been personally affected by Julia Louise Robertson's death. But maybe his apparent dissolution was the normal state of affairs.

"How did things end between the two of you?" Margie asked once they were seated.

"We both agreed that it was time to end things. We didn't get along so well together. We had gone in separate directions over the years. Didn't really have anything in common anymore."

"It happens," Gagnon said understandingly.

Calver looked toward him and seemed to connect with him better than with Margie. "People don't expect to stay together forever these days. Even though you're showing your commitment through marriage, you know it isn't likely to last more than a few years."

"Twenty years is a good run."

"Yeah, that's what I thought. We gave it our best shot but, eventually... well, things happen. She had her career, which didn't leave much time for anything else. Our politics were different. We didn't share the same friends. We didn't share much, to be honest."

"So it made sense to formalize the separation."

"Yeah. Neither one of us really wanted the divorce, but we didn't want to stay together, either."

"Might as well be legally free of each other," Gagnon agreed. "Split the assets. Be able to see other people without complications. Go your separate directions."

"Yeah."

"Did the two of you stay in touch?" Margie asked.

"I kept track of what she was doing. And we did have a few friends in common that would mention her now and then. But direct contact... no. There was no need. Neither of us had any desire."

"So it was a pretty clean break."

He nodded. "Yes. I think it's nonsense, the whole business of 'staying friends' and still getting together for coffee or seeing each other socially after the divorce. I didn't want to have any more contact with her. That was the whole point of the divorce."

"Sure."

"I was shocked to hear about what had happened to her, very sorry to have her go that way. But there isn't anything I can help you with. I wasn't a part of her life anymore. What she would have been doing in Bowness Park or on the river—" he shook his head, "I have no idea. That wasn't her kind of thing. Very out of character."

"She didn't go for walks?"

"No. If you've seen pictures of her, you know she wasn't exactly a lightweight. She wasn't interested in exercise. Not walking or going to the gym. She drove everywhere or had a service take her. She wasn't into parks and nature."

"What was she into?"

"It was all about her work. She was into whatever she was investigating at the moment. She worked, ate, and slept whatever story she was investigating. It was all about revealing the truth."

"And you don't know what she was working on recently? What story she might have been running down?"

"No, sorry. No idea."

"Did she ever say anything to you about an iceberg?"

He shook his head, brows drawing down. "Do you mean, like, an actual iceberg?"

"We don't know. That's what we're trying to figure out."

"We didn't talk. I don't know when the last time was that I had a conversation with her. Nothing about an iceberg."

Margie nodded understandingly. She looked at Gagnon, who took up the next line of questioning.

"What were things like when the two of you were together? I notice that there were a few domestic violence charges."

"I was never convicted," Calver said immediately. "Nothing ever stuck. The cops, they're told that they have to lay domestic violence charges whenever there is a disturbance call and a couple is arguing about something. It doesn't mean there was any actual violence."

"The two of you only argued?" Gagnon asked.

"We were a married couple with separate interests. Of course we argued. That's pretty much the only kind of conversation we had in the final months. It doesn't mean that I was beating her."

"You never laid hands on her?"

"I was never convicted of anything. What does that tell you?"

It didn't tell Margie that he *wasn't* guilty of intimate partner violence. It just meant there had not been enough proof to do anything about it.

Maybe Julia had refused to testify against him, so the prosecutor hadn't had anything but the report of the police officers who had responded that she'd had a fresh bruise on her face. And that wasn't proof of anything but that she'd hit her face on something recently. She could have walked into a door like she told them. Or hit herself. Or been in a fight with a neighbor. Or the subject in a story she had been investigating.

It was almost impossible to get a conviction against a husband when his victim was shielding him.

"How many assaults?" Gagnon asked.

"What?"

"How many times were you charged? I can look it up."

Calver hesitated. He could tell Gagnon to go ahead, look it up, to be belligerent and refuse to answer. But he was trying to give the impression that he felt bad about Julia and was being helpful and cooperative. And maybe he didn't want them digging into his history and could avoid it by answering the question.

"Four times," he answered finally. His tone was flat. It was just a fact. Not something that he had to defend himself about. Not something to get excited about. It didn't mean he was a bad person. He and his wife had grown apart and had neighbors who felt it necessary to intervene when they argued.

But four was over the edge, in Margie's opinion. It was easy for a man to have the police come down on him once when he was completely innocent. Maybe his wife *had* scratched herself. Maybe he'd been drunk and taken a swing at her in front of the police, even though he had never connected and never intended to. Maybe she had simply made accusations when he had never laid a hand on her, and the police had done their duty in taking the statement.

But after that, he would be more careful. Maybe he'd get another accusation from another girlfriend ten years later when they were in the midst of a breakup.

But being charged four times for violence against his wife, that was a lot. And only the tip of the iceberg, if Margie were to borrow a term from Julia. There was no chance he had been charged every time he had been violent toward his wife. Or even half the time. They should probably check emergency room visits and see how often Julia had been treated for injuries that might have been the result of a domestic assault.

"Where were you the night before last?" Gagnon asked in the same flat tone as Calver had used.

Calver looked like he would object, would raise a fuss to point out how stupid they were being, since he didn't have anything to do with Julia anymore and had been nowhere near Bowness Park. But he schooled himself, pressing his lips together and maybe counting to ten before responding. His chin lifted a little.

"Having a drink with some friends."

"Mind if I get their names and phone numbers to confirm that?"

"That's an invasion of privacy," Calver objected. "You can't go around bugging my friends…"

"We will be discreet. But we would be remiss not to check your alibi."

Calver made more noises of objection, mostly to himself, but he pulled out his phone and gave Gagnon several names and phone numbers. The fact that he had them at hand was a good sign. They would call as soon as they separated from Calver to ensure he didn't have a chance to call them and encourage them to give a false story. If the alibi checked out, they could take Calver off of their list of suspects. Chances were that he hadn't hired or encouraged someone else to kill her so long after the divorce was over and done. People who wanted their wives killed did it while they were still married.

CHAPTER NINE

*W*here next?" Margie asked.

"Her workplace. The network."

"Oh, that's going to be fun."

They would be juggling competing interests. The network wanted Julia's death to be investigated by the police and the culprit brought to justice. Still, they would also be asserting their right to keep sources confidential and to keep any information they had that might relate to Julia's death to themselves so that they could have an exclusive exposé on her story.

And television networks were not the calmest, most sane places to work or conduct an interview to begin with.

"Do we have the name of someone to talk to?" Margie asked.

"We've been getting all kinds of phone calls. I have a few names."

Margie snorted and shook her head. Of course. The network had not sat quietly waiting for them to make the first move.

Outside the network's office, Margie and Gagnon stood for a few seconds, looking in at the bank of televisions inside the glass doors, showing what was currently playing, what was available for replay, and what was coming up. She wondered how much viewership they actually got from foot traffic walking by the building. Certainly enough to pay for a few extra monitors and feet of cable. The bright, flickering screens would suck in anyone who was walking by or waiting for the next bus or train.

Gagnon shrugged and pushed through the glass doors. They went in and found a reception desk. The woman manning it with a wireless headset was absurdly tall and thin, with short, spiked, bleached white hair and a sheath dress that belonged on a runway rather than at a reception-ist's desk. Margie wondered how long the receptionist had been trying to break into network TV herself.

"We're here to see DeeDee Strong," Gagnon told her.

She waved him to silence for a moment, listening to something on her headset. She said okay a few times, then tapped to end the call.

"So sorry," she apologized. "DeeDee? Is she expecting you?"

"We're with the Calgary Police Service," Gagnon explained. "About Mrs. Robertson."

"Oh," the receptionist drew the syllable out long. "We are all in shock here. I can't believe... None of us could believe it when we heard. Like, I was sure it had to be some other Julia Louise Robertson... There are others. It's not that uncommon a name."

"I'm sure," Gagnon agreed. "It was very shocking. Now, if you could please direct us toward Mrs. Strong..."

"Are you talking to everyone who knew her?" the woman inquired. "That must be so fascinating. I'll bet you could write a book about her after that. Though you're not allowed to, you know..." She waggled her finger at them. "We have the exclusive rights to Julia's story."

"To her authorized biography, maybe," Gagnon said dryly. "That doesn't mean no one else can write about her."

The woman's mouth dropped open and she searched for something to say. Margie had to chuckle. "We wouldn't be allowed to write it as active police officers anyway," she told the woman. "I don't think you need to worry that we'll scoop you."

"Well, it's not *my* story," she muttered as she tapped numbers into the base of her phone. "Boy, if I was given *that* job..."

She interrupted herself as the call she had placed went through.

"DeeDee, honey, I'm sorry to bother you. I know you didn't want to be interrupted, but there are a couple of police officers here asking for you. They want to talk to you about Julia."

She listened attentively, hand up to prevent anyone from asking her anything. Then she nodded.

"Yes, of course, DeeDee. I'll look after everything."

She tapped to end the call and smiled at Gagnon and Margie.

"If you'll come with me, I'll get you set up in an interview room. DeeDee will join you just as soon as she is able."

They followed her into a well-appointed room, a small boardroom or large meeting room. Two walls were glass, with tiny Venetian blinds letting in light but still allowing a measure of privacy. The other walls held a stand for coffee service and a very large screen. The table and chairs were in a beautiful rose and silver theme, with a matching silk flower arrangement on the sideboard. The receptionist motioned for them to see down. "What can I get you to drink? Coffee? Tea? Cold drinks?"

"Just a water for me, please," Margie requested. She'd had her fill of coffee for the morning, but was finding herself dry after talking to Calver. Calgary's winter air was so dry, it seemed to suck the moisture out of everything.

Gagnon looked like he would refuse, then gave a little shrug with one shoulder. "Coffee," he requested.

"Certainly. DeeDee will be with you shortly."

She slid out of the room as smoothly and silently as if on rollers. Margie looked at Gagnon.

"Julia certainly climbed the ladder a little farther than her husband."

"Probably half the reason they divorced. Husbands don't like their wives being so much more successful than they are."

Margie would have liked to argue the point and say that was a biased viewpoint and certainly didn't apply to all couples. But it was true of most of the couples that she knew well. And from what she had seen of Calver, it was probably true of him. He was a journalist too. He didn't want to stand in his wife's shadow.

The receptionist returned with water and coffee and set them on the table. "Can I get you anything else?"

"No, thank you."

She looked hesitant about leaving but, eventually, she nodded and drifted away again like a ghost.

The next person to come into the room was not DeeDee, but a man in a vest and rolled-up sleeves, straight out of central casting. He stuck his head in the door and looked at Gagnon and Margie.

"Are you the detectives? Someone said that the detectives were here to talk to us."

"Well, yes…" Margie didn't want him to invite himself into the room when they were waiting for DeeDee. Yes, they were there to conduct interviews, but they wanted to keep everything under control. Not to spend their time with people who had nothing to do with Julia's death and didn't know anything about what cases she had been working on. "But…"

"Sebastian Doucet," he introduced himself, coming the rest of the way into the room. He put a foot up on the seat of the chair and leaned an elbow on his knee. Casual, or pretending to be casual. Not sitting down with them for an interview, but just happening to be there to exchange some gossip.

"Terrible, what happened to Julia," he said with relish.

"Yes, it is," Margie agreed. "I'm sure that you are devastated about it."

"Of course," he agreed, with no show of remorse whatsoever. "You must tell me everything you know about what happened to her. It is just unbelievable. It really is."

"We're not here to tell you about everything we have," Gagnon said in a measured tone. "We are here to make inquiries to find out what her coworkers might know about what she was working on."

"Oh, I doubt if anyone knew what she was working on. We are all very suspicious of each other and don't want to get scooped. So we don't share what we are working on until it is done and in the hopper."

Margie nodded slowly. "But her boss must have known what she was working on. The editor. Her cameraman. Whoever arranged for inter-views for her."

"Julia did not get to be where she was by having loose lips. She played her cards close to the vest and made some very big stories. I'm sure you've read through the extremely long list of awards she had been given over the years. She was the cream of the crop. The network's pride and joy."

Gagnon looked Sebastian Doucet up and down. "Unlike you, who I don't remember hearing of before. What is it that you report on?"

"Oh, you've wounded me," Doucet said flamboyantly, with a hand to his breast. "I am following in Julia's footsteps! Maybe I'm not there yet, but I intend to be someday. I will be someday; you can count on that. No one is going to stop me."

A threat?

Had Julia been in his way? Someone that he perceived as blocking him from what he wanted to achieve? He certainly sounded like a jealous rival.

They both just looked at him, weighing his words. Margie got out her notebook and wrote his name in it. There. Now, he could revel in being a suspect. His name was in her notebook.

His eyes followed every movement, and he looked pleased—someone always glad to be in the spotlight.

CHAPTER TEN

$\mathcal{A}$ woman came to the door. Polished, chunky silver jewelry that coordinated and complemented the power suit she was wearing, navy, well-tailored to her shape. DeeDee Strong.

"What are you doing here?" she aimed the query at the man standing there with his foot on the chair. She looked as if she were searching her memory for his name. "Sebastian."

He cleared his throat and quickly removed his foot from the chair. "Ah, Miss Strong. Sorry, I was just… talking to the detectives. It's terrible what happened to Julia…"

"Yes, it is," the woman said. "And if you don't shove off, something could happen to you."

He made a movement halfway between a nod and a bow, and backed out of the room, nodding to each of the detectives. DeeDee watched him go and closed the door. She looked around the room as if to make sure it was secure. No one else there, no one watching, no recording devices or cameras. She let out a breath.

"I'm sure I wasn't that desperate and needy when I was a junior," she said, indicating the direction Sebastian had disappeared in. "But… it is a highly competitive business. People are always looking for a way to get one up on everyone else. To prove that they're the next big thing. It's just tooth and nail, pulling yourself up hand over hand to make something of yourself and get out there in front of an audience."

"So he's a junior?" Margie repeated. "He didn't actually know Julia?"

"Know her? Goodness, no. Not a chance. She wouldn't have had anything to do with him. The closest he might have gotten to her was to bring her a cup of coffee."

"And would she have thanked him for it?"

"Not likely," DeeDee sighed. "I'm sorry to portray the business in such a poor light, and maybe it's different at other networks, but we really can be…" She shook her head. "Selfish and self-centered, to put it politely."

"Won't you sit down?" Gagnon indicated the empty chairs at the table. "I got the names of several people at the network that want to talk to us or who might know something about Julia… But I picked you out as the person most likely to be able to help us. If you can't, hopefully you can point us in the right direction."

"I'll do my best."

"I got the feeling that you and Julia knew each other quite well. I'm not sure whether you were friends or rivals."

DeeDee spread her hands apart. "Both, I guess. We loved each other and were the best of friends. Loved to go out and do things together. But we were also always in competition. In everything. Breaking a story. Finding the perfect Christmas gift. It didn't matter what it was. We couldn't help ourselves."

"Is that because you were so much alike?" Margie suggested.

"Yes, I would say so. We were always after the same prize. Tended to think the same way. So it was pretty hard to stay out of each other's way. I don't know what I will do… now that she's gone. Things will be boring around here."

"You won't have anyone to compete with?"

"Well, there are still plenty of people to compete with, but it won't be the same. There aren't very many other people at my level. You might think I'm being egotistical, but it's the truth. People recognize our faces. We are household names. People know that if we bring them a story, it's going to be big. It's breaking news, and we will have uncovered something no one else could have. We're the best in the business."

Not egotistical at all.

"I wonder if you know anything that was going on in Julia's life. Anything unusual or concerning," Margie asked.

"Well, no, can't say I did. Everything seemed pretty normal. I mean, it was business as usual. She was working on an investigation. I was working on an investigation. As long as they don't intersect, you're golden. But if they collided with each other and we both ended up trying to chase the same lead, that was a problem."

"And did that happen? Do you know what she was working on?"

"No. I'm not sure what Julia was working on. It was something to do with Winnipeg." DeeDee mused on this for a minute. "Or, it was Manitoba, anyway. Maybe not Winnipeg. I don't remember—some kind of… financial scheme. I don't know. Maybe it was insider trading or something."

"In Winnipeg?" Gagnon questioned doubtfully, his French accent making him sound even more incredulous. What of any importance could come out of Winnipeg? Insider trading on what market?

"I didn't get the details," DeeDee said, brushing it aside. "Of course not. Neither of us would tell the other about anything we were investigating. No details."

"Did she say if she was dealing with anyone… dangerous? Did she have any concerns about it?"

DeeDee shook her head. She tapped the table with an acrylic nail as she thought about it. "I don't know. There was something. Something that she was excited about. But she didn't tell me what it was. She said that it was just the tip of the iceberg. Laughed about it."

Gagnon raised his brows at Margie. Another iceberg reference. But had Julia just been making a joke? Teasing her friend about the great new lead she had?

Margie opened the phone and thumbed over to the photo of the last page of Julia's notebook.

Encounter with the iceberg.

"What's that?" DeeDee asked. She squinted at it, frowning. "Is that Julia's notebook? Do you have it? I need to see that. We don't know what stories she might have been working on that we need to bring in. You need to get that to me. And her laptop, do you have that?"

"Somebody will be going by her house today," Gagnon told her.

"We're just trying to find out who has access to her house. We can't just bust the door down like some TV show cops."

"I don't know who has access to her house. Maybe one of her neighbors. She didn't live with anyone."

"Did she date anyone after Calver?"

"Calver." DeeDee rolled her eyes. "Now there is a real winner. She dated, yes, but nothing long-term. No commitment."

"Was she afraid to after Calver, or did she just not have enough time?"

"It was all work with Julia. She didn't like to waste her time socializing. Me, I still like to have a little fun now and then. But Julia was married to the work. She would rather be working than anything else and didn't want anything to get in the way of that. Great work ethic. Horrible social life."

"If you have the names of anyone she was seeing lately…"

"No. I mean, you can check her phone. I don't have any names. It was all pretty casual. I doubt she went on more than one or two dates with anyone."

They would check her phone logs, and that should give them the names of anyone she had had social or professional contact with lately.

"Did she go with anyone at the office?"

DeeDee looked around her. "Maybe a thing," she said. "I don't know. Nothing formal."

"What do you mean, a *thing*?" Gagnon questioned.

"You know, just a thing. Two people working decide to let off a little steam. Not dating. Not seeing each other. Just…" she shrugged, "a thing."

"And that wouldn't have any repercussions? Problems at work? With spouses? Having an affair at work could cause all kinds of problems."

"No. Julia didn't have any problems." DeeDee shook her head. "I don't get where you're going with this. I thought… Julia slipped and fell. Died of hypothermia. Why are you asking all of these questions? You're making it sound like…" she trailed off.

"We're just investigating," Margie assured her. "We don't know anything. The ME has not yet made a ruling. We don't know that it was anything more than an accident."

"But it could be more. That's why you're asking."

"We don't understand what she was doing in the park. Why she would have been close to the river. We're just hoping to get the answers to some questions."

"But you're not asking any of those things. You're asking about work and affairs and jealous spouses."

"Just in case there was something more than met the eye."

DeeDee eyed them thoughtfully. "So you've buried the lede," she suggested. "This is a much bigger investigation than you are letting on."

CHAPTER ELEVEN

*D*eeDee did her best to pry the story out of Gagnon and Margie, but they succeeded in getting out of the network offices with their secrets still intact. Margie shook her head. She had never been questioned by an investigative journalist before. Not like that. She'd certainly had reporters yell questions at her before, and had one or two interviews after a case was solved, feel-good stories outlining what they had done and that the world was a safer place now that the criminal was off the street. But being questioned by someone like DeeDee Strong was an entirely different experience. It made Margie think about the stories she'd heard of intelligence agents undergoing grueling interrogations in training so that they would be able to withstand torture if they were ever actually captured by the enemy.

DeeDee Strong would have been a great interrogator.

While there were more interviews to be done, they headed back to the office to review the surveillance footage that Siever had gone through. He was good with tech and always the first to volunteer for tedious duties like reviewing video or compiling or searching large amounts of data. Margie was relieved that he enjoyed it, as she did not, and like everyone else in the department, she was content to let Siever take charge of such tasks.

They walked by MacDonald's office on the way to the boardroom to view the video that Siever had compiled, but didn't make it without MacDonald noticing.

"Gagnon. Detectives."

They stopped and turned toward his door, exchanging looks. No one particularly wanted to fall under his scrutiny. Not when they hadn't really accomplished anything yet.

"I thought you were out doing interviews," MacDonald addressed Gagnon. "Have you made any progress?"

"We've been interviewing all morning," Gagnon confirmed. He quickly wiped his forehead, glistening with sweat, even though they had just come in from the cold. Margie hoped it was nervousness and not COVID that was giving him the sweats. He hadn't said that he was having any other symptoms.

"Any progress?"

"Not a lot, sir. Got an alibi statement for the ex-husband that seems to hold out. There are rivalries at work, but I don't get the feeling that anyone would physically assault her to get a story. But still no explanation as to why they would be at Bowness Park. Detective Siever has some surveillance video that we're just going to view."

MacDonald looked at Siever. "Does it give us a suspect?"

"Uh… not yet," Siever admitted, shifting his weight from one foot to the other. "I haven't been able to identify anyone suspicious. But I can see the victim walking into the park and part of her travels around it. She doesn't come out," he cleared his throat awkwardly, "Uh, obviously. And I don't see anyone behaving suspiciously. No one skulking around or following her but, after Gagnon and Patenaude take a look at it…"

"Do you think they'll find something you missed?"

"No. But I might have missed something. Or it might give them an idea of another direction to pursue. At any rate, we should all see exactly what happened during the last hour of her life. If we're going to solve it."

MacDonald stared at Siever for a minute. Siever swallowed and nodded, reemphasizing his words.

"Very good," MacDonald said. "We should all see it. Someone might have a brainstorm."

On MacDonald's advice, they gathered together everyone in the bullpen to watch the video surveillance that Siever had compiled. This served to make Siever anxious. He didn't like having to present to the whole room.

"Just talk to me," Margie told him as they walked to the boardroom and waited for everyone to assemble. "Don't worry about anyone else. You were going to show it to me and Gagnon, so pretend that's all you're doing. If anyone has any comments or questions, that's great. You can deal with them when they come up. That means they're engaging with what you've prepared, and that's what you want."

"And if they ask stuff that I don't know the answer to..."

Margie understood this was one of his biggest worries. They had talked about it before. "Then you just tell them that the surveillance doesn't show that, or it will have to be investigated further. No one expects you to have everything analyzed. We're just moving forward as quickly as we can on what we have gathered so far. If you hadn't pulled this together, I would have to stay late tonight, scrubbing video instead of being with my daughter, and I still wouldn't have everything pulled together like you have in the morning."

"You haven't even seen what I've done," Siever pointed out.

"I've seen it before. Your video work is always top-notch. I know it will be."

Siever smiled at this and nodded. His shoulders relaxed a little.

"You've got this," Margie told him. "You're ahead of the game, not behind."

CHAPTER TWELVE

*I*n a few minutes, everyone in the office had assembled and was waiting for the video, a couple cracking jokes about needing popcorn.

Siever looked at Margie once more, and she gave him a reassuring smile. He turned to his computer and brought the video up on the screen.

"So I found our victim entering the park through the main entrance and parking in the main lot. Her car has been identified and the crime scene techs will look at it to see if there is anything of forensic value inside the car. But we know that she drove there under her own power and that no one else was in the car with her."

They watched the video as Julia's car drove past one surveillance camera and then another angle following her farther into the parking lot. Siever had spotlighted the car so that it was clear what they were supposed to be watching. They saw Julia get out of the car, bundled up for the cold. She looked around. It was apparent that she hadn't seen anyone or anything in the parking lot that concerned her. She locked her car and walked toward one of the pathways. She hesitated, maybe unfamiliar with the terrain, but remembering instructions she had been given or what she had looked up on a map before arriving.

"I cataloged everyone who came into the park the hour ahead of her and an hour behind her," Siever said. "There is little traffic at that time of the night, so there weren't a lot of subjects to follow. Most of them are dog walkers. A few people who are just there to walk by themselves, and those are the ones I focused on."

He brought up a display that showed the best facial shot he could get of each person.

"The pictures from the surveillance camera are not good enough for facial recognition. But I followed each one across surveillance cams as much as possible, and mapped their routes around the park. People didn't generally stay for very long; it was cold. Just a half-hour walk around the park, generally, along well-marked pathways."

He brought up a map showing the routes that the various people had taken, mostly confined to the same loop.

"But that's different from our victim, who did not stick to that main loop," Siever pointed out. He brought up another map, which showed the locations of each camera that had caught Julia Louise Robertson and the implied route she had taken between them.

"There are, unfortunately, no surveillance cameras when you get off of the main trails and down to the water's edge," Siever told them. He marked the last point he had been able to catch Robertson on camera and then the point at which her body had been discovered, some distance downriver.

"I've compiled all of the video that I could get of Robertson walking through the park, as she moves from one camera to another."

There was a pause as he selected the video and then played it. As Margie had expected, his presentation was much better than she would have been able to pull together in twice as much time. Siever had managed to compile it all very professionally and had gone a lot further with it than she would have been able to, following potential suspects and mapping their routes. It was in Siever's wheelhouse. Tedious, meticulous work, all pulled into a form easily digestible by the rest of the squad.

There was not a whisper as they all watched the compiled video, watching Robertson walk from one video camera to another and then off the edge of the screen each time. Margie tried to discern everything she could from the woman's walk across the screen. She was dressed for the weather. She hadn't just gotten out of her car in Bowness Park on an impulse to relive childhood memories. She walked at a good pace. Not a slow, meandering, exploratory route, enjoying all of the wonders of nature. But not too brisk, either. She was a big woman, not in good physical shape, and she didn't move quickly enough to get out of breath.

There wasn't anyone on the surveillance tape in front of or behind her. If someone had been following her or waiting for her, he'd known enough to stay off of the camera feed. No dark shadow dogged her along the route.

"Why would she go to the river?" Jones was the first to speak after they had watched the entirety of the video compilation. "That's what I don't understand. She wasn't just there for a walk. This wasn't part of her normal routine." Jones looked at Margie and Gagnon, sitting beside Siever. "Was it? She didn't even live in the area."

"No," Margie said, "She lived in Bearspaw, a good fifteen-minute drive away, and we haven't found anyone who suggests that she went there regularly or had any kind of emotional attachment to the park. Maybe she had been there as a kid, like many of us, but no one has said anything about her going there or mentioning it recently."

"Then why? Was she meeting someone? Looking for something? Throwing something in the river?"

Margie frowned, thinking about it. She hadn't considered the possibility that Robertson had thrown something away in the river. But she hadn't been carrying anything bigger than what she might have in her pockets. And if she wanted to get rid of something that small, then surely there were plenty of places in Bearspaw where she could have thrown it away. Ponds, wells, irrigation ditches, dumpsters, forests, and open fields. There was an excess of places she could have gotten rid of something small and no one would ever have been the wiser.

Nor had she gone there to pick something up. What? A river rock? There was nothing in the park that an investigative reporter would have been interested in.

Years before, Bowness Park had been a center of social entertainment in both the summer and the winter. It had boasted a midway, with a carousel, Ferris wheel, and other rides, a dancing hall and restaurant, boating, cabins, playgrounds, a zip line and, of course, skating in the winter. But most of that was gone now. Now, it was mostly just a natural park. The restaurant, picnic areas, and playgrounds remained, but there was little to do in the winter other than skating on the lagoon and walking around the pathways. Margie could think of nothing that would have attracted Robertson to the river's edge.

CHAPTER THIRTEEN

S he had to be meeting with someone," Margie posited. "What else would she have been there for? It wasn't her normal stomping grounds. There was nothing to do. She didn't stay on the loops everyone else did. She must have been there to meet someone."

"But she didn't," Siever insisted, motioning to the screen. He pulled up the routes that the non-dog-walkers had taken. "These are the routes taken by those who were closest to the river, where Robertson deviated from the main trails. And the timing just doesn't allow for any of them to have met her. I recorded the time that they passed each surveillance camera, and they didn't have enough time to leave the routes I marked. They were all walking at a consistent pace, with only minor variations of a minute or two."

"What if someone had been waiting for her for over an hour?" Cruz suggested.

Siever looked at him. "It's possible," he said, "but do you really think someone was standing around out there for more than an hour? It was cold. And if someone had set up a meeting with her, why would they arrange it so that they had to wait for her outside for more than an hour? Maybe they'd make it so that *she* had to wait longer, but why would he make himself wait out in the cold for that long?"

Cruz shrugged. "Just spitballing."

Siever nodded. "It's possible, but in my experience, people don't like to stand out in the cold for longer than an hour."

There were some chuckles around the room.

"Any other thoughts?" MacDonald prodded.

"A boat in the river? A helicopter? Ski-Doo? Someone hiking in from somewhere other than the main entrance? Down the river on skis?" Margie tried to think of as many different possibilities as she could. None of them seemed too likely.

No one around the table took any of them up as being likely. Siever shook his head but didn't say anything.

"There were ski and Ski-Doo tracks along the river," Gagnon said eventually. "That's always a possibility. But there's no way to verify if someone came in that way. No cameras."

"We could check traffic cams," Margie suggested. "See if there are any on the bridge that capture part of the river. It's a long shot, but if we can see someone coming or going around the time that Robertson was there..."

Siever pursed his lips and nodded. "I'll get footage, but I don't think anything captures the river. And it wouldn't be close. Someone on the bridge saw her caught up on the log, but that's downstream from where she went in. She was carried there by the river."

"And there's no evidence we could use where she went into the river?" Cruz suggested. "Footprints? Those ski tracks? Do we have a clear indicator of her going into the water intentionally, accidentally, or at someone else's hands?"

Margie and Gagnon shook their heads.

"There is a mess of tracks in the snow on top of the ice," Gagnon said. "Lots of animals going down to drink, some human footprints or ski tracks. Nothing that is identifiable as the victim's boots, nothing that clearly identifies the point where she went into the water. Forensics did their best to narrow it down, but...?" He shrugged. "No luck. The ice may have broken under her weight and taken any evidence of what happened into the river with her. An accident, if that was what happened." He looked sideways at Margie. "And our best Indian tracker wasn't any more helpful."

Margie snorted. There were a few snickers around the table, but no one knew whether they should laugh at the politically incorrect joke.

Margie called Gagnon a name she normally didn't use at the office and moved on. She had already been branded overly sensitive about comments that had been made about Indigenous people in other investigations. There was no point in telling him that he was making a racist joke when he already knew it. She had been open about her heritage with him, about their shared language base, and maybe it was his clumsy attempt to connect with her through a joke, as men often did.

"I have to say, from all of the work that Siever has done, it looks like an accident," she said to the room. "We'll make sure that the medical examiner gets a chance to review it as well, to take into consideration in his findings. The only thing that makes me hesitant to call it an accident is that I can't figure out *why* she went there in the first place. Why go to the river? Why go to Bowness Park? If I had a satisfactory answer to that question, maybe I would be satisfied with it being an accident."

MacDonald nodded briskly. "Yes. That all makes sense," he agreed. "How have the interviews so far gone? Anything interesting? Any indication that she was suicidal or having problems with someone?"

Margie looked to Gagnon to answer the question. He was the lead, after all, and she had just shared her opinion.

"Not much joy," Gagnon filled in. "There are definitely jealousies and rivalries to be considered. Her ex is violent, but his alibi seems solid, and it is doubtful that he would hire anyone to kill her after the divorce was finalized. She earned quite a bit more money than he did, so I assume if there was any alimony, she was paying him. No reason to kill the golden goose, unless he happened to know that he was named as a beneficiary in her will."

"And I doubt if he was," Margie contributed.

Gagnon nodded his agreement. "At the office, there was a lot of rivalry. It has been referred to more than once as being a cutthroat business. But then, her throat wasn't cut." This joke fell flat, no one even smiling at it. "There is a lot of competition for stories. Even her self-professed best friend was a rival, trying to beat her out for the biggest investigations. I don't get the feeling that any of them would actually do violence to get the better story, but we have all seen cases where rivalry has gotten the better of people in unbelievable ways. Soccer moms killing other players. Kids killing other kids for toys or treats, or just because they were a teacher's favorite. So I don't *see* any real motive, but sometimes..."

Margie had to agree that it was a possibility, but a doubtful one. "We could see whether any other reporters at the network live in the Bowness area."

Gagnon nodded unenthusiastically. "Might be worth it on an outside chance."

"Anything else?" MacDonald asked. "Any leads on the stories she was working on?"

"Oh, her friend at the office said she thought it was some financial scam in Manitoba. But she didn't have any details. Worth following up on. Did we get her laptop?"

"Got it this afternoon," Siever advised. "The techs haven't sent me anything yet. Once they have, I'll see what the most recent documents created or modified were. And I'll see if there is anything in Manitoba."

"Winnipeg, she thought," Margie advised, "but she wasn't sure."

"Okay," MacDonald said, in his "wrapping it up" voice. "We've all got information to follow up on. Please keep talking to her family and friends. Following up on her cases and anything on the computer. I think Bowness Park itself is a dead end. Unless we get some additional footage that we don't already have. Any current boyfriends? Girlfriends?"

"She might have had office romances," Margie told him. "I don't have any names, but it sounds like it was a pretty common occurrence with people working late. DeeDee said that she didn't have anyone steady. The occasional date, but nothing that ever went anywhere. Nothing past a date or two."

"Dating apps?" Siever asked.

"I don't know. Maybe. Did you get her phone?"

"No phone on the body or in the stuff they brought back from her house. Probably in her purse at the bottom of the river now."

"Well, you could see if you can find anything on the computer about a dating site. Most of them are on your phone these days, but she might have a site she could access from both, or there might be something in her email or messenger service that tells us if she was using one or what profiles she had looked at or connected with."

Siever nodded. She probably didn't need to tell him what to look for; he was better with the tech than she was.

"Other family or friends?" MacDonald asked. "Neighbors? They found a neighbor with a key to get into her place. Might be worthwhile to follow up with her to see if she noticed anyone new visiting the victim or hanging around the neighborhood lately."

"Got it," Margie agreed, jotting down a note. Bearspaw was out of her way, but maybe she could then pick up some ice cream at MacKay's in Cochrane to take home to Christina. They would both enjoy that.

CHAPTER FOURTEEN

*T*he homicide team moved cases forward as quickly as possible, but things did not always move as quickly as they would have liked. There were many times when they were stuck waiting for tests to come in, witnesses to call them back, or for something to just fall into their laps when a case was not going well. And as other cases came along, they pushed the previous cases aside, as they diminished in urgency every day.

The press and politicians kept Julia Louise Robertson's case in the forefront as much as possible. Margie kept an eye on the media and was still seeing front-page articles on Robertson, even though they really hadn't found anything worthy of reporting.

There were memorial articles. Remembering all that she had done in the community, which, as far as Margie could tell, wasn't very much, but they were trying to make it sound like more than it was. Remembering the big breaks she had made, the stories that she had broken that changed the world or, at least, some small corner of it. Timelines showing the milestones in her life. They omitted milestones like getting married and divorced, but included birth, graduation, earning the letters behind her name, first article published, and first nomination for a Pulitzer.

Julia had lived an eventful life. Until she had shown up caught on a log in the Bow River.

They were still trying to crack the files on her computer. The drive was encrypted, which made it difficult to access the files she had written, even though they were able to make a copy of her drive and access the files without a login.

Margie wasn't sure where to begin making inquiries in Manitoba. But she had come from there and had contacts she could call upon. If Robertson were investigating a financial scheme in Manitoba, then it stood to reason that the Financial Crimes Unit of the Winnipeg Police Service might know something about it.

She tried Bud Webber, a mentor of Margie's, someone who had helped her get into law enforcement and kept an eye on her while she had been in Manitoba, making sure that she was getting along all right.

"Margie!" Bud was delighted when he heard who was calling. "Or should I say, Parks Pat?"

"Oh, you heard about that, did you?"

"Google Alerts still sends me all the clippings," he advised. "Any time your name is in the news, I read about it."

Margie's cheeks warmed. She hadn't thought about Bud following her career from such a distance.

"Well… I guess I don't need to catch you up, then," she chuckled. "I'm on a new case, and this one could have a connection with Manitoba, so I thought I would start with you, and see if you've heard anything. If you can point me in the right direction."

"Well, you know I will help if I can."

"I don't have much to go on. Just that an investigative journalist, Julia Louise Robertson, was looking into some kind of financial scheme in Manitoba. Probably Winnipeg."

He waited for more.

"That's about it," Margie said uncomfortably. "I don't know much more than that. She's a big name, so it isn't going to be about something small. It would be something pretty important or far-reaching. Maybe… I don't know. Maybe organized crime? Financial market manipulation? Something in the millions."

"That's not much to go on," Bud said, "and most of it is guesses."

"Yeah. I know. I didn't know where to start, so I called you. Maybe you can ask a few of your colleagues. See if they know a new player in town or some big deal going down soon. Or if anyone has been making inquiries. Maybe Robertson called the Financial Crimes Unit to make initial inquiries. Or tried to get access to certain documents or files."

"Well, it's possible. I'll ask around, but I'm not sure I'll be able to help you."

"I appreciate that you're even willing to try with how little I have. I wish I could give you more. I'll keep digging. We're trying to access her digital files, but they are encrypted. And I have her notepad, but it is mostly in shorthand, just using single initials for people's names and cryptic comments that don't lead us anywhere."

"You might want to scan that and send it to me. You never know; it might trigger something if it is related to a case that someone is working on."

"Okay, I'll see what I can do."

Of course, Margie had to be careful where she sent copies of documents that were evidence, and she would be sure to get MacDonald's permission first. Still, there wasn't usually a problem with sending it to someone else in law enforcement so that they could collaborate.

"And how is your family?" Bud asked before Margie could say goodbye. "Everybody keeping well?"

"I haven't talked much to anyone in Winnipeg," Margie admitted. She felt guilty about how she had left them behind and rarely even emailed or called. But she had her own life in Calgary and she had done her best to keep Christina away from any of the old influences. And some of those influences had been extended family members.

"And Christina?"

"Christina's doing really well. She's organized an Indigenous Fair at school here, and I think it will be a great event."

"How old is she now?"

"Sixteen."

"How quickly they grow up. I remember bouncing her on my knee." Bud paused. "I remember bouncing *you* on my knee!"

"Yeah, but I was twenty-five," Margie joked.

He guffawed. "Oh, I miss you. It's nice to hear from you again, even if it is just to try to squeeze information out of me like a ripe fruit and then throw me away."

"I'm not doing that. I just... well, you're the first one I thought of who might be able to give me some guidance. You've always been very helpful," she cajoled.

"You know you can call me for help any time. Even if I can't help you, I'll at least try."

"I appreciate it. You'll let me know as soon as you hear anything that might be helpful? There's a lot of pressure on this case, with the victim being something of a celebrity."

"I'll let you know the moment I hear anything," he agreed.

CHAPTER FIFTEEN

I think I saw something out on the ice that day."

Margie played the message back once more, listening for any special accent or inflection, any indication of who might have left the message. Whether it was someone she had previously spoken to. If the caller really had new information, or it was just a hoax or someone who wanted attention. The caller had not left any contact number. When they traced it, they would probably find that it came from a public phone that a number of people had access to. An airport or hotel courtesy phone, an office phone in a company that employed 3,000 people. People generally knew now that even if they told their cellphones not to display their caller ID, the police could still track a call back to the owner of the phone.

"Is it someone you know?" Gagnon asked impatiently.

"No, I don't think so. Doesn't sound like anyone we interviewed. Siever identified a few of the people from the surveillance video. It could be one of them."

"But then why not just tell us they saw something when we call them? It doesn't make sense to hold back in person and then call and leave a message like that."

"Since when do people make sense? I agree, though. I think it's probably someone who has been reading about the investigation in the news.

Whether they actually know anything or not is doubtful. But they'll have to leave a number to call back if they want to talk to us."

Gagnon nodded his agreement. "Well, we'll see whether it can be traced back to a number we can reach. Probably just some crank."

Margie nodded.

Her phone rang, making her jump. Was it the anonymous witness calling back? Maybe with the realization that he had not left a number where he could be reached? But when she glanced at the display, she saw that it was Sergeant MacDonald. She picked it up.

"Yes, sir?"

"Can I see you for a moment, Patenaude? In my office?"

"Sure. I'll be right there."

"Gagnon too, if he's out there."

"He is. We'll both be right there."

Margie looked at Gagnon, who had undoubtedly seen MacDonald's name on the display. He nodded, and they walked across the bullpen to MacDonald's office.

The door was open and, when Margie reached up to knock on the frame, he looked up from his paperwork and motioned for them to come in.

"Come, come."

"What's up?" Margie asked, once they were stationed in front of him.

He seemed distracted or irritated, shuffling through a few of the stacks of paper on his desk without really looking at them and then dropping them in a pile with a thump.

"How is the progress on the Robertson case?"

"Not much," Gagnon said. "Not really anything new since this morning's briefing. We received a call from someone saying they saw what happened, but no number and obviously if she saw what happened to Robertson, she has to tell us about it before we can do anything."

MacDonald nodded. His eyes flicked to Margie, but she didn't have anything to add.

"I understand that you have been stirring things up in Winnipeg."

"Stirring things up?" Margie repeated. She thought about the few discreet calls she had made to law enforcement officers with whom she had a personal relationship. None of them had complained, and none had come up with anything that had assisted their investigation.

"We've been asked to back off. Stop calling law enforcement in Winnipeg and keep our investigation focused on Calgary. This is where she died. This is where we are going to find the clues. Or not, as the case may be."

"Who complained?" Margie asked. "I didn't know anyone was upset about it."

"I don't know. I don't get the whole story; I'm just told to stop making waves. That they don't want us messing up their investigations in Winnipeg. Whatever happened to Robertson happened to her here."

"Had she been to Winnipeg recently?" Margie asked, finding his wording curious.

"Not that I'm aware of. But everything to do with this case seems confined to Calgary, so let's keep it the focus of our investigation."

Margie shook her head. "It has been our focus… but Robertson's next big story was supposed to be from Winnipeg, so that's what I have been inquiring about."

"You have any details about what that story was?"

"Just that it was something financial, that it was based in Winnipeg or Manitoba. I've just been checking in with a few LEOs I know to see if they're aware of anything or if Robertson had reached out to them for information or confirmation."

She had already explained all of this to MacDonald earlier, but he seemed to have forgotten those conversations or decided they were unimportant. She wasn't *trying* to cause any trouble.

He tapped his pen on the top of the desk. "Well, you've made your inquiries, and nothing has come from it, so let's drop that line of investigation and stay focused on Calgary. Maybe this anonymous caller will have something."

"We'll do our best to trace her," Margie assured him. She wondered if he would just gloss over her answer and not notice that she hadn't agreed to the rest. She was responsible for following up on all leads, whether they were in Calgary or another jurisdiction.

"Good," MacDonald approved. "I think that after that… we'll have exhausted most of the leads. OCME is leaning toward classifying it as an accident, so I think that will be the end of it. Once the manner of death is determined to be an accident, there isn't much more we can do."

"No, sir," Margie and Gagnon agreed together.

She wondered if Gagnon felt as off-balance after hearing MacDonald's instructions as she did. A tight knot in her gut told her that Robertson's death wasn't a simple accident. Why had she been out on the ice? Margie wouldn't have gone out there. And she wasn't a big woman like Robertson. Surely Robertson would have recognized the danger of getting too close to the edge of the ice, where it thinned out. She wouldn't be there for no reason.

And if the anonymous witness did know something, then there had been something to see. Was she going to claim that it had been suicide? Margie really couldn't see anyone in their right mind deciding that drowning in icy water would be a peaceful, easy way to go.

But then, someone who would do such a thing obviously wasn't in their right mind.

MacDonald shuffled a few more packets of paper.

"That's all," he snapped. "You're dismissed."

Margie and Gagnon both nodded and retreated from his office. Gagnon stopped at Margie's desk, his brows drawn down.

"What was that all about?"

"I don't know," Margie said, shaking her head. "I guess I got on someone's nerves with my calls, but it isn't like I've been making a lot of them or keep calling back to harass them. I certainly haven't made any accusations."

"Have you found out anything in Winnipeg? Even a hint?"

"No. Nothing."

It was all just a dead end.

Or that's what Margie thought.

CHAPTER SIXTEEN

*M*argie was almost falling asleep in front of the TV. Christina, leaning against her, was also slack and breathing heavily. The two of them were certainly a pair.

Her phone vibrated in her pocket, making Margie jolt awake. She looked first at the TV to see what was on and to mute it so that it wouldn't interfere with the call. Then she looked at the phone screen.

Bud Webber. She smiled and swiped to answer the call.

"Bud, how are you?" she asked warmly.

She looked at Christina to see if she were awake and to tell her who it was, so she could say 'hi' to an old friend, but Christina's head was tipped back and she breathed heavily.

"I've been looking at the notebook you sent me."

"Oh, was that helpful?" Margie perked up a bit at that. She hadn't found anything in the notebook that had been at all enlightening to her, but maybe something had caught Bud's eye that meant something to him.

"Actually… yes, possibly. I might have a connection for you."

"What was it?"

"The key was on that last page you sent to me."

"Encounter with iceberg?" Margie asked, laughing. It was such a strange headline for Robertson to write about, especially if it were related to Manitoba. It had stuck in her mind. Obviously, there were no icebergs in the landlocked prairie province. It wasn't like it was Newfoundland, which had a rich history of iceberg encounters.

"Yes," Bud said. "Encounter with iceberg."

"Okay. That meant something to you?" Maybe iceberg was a code name for a police operation in Winnipeg. Most police departments gave undercover operations names that were randomly generated and had absolutely nothing to do with the operation itself. It could be Operation Stapler or Operation Magpie.

Or Operation Iceberg.

"You said that you thought your reporter's investigation could somehow be related to finance."

"Yes."

"Iceberg is the nickname of a Russian mobster."

Margie caught her breath. Her heart rate quickened.

"Really?"

That could be it. A meeting with a mobster. Not a boat running into an iceberg like the Titanic. Not the very tip of a huge operation that was mostly hidden from sight.

A person. A meeting with a real person.

"Tell me about this mobster," she told Bud, her voice hoarse.

"Okay… his name is Victor Petrov. Born and bred in Winnipeg to an immigrant family. Into a poor Russian-Canadian community. His family wasn't anything to speak of in the mob. Maybe they had some distant connections. Maybe they'd done some messengering or muling for the organization, but nothing that was big or important enough for them to be arrested and connected to the mob."

"Yeah." Margie looked for a piece of paper to jot some notes on, having already changed out of her work clothes and left her duty notepad in the bedroom. She laid her hands instead on Christina's laptop and, after a glance at her still snoozing away, opened it up and started a new document.

Bud went on. "Victor himself did get involved with the mob as a street-level soldier and worked his way up through the ranks. He's smart. Ruthless. Good at flying under law enforcement's radar. We hear things about him, but no one ever has the proof to nail him."

"No convictions?"

"A few for low-level stuff. And some arrests that never led to anything.

291

I've suspected more than once that he had some connections *inside* law enforcement. I have no proof of that or any way to know what organizations he might have his feelers into. I'm talking to you unofficially. You can bet that I will not be making a report that I've passed anything on to you."

Margie breathed slowly, trying to calm her rapidly beating heart. "This is it. This is who Robertson was investigating."

"It's possible," Bud agreed cautiously. "I wouldn't swear to it, but you don't see a lot of icebergs in Manitoba."

"What's with the name?" she laughed. "Why Iceberg?"

"Cold as ice. A lot more dangerous than he looks."

"What does he look like? Can you send me a picture?"

"I'm sure you can get something on your end. I don't want to be connected to your investigation. You found this yourself. You searched the databases for a criminal with the known nickname of Iceberg."

Margie could do that. Had she realized that Iceberg was a person rather than part of an interesting headline then, of course, she would have searched the criminal databases for him. And now she would.

"Sure, of course. I'll do that. Does he have any connections with Calgary? Why would he have been here?"

"I don't know if he was, or if he sent someone else to take care of the problem. All I can gather from your victim's notebook is that she was supposed to be meeting with someone, whether it was Petrov himself or a witness who was going to tell her about a meeting he'd had with Petrov. And during that meeting, she ended up in the water."

"Would she have been a danger to him? How much could she have had on him? If the police could never get anything on him, what are the chances that a reporter could have uncovered enough to worry him?"

"You've seen some of these exposés on TV. People will talk to reporters when they won't talk to the police. And they're very good at what they do. Your victim was at the top of the game. She'd produced some really good stuff in the past. If he'd even gotten wind of the fact that she was investigating him, then I don't think it would matter if she had anything on him yet. He would want to get her out of the way."

Margie nodded slowly. She typed notes into Christina's computer, her mind racing, trying to get down all of the information Bud had given her and to make lists of the things she would need to investigate on her own.

"You need to keep this quiet," Bud warned again. "You don't want to attract attention to yourself, and if he's got people inside the police department, they may be notified when you access Petrov's records. You're going to need to make it look routine. You just happened to run his records because of the word iceberg, but once you looked at his files, you didn't think there was anything there. You discounted him because he's in Manitoba and you can't connect him to Calgary."

Margie was already keeping her continued investigation into any Manitoba connections quiet. It would be easy enough to say that once she saw that Petrov was in Manitoba, she backed off because her sergeant had already told her to stop investigating any Manitoba connections. There was no Calgary connection, so she didn't pursue it any further—an abandoned investigative angle.

If she were lucky, maybe there was more than one criminal with the alias of Iceberg, and she could spend more time on the other one. Bury her interest in Victor Petrov.

"Be careful," Bud emphasized.

"I will."

"I don't want to hear that something has happened to you. I would never forgive myself."

"I really appreciate you bringing this to me. I'll be careful. Nothing is going to happen."

"You think about your little girl. You want her to have to grow up without a mother?"

Margie put her arm around her sleeping "little girl," already taller than she was and champing at the bit for more independence. However much Christina thought that she was ready for the adult world, Margie did not want her living the rest of her life without a mother. Margie herself had cut off most of her contact with her own mother at Christina's age, and living in the adult world had been much more difficult than she had ever anticipated.

"I'm not going to let anything happen to Christina. Including losing her mother," she assured Bud. "Thank you for the warning. I'll be careful."

He gave a heavy sigh. "I'm already regretting telling you. I should have just stayed out of it. If Petrov is your guy... I wish we could just leave him for someone else to take down."

"Well, I'm not the lead on the case. If we do end up being able to connect him to Robertson's death, my name doesn't have to come into it." Was she throwing Gagnon under the bus? Did that mean that some shadowy figure from Manitoba or the depths of the police department would come after him? "And Petrov's name isn't going to come up unless we have something solid on him. Something we can arrest him for. Otherwise, it will just be one search I did for an alias in the course of the investigation."

"You make sure of it."

"I will."

CHAPTER SEVENTEEN

argie rubbed her eyes and considered whether to take a break, go for a walk and get some lunch, or grab another cup of coffee from the breakroom, hoping that the caffeine would give her the boost she needed.

It had been a long week. She had officially relegated the Robertson case to second place while she and Cruz reactivated a series of youth gang deaths as threats of further gang violence had been heard over ALERT's informant networks. If they could find some information that the original investigation hadn't managed to turn up, maybe they could grab up the culprits and prevent further unnecessary deaths. She always hated it when she knew that teens were at risk. She couldn't help thinking about Christina and her friends. Even though they were not involved in any gang stuff—and Margie had her eyes open and was sure they were not—she knew that innocent children were never truly safe. There had been some tragic deaths of bystanders who had happened to get caught in the crossfire. No one was safe from gang violence and, if it went down at the schools, a lot of innocent people were at risk.

And that meant that her investigation of the Robertson case had to go on the back burner. As far as anyone knew, there wasn't any risk of additional deaths on the file. Not as far as Gagnon or MacDonald were concerned. They were both of the opinion that it had just been a bizarre accident. Only Margie thought it might be a homicide. She kept her inquiries to after-hours and tried to keep it below the radar of the rest of the department. She couldn't use the work servers and databases without leaving a trail. Still, she could do public records searches, internet research, and phone calls in the evening without anyone being aware.

But that meant she was putting in much longer hours than usual, which was wearing on her physically.

Not only that, but Christina's Indigenous Fair was coming up quickly. Margie had agreed to make bannock and to talk with the students about Indigenous people and law enforcement.

Moushoom would also participate, telling old stories, talking about his time learning from his parents and elders, in residential school, and then trying to reconcile the two worlds and find his place in them. He would talk about the things he had grown up with—hunting and foraging, eating bannock, wearing and using a Métis sash, and the other traditional practices. Margie would need to transport him from the nursing home to the school. It was going to be a very busy day.

So she was not just tired out by the double duty she had been doing as a detective, but also with preparing her presentations and helping Christina make all of the final arrangements for the fair. It was sometimes hard to get the members of her community to show up at the expected time. They tended to have a looser interpretation of "on time." Margie gave Christina as much helpful advice as she could on how to get people to show up for the presentation slots they had been assigned.

She elected for another cup of coffee. A walk would have to wait. Siever was in the breakroom when she refilled her mug. Margie paused, thinking about the work she had been doing.

Things had been pretty quiet over the last week or two. Everyone seemed to have forgotten about the Robertson case. Maybe she could do a little work from the police servers and make some progress.

"Hey, Siever…"

He stirred creamer into his coffee, looking intent. After a minute, he looked at her and flicked his stir stick into the garbage.

"Eh? What?"

"I was wondering. You know all of that footage that we have of Bowness Park?"

He blinked, considering. "You mean for the Robertson case?" he asked finally, making it sound like it had taken place fifty years ago.

"Yeah."

He shrugged. "Okay, sure. Yeah, we have lots of footage. Not that it did us any good."

"If I had a face, would you be able to find some time to look through some of the surveillance video to see if he shows up?"

"Yeah, sure." He took a sip of his coffee. "I didn't know we had a suspect."

"Well… let's say a person of interest. Maybe not even that right now. Just a hunch. Not even something that we are ready to put down on paper. But if you could spend a few minutes looking at video…"

"It would take more than a few minutes," he pointed out. "There are hours of video."

"Well, yes. But not all of it shows faces. You would only need to review footage that shows faces. And from what I remember, only a couple of cameras tended to catch people's faces as they arrived or left."

"Yeah." He shrugged. "I can find some time. I don't know how long it will take, and it won't be top priority."

"No. I wouldn't want you to spend a lot of time, or to let anyone know that you were working on it."

He didn't ask her why. Any other detective would have either asked or given her a knowing look, understanding that she was pursuing something she wasn't supposed to. But Siever just nodded and accepted this.

"Sure. Just send me the picture."

"Thanks. I appreciate it."

Margie hadn't been able to find anything showing that Petrov had flown from Winnipeg to Calgary. No known aliases had been used to book a commercial flight. But that didn't mean that he hadn't used a private plane. Or driven from Winnipeg to Calgary, as Margie and Christina had done. It was a thirteen-hour drive without breaks, but it was doable. She couldn't imagine a mobster choosing to drive instead of flying, but he wouldn't necessarily have done the driving himself. There were bound to be plenty of underlings to do that kind of thing. Petrov could sit in the back of a limo with his computer or TV and be perfectly comfortable with a couple of well-timed breaks.

He could still have been in Calgary the day that Robertson had died.

The only way they could know if he had been in Bowness Park that day was to find him on the security video.

Margie's phone rang as she returned to her desk with her coffee. The coffee had been made some time ago by the smell of it, and she wasn't sure whether she could actually stomach it. But she hadn't wanted to take the time to make a fresh pot.

She picked up the phone without looking at the caller ID.

"Patenaude."

"Oh, is this Detective Patenaude?" a woman's voice asked pleasantly.

Margie rolled her eyes. She wasn't sure why people had to ask when she had just said her name. It wasn't like they couldn't understand what she said.

"Yes, this is Detective Patenaude. How can I help you?"

"This is Estelle Sinclair from the mayor's office…"

Margie thought that Estelle expected her to recognize her name, but it wasn't someone she had dealt with before. And it wasn't like she dealt with the mayor's office very often. That was above her pay grade.

"Yes?" she asked, clipped.

"I wonder if you and I could get together for a few minutes for a chat."

"Can I ask what this is about?"

"It's about a case that you are working on." There was a pause and, when Margie didn't jump in to guess what case it was, she went on in a tentative tone. "The Robertson file?"

"Oh? Do you have information on the Robertson file?" Margie asked. Where did Estelle think she was going with this? Their anonymous witness had never called back, maybe deciding it was too dangerous to talk to the police. But Margie didn't think it had been Estelle's voice on the voicemail message. Though, of course, she might always have been trying to disguise it, speaking in a lower register than usual.

"I would like to talk to you about it," Estelle told her, not clarifying.

"Well, I suppose, but I am working on other files with a higher priority right now. Maybe you and I could get together after the Christmas break…"

"We need to talk today."

"Today? This is a low-priority file. I don't think I can get together on it today."

"Did you hear me tell you I'm with the mayor's office? I think you might want to reconsider."

Margie sat down in her chair. She looked at the caller ID on the phone to ensure that it did say City of Calgary on it. A lot of crackpots might be running around saying that they were with the mayor's office. She wasn't going to meet with all of them.

"Can you tell me why the urgency?"

"I will discuss that when we meet."

Maybe they were going to issue some statement on the status of the file. Maybe Robertson's extended family was pressuring for some resolution, or at least an update statement. Robertson had been an important person in some circles. Influential. They didn't want it to look like they had forgotten about her. The city might want to name some scholarship after her. Or a piece of public art or a memorial marker.

"I supposed I could give you a few minutes this afternoon," she agreed finally. "When can you be here?"

She was pretty sure that Estelle would turn around and tell her that the meeting needed to be done at the City of Calgary offices, and however quickly Margie was able to get there would be just fine. But Estelle surprised her.

"I don't want this meeting to be at your offices or mine," she said firmly. "A private room... maybe at the Pete Club?"

"Uh... okay. You can get one for us?"

"Of course," Estelle agreed. "If you want to head over there now..."

"Now?"

"I'll get a room reserved and be over there before you. If you could grab a cab and get over there as quickly as possible..."

Margie blew out her breath in disbelief. Who did this woman think she was to just be ordering a homicide officer to drop everything she was doing and get over to a meeting?

She wasn't even the lead investigator on the Robertson case. It was Gagnon's case.

"Detective?" Estelle prompted.

"Okay. But I expect you to tell me why it was so urgent when I get there."

"I'm sure you will understand."

Margie looked at the papers she had spread out over her desk. So much for the advent of the paperless office. "I'll get there as soon as I can."

"Thank you, Detective."

Margie shrugged and hung up. She took a few minutes to sort through the papers on her desk and get them neatly compiled and locked up so that she would be able to pick up where she had left off later.

CHAPTER EIGHTEEN

Margie doubted that she would get reimbursement for a cab to the Pete Club, but she called one anyway. She didn't want to spend her time driving around the downtown core looking for the Pete Club and then looking for parking nearby. If she did find parking, it would be as expensive as taking a cab anyway.

She went in the nondescript entrance to the Petroleum Club and found herself in a plush lobby. She had no idea where to go. She approached the reception desk, and a woman with a snowy white mask snapped to attention and leaned forward to engage with her, immediately helpful.

"Are you meeting somewhere here today?"

"I... yes. Umm, Estelle from the Mayor's office. What was her last name..." Margie tried to recall it, patting her pockets for her notepad or phone. She must have written it down on one of them.

"Estelle Sinclair is waiting for you in the Shaunavon Room. I will have someone escort you there. One moment."

Margie was escorted to the room by a dark-suited, masked man who said nothing, but nodded politely to her. The Shaunavon Room turned out to be a bright, airy room with a table and chairs and coffee service waiting, along with a pinched-looking dark-haired woman who had to be Estelle.

"Ah, Detective Patenaude." Estelle stood up to greet her, then decided not to shake hands and sat down again, motioning for Margie to sit across from her.

"Help yourself to a cup of coffee."

Unsurprisingly, it was much fresher and of much better quality than the coffee from the breakroom, which Margie had dumped down the drain. Margie helped herself and sat down.

"So, can you tell me exactly what this is about?"

Estelle screwed up her face like she had bitten into a lemon. Maybe Margie should have eased into the conversation more diplomatically, but she didn't have the time to play politics with the mayor's office. She sat back and waited for Estelle's response.

"We have tried to reach out before to address issues of... resources being put into avenues of investigation which are not... profitable."

Margie frowned, taking a moment to consider Estelle's response. "Yes...?"

"I believe you are still pursuing a Manitoba connection with Julia Louise Robertson's unfortunate death."

"No," Margie said flatly. There was no way for Estelle's office to know who she was talking to or what inquiries she was making when she was away from her office computer and the police department servers. Unless they had her home network bugged or tracked, which Margie thought was extremely unlikely. The mayor's office didn't have that kind of money or technology. If they felt that she was still pursuing a Manitoba connection, it was just a guess.

Estelle looked taken aback at the flat denial. "Really. I understand you're from Manitoba, so, understandably, you were interested in the possibility of a connection with your home province."

"Uh-huh. I think I told you on the phone that the Robertson investigation is lower on my list right now. There isn't much we can do to prove that she died one way or another. Unfortunately, we've run out most of our leads and it's going cold."

Estelle nodded, but looked unconvinced.

"You still have family in Manitoba, don't you? Family and friends?"

"Yes." Margie swallowed. She waited for Estelle to warn her off, to tell her that if she continued to work off-books on the Robertson file, things would happen to people she knew and loved. Bud had warned her about this. He had warned her that Petrov had connections and that if Margie left any trail, they would know about it and retaliate.

Who had they talked to? How much did they know and how much were they just being cautious and trying to keep her from becoming a problem?

"You must miss them," Estelle said. "Even with all of the communication methods available to us right now, it's not the same as having dinner together. Dropping in on friends or loved ones for a chat. And your people have such a strong sense of community."

Which was both true and not true. There was a strong Métis community, both in Winnipeg and in Calgary. But Margie's immediate family had not been a part of her life since she had become pregnant with Christina. And that was a long time ago. It had been a relief to leave Winnipeg behind and to reconnect with Moushoom, who had never said a judgmental word about her becoming pregnant so young. He adored Christina and would never say anything negative about her birth or existence.

Estelle swirled her drink, which was not coffee, but a glass of ice and clear liquid. Water or liquor? Margie felt cold just looking at it.

Ice.

Iceberg.

Icy water.

She tried not to think about Robertson's death and how she must have felt in those last few minutes or seconds of her life. How long had she been conscious? How long did she know she was going to die?

"I've been hearing wonderful things about this Indigenous Fair that your daughter has been organizing," Estelle commented.

Margie felt even colder, goosebumps standing up on her neck and arms.

"My daughter—my teenage daughter—has nothing to do with the investigation. Why would you bring her up?"

"I was just thinking… how nice it would be for her if the mayor made an appearance at the fair and said a few kind words about it. Maybe brought the press with him. That would be nice, wouldn't it?"

"Of course it would," Margie agreed. She knew that Christina had reached out to the mayor and other civic leaders, hoping that some of them would acknowledge the fair in some way and get it some good publicity.

"On the other hand, there are a lot of people these days who are sick of hearing about the privileges that should be afforded the Aboriginal community. This country has put billions of dollars into reparations for wrongs that were done generations ago. We keep hearing about all of the problems in the native communities. The alcoholism, drug abuse, abuse, and neglect of their children, Indigenous people killing each other. We see them all around us, drunk on the train or at bus stops, panhandling and making a nuisance of themselves. Calgarians have had enough."

Fury boiled up in Margie. She had, of course, heard it all. Estelle was right; there were plenty of people who were tired of hearing about Indigenous rights. About the lands and culture that had been stripped away from them. The genocide all across the Americas. People were tired of it and didn't hesitate to express their opinions.

"Something like that could poison this Indigenous Fair," Estelle commented. "If the wrong people showed up, if the mayor happened to say how it was a kind of racism against whites, Muslims, and Blacks in Canada. Asians, Hispanics, other immigrants. How maybe we need to stop cosseting and promoting the cause of the First Nations in Canada and start treating them the same as anyone else, not as a separate, special culture deserving of our pity and our pockets."

"The mayor would not say that," Margie asserted. "He would be lynched."

Estelle gave a little shrug.

And maybe the mayor wouldn't say anything like that. Still, perhaps he would say that he hoped other cultural groups in the school would offer similar educational opportunities about their heritage, pointing out that the focus shouldn't all be on the Indigenous cultures and that he would like to see something else. He could say something else that would encourage the closet racists to make their opinions known. Someone from his office, like Estelle, could put the word out to neo-Nazis and other groups, who would make trouble for them. Christina's event, the project she'd put her heart and soul into for weeks, would be ruined.

"So the reason you asked me to come here was to threaten me," she said, looking Estelle in the eye.

"It's not a threat. Just an observation. How easy it is for something like this to go the wrong way, especially in today's political climate."

"You think that I'm not paying attention to what I've been told and investigating something that you don't want to be investigated, so you threaten my kid."

"*I* don't care what you investigate. You can investigate whatever you like. I have no skin in the game. I'm not your boss. I don't know what he's told you. And I don't know what you're doing." She looked at Margie, and her gaze was cunning.

Margie didn't know how she knew or guessed that Margie was still working on the Robertson case, still looking in the "wrong" direction. But she knew. And she, or someone she was connected to, wanted to put an end to it.

Someone had figured it out. There was a mole at the office, or someone had access to her internet history or phone logs. Maybe the idea of someone bugging her house wasn't as crazy as she had thought.

"So." Estelle sat back in her chair and tipped up her glass, ice cubes tinkling. She put it down on the table. "Do we have an understanding?"

"I understand you perfectly," Margie told her.

"Good." Estelle smiled. "I'm delighted to hear it."

Margie stood. "You can tell the mayor that he doesn't need to worry. I will put the Robertson case to bed. One way or another."

CHAPTER NINETEEN

*I*t was a few days before Siever got back to Margie on the surveillance video. She was so busy with other work and helping Christina with the final arrangements for the Indigenous Fair that she hardly even thought about it. There was no longer any urgency to the Robertson case, and it would be better if she put it on the back burner, at least until the Indigenous Fair was over. She could pick it up again after the Christmas break. Then, she would look at the case with fresh eyes, and maybe she would be able to identify something she had missed.

Siever stood by Margie's desk for a minute, waiting for her to finish what she was working on and look at him. Margie pushed away the file she had been staring at. Her eyes were scratchy from staring too much at the fine print and too much dust. She felt like she hadn't blinked or slept in a week. She rubbed her eyes, even though that was probably more likely to rub dust into them than to produce cleansing tears.

"Detective Siever." She held her palms cupped over her eyes. "What've you got?"

"I found him."

"What?" She uncovered her eyes. "You found who?"

"The picture you gave me. You wanted me to look through the surveillance video for the man in the picture."

"Right." Margie blinked. The picture of Petrov.

Siever had found Petrov on the surveillance video?

How had they missed it the first time? If Petrov was there to meet with Robertson and had been instrumental in her death, how had they missed it the first time they had examined the video surveillance?

"You found him?" she demanded. "You found him in Bowness Park the day that Robertson was killed?"

Siever nodded, looking smug. "I found him."

Margie swore under her breath. "Show me! I have to see this!"

He grinned at her, as delighted as a kid that she was so excited about his discovery. He bent over Margie's keyboard and navigated to the shared workspace for the Robertson file. He found the video he wanted and scrubbed through the first portion of it. Then he let it play.

Margie watched the video playing with eagle eyes. She watched people come and go from the screen, but didn't see Petrov.

"You missed him," Siever told her.

"What? I was watching. How did I miss him?"

Siever rewound it and played it again. Margie looked at each face carefully.

Siever paused the video. He pointed to a dog walker. Margie had been looking only at the lone walkers. She focused on the dog walker and Siever pressed play to restart the video. As he looked around, Margie got a good look at his face. She got out her phone and brought up the picture. She held it up while she looked at him on the video. Siever was right. It *was* Petrov. And they had missed it the first time because they had discounted the dog walkers. They had only been looking for an isolated person walking, following Robertson or preceding her into the park.

"He has a dog!"

Siever nodded. "We didn't look at the dog walkers. We assumed that anyone who met with her or did anything to harm her would have been one of the solitary walkers. A bad assumption."

"Yes," Margie agreed. She looked at the time stamp on the video. "This was before Robertson got to the park, right?"

"Yes."

"So he could have gone wherever he wanted to set up an ambush, and then given her directions to get to him."

"Yup."

"Can you follow him through the park? Establish where he went? Where he might have attacked her?"

She should have known that Siever would be prepared for this question. He brought up a map and showed her the timestamps indicating when he had been at each camera location. And a dashed line when he was away from a trail for an extended period of time. Close to the river.

As a dog walker, he could claim that he had been letting his dog run off-leash for a while, playing a game with him so that he got proper exercise and would settle down for the night. Even if off-leash dogs were prohibited, he could shrug that off in embarrassment and admit that he had broken the rule. People did it all the time. How often had Margie gone to a leash-restricted park with Stella properly secured, and had other dogs run up to her with no leash, their humans lagging far behind? It happened all the time. Every park. At least once, if not multiple times each visit.

"He was out of camera range at the same time as Robertson," Margie commented, "Except he returned to camera and she never did."

Siever grunted and nodded.

"Somehow, he got her into the river. Attacked her and bound her? Hit her over the head and knocked her out? Pushed her into the water? Held her under?"

Siever watched her as she tried to come up with a likely solution.

"She didn't have any injuries like that," he pointed out. "No blunt force trauma. No ligatures. No bruises."

"She had some bumps and scrapes on her face."

"A few of them," he admitted.

But he was right. There was nothing to indicate a struggle. Or a knockout. Nothing to indicate how Petrov had overpowered the large woman.

A drug? Chloroform? An injection? Something he had put in her water bottle before she got there? A drink at a bar before they went to the park? Was it supposed to be some kind of assignation and he had turned on her?

But Robertson had known him as the Iceberg. That was what she had written in her notebook. She would have known where the nickname came from. That he had ice water in his veins. He was a dangerous man, even if he didn't look it. He had promised her a story, not a romantic encounter. He had convinced her that he was going to be her source. He would spill details about his criminal organization and how things worked —or didn't work—in the criminal justice system. How money was laundered, if she had only been interested in the financial fraud aspect of the organization.

Russian mob. Had Robertson really planned to meet a Russian mobster by herself, far away from anyone who could help her? Had he convinced her that he was harmless, that she had nothing to worry about? He must have a silver tongue.

Siever forwarded to the end of the surveillance video, to Petrov walking back out of the park. Margie watched him critically. Was this how a man looked after killing a woman? His walk was calm. He wasn't looking around in fear as if afraid of being caught. The Iceberg seemed as cool as his name implied.

She continued to stare at the screen after he had disappeared from sight. Another dog walker followed him. A woman with a smaller dog. She looked guiltier than Petrov. Her movements were jerky. Her eyes were wide, and she was clearly trying to act normal when something was very wrong.

An accomplice? Had the two of them been working together? Surely not. What reason would he have to align himself with an amateur? Someone who could give away the game and, by the look of her, was likely to do just that. If he had been working with her, they would have found a second body. He would have eliminated her, too.

Margie remembered the anonymous witness. The message on her voicemail.

"I think I saw something out on the ice that day."

She turned and looked at Siever.

"We need to find this woman."

CHAPTER TWENTY

*M*argie agonized for several days over what to tell Christina, if anything, about what Estelle had said. Ultimately, she decided it was better if Christina knew ahead of time. At least she would be mentally prepared if something happened at the Indigenous Fair and wouldn't be devastated.

They had gone out for pizza not that long ago, so Margie suggested A&W instead. Christina ordered a veggie burger, and they sat inside the restaurant to eat. Margie felt like it was a discussion that would be easier to have away from home.

Margie explained to Christina, as gently as she could, about the threats or warnings that had been received from Estelle, though she didn't mention the mayor's office. Margie wouldn't be surprised to discover that the mayor had no idea what Estelle was doing in his name. While Estelle might have some control over his itinerary, Margie doubted that the threat had originated from him or that Estelle could guarantee he would make either the positive or the negative comments she had suggested. But that didn't mean she couldn't target the Indigenous Fair and make sure it was a fiasco.

Christina ate her burger slowly, looking at Margie and thinking about it.

"It isn't like I haven't heard all of that before," she said finally. She seemed reluctant to disclose this to Margie. "Not everyone has been real positive about the fair."

"Well, I guess I wouldn't have expected everybody to be excited about it," Margie admitted. "Have you had a lot of negative feedback? People who don't want to see it happen, as opposed to those who are just apathetic and don't care if you do it or not?"

"Yeah. I've had threats."

"You've what?" Margie struggled to keep her voice steady. Why was this the first time she was hearing about it? She wanted to know who had made threats and where they lived. She was going to see that they were prosecuted personally.

Christina shrugged. "Don't tell me you've never been threatened before," she said.

"Well, of course, but…"

"Did you think I wouldn't be? What? Because my mom is a cop? Because I'm just so cute?"

Margie chuckled. "Well yes, two excellent reasons."

"It's gonna happen. Whether I'm pushing for Indigenous rights, education, or just riding the train. People are going to speak up. I don't like it, but most of it I can just ignore."

"Have you had… any physical harassment? Anyone putting their hands on you?"

Christina swallowed. "Not usually. And most of the time, I hang out with Tracy and others. I'm not by myself. So mostly… I can avoid it."

"You need to tell the school if you are being physically abused. That can't be allowed to continue."

"Yeah." Christina shrugged in a "That ain't gonna happen" way. "I'll keep that in mind."

"How bad has it been? I can't believe I didn't even know. Why didn't you tell me?"

"I'm a big girl, and I look after myself. It hasn't been so bad. Pushing, usually. Pulling on my braid. Grabbing my—grabbing me. You know. I can handle it."

"Oh, honey." Margie sighed and put her hand over Christina's. "I'm sorry. And I'm sorry I didn't know about it."

"It's fine, Mom. I can deal with it. And I'm not afraid of whatever these guys you were talking to do. If they want to send protesters or talk smack about the Indigenous Fair, that's just fine. Don't they say that any publicity is good publicity? They'll just bring more attention to the fair. And if it's something controversial and they get people riled up, maybe that will make our people take it more seriously. See that it is important and not just shouting into the void."

Margie allowed a small smile. "That's a good attitude," she agreed. "We can't do anything if they decide that they are going to protest it. So we'll just have to deal with whatever comes. Or you will. I doubt it will be directed at me, even though I am the person they are trying to influence."

"What don't they want you to investigate? And why not?"

"I can't say much about it. But there are organized crime connections. And maybe some powerful people leaning on politicians, or moles in law enforcement. Bad players who want to influence the outcome and make sure that I can't solve the case or get enough evidence to arrest the guy who I believe is responsible."

"Responsible for killing someone?"

"Yes."

Christina frowned. "Well, you be careful. I don't want you getting mixed up in something dangerous. If they are that concerned about what you are going to find out…"

They had been there before. A threat to send protesters to Christina's school was nothing. The real worry was their sending an enforcer or hit man to her school or their house. And if they had already bugged Margie's house, they were way past the need to find her address. She had searched for bugs once and was reasonably convinced there weren't any, but she couldn't be sure. They were getting smaller and more sophisticated all the time.

"I'll be careful," she assured Christina. "I'm not even working on it this week. We need to focus on your event. I need to review my notes again, make sure I'm ready for my presentation, and we still have a few errands to run to pick up displays."

Christina nodded and tapped her phone to get to her project plan and see what remained to be done.

CHAPTER TWENTY-ONE

*A*nd then the day arrived. Margie and Christina slept little the night before the Indigenous Fair. Both of them were checking and rechecking their lists. Margie knew that there would be hiccups. There would be latecomers and no-shows. There would be fewer kids than they expected at the event since school would let out for the Christmas break the next day. Families who wanted to get a head start on their vacations would already be gone. Kids who figured that their classes wouldn't cover anything important when people were already on vacation and who thought that the Indigenous Fair was lame would skip, going to the mall for some last-minute holiday shopping or five-finger discounts rather than school.

But it had been well planned. Christina and Tracy had worked hard on it. Margie had her talks and bannock-making demonstration prepared, as well as small bags of baked bannock ready to hand out.

There had been an article in the Calgary Herald about the planned event, and there wasn't anything negative in it. No suggestion that Indigenous people were being favored over other cultural groups or that they shouldn't be given a podium to express their grievances when so much had already been done for them. The press used all of the right words and the article had clearly been vetted for anything that could be construed as even a little bit racist.

If there were protesters, then there were protesters. That would just make the apathetic students more interested in seeing what was going on.

"I guess it's time to go get Moushoom," Margie announced, checking the time for about the fiftieth time in the last hour.

"Let's do this!" Christina agreed, and gave a nervous giggle.

They drove the route that they usually walked to get to the nursing home, and Margie parked in the loading zone in front of the building.

She had thought that she would have to go up to Moushoom's room to get him ready and bring him down, but he was waiting in front of the doors in his wheelchair, wearing his traditional garb with Métis sash proudly on display. A male nurse stood beside him, playing on his phone. He looked up from the screen when Margie pulled in front of the doors. He slid the phone into his pocket, and took the handles of the wheelchair to push Moushoom up to the car. He set the brakes and opened the car door.

"I can do it," Moushoom told the nurse when he attempted to help him into the car. He only needed to stand up and turn around to get into the car seat. He mainly needed the wheelchair when he got tired or lost his balance. He could walk short distances as long as he was not too tired.

Margie watched Moushoom carefully maneuver his body into the passenger seat. He smiled at her and the nurse.

"You see? I might be an old man, but I can still get from one place to another."

The nurse agreed. He folded the wheelchair and Christina got out of the back seat to put it into the trunk of the car. It was a tight fit, but they had cleared everything else out of the trunk before leaving the house to ensure they would have room. Christina slammed the trunk shut and got back into the car.

"You have a good day, now," the nurse told Moushoom, shutting the car door after ensuring that Moushoom's elbow was tucked in and would not be hit by the closing door.

"How are you today?" Margie asked, twisting around to give him a hug and a quick kiss on the cheek. "Ready for some fun?"

"Who thought I would be going back to school at my age?" Moushoom joked.

"As a teacher," Christina pointed out, "not a student. You've always been a good teacher."

"We are all students, too," Moushoom told her, "even a tough old bird like me still has things to learn."

❧

THERE WERE no protesters outside the school with signs. There was no graffiti smeared across the side of the school, the cars, or chalked on the pavement. Everything seemed to be quiet. Just a typical school day. Or a quieter-than-normal school day, the parking lot only half full.

Margie found a parking space near the doors so Moushoom would not need to walk too far. There were a few other cars and trucks around filled with dancers from the various bands around Calgary in their colorful costumes, from children who were barely walking to men as old as Moushoom or older, all ready to participate in the opening of the Indigenous Fair. Margie had been worried about putting them right at the beginning, since they would have to get there early, but there were a good number of people there. Enough to keep everyone entertained, even if they happened to be missing one or two acts. The Nakoda chief doing the opening prayer stood outside his car smoking as he awaited their directions.

CHAPTER TWENTY-TWO

*B*efore Margie knew it, the fair was all finished. The dances and other presentations were done. Students had been able to go from kiosk to kiosk to see arts and crafts, study ancient artifacts, or sample traditional foods. The food had been a popular draw, of course, but the students had also sat quietly, mesmerized and not looking at their phones when Moushoom had told them stories. They were not quite as quiet and attentive for Margie's talk about law enforcement of and by Indigenous peoples, about the National Inquiry into Missing and Murdered Indigenous Women in Canada, and about her experiences in the Winnipeg and Calgary police departments. But they had been respectful, and Margie thought a few of them had been making notes on their phones during the presentation rather than texting each other.

"I am so tired!" Christina said, flopping down onto the couch. "I swear, I'm going to sleep for three days."

"Well, you can if you need to," Margie agreed. She and Christina would have Friday, Saturday, and Sunday to relax and recover. Days when she didn't have to do anything else if she didn't want to. Maybe turn on a couple of Christmas specials on the TV and veg out eating leftover bannock. Then, on Monday, Margie would return to work, getting in a few more days before Christmas.

The time between Christmas and New Year's was always a busy time for the homicide unit. Stresses were high, money was short, family members were together who normally couldn't stand each other. Depressives who had made it through Christmas for the sake of their families gave up and tried to slip quietly away. And then there was the drinking. Alcohol flowed freely at family dinners, get-togethers of friends who lived or went to school in other cities, and widowers and singles trying to numb the pain of loneliness. Almost without fail, New Year's Eve or Day would kick off the year with a hit-and-run, a gang shooting, or some other death for the department to investigate. New Year's was not a holiday in Homicide.

But this time before Christmas, when the kids were out of school, people were occupied with baking cookies, shopping, gift wrapping, and going to Zoolights, the department was quiet and peaceful. They would pass the longest night of the year, and after Winter Solstice, the days would start to get longer again.

It was a good time to tie up loose ends and clear the decks for what was ahead.

On Friday, Christina wanted to spend some time with Tracy and his family. They were not Christian, but still enjoyed Christmas traditions of their own. With her daughter out of the house for the evening, Margie decided to take advantage of the opportunity to canvass Bowness Park for her witness. The woman would, presumably, follow the same routine every day, so she should be in the park at roughly the same time as she had been the night of Robertson's death.

While they had a good circumstantial case against Petrov, they didn't have proof that he had harmed Robertson. He might argue that he had wanted to meet with her, wanted her to publish his story, showing off the hard work of his Russian family and leaking some information about a rival family. He could claim that someone else had gotten to her or that a tragic accident had occurred.

Margie needed to find that witness.

Margie informed Christina that she would be doing a little work after hours but was still reachable on her phone. Christina wouldn't call. She would be watching a movie with Tracy and his parents, playing a game, decorating, or making cookies. Christina wouldn't worry about what her mother was up to.

THE AIR WAS CRISP. It wasn't too cold yet; Margie would be fine as long as she bundled up for the weather. But the wind was picking up a little and there were warnings of an impending snowfall. For the moment, there was only a light snow, pretty, a fine sprinkling of flakes.

If things didn't work out tonight, Margie could return the next day. The pathways would be cleared quickly by Bobcats once the snow stopped falling. Dog walkers needed a place to walk their dogs. They would, Margie was sure, make irritated calls to the city to have the pathways cleared if they were not done quickly enough.

Stella was excited to be in a new place, walking outside with her person. She sniffed everything and wanted to meet all the other dogs and people there. She was well-behaved and didn't try to jump up on anyone or strain on the leash as Margie tried to talk to the other dog owners before allowing the dogs to smell each other. Margie had figured that other dog walkers would be more accepting of a stranger's presence if she were there walking Stella than if she were a solitary walker stopping to talk to the dog walkers and asking questions about whether they had been there the night that Robertson had been killed.

But with Stella there to break the ice, the questions came naturally. Margie expressed concerns about the safety of walking in the park after that woman had fallen through the ice and drowned. She wanted assurances from people who had been there that night, and they were eager to oblige.

She knew the woman she was looking for, had studied her picture many times since she and Siever had reviewed the video footage and they had identified her as a person of interest. But Margie was only assuming from the woman's expression that she had seen something that night, that she was the anonymous witness who had called in and then chickened out. She could have been upset about something else. Their witness might be someone else. In fact, they might have several witnesses who had seen parts of what had happened, and cobbling together their stories would provide an overall picture.

So Margie kept asking questions. Who had been there? Had they known the dead woman? Had they seen what had happened or seen anything else weird that night? Stella made friends with the other dogs and Margie asked her litany of questions, gradually eliminating dog walkers who had not been there or who had been there but not seen anything.

It was dark, of course, full dark by six o'clock, so the walkers stayed close to the streetlights or used flashlights or headlamps as they navigated the park. Margie studied everyone's faces, looking for the woman who had been on camera.

The temperature dropped by a few degrees, the snowfall was getting heavier and the flakes bigger. Stella was enjoying the fluffy snow, dancing around and using her snout to toss the loose piles of snow into the air, biting at the snowflakes as they fell back toward the ground.

Margie knew she should probably turn around and head back to her car. Come back tomorrow or the next day after the snow had stopped. But tonight, Christina was occupied, and Margie didn't want to have to leave her alone in the evening later in the week, with Christmas close at hand and only a few nights for them to enjoy her school break together.

Margie saw the dog first. A shepherd cross, by the looks of him. Coming toward them. Margie thought he looked like the dog she had seen on the tape. She looked at the woman's face and, when she studied it, accounting for the scarf, she was pretty sure it was the woman who had been following Petrov out of the park. On her way home now, going back toward the parking lot.

Margie steered Stella closer to the shepherd and pretended to be lost in thought or absorbed by Stella's antics until they were only a few steps apart. Then she smiled at the woman and Stella pulled in the shepherd's direction.

"Is he friendly?"

"Yes, he'll be good."

They let the two dogs sniff and circle, getting to know each other.

"Do you come here regularly?" Margie asked.

"Yes, almost every night. Twice a day, if we can, but sometimes the morning gets a bit… frantic."

Margie recognized the woman's voice. She was definitely the person who had left the message on Margie's voicemail. She had seen what had happened out there on the ice.

Margie chuckled. "Oh, I hear you on that one. We go for a morning run if I can get up and get myself out the door, but it doesn't always work out."

"You don't run in this weather, do you?" the woman looked slightly alarmed at the thought.

Margie looked at the snow now falling thickly around them. "No, not like this. And not if the pathways haven't been cleared. Sometimes, it takes the city a couple of days to get them cleared."

"Yeah. They're pretty good about getting the main ones in the park done. But if there's a heavy snowfall for a few days, and then it doesn't get cleared for a few more days… it's disappointing. Harry doesn't understand why we can't come like usual."

Margie nodded. "Stella is the same way. She's very good about it, but she doesn't understand why she doesn't get to go for a run every day."

The woman started to move on, heading back toward the parking lot. Margie had been walking in the opposite direction, but now she looked at the increasing snowfall and decided to walk out with the woman, acting as though the incoming blizzard had changed her mind about the walk.

"It's really coming down," she observed. "Did you happen to be here when that woman fell through the ice?"

The witness looked at her, eyes widening. She looked around, wondering if it was an ambush. Which of course, it was, but not because Margie wanted to harm her or eliminate the witness, but because she needed to know what she had seen. If Margie were going to arrest Petrov, she needed more than just conjecture about what had happened.

"Who are you?" the woman demanded.

CHAPTER TWENTY-THREE

*M*argie didn't answer immediately. She studied the woman's face, trying to pick up every tiny indicator of expression.

"My name is Detective Patenaude," she said finally. "I am a homicide detective."

"Oh."

The woman's face was pale. Maybe it was just the cold or her natural pallor. But she looked scared, uncertain as to the correct course of action to take now. She wanted to run, but she also wanted to unburden herself. She probably had conflicting ideas about the right thing to do. Help the police, of course, help see justice served. But also to protect herself, her family, and her quality of life.

But she had witnessed something frightening. It was hard not to talk to someone about it, but it probably also felt unsafe. If the man knew who she was and knew she had talked, he might come after her next. And Margie knew that if the woman agreed to testify in court, her name would be revealed, compromising her safety. She might put the Russian in prison, but what about the rest of the organization? She couldn't put them all in prison.

"You called me," Margie said. "You saw what happened out there and were going to tell me what happened. Then you didn't leave your name or number. You didn't call back."

"I was afraid. I wasn't sure… what I should do."

"A woman is dead. Everybody is telling me that it was just an accident. But do you know what? I don't think it was. I don't think she just happened to walk out on the ice and fall in."

The witness snorted. "No. That's not how it happened."

"Then I need you to talk to me about it. Let's talk about what happened out there. What you saw. And then we can work on making sure you are safe."

"I don't know. It all happened so fast. It was nighttime; you see how dark it gets." She lifted her hands to indicate the world around them. Dark as pitch outside of the lights and flashlights. "Maybe I'm not sure what happened."

"What's your name?"

The woman hesitated. It was a big ask. But she had also grown up being taught to give her name when required. She had been taught to do what the cops told her to do. She wanted Margie to do something for her in return. To make her feel safe again. She couldn't ask for protection if she wouldn't even give her name.

"Lacey," she said eventually. "Lacey Brown."

"Well, Mrs. Brown, I appreciate you calling us to tell us something happened that night. There has been a lot of speculation, and it will be nice to talk to someone who saw something, who knows something concrete."

"I don't know what I saw."

"Let's talk about what you do know. Tell me about it, and then we can discuss whether you want to make a formal, written statement. We'll start with just talking."

"Okay." Lacey rubbed her chin, pushing her scarf around. Touching her face was a nervous gesture. Harry, her dog, bumped against her leg and whined. Lacey's hand dropped down and she scratched his ears, which calmed her.

"You were out here that night walking Harry. Who did you see first? The woman or the man?"

"The woman, I guess. I must have walked into the park behind her. I wasn't paying much attention at that point. She was a big woman, didn't move very fast. Harry always has to stop and sniff everything, so we weren't going anywhere very quickly either. A few times, she turned around to look at us or around the park. I thought she was looking for someone. The rest of the time, she was looking at her phone. It's dangerous to walk around a wild, dark place like this looking at your phone. It dazzles you, eliminates any night vision. If you're not watching where you are going, you could accidentally step off of the pathway or into a depression in the pathway and twist your ankle or fall." She looked rueful. "If anyone knows that, it's me!"

"We're all so dependent on our phones, I think anyone can relate. We've all done something stupid—walked into a newspaper box, accidentally stepped out into traffic without looking, or just stepped on the heel of the person walking in front of you."

Lacey nodded. She looked at Margie, uncertain about going on. Margie motioned for her to continue, not wanting to derail her description with any questions.

"So… I thought she was a little strange because I hadn't seen her here before and she spent the whole time looking at her phone. But, like I said, I figured she was here to meet someone. Getting directions or answering text messages. I just kept going with Harry on our usual route. Then, when we got toward the river… she left the pathway. I didn't know what to do."

"Did you call out to her?" Margie asked. "Warn her that the river was dangerous or that she should stay on the pathway?"

"No. I thought maybe I should, but it was obvious that she had a specific destination in mind, so she knew what she was doing. I didn't want to poke my nose into anything that wasn't my business, but I was worried about her, too. I didn't want someone unfamiliar with the area wandering in the dark. Even if she had directions, it's easy to get turned around in the dark or to misunderstand a direction."

Margie nodded her agreement. She was the master at getting lost and knew how easy it was to get lost even using a GPS with the roads highlighted on the screen right in front of her.

"So…" Lacey shifted uncomfortably and looked around. "We should keep moving; it's getting pretty fierce."

Margie had barely noticed the snow swirling around her, but it was getting heavy. Both dogs were gathering snow in their fur, and it was collecting on Lacey's hat and shoulders. Margie brushed and shook herself off, and they walked slowly toward the parking lot while continuing their conversation.

"I decided to follow her," Lacey admitted, finding it easier to talk while they walked side by side instead of looking Margie in the face. A lot of witnesses found too much eye contact uncomfortable even if they hadn't done anything wrong.

"She went out to the river?" Margie suggested. She wasn't worried about planting false memories with the suggestion. It was clear that Robertson had gone to the river. That was where she had died. Lacey had said she had seen what happened out on the ice that day.

"Yeah. I was a little nervous. I didn't want to get caught following her, but I didn't want to let her walk into danger if she didn't realize where she was going or couldn't see a danger in front of her. She just had the LED on her phone for a flashlight. Those lights aren't really strong, and it would run her battery down quickly."

Lacey looked around.

"It was a clear night, not like tonight. The sky was clear, so there was some light from the moon. She walked down to the river, and then I saw her boyfriend. Or whoever she was meeting for her assignation. I didn't know what kind of a meetup it was. She didn't hug him. They approached each other slowly, like they didn't know each other but had been set up to meet. Maybe it was a blind date or something; I didn't know for sure. The man had a dog. A black dog. Maybe a lab. So I figured he was a park regular, even though I didn't recognize him. They were a little distance away, so I couldn't see his face clearly. Maybe he usually walked there at a different time of the day, but he still knew his way around. I got ready to leave. Figured that they had met each other now and he knew his way around, so she would be safe."

Margie was disappointed. "Was that all that you saw, then?"

"No." Lacey cleared her throat. She scratched Harry's ears. They were out to the parking lot now, so there was more light and Margie could see the woman and her dog more clearly. Lacey turned away a little, still uncomfortable with direct eye contact. Still with more story to tell.

Margie nodded.

Lacey went on. "I was turning around to go when I heard raised voices. I couldn't tell what they were saying, but they certainly weren't lovers or on a blind date. I turned back and watched them, thinking that she might need help. I could do something if he turned... violent."

"That was very brave of you."

"I should have called 9-1-1. Gotten the police out there."

"Because two people raised their voices? I probably wouldn't have."

"No. But then... they were moving apart, but the man wouldn't let the woman return the way she had come. He kept moving in her way to block her. She had to keep retreating and going farther down the river, trying to find a way to get back to the pathway. I even left the pathway to get closer so that I could see."

"There was not much you could have done," Margie reassured her.

"No. I really wanted to. I wanted to help her. But... this guy was starting to get really aggressive. I could tell he was threatening her. I knew he was dangerous. But I was too involved. Frozen."

Petrov with ice in his veins. Lacey frozen where she was. And the ice crackling beneath Robertson's feet.

CHAPTER TWENTY-FOUR

*H*e shoved her and was yelling at her. She was trying to get away from him, backing toward the middle of the river. At the shore, you're safe. It's ice all the way down to the ground and perfectly stable. But the farther you get out, the thinner the ice is, and there is no land underneath it, just the river. And then." Lacey swallowed strenuously a few times. "Then he sicced the dog on her!"

Margie opened her mouth, but had nothing to say. Nothing that would make Lacey feel better. Nothing to ask. She just waited, holding her breath, for the rest of the story.

"The dog went after her, chased her across the ice. She was running as fast as she could. She was not in very good shape, but she was really moving. Trying to stay away from the dog. It was barking and snarling at her, snapping at her heels. She was screaming and flailing her purse at it. But she was running straight toward the middle of the river, where the water isn't even frozen. And she just… the shelf of ice that she was on cracked, and she went through it. I wanted to go out there and help her, but… she was so far away, and she was in the water, and I knew if I jumped in the water, I would never get back out. It paralyzes you when it's that cold. You can't move and you can't think, and you just go down and drown."

"I don't blame you. I don't see how you could have been expected to rescue her."

"And if I called 9-1-1… even if they got the river rescue out there, she would have been gone long before they could even find her."

"Yes." Margie knew the stats about drowning in freezing water. If someone wasn't right there to help—and often even if there was—the chances of survival were practically nil.

Lacey cleared her throat again. Harry was rubbing against her, still looking concerned. Margie was sure he knew his person was distressed and wanted to comfort her. "And then the man… he called his dog to him. They were turning around. I turned off my flashlight as fast as I could. I was too afraid that he would still be able to see me, so instead of going back to the pathway, I hid in some trees, where it was very dark. I stayed as still as I could. He never even looked in my direction. His dog did. The dog wanted to come and investigate and find out what I was doing there. But the man clipped the leash back on its collar to make sure that it stayed with him, and he wouldn't let it explore the bushes. He was quick to get back to the pathway and headed around the loop back to the parking lot."

"And after he was past you, you went the same way to the parking lot."

"It was the shortest way, I didn't want to go around the long way. I was pretty sure he hadn't seen me or realized he had been seen." Lacey looked down at the ground and petted Harry, taking a few shuddering breaths. "I read about that reporter in the news. And I called you… but I couldn't follow through. I was too afraid that if I revealed myself as a witness, he would come after me."

"We want to get this guy. I'll have you come down to the office to look at some pictures so that you can identify him for me."

"I'm afraid…"

"We can't just let a killer go free. He lured her there and killed her, just as surely as if he had shot her. We don't have enough evidence without your testimony. All that we have is circumstantial evidence. A good theory. We need you to tell how it happened."

"He was… so menacing. I can't imagine having to look across the courtroom at him. He would know who I was, and I just can't.…"

Stella turned suddenly, growling. Margie whipped her head around to see what Stella had seen.

And he was there.

Victor Petrov.

He wasn't back in Winnipeg, where he should have been.

He was right there in Bowness Park.

Lacey gave a yelp and moved away. Harry stayed between the threat and his master, watching warily and growling. Stella was a smaller dog than Harry, and she barked and growled at the threat.

Not just Petrov, the ice-cold killer. But also his dog, a coal-black demon dog who stood there slavering and snarling.

"You were warned," he told Margie. He didn't spare a look at Lacey, who was melting down somewhere behind her now. She was crying and protesting that she didn't know anything and trying to put as much space between her and Margie as possible. Which was undoubtedly a good idea. Petrov had his target. He knew who the threat to his freedom was. And it wasn't Lacey, it was Margie.

Without Margie, nothing would ever come to fruition. The other detectives would deep-six the case, knowing that there were no more leads to follow up, no way to prove that it hadn't been an accident or suicide. They wouldn't find Lacey again. Even if they did, she would not tell her story and would not testify against Petrov in court.

"You killed a woman," Margie told Petrov. She was trying to calculate her chances of survival. Could she get back to her car? Make a phone call? "Did you really think that I would drop the case?"

"You should have. A woman fell into the river and drowned. Why make such a big deal of that?"

His voice was higher than she had expected. A tenor rather than a bass. Not low and gravelly like a TV villain. But the killers she arrested were rarely like comic book or TV show killers. They were complex people. Most of whom confessed what they had done in the end. Many of them cried. Even the gang members tended not to be ice-cold killers. They were hotheaded, scared, drunk or high.

"Murder is murder," Margie told him, feeling for her phone in her pocket with clumsy, gloved hands. She would need to take off her gloves to call 9-1-1. And to see the screen. Unless…

"I can't just let it go," Margie said flatly.

"You could. Just like everyone else. I never laid a finger on her. How could it be murder?"

"We both know you took her life," Margie argued. "Right here in Bowness Park. Julia Louise Robertson never had a chance. Victor Petrov and his demon dog. How could anyone expect to stand up to you?"

"That's right," Victor agreed smugly, advancing toward Margie. "No one dares. No one does and survives."

"You make sure of that. You find a way to silence them. Just like Julia."

"Just like you," he corrected.

Margie stood her ground. He wasn't going to chase her into the river. She might not have a much better chance if he decided to pull a gun on her and shoot her at point-blank range. But people did survive gunshot wounds to the head or the heart. She wouldn't survive in the freezing cold water in the dark, with no one around.

She looked around, hoping to see crowds of dog walkers and fitness buffs out for their evening walks. But the storm had chased them away. The snow was swirling thickly around them. The wind was picking up. Snow was drifting along the edges of the pathways and curbs of the parking lot. The wind cut into Margie, even through her warm winter coat.

"Get her!" Petrov ordered his dog, which was not on leash, pointing at Margie. The black dog took a couple of bounds toward her, snarling like a demon. Stella released a volley of threatening barks and growls, baring her teeth and screaming like a banshee.

The black dog was stopped in its tracks. It slunk around, circling, trying to get around behind them for a better opportunity to attack. Margie turned, not allowing it to get behind her. If she kept turning, that would put Petrov behind her, so she stepped backward, trying to keep them both in sight and put more distance between herself and the two threats. Petrov still had not seen the need to draw a gun, but was shouting at the dog, berating it, trying to whip it into a frenzy so it would attack.

Margie talked to the dog in a quiet, calm voice, though she knew in her heart of hearts that there was no way she would be able to calm it down and counteract Petrov's orders. The dog knew who its master was.

The dog had killed before. Multiple times, if Margie was right. She was sure that Robertson's death wasn't the first that the dog had been responsible for. And probably the other attacks had been more up-close and personal. Not everyone would obligingly fall into the icy river.

CHAPTER TWENTY-FIVE

*A*t first, Margie wasn't sure she could actually hear sirens over the noise of the wind and the barking, snarling dogs. She was listening for them, hoping, but not sure they would come.

Stella looked around. Petrov's demon dog finally managed to reach Margie as she looked down at Stella, both distracted by the sound. Both reacting instinctively to the sound of a siren.

The dog went first for the back of Margie's calf. Margie kicked out, trying to escape it and force it back at the same time. Stella screamed and snarled, her teeth ripping into the shoulder of the black dog when it moved in.

Margie tried to bar it with her arm when it jumped up at her on its next attempt. The dog's teeth sank into her puffy sleeve, finding more fiberfill than flesh. There was the sound of tearing fabric as the dog tried to rip at her. Stella struck again and the other dog yipped and whirled around, trying to defend itself as well as attacking its target.

The sirens got louder. There was no mistaking them now. Petrov shouted for his dog, trying to call it back. He looked for the best avenue of escape. Into the darkness of the trees? To his car? There was a gun in his hand now; he wouldn't be going down without a fight.

The police cars rolled into the parking lot, sirens screaming. As much as Margie wanted to collapse or relax her focus, she fought to stay in control. She could not let down her guard until she knew that she and Stella and anyone else around them were safe.

A couple of shots were exchanged between Petrov and the arriving cops. Margie didn't even have her sidearm with her. She had come to the park to walk her dog and search for witnesses, not to fight a madman and his mad dog.

Petrov fled into the trees with his dog. The darkness and drifting snow swallowed him up. Several cops pursued, flashlights in hand. Margie didn't know if they would be able to catch up or find them in the inky darkness. It was a big park.

"Are you okay?" A couple of the responding officers approached Margie. They reached for her, held her steady as they walked her back to one of the cars to sit down.

"I'm fine," Margie insisted. "Fine, fine."

They ignored her, herding her back to safety. Sitting in one of the squad cars with her feet out the open door, Margie looked down at herself as they ministered to her. More sirens were audible, more police cars and an ambulance pulled into the parking lot.

"You should look for a woman with a dog," Margie said. "Her name is Lacey. She's a witness. I don't think she was hurt, but…"

"I think we've got her farther up the road," one of the officers assured her. "She made it to her car and called 9-1-1."

"So you got *her* call," Margie said.

"We got yours too. The emergency operators were able to use both to get a clearer picture of what was going on and dispatch multiple units."

"I wasn't sure if mine went through. I've drilled on making emergency calls on my phone with just the hardware buttons. They tend to change the settings every time you update the operating system. I've never actually had to do it before."

"Well, it worked. Not the clearest call. Lots of background noise. But that, together with the second call, was enough."

Margie's heart was starting to slow. She pulled Stella against her, scratching her ears and petting her head, murmuring to her. "Good girl. Who's my good girl?"

She wanted to wipe the blood from Stella's muzzle, but didn't dare. The crime scene techs would want to swab her to take samples.

"Let's have a look at you, then," one of the cops said, pulling at Margie's sleeve. She had to unbutton her coat to get her arm out of the sleeve, and felt a chilling rush of air.

She was surprised to see a small amount of blood and puncture marks in her arm. She hadn't thought that the black dog had actually hurt her. She hadn't felt it. Still couldn't feel it. But she started to shake, a combination of the adrenaline rush and the cold air on her body.

The black-masked paramedics were allowed onto the scene, since the shooter was not in the immediate area. They looked at Margie's arm and bandaged it, but told her that she would need to have it looked at at the hospital and to have shots. They were initially nervous of Stella, blood on her muzzle, thinking that she was the one who had bitten Margie, but she assured them that Stella had only defended her, had only slashed another dog, not a human.

"She wouldn't ever hurt anyone, would you, Stella?" Margie asked Stella in her "good dog" voice.

"Detective Patenaude," a familiar voice intruded into the conversation with the paramedics. "What have you gotten yourself into?"

Margie looked up and saw Detective Cruz, bundled up in a thick winter coat, a scarf wrapped around the lower part of his face.

"What are you doing here?"

"Well, I heard some action on the police scanner and it sounded... suspicious. A couple of calls confirmed that one of the members of my department was involved."

Margie's face warmed in embarrassment, but she was grateful to have someone familiar there with her. She was glad that he had come.

"Things went in an unexpected direction," she admitted.

"I guess so. What is this all about? What are you even doing on this side of town?"

"I was looking for a potential witness. The one who had called in anonymously. Siever and I found her on the surveillance tapes, and I was hoping she might walk her dog here regularly."

Cruz looked down at Stella and at Margie's bandaged arm. "And her dog attacked you? Are you suggesting that she was involved with Robertson's death, not just a witness?"

"No. No, this wasn't her..."

"Your own dog bit you?"

Margie shook her head emphatically. "Stella wouldn't hurt a fly. No, it was... Victor Petrov was here with his dog." She shuddered, remembering how it had looked at her. How he had sicced it on her after Margie had heard the story of how he had chased Robertson to the edge of the ice, causing her to fall in and drown in the frigid depths.

"Who?"

"Uh... Russian mob from Winnipeg. That's who Robertson was supposed to be meeting with. Nickname Iceberg."

"Encounter with Iceberg."

"Yes."

Cruz raised his brows, but didn't follow this up with another question about Petrov. Like how had Petrov known that Margie was going to be there? How had he just happened to be there at the same time as Margie? All of those questions that she couldn't answer.

"Are you okay?"

Margie nodded. "Fine. It's nothing. Very minor. It helps to be bundled up like a mummy." She looked down at her winter gear. "It's not that different from the body suits they wear while training police dogs in takedowns. He could hardly find my arm underneath all of the padding."

"That's lucky. What happened? Did you attempt an arrest?"

If Cruz had been listening to the police channel and had talked to whoever was in charge of the scene when he arrived, he probably knew more details about it than Margie did. But he was letting her tell her story in her own way.

"No... all I could do was call 9-1-1. I didn't come here expecting to find him. Wasn't armed. He just showed up out of nowhere. Then he rabbited when the cavalry arrived."

Cruz nodded. He looked off into the distance. Standing, he had a much better vantage point than Margie.

"Did they catch him?" she asked.

"Still working on it. They have a perimeter. But I don't know how secure it is. With all of the green space, there are a lot of places to hide. And there are probably a lot of places you can come out on foot that can't be blocked like the main roads. And if you don't know where he came from, it's even possible that he has a house in the area that he owns or stays at when he is in town. Maybe that's why he was here the night Robertson died."

"It was murder," Margie told him. "I found the witness."

"How?"

Margie explained it to him. Cruz pulled his coat tighter to him, shaking his head. "Hard to believe."

"It matches up with what is on the surveillance tapes."

❧

THINGS PROGRESSED SLOWLY, as they always seemed to. Crime scenes took time to process. Witnesses were interviewed and reinterviewed. It was cold, windy, and snowy, obliterating the crime scene. They did manage to get a couple of crime scene techs out to process a few footprints and the blood on Stella's muzzle. Coordinating the search for Petrov would take long hours and, not only was Margie not required to be part of it, she was barred from participating.

"I'll take you to the hospital," Cruz told her. "You should get that taken care of tonight."

"It's not that serious."

"Didn't they say it needed further treatment?"

"Well… yes."

"Then I'll take you to the hospital."

"I can drive myself."

"Not like this, you can't. You were attacked, and the adrenaline will probably have you all wobbly. Your brain is in fight or flight mode, not driving calmly and noticing all the hazards. And in case you didn't notice, we're in the middle of a blizzard."

Margie laughed. "Which means that the person from Winnipeg is probably a better bet for driving safely than the person from the Philippines."

"I'm qualified," he told her sternly. "I've lived here long enough to learn to drive in all weather conditions. Come on. Bring Stella, and we'll go in my car."

"What about my car?"

"We'll deal with that tomorrow. I'll bring you back, or we'll get one of the others to pick it up. But you're not in any shape to drive tonight."

"Jason Bourne always does his own driving."

"Not when he's been bitten by a dog and it's snowing."

They both laughed, and Margie conceded, letting Cruz take her back to his car. Stella was eager to get out of the storm and had no qualms about jumping into the back seat of a strange car when Margie opened the door for her.

CHAPTER TWENTY-SIX

There was a wait when Margie and Cruz got to the emergency room at the Lougheed Hospital. Apparently, even injured police officers had to follow proper triage protocols, and a non-life-threatening dog bite was well down the list in terms of urgency. Margie would have preferred to go home and seek further care the next day or in a couple of days when she could schedule an appointment at one of the medical clinics rather than dealing with the emergency room. But Cruz didn't give her that option.

While waiting at the hospital, she called Christina and explained that she'd gotten a dog bite while walking Stella.

Christina was bright enough to know that there was something more going on. "What were you doing walking her in a blizzard?"

"Well..." Margie tried to come up with a logical explanation that didn't involve telling Christina that she'd been working on a homicide investigation at the time.

"You were working," Christina accused.

"I was looking for a witness, who I figured would be out walking her dog."

"And her dog attacked you?"

"No. It was another dog. Do you want to just stay there with Tracy's family, and then I'll pick you up when I'm finished here?" Margie ignored the fact that she didn't have her car with her. Cruz would take her to pick up Christina. Or she could get a ride share if she could convince him to go home to his family.

"No, I'm coming there," Christina asserted. "Tracy can bring me."

SOME TIME after Christina got there and was reassured that Margie did not have any serious injuries, Margie looked up from her bored scrolling on her phone to see Staff Sergeant MacDonald striding toward her, his long legs eating up the distance. She shifted to get to her feet, but Cruz pushed her shoulder down and MacDonald motioned for her to stay put. He sat down in one of the chairs facing hers.

"So, do you want to tell me exactly what happened in Bowness Park, Detective Patenaude?"

Margie explained as succinctly as she could, not trying to excuse herself. She had, after all, only been trying to follow up on a witness. That was her job.

"Didn't I tell you to let the Winnipeg connection go?" MacDonald asked.

"Yes, sir. This was a witness in Calgary. Someone who had called in to say that she had seen what had happened."

"I don't remember you telling me you had identified that potential witness. Exactly how did you do that?"

"I... I identified Petrov going in and out of the park and, when he left, she was behind him."

"So you *were* working on the Petrov connection."

"He was here in Calgary. He did kill Robertson."

She could see that he wanted to reiterate that she wasn't supposed to be following the Winnipeg connection. But she had found the killer, and what could he say about her investigating a line of questioning that was not, in fact, a dead end? Detectives didn't stop investigating certain lines of inquiry just because they were politically fraught.

"Why was Petrov at the park?" he asked instead. "Did he know that you were going to be there? How?"

"I don't know how. I thought I was pretty careful. I was worried about the possibility of leaks," Margie wasn't sure how to put this in a way that didn't indicate that there might be a police department mole, "so I was really careful. I didn't do any searches that would be logged on our systems."

"How do you do that? I thought any database record access was part of the audit log."

"Yeah. So I didn't do any police database searches. Only public search engines and commercial databases."

"On our computer network?"

"No... I used my daughter's computer," Margie confessed.

"Did you use it to log into our network?"

"No. Completely separate."

MacDonald shook his head. "Well, something you did must have tipped him off. Talk to Siever. Maybe he can figure out where the tripwire was."

"I'll talk to him," Margie agreed. Siever was the most likely one to be able to help her sort out technological issues. But she also worried that he was the only one who had known that she had found the witness and was going to question her, and that information had somehow made its way to Petrov.

It couldn't have been a coincidence that Petrov had just happened to be in the park.

CHAPTER TWENTY-SEVEN

*B*y the time Margie had finally seen the doctor to get her wounds treated and rebandaged, as well as getting her first shots and the instructions for the protocol she should follow, the emergency room had quieted down quite a bit. Christina was still there, playing on her phone and waiting in the chairs, accompanied, not by Cruz or MacDonald, but by Detective Kaitlyn Jones. Stella lay at their feet and, when Margie approached, gave a bored sigh and eye roll.

"Yes, we can go," Margie told Stella. She smiled at Christina and Jones. "Sorry to be so long. You must be tired of sitting here."

"You can't control how long you wait in a hospital emergency room," Jones said with a philosophical shrug. "It's like stepping into a different world where time is suspended. Things just happen when they happen."

"You didn't have to come," Margie told Jones.

"What? My fellow officer was injured in the line of duty. Of course I had to come."

"It's just a bite. A few puncture marks."

"Can I see?" Christina asked.

Margie's arm was bandaged up so she could not, but Margie had taken a picture before the bandage was applied, and showed off a picture of her war wounds to Christina and Jones.

"That doesn't look too bad," Christina said tentatively.

"No, it really isn't. I've got a bruise where he bit the back of my calf, too, but he didn't break the skin there. And… I have to get shots."

"Rabies?" Jones asked.

Margie nodded. "Unless they find and test the dog. And I think to do the tests, they have to kill it and examine its brain. They said the protocol isn't as bad as it used to be. I'd rather just do it and not worry about them having to put the dog down."

"No," Christina agreed, covering Stella's ears. "You couldn't let them do that!"

Margie stretched her sore muscles. She had been tense for a long time, and the cold weather had not helped, nor had sitting in hard chairs and then having to be still, with her arm at an odd angle, while the doctor treated the punctures and put a couple of stitches across them.

"I don't suppose you've heard whether they caught him."

"The dog?" Jones asked, eyebrows up.

"Well… the dog too, I guess. But Petrov? Did they find him?"

Laughing, Jones nodded. "They got him. Footprints in the snow. It was coming down pretty good but, once they found fresh tracks, they were able to run him down."

"So he's in custody?" Margie checked.

"He'll probably be tucked into bed before you are."

Margie let out her breath. "Thank goodness!"

"They just booked him on assault of a peace officer today, but once you get all of the paperwork in and your witness corroboration, they'll charge him with the murder."

"So much for him being untouchable."

"We get them all, sooner or later."

"I hope so," Margie said. But she knew there was a small percentage that slipped through their fingers. With new DNA testing technology and genealogical tracing, they were getting some of the criminals who had escaped the net forty years ago. Still, Margie wasn't sure that putting a seventy-year-old in prison for the rest of his days was quite as satisfying as getting someone like Petrov within weeks of committing the crime. Now he would serve time for what he had done. Not enough, she was sure. The Canadian penal system was way too quick to let criminals back on the street again. But at least he would be away for a few years, unable to cause more havoc on Calgary's city streets.

"Now you can relax for Christmas," Christina said firmly. An order, rather than a request or suggestion.

Margie hid a smile and saluted. "Yes, ma'am."

EPILOGUE

Usually, Margie and Christina visited Moushoom at the care center. When the weather was nice and he was feeling good, they sometimes went for a walk from the home to the top of the irrigation canal that ran alongside Twenty-Sixth Street for some fresh air and a bit of nature, though the well-traveled strip of green space was far from being a wilderness area.

The weather had warmed rapidly in the early morning of the Twenty-Third, going from -17 Celsius to a balmy six degrees and, while it hadn't held there until Christmas, it was still a few degrees above freezing and refreshingly bright and clear.

Margie and Christina had gotten up early Christmas morning and taken stockings to the nursing home, where they had all opened their little gifts and recounted memories of Christmases past. After Moushoom had eaten his breakfast, they were allowed to take him out. It was a short drive to the house, and then, with Christina and Margie both standing close by to help if he had any problems, Moushoom was able to get up the three stairs to the front door and into the house. There, he delighted in the Christmas tree decorated with some of his family's heirloom ornaments and a few new ones with Métis flags or symbols.

Moushoom gave the traditional Métis retelling of the Christmas story of Marie and Joseph and the birth of Emmanuel. He wasn't up to dancing jigs with Margie and Christina, but he clapped along to the music and whooped and laughed as he watched them. They all had the dinner Margie and Christina had prepared of bannock and fresh fish, then settled in front of the TV to watch *A Christmas Carol* and *It's a Wonderful Life*. Alexander, who had been married to Margie's cousin, and his son Quinn would join them later in the evening to do some crafts and have another go at the bannock and fish, and some wild game that Alexander had promised to bring.

Margie was thankful to have her family around her, and was at peace, knowing that Julia Louise Robertson's killer was behind bars and, for the moment, there were no burning cases on her desk.

It was the end of December, and those would come soon enough.

"*Gayayr Nwel*," she murmured to Moushoom and Christina, both drowsing in front of the TV.

"*Gayayr Nwel*," Moushoom repeated, rousing himself. "*On veut la paix sa terre.*"

Merry Christmas. May there be peace on earth.

BOWNESS PARK

In its early days, the park was a bustling recreational hub featuring a variety of attractions including a swimming pool, lagoon for canoeing and boating with musical accompaniment, a large dancing pavilion, a merry-go-round now housed in Calgary's Heritage Park, picnic areas, swings, teeter-totters, camping sites, and rentable cabins. From the 1920s to 1946, families often rented summer cottages there for retreats. However, many of these amenities gradually disappeared over time.

During the warmer months, visitors can enjoy paddle boating on the shallow lagoon, wading pools, boat rentals, and a children's train ride. The park is also equipped with numerous pathways, and firepits and BBQ stands, making it a popular spot for picnicking along the Bow River. In winter, Bowness Park transforms into a hub for outdoor skating on the lagoon.

The author recalls family reunions and church activities at the park, eating BBQ and playing in the playground and on the zip line. In her early years in Calgary, there was a small midway. In the winter months, she remembers skating, warming herself by the fires, and drinking hot chocolate.

Did you enjoy this book? Reviews and recommendations are vital to making a book successful.

Please leave a review at your favorite book store or review site and share it with your friends.

Don't miss the following bonus material:
Sign up for mailing list to get a free bonus
Read a sneak preview chapter
Other books by P.D. Workman
Learn more about the author

Get the Parks Pat Survival Pack!

Sign up for my newsletter and receive the **exclusive Parks Pat Survival Pack**, packed with bonus materials and extra goodies you won't find anywhere else.

Stay in the loop on new releases, special offers, and insider content—all delivered straight to your inbox.

Sign up today and start your adventure with Parks Pat!

https://shop.pdworkman.com/products/parks-pat-survival-pack

Here's what's inside:
- **Out with the Sunset (Book 1, eBook)**
Begin Margie's journey with her first gripping case as a Calgary homicide officer in the Parks Pat Mysteries.
- **Out with the Sunset (Book 1, Audiobook – Computer Narrated)**

Take the mystery on the go—perfect for your commute, workout, or a walk through the park.

- **Bonus Prequel Story:** *Flight of the Bluejay*

Discover Margie's *true beginning*. Before she was a sleuth, she was a pregnant teen on the streets—fighting to survive and find her place in the world.

- **Discover Calgary's Treasures – Photo Minibook**

Step into the beauty of Calgary with this exclusive photo album showcasing the first 15 parks that inspired the series.

- **Digital Wallpapers**

Bring the beauty of Calgary's parks to your phone, tablet, or computer with stunning photography.

SNEAK PEEK AT GROUNDED
IN THE WIND

CHAPTER ONE

The day began like any other. Things had been pretty quiet on the homicide front, so the team had been working other Major Crimes cases, reviewing some cold homicides for any old evidence that might benefit from modern technology—such as more sophisticated search techniques, cutting-edge DNA testing, or an appeal to the public through social media. Margie looked forward to going home and spending some time with Christina at the end of the day. Her teenage daughter was getting older and more independent, and they didn't get nearly as much time together as Margie would have liked. Between Margie's work, Christina's school schedule, and Tracy, Christina's "friend who was a boy," it could be hard to connect for any meaningful length of time.

Margie had reached out lately to her cousins, now that more public gatherings were allowed, and was trying to arrange some extended family activities to reconnect them with some of the tribal "brothers" and "sisters" she had lost touch with since she had been Christina's age. She wanted to keep Christina connected with the Métis community, something that had not been easy during the early COVID months when they had first moved from Winnipeg to Calgary.

But tonight, they were planning a movie marathon, just Margie and Christina, bingeing Batman movies. Margie honestly wasn't that excited about the newest Batman, but was looking forward to some of the cheesier early TV episodes and movies.

Staff Sergeant MacDonald came out of his office and whistled to get everyone's attention, something she had never seen him do before. The effect was, therefore, instant. Everyone froze. Any banter between the detectives ceased, fingers froze over keyboards, and everyone looked at the tall, gray-haired man to see what was happening.

"We've got an incident," MacDonald announced. "A possible attack directed at the airport. A drone has been launched and has disrupted flights. The airport is locked down, all flights in and out have been suspended until the drone can be neutralized. Police all over the city are being scrambled to deal with the threat to public safety and ensure that the public does not panic. Messaging is that the source and intent of the drone are unknown, but there is no apparent danger to the public."

"*Is* there a danger?" Cruz asked.

"If there was going to be a weapons attack, it would likely have been deployed by now. It may be that the pilot lost control of the drone, it is being directed by someone without any real training or understanding of the restrictions they operate under, or that it is an act of mischief."

"Are they going to shoot it down?"

"They have methods to deal with it. Our job is to check out a potential launch area and see if we can locate the point it went up from and the pilot."

Margie's heart was pumping hard and fast. Even though it didn't sound like the drone was actually any threat, it was still very different from what they handled on a day-to-day basis and would unfold quickly. It was a dynamic situation that would require all of them to be at the top of their game to see that the public wasn't put at risk and didn't panic over nothing.

"Where are we going?" Kaitlyn Jones asked as everyone rose from their seats and quickly pulled on jackets, preparing to go.

"Prairie Winds Park is the apparent point of origin," MacDonald announced, "given the reported sightings."

Margie glanced around at the others, hoping they had a better idea of where Prairie Winds was than she did. She vaguely remembered it as a park the Calgary cousins had spoken of sledding at when they were all still kids. But Margie had rarely been to visit Calgary during the winter.

When she had, they had found smaller hills close to home or gone skating at Bowness Park.

"I will send you all the GPS coordinates and you can use your maps apps if you are not familiar with it," MacDonald advised. "We will all be heading out at the same time and can probably travel as a convoy, but if you get separated we don't want anyone getting lost."

"You're going too?" Margie asked, surprised. MacDonald generally worked from the office and dealt with the mayor's office or other political situations rather than going to crime scenes.

"In this case, I think it is best that I be on site to deal with any communications issues immediately."

Margie nodded, as did the others, and they quickly prepared to leave. Margie's phone chirped, and she saw the GPS coordinates MacDonald had broadcast, underlined as a link that meant her phone recognized the data format and would open it in her maps app, as MacDonald had suggested.

"Do you want to go together?" Jones asked Margie.

Margie grimaced. Unfortunately, her poor sense of direction had become legendary in the department. Even with GPS directions, it would not be unusual for Margie to miss an exit or take a wrong turn and add an extra twenty minutes to the trip to a location that should have been easy to find. Margie was sure that neither the French explorers nor the Cree making up her Métis heritage would have been very impressed by her ability to navigate by map or by memory.

"What part of the city is it in?"

"Northeast. If you started at your house and went north up Fifty-Second—"

"Uh, right." Margie nodded. Considering the time and the fact that Jones would have to drive Margie back downtown to pick up her car after however long it took them to deal with the drone incident, Margie thought it was best not to impose on Jones. "I'd better take my car. Who knows how long this will take. We will probably be heading straight home afterward."

Jones nodded and pushed back a curled lock of blond hair that had escaped her bobby pins. "You're probably right. It shouldn't be too hard for you to get to, even if we get separated. We'll probably take Deerfoot, turn off at McKnight—"

"I'll just follow everyone else or the GPS," Margie interrupted. "There's no point in telling me the route ahead of time."

"You should just ride with someone else," Gagnon told her as he headed for the door. Though Margie noticed he did not offer to drive Margie as Jones had.

CHAPTER TWO

*W*ithin a few minutes, they were down to their cars and headed out in a convoy to the park.

No one had made any jokes about Detective "Parks Pat" being on this call. It was not her usual callout to a park because she had been specially requested by someone who thought she should be there to investigate a homicide in a park, since that was *her specialty*.

Not that Margie *had* any particular talent for solving murders that took place in parks. She couldn't track and was more likely to get lost than anyone else if she set off on a hiking trail alone.

She kept focused on Jones's car in front of her, following as closely as she could without putting herself in danger of rear-ending her at the speeds they were traveling. Deerfoot had a speed limit of 100 kilometers per hour, and escorted by patrol cars with flashing lights, they were quickly passing all other traffic. They would beat the 18 minutes predicted by her maps app.

Margie let her eyes stray to the sky once or twice, wondering whether she would be able to spot the drone or any military aircraft sent to take it down. Surely they wouldn't shoot it down over the city, even over an airport runway.

Would she even be able to see it? They hadn't been given any details on the size of the drone, whether it was a child's toy, the type that could deploy a missile, or something in between. She assumed it wasn't the missile type, if it had been launched from a park. But she couldn't imagine a child's toy causing a panic at the airport, either.

The other cars in the convoy were exiting, so Margie followed suit. At the speed they were driving, she probably would have missed the exit if she had been on her own. So much of the time, it seemed that her maps app did not inform her of an exit until she had passed it. It couldn't just be hers. Did everybody else experience the same thing, and they were just better at anticipating a turn or recovering from a wrong move? She didn't understand how she could be that much worse than anyone else when she was being directed by a computer. She also had the ability to make several wrong turns in a row trying to get back on track, while others recovered after the first one.

They had to slow down considerably to crawl through the curving, single-lane roads in a retail shopping area, so she figured she would be able to stay with the rest of the convoy without getting lost.

In a couple of minutes, they were pulling into the parking lot of Prairie Winds Park. They didn't take the time to find individual parking spots, but instead pulled onto the grass. Margie looked around. It didn't appear to be a large park. Not like Glenbow Ranch, Fish Creek, or Nose Hill. There was a splash park and some playground equipment. The big sledding hill was the central feature of the park, and Margie figured that was the most likely place to launch a drone. It had only a few trees at the top, with wide grass expanses encircling it. It was higher than anything else in the area. A good reason for the authorities to suspect this was where the drone had been launched from. MacDonald gave directions, sending his detectives around and up the hill from various directions. They would all converge at the top, having covered most of the park so they could report anything suspicious and work out a plan of action.

Margie and Detective Jones took the right-hand trail after walking through the playgrounds. They encouraged people to leave as they walked through, trying to make their warnings sound stern but not frightening enough to make people panic. "We are investigating a situation. We need people to return to their cars for their own safety. Please move along…"

More law enforcement officers would be arriving to help evacuate the park, so they didn't spend much precious time encouraging those who were resistant. They had a situation to investigate. Margie kept her eyes peeled for anything that might be a remote control for a drone, for any weapons, and for anyone who looked suspicious.

It wasn't the kind of situation where they could weed people out by whether they had children with them or not. There were plenty of people who went to the park alone, from athletes obviously training for their particular sports to seniors with walkers or hiking poles walking only the flat areas or the gentle slopes. Some children didn't seem to be attached to any of the adults present, but Margie figured that if anyone were to approach them and try to engage them or remove them, their parents would quickly make themselves known.

They walked along the pathway, heads on a swivel, checking 360 degrees around them for anything out of place or that might flag the launching point of the drone.

Margie had expected it to be pretty clear who was involved. She had thought the culprit would be showing off, making a big deal of what he had done, even if he knew it was illegal. But there was no launchpad that she could identify. No man or group of teens standing around a controller or staring up at the sky. Margie and Jones had worked small drones with cameras when they had been looking for evidence in Edworthy Park on a previous case, so she had some idea of what to look for.

"Have you seen anyone with a drone or controller?" they asked various people they encountered on the path, before directing them back to the parking lot.

"What is this?" demanded a dark-skinned man in a gray hoodie. "Where did you all come from, and what is this all about? I have a legitimate reason to be in the park; you can't just kick us out of a public place."

Margie looked him over. His racial origins weren't clear. He could be Hispanic or Indigenous, or a mix of any number of races. Was it possible he was Middle Eastern? Was it bad that her mind went there when they were investigating a potential terrorist act? His loose hoodie could be hiding weapons in his waistband or pockets. She didn't like the way he moved his hands as he talked or how confrontational he was.

"Sir, could I get you to put your hands on your head, please?" Margie instructed him in a steely cop voice, "Interlace your fingers."

"What?" he blustered, "You don't have any right to come around here and order me around. I'm not doing anything wrong, working out at a public park." He still gestured as he spoke.

"Hands on your head, now!" Jones ordered, her voice a shade louder than Margie's. They wanted to control him, but not cause concern or panic among the other park users. They didn't even know if he were anything to be concerned about at this point. They could be putting themselves at risk from another direction by focusing on an innocent bystander not accustomed to following orders.

The man's eyes widened and he tried to watch them both as they approached him from different directions, each with their hands on their service weapons.

"Whoa, whoa, whoa," he said defensively, bringing his hands up to ear level and no longer gesticulating. "No need to overreact, here."

"Hands interlaced behind your head," Margie told him.

ॐ

Grounded in the Wind, Book #13 of the *Parks Pat Mysteries* series by
P.D. Workman
can be purchased at pdworkman.com or at your favorite online retailer

ॐ

ABOUT THE AUTHOR

P.D. Workman is a USA Today Bestselling author and multi-award winner, renowned for her prolific output of over 100 published works that span various genres. With a knack for crafting page-turners, Workman captivates readers with everything from cozy mysteries like the Auntie Clem's Bakery series to gripping young adult and suspense novels.

A prolific reader and writer since childhood, P.D. Workman crafts emotionally powerful stories that don't shy away from hard topics. Her books tackle mental illness, addiction, abuse, and trauma with raw honesty and compassion, giving voice to the often unheard. If you crave authentic, character-driven page-turners that hit deep and stay with you long after the final page, you're in the right place.

With each new release, fans eagerly anticipate another thrilling blend of thought-provoking storytelling and relatable characters that define P.D. Workman's brand as an author of unforgettable page-turners—gripping tales that leave a lasting impact long after the last page is turned.

> P. D. Workman, does not shy from probing the deep psychological scars of childhood trauma, mental illness, and addiction. Also characteristic of this author, these extremely sensitive issues are explored with extensive empathy, described with incredible clarity, and portrayed with profound insight.
>
> — —KIM, GOODREADS REVIEWER

Some of Workman's titles have been translated into Spanish, French, Portuguese, German, and Italian.

Workman began writing at an early age and is a prolific reader as well as writer. She is also passionate about teaching and learning, expresses her creativity through art and cooking, and loves exploring the Calgary parks and green spaces where the Parks Pat Mysteries are set. She was a legal assistant for many years and has done extensive charitable work.

Workman was born and raised in Alberta, Canada, and is married with one adult son.

Please visit P.D. Workman at pdworkman.com to see what else she is working on, to join her mailing list, and to link to her social networks.

If you enjoyed this book, please take the time to recommend it to other purchasers with a review or star rating and share it with your friends!

tiktok.com/@pdworkmanauthor

facebook.com/pdworkmanauthor

x.com/pdworkmanauthor

instagram.com/pdworkmanauthor

amazon.com/author/pdworkman

bookbub.com/authors/p-d-workman

goodreads.com/pdworkman

linkedin.com/in/pdworkman

pinterest.com/pdworkmanauthor

youtube.com/pdworkman

Find P.D. Workman's books at

PDWORKMAN.COM

Scan the QR code below